HOUSE
OF
MASSAN

THE EDGE OF TIME

KARL LOVERIDGE

 GLASSSPIDERPUBLISHING

Cover design by Karl Loveridge
with special thanks to Judith S. Design & Creativity
Chapter illustrations by Karl Loveridge
www.karlloveridge.com
www.judithsdesign.com

Published by Glass Spider Publishing
www.glassspiderpublishing.com

To Janna, for unfaltering support.
Without her, this story would never have been told..

Prologue

The end of the world isn't something to fear. The end of one world is simply the beginning of another. Time is a good mother who cleans up after her children. She heals every scraped knee, blunts every thorn, and wipes away every tear.

Chapter 1
Hermit Cove

Micah Fennly's life had been spinning in an eddy of self-wallowing for months. He had so looked forward to that summer after the end of fifth grade—no more homework or demanding teachers. But this summer had been different. It had been lonelier than any previous summer. Perhaps that was the way it was meant to be. The punishment fits the crime.

A perfect day had been reduced to sitting alone in his bedroom playing video games. If Micah was feeling adventurous, he might ride his bicycle down to the gas station for an ice-cold pop and a salty snack. Those always paired well. And on a few fortunate occasions, it would rain. The rain lessened the chances his mother would think of a chore or want to do something absurd like go to the beach or, worst of all, take him shopping.

When Micah's parents gave him a puppy last Christmas, he wasn't sure if the brown dachshund pup was a blessing or curse. Micah named him Grubb for his tendency to bury himself in blankets. Grubb had big floppy ears and an extra-long tail that sprouted like cotton at the tip. He instantly loved Micah and followed him around like…well, a lost puppy.

If appreciating cuteness was all that was expected of Micah, Grubb would have been the perfect companion. But Micah quickly learned that owning a pet was more work than he'd bargained for. Grubb's constant need for food and attention nickeled and dimed precious time away from Micah's video game habit. As Grubb grew, complications set in. He barked at everything. He gobbled up Micah's snacks and tipped over his drinks too many times to count. He even chewed up a couple of game controllers. Grubb was exhausting.

Micah looked out the glass kitchen door and sighed. Another interruption. It was hot outside, and he had a video game paused up in his bedroom. Hastily, he filled Grubb's chewed-over dog dish with too much food and waited. Grubb usually was punctual when it came to his mealtime.

Growing impatient, Micah cracked the door and shook the dish outside.

With no sign of Grubb, he slid the glass door open and stepped out onto the porch.

Grubb often hid in the bushes to ambush birds or squirrels that wandered into the yard. He was good at catching them, too. But at mealtime, he'd blow his cover. Where was he?

Searching the bushes, Micah fixated on the oak tree that rose from the middle of the yard. A gust of Pacific wind blew through the boughs, and the tree came to life like a welcoming friend. Between the oak and a stir of lilac in the air, the memory of his sister pushed the cares of the day aside. Today, it had been one year since the accident, and the guilt hit him like a punch in the stomach.

He went to the tree's shadow to escape the afternoon sun. Leaning against the sturdy trunk, he continued his leisurely search for Grubb.

Idly, he reached up and touched the lowest branch without standing on his toes. He had grown three inches over the summer. The oak had become his favorite place to disappear when his mother threatened to clean the house. He looked up into the branches where he and Mariam once played and felt a mixture of nostalgia and sorrow.

When Micah and Mariam had fought, she would often escape up into the oak tree with his favorite toys. With Micah's fear of heights, the branches were a perfect way to declare a victory. But Mariam was kind by nature. She started to feel sorry when her younger brother stopped caring.

"I'm going to get you to climb this tree if it's the last thing I do!" Mariam had threatened. She carried through with that threat by taking his beloved video games up into the tree. Micah had no choice but to face his fear. After the many battles they fought, he eventually found the bravery to conquer the tree and his fear of heights.

Mariam may have lost her advantage of the tree, but she was proud of her younger brother. "See, you can do anything if you want it bad enough," she told him, hugging him like he had conquered the world. To celebrate, they ate lunch perched on the highest branches: a peanut butter and jelly sandwich and a couple of juice boxes.

It was a cruel irony that shortly thereafter, Micah chose to use Mariam's trick of climbing the tree when they fought again. He had scrambled up with her favorite hairbrush. Reluctantly, she followed, even after complaining that she didn't feel well. Micah did not believe her and showed no mercy in proving he could climb higher than she could.

That was when she fell.

Even after countless assurances from his grief-stricken parents that the accident wasn't his fault, time had only managed to dull the shock of the memory, but the guilt was still an open wound. He missed Mariam.

"Trees don't eat dog food, you know!" Ben Farnsworth shouted over the white picket fence separating the two backyards. He hung over the edge, swiping a rake back and forth through the Fennlys' rose bush. With each violent swing, rose petals erupted, carpeting the grass in crimson.

Micah blinked. He was holding Grubb's dog dish like it was an offering to the tree.

"Earth to Micah!"

Micah set his jaw. "You better not be teasing Grubb again."

Ben scoffed as he plucked the sparse remaining roses with the rake. "Why don't you teach that mutt not to bark so much?" he said, flinging the mangled flowers at Micah.

Ignoring Ben, Micah shook the dog dish as he searched the yard. "Grubb, come here, boy."

"Is something missing?" Ben grinned, motioning to the open side gate entangled with grapevines.

"You opened our gate!"

Ben cackled as he used the rake like a sword when Micah raced up to him. With a swift jerk, Micah yanked the rake out of Ben's hands.

"Hey! That's ours!"

Ben was eight years old, and Micah was almost twelve. Their age difference suggested that Ben should respect Micah, but he didn't. Between Ben and his older brother, Jack, the two took every opportunity to cause trouble.

"When did you let him out?" Micah demanded.

Ben grinned with his usual overconfident smirk. Micah struck the fence with the rake close to Ben's knuckles, causing him to fall back into the grass.

"How dare you, Micah!" Ben's mother shouted through her kitchen window. The back door banged open, and Margot Farnsworth rushed out, waving a wooden spoon dripping with batter.

"Ben let Grubb out of our yard!" Micah protested.

"You have no proof of that. Benny's been with me the whole afternoon, haven't you, sweetie?" Margot said, helping Ben to his feet.

"I was raking up pine cones like you told me. I was just trying to tell Micah that he left their gate open—"

"Oh, he's lying!" Micah said, striking the fence again with the rake.

"Don't you threaten us, young man! If I ever see you raise a finger at Ben again, I'll…" Margot trailed off and took a deep breath. She reached over the fence and calmly said, "Hand me my rake back and apologize this instant."

Ben stepped behind his mother and stuck out his tongue.

Micah glowered at Ben as he surrendered the rake and folded his arms.

"And the apology?" Margot demanded, putting her hands on

her hips.

"Micah! What's all the shouting—oh, it's you, Margot," Micah's mother said, poking her head out the second-floor window. She had been brushing her teeth.

"Hello, dear!" Margot said. "Micah's just upset about—"

"Ben let Grubb out of the yard," Micah shouted over his shoulder.

Margot stomped her foot, about to let loose when Lorna said, "Grubb's running around the front yard. Just go get him. We're in a hurry."

"Not until Micah apologizes to Ben," Margot insisted.

"Apologize? For what?" Lorna said, wiping toothpaste from her lips.

Margot sighed. "Lorna, sweetie. I've worried about you and Kimble since Mariam's accident."

"And what does that mean?"

"Well, dear, it just means Micah has developed a bit of a temper lately. He has too much free time and nowhere to vent his frustration except on my boys. I can imagine that it's been difficult since the accident. But it might not hurt to keep him occupied with some chores." Margot glanced around the Fennlys' backyard. "Perhaps Micah could use some of that aggression to fix up your yard?"

With every word that fell from Margot's lips, Micah added more colorful adjectives in his mind to how he really felt about Margot and her bratty son. As he watched Ben nodding with his smug grin, he could feel the sentence being cocked behind his tongue.

Margot was correct about one thing. The Fennlys' backyard was a gardener's worst nightmare. The truth was, Micah's mother liked the shabby bushes, uncut grass, and weeds. She had even given the plants their own special names like they were her pets.

"Oh, and while I have you, what did we decide to do about that eyesore?" Margot added, pointing the rake at the tree house in the oak tree.

Micah and his father had built the tree house shortly after Mariam's accident. The simple wooden platform with a guardrail and dangling knotted rope had become the centerpiece of every conversation Mrs. Farnsworth had with his mother. Micah knew why. When the weather allowed, he slept out in the tree house. During one of Margot's endless nightly parties, Micah had overheard her gossiping. "Isn't it strange they have such a young son? I mean, really, what are Lorna and Kimble…in their seventies? Was Micah adopted? It would have been more responsible for them to plan their funerals than to have another child." As her guests laughed at her snobby comment, Margot was mortified to see Micah eavesdropping from the tree.

"I don't know why it bothers you so much, Margot," Lorna said. "You can barely see it."

"Oh, Lorna, please, I beg of you to take it down. Considering your age, wouldn't it be wonderful to have one less worry? What if Micah had an accident like Mariam?"

"Micah, get Grubb and be ready in five minutes! We're going to be late," Lorna said, slamming the window shut.

"Well!" Margo exclaimed, shaking her head at Micah with a sniff. She leaned back on her heels and said, "Come along, Benny."

Following in the shadow of his mother, Ben picked up a handful of pine cones and lobbed them over the fence at Micah.

Fuming, Micah ignored him and started for the front yard. On his way, he nearly tripped over his bicycle lying in the tall grass. He had a paper route that he shared with his best friend, Richard Sommers. Thanks to another nightmare that kept Micah awake all night, Richard had excused him from today's torture. Micah had never wanted a summer job, but Richard had tricked him into being his partner by begging him to death.

The jingle of Grubb's collar led Micah to the Dickersons' yard next door.

"Grubb," Micah called with a whistle.

Grubb scampered from the flower garden, wagging his tail. Two crows dove from the roof, squawking angrily as they soared away. Grubb sat on his haunches, panting like his work was done for the day. His floppy ears suddenly perked when a change in the wind kicked up a swirling of leaves in the street. The hairs on Micah's neck prickled when he heard familiar, infectious laughter carried on the wind.

"Mariam?" Micah called, feeling foolish for saying her name out loud. Of course it couldn't be her, but something caught Grubb's attention, and he took off up the street.

"Grubb! Your dinner!" Micah shouted. It was no use. He tossed the dish aside. If Grubb wasn't interested in food, it was certain he was sniffing for trouble.

The laughter grew louder as Micah ran up Albatross Avenue. Huffing, he soon found himself in the older neighborhood where the summer rental clapboard houses had a front-row view of the Pacific Ocean. Grubb stopped, took a bearing with his nose, and sniffed down a side trail.

Micah slid to a stop on the sand-covered sidewalk to catch his breath. He hated running. It was so deceptive that a video game character could run all day and never get tired. Running felt like death in real life.

The weedy path led to a leaning fence made of wood slats and wiring. A prominent sign made of driftwood read HERMIT COVE—NO TRESPASSING. Grubb scurried under the fence and disappeared over a sandy rise.

"Ah, man, don't go down there!"

Micah stopped at the fence and listened for the laughter. All he heard was the rustle of beach grass and the distant roar of the surf. This whole situation was ridiculous. Mariam had been on his mind all day, and his imagination had filled in the rest. Grubb running off had caused the urgency.

Grumbling, Micah punched the no-trespassing sign. The sign glared back, daring him to challenge its authority. He considered heading back home. Grubb had run away before and always returned. But Micah knew better because of his mother. He also knew the Stonehelm Bluff trails were dangerous from when he and Mariam used to go on their adventure hikes together.

"Stupid dog," Micah muttered, crawling under the fence. He jogged through the waist-high grass and stopped when he found Grubb panting at the trailhead. "Where do you think you're going?"

The blast of a ship's foghorn came from the sea, distracting Grubb. Micah crept forward and dove. Grubb escaped with a countering leap. For a wiener dog, Grubb was quick. He trotted down the trail, indifferent to the danger.

Lying in the sand, Micah's brow rose when patches of fog blew over the cliff edge. He crawled forward to get a better look and saw a peculiar cloud in the cove below.

He stood and dusted himself off. Grubb showed no sign of slowing his descent down the trail. Micah frowned. "Get back here right now!"

Grubb stopped and looked back.

"That's better," Micah said. He waited, but Grubb sat defiantly on the trail like a rock.

Mariam had always been a risk-taker, but even she hadn't dared take the bluff trails. Could Micah do it now that he was older and had conquered his fear of heights?

Micah started confidently down the path until it narrowed. He could feel the strength in his legs weakening when he was forced to side-step with his back against the cliff wall. He had an excellent view of the two-hundred-foot drop. The cliff was sheer, formed from loose earth packed around enormous rock outcroppings. Moss and lichens made the rock slippery. The rocky trail was nothing like climbing the oak tree.

He halted at a section where the trail sloughed off. Grubb had somehow managed over this part, but Micah wasn't so confident. He spun around and, with both hands, grabbed a tree root above and stretched his foot out to test a rock outcropping. In doing so, he disturbed a hairy spider that scuttled onto his hand. Surprised, he shook off the spider, leaving only one hand gripping the root. Off balance, he dangled backward, desperate to keep his footing. He looked down, and fear gripped him like a vise. If his mother saw him now, she'd ground him for a month.

The ship's horn blew again, closer this time. The blast rolled up the cliff, sending a peppering of sparrows fluttering from the hemlocks below. Micah clenched the roots until his hands burned.

At that moment, all the troubles in Micah's life came in like a tidal wave. Every trouble battered the calm he desperately guarded in the quiet harbor of his bedroom: Grubb, the paper route, Ben and Jack Farnsworth, and school about to start up. It was too much. Life was determined to take him out into uncertain waters.

Then there were the dreams. The nightmares visited every night. Last night was the worst. The months of poor sleeping were adding up.

Lastly, the guilt of his sister's accident brought tears to his eyes. Why did she have to die? A storm of guilt and self-pity washed over him. In this whirlwind of emotion, he stared at his hands gripping the roots, and a serenity came. What if he let go? Would death excuse him from the guilt he had lived with for so long?

A jingle came, and this dark thought flitted away. Grubb stood nearby, peering up with his innocent golden eyes.

"This is all your fault," Micah sobbed. He reached out to grab his wayward pet, but Grubb bolted back down the trail. "Come back here!"

How dare Grubb put his life at risk with such indifference! Through teary eyes, Micah swung to the other side of the washout, chasing after Grubb with blind anger and disregard for the danger of the cliff. He ran into the dense, soupy cloud that shrouded the cove.

Robbed of his sense of sight, he became disoriented. He ran off the trail and fell with a terrified scream. The fall was mercifully short. He landed on a slope of dirt and stones, tumbling down until finally sliding to a stop at the bottom. Nothing was broken, but as his chest heaved, he decided taking risky trails should be avoided in the future. The forest of trees creaked in a light breeze, accompanied by the distant cries of seagulls and crashing waves.

A flash of light caught his eye.

Was that lightning?

Micah stood and shook the dust from his unkempt brown hair. Two crows fluttered down, landing on a dead branch nearby. They squawked as if they were laughing at him. He gave them brief notice when he saw one had an unusual pink crown of feathers.

Looking into the fog, an uneasy feeling came.

"Grubb?" Micah called timidly, ignoring the mocking crows.

Another light flash came and faded away.

Unable to locate the trail, Micah pushed blindly into the fog with the thorny undergrowth scratching and jabbing through his jeans. He spat out the bitter taste of pine as the conifers brushed his face. He reached a rocky embankment and climbed down. His feet sank in the wet sand of a tide pool filled with barnacle-encrusted stones. Shrouded in fog, two colossal rocks rose up, flanking the cove like sentinel guards.

The light flared again, revealing a shadowy, tangled web rising up from the water.

Micah took cautious steps forward until water foamed over his feet. The air carried the briny scent of seawater mingled with the muskiness of wet sand. His imagination played tricks on him as he squinted into the gray. Was that a shadow darting to his left?

His senses buzzed with anticipation. A pocket opened in the billowing fog, revealing a grand ship a stone's throw away. Three masts speared the sky with a web of ropes reaching the tops. Anchored, the vessel rocked gently on the water as it rose and fell in the quiet surf. Carved in ornate script along the swooping nose was the name *Miss Darby*.

Was it just a coincidence this ship was just like the one in his nightmare last night?

Micah backed away from the water. Though he was sure he wasn't in danger of a shark attack like in his nightmare, the cove conjured up a deep sense of déjà vu.

"Hello? Is someone there?"

The ship creaked, and the ding of a bell rang from the mainmast.

Another flash of light. A distant red-and-white-striped lighthouse sat perched on a craggy rock. An ocean swell struck the rock, erupting into an explosion of sea spray.

Was there a lighthouse down here before? Micah wondered.

The two crows fluttered down and landed in the wet sand, skittish and uncertain. The crow with the pink crown of feathers had something shiny in its beak. It dropped it into a shallow mossy pool of water at Micah's feet.

Moments later, Grubb emerged from the fog, licking his chops. Noticing the crows, he charged and barked after the one with pink feathers. The crows flapped away frantically, barely escaping Grubb's snapping bite. They landed on a large boulder, ruffling their feathers.

"Way to go, Grubb. You almost got that one," Micah said, patting his huffing friend.

A torrent of wind rushed from the forest, pushing the fog out to sea. The crows squawked as they leaped from the boulder and flew toward the ship.

Watching them fly over, Micah was stunned when the ship and the lighthouse suddenly disappeared in the blink of his eye. The crows panicked in their flight, retreating back into the woods.

"Micah?"

"Mom!" Micah exclaimed, spinning about.

His mother, shrouded in swirling fog, stood above him on the rocky embankment with her arms raised to the sky. Noticing Micah, she quickly lowered her arms and removed her cell phone from her pocket. The screen glowed an ominous red. She tapped the screen and discreetly tucked it back away.

"What possessed you to come down here? I told you we were in a hurry. You were just supposed to get Grubb and put him in the backyard. Now I'm going to be late!"

Micah stared with disbelief. His mother was seventy-two years old and had difficulty with the stairs in their home.

"How did you get down here?" he asked with his brow raised.

"No, why are *you* here?"

"Grubb ran away. There was a pirate ship down here. It was here just a moment ago, I swear!"

Lorna looked confused. "A ship? It must have been your imagination."

Micah scanned the cove, scratching his head. "It was right in front of me."

"Oh, pishposh! You should have come and got me. Lots of junk floats into the cove, and you could have been hurt," Lorna said as she paced about, looking around the rocks and crevasses.

"No, Mom, it wasn't junk. It was a ship—a galleon. It even had a name. It was *Miss Darby.*"

Lorna's expression hardened as she continued to look around the cove.

"What are you looking for?"

"Never mind that. Was there anything else you saw down here?"

"There were just a couple of crows. They…"

"Crows?" Lorna shot back. She scanned the woods around her.

Micah knelt over the tide pool. "They dropped something here in the water." He fished around the moss until a glint of gold caught his eye. "Look at this! It's a locket… It's Mariam's!"

"Let me see it." Lorna hastened down the rock embankment without the slightest hint of difficulty. Taking the locket, she looked disappointed. "Did you notice where the crows went?" she asked casually.

Micah gestured at the forest. "They flew off that way. What do you think about the locket they gave me?"

Lorna examined it, looking skeptical. She removed her phone and took pictures of the gold disc.

"Why are you taking pictures?"

She was quiet as she thumbed through the images. Curious, Micah looked over her shoulder.

"Hey, it just looks like a rock on your phone," he said, taking back the locket.

Lorna tapped the screen, and the image cycled through a

rainbow of colors. Finally, she declared, "That's because it *is* a rock. Why would you pretend it was her locket?"

Micah looked surprised. "It's her locket, Mom, I'm sure of it. Look, it has the *M* engraved on the outside." Prying it open, he found a small colored photograph of himself from second grade. "It even has my picture inside, see?"

Lorna let out a heavy sigh. "Micah, I'm in no mood for this."

Micah watched with disbelief as his mother struggled back up the embankment. "Mom, it's Mariam's locket. Why don't you believe me?"

"Micah, son. I know it has been hard lately, and you've always had an active imagination. Maybe Margot is right. Perhaps all of this is our fault for not spending more time with you since Mariam's death. Things will get better, I promise."

"It's not that, Mom. It *is* Mariam's locket, just look!" Micah insisted.

Lorna turned and walked away. "It's just a pebble, Micah. We need to get back."

Frustrated, Micah dangled the locket before Grubb's nose and whispered, "Pebble? I don't care what she thinks. It's her locket, isn't it, boy?"

Grubb sniffed the locket, wagging his white-tipped tail. Micah stuffed it away and followed his mother.

Chapter 2
Special Delivery

The hike back home from Hermit Cove was unpleasant.

Micah hadn't had a browbeating like the one he got from his mother since he was caught playing in the street when he was five. If he hadn't witnessed it himself, he wouldn't have believed his elderly mother could have climbed the steep trail.

Perhaps the adrenaline combined with her anger gave her super-powers. She had been anxious to get to the back-to-school night, and she made sure Micah knew it.

After they arrived home, she gave him strict instructions that he was to wash up and change his clothes. No snacks. No video games. No excuses. They needed to be on their way.

As they were about to leave, Lorna's cell phone rang. "It's Shiela. Go get in the car. I'll be down in a moment," Lorna said, motioning Micah away and taking the call.

Micah went downstairs with Grubb in tow. Hermit Cove troubled him, especially his mother's reaction to the locket in his palm.

Where had the crows found Mariam's locket? Unlike his mother's assessment of it being a pebble, he was sure it was the locket he'd given his sister on her twelfth birthday. She never took it off. If there was anything unusual about the locket, it was that it was heavy. He shook it and heard something rattle inside.

With his pocketknife, Micah peeled out the picture from the locket, and a jolt of excitement hit when he discovered a nickel-sized silver coin hidden inside. Micah had collected coins ever since his Grandma Hazel had given him her change from a trip to Mexico. The primitive coin had unfamiliar markings, except for one: a prominent cross with a loop at the top. An amber crystal was set in the loop's eye. Ancient Egypt fascinated Micah, and he knew the symbol was called an *ankh*.

The doorbell rang.

A hulk of a man with a thick gray beard and mustache greeted Micah at the front door. He wore a drab soldier's uniform that snugly fit his wide build. A pack was casually slung over his shoulder, partially veiled by the folds in his cloak.

"Is this Kimble Fennly's home?" the man asked gruffly. Seeing Grubb grumbling at Micah's feet, a smile appeared under his thick beard. "You must be Micah. Is your father home?"

Grubb huffed, curiously sniffing at the stranger. Micah pushed Grubb away from the door with his heel and said, "No, but he usually gets home about now."

The soldier shifted his bag and said, "I have a package for your father that I am to deliver personally. But I'm in a hurry. Can I trust you to get it to him?" He bent over to scrutinize Micah under his thick eyebrows.

"Yes, sir," Micah said, trying to hold a straight face. The man's bad breath rivaled Grubb's.

The soldier straightened up, eyeing Micah as he stroked his beard. Finally, with a dismissive exhale, he opened his pouch, revealing several identical brown packages, and took one out.

"This is important. Promise me you'll get this to him *first thing*."

Micah nodded.

Surrendering the bundle from his calloused hand, the soldier poked Micah's chest. "First thing, got it?"

Grubb growled, and the soldier's expression softened. "He's a fine animal, son. I had one myself when I was a boy," he said, buttoning up his pouch.

The soldier dismissed himself, his cloak swishing as he walked off. The cloak mesmerized Micah as its color changed. When the soldier walked past a red car parked up the street, the cloak turned red, camouflaging against the car. Soon, he passed a grove of trees and disappeared from view.

Micah closed and locked the door. He would have been more curious about the soldier, but after the events at the cove, the cloak was the least strange thing he'd seen all day.

Looking over the package, he found it had no markings other than a dull red star. He placed it on the fireplace mantel, where he promptly forgot about it.

On the mantel were family photos of his elder siblings. He and Mariam were the youngest and had often been jokingly introduced as his parents' second family. In the collection of photographs were pictures of Mariam taken months before her death. In each photo, she was wearing the locket.

One particular picture caught Micah's eye. It was a professional portrait taken of Mariam on her fifteenth birthday. The locket was clearly visible, including a small dent near the hinge. He ran his fingernail over the locket in his palm and could feel the same indentation.

An absurd thought crossed his mind. *Could Mariam still be alive?*

His mother honked the car horn impatiently from the garage. Still bothered by her reaction to the locket, Micah hastily stuffed it back into his pocket and made his way to the garage.

Lorna backed their old Lincoln out of the driveway onto Albatross Avenue. The steep street was quiet, with a majestic view of the ocean. The neighborhood behind the Fennlys' home bloomed with leafy trees and pines. Older homes like theirs, all of unique shapes and colors, interrupted the otherwise rich, green view. Micah sat in the back, feeling spent now that the adrenaline had worn off. He wasn't about to mention the coin after the lecture he got about his overactive imagination.

"Micah, I want you to promise me you'll never go to the cove again. It's dangerous."

"I know, you told me a thousand times," Micah said, annoyed. When his mother got on something, she didn't know when to quit. "I still don't know how you got down there."

"Your old mom can do many hard things when she puts her mind to it. No matter what that rude Margot Farnsworth thinks."

"The Farnsworths have never liked us," Micah yawned.

"I still shouldn't have lost my temper. The Farnsworths aren't the most considerate neighbors, but we should always be respectful, even if they're sometimes rude."

"Sometimes?" he breathed to himself.

"Who was at the door?"

"A delivery man dressed like a soldier."

"A soldier?" Lorna asked, looking at him in the rearview mirror.

"I think he was a soldier. He was wearing a cloak that changed colors. I've never seen anything like it before."

"Really? A cloak that changed colors? I suppose that's not too unusual these days. It seems like something new is invented every day," she said, taking a hairpin turn. "What did he want?"

"He delivered a package for Dad with a star on it."

"A star?" Lorna said, this time turning her head to look back at him. "What color was it?"

"Red." Micah saw his mother's lips tighten when she glanced at her watch. "Is that important?"

"Are you sure the star was red?"

"*Yes,*" Micah said with an edge to his voice.

Reaching the stop sign at Highway 101, Lorna looked both ways and merged onto the highway. "It'll just have to keep," she said.

Micah noticed his mother had turned the wrong way. "This isn't the way to town," he said.

"Sheila needs us to stop and pick up Richard and Angela."

"Not Angela," Micah groaned.

Micah yawned and closed his eyes as they sped down the highway.

Chapter 3
Richard's Gift

"Wake up!"
    Micah was startled awake to find Angela, his best friend's bucktoothed sister, grinning at him.

"Go away," Micah said and turned his back to her. He shut his eyes, hoping she'd ignore him. Suddenly, a wet finger was jammed into his ear, followed by an outburst of giggles.

Richard slid into the back seat, sandwiching Micah in the middle. His mother had given him a new haircut for school. The sides were uneven, and there were nicks in his black hair, but it was free, and Richard cared little for his appearance.

"I see you're still stickin' to the story you were too tired to help with the paper route today, huh?" Richard said.

Micah wiped his ear on Angela's shirt as she batted him away with a barrage of slaps. "I told you, I didn't sleep last night."

"You're just lazy," Angela said, scowling at the wet spot.

"It took an extra hour to deliver the papers without you," Richard said, pointing to the four empty bags scattered around his bike in the front yard. "I got stuck at Morty Crowther's house. He was worried he missed your birthday. I told him five times your birthday was tomorrow. I don't care if you have more nightmares. You're gonna help me with the paper route tomorrow!"

"Yeah!" Angela added.

"Alright, alright! I'm sorry," Micah said, pushing Angela out of his face.

After several moments of uncomfortable silence, he sat up, wondering what was taking his mother so long. She was talking to Shiela, Richard's mother, on their front porch.

Micah took out the coin and locket. "What do these look like to you?"

Angela looked over to see. Richard ignored him, saying, "I don't feel like playing games right now."

"It's a locket and a coin. Are those for a girlfriend?" Angela giggled.

Micah sneered. "No, the locket was my sister's. I found it at the beach today."

"The beach?" Richard spat. "So you couldn't help with the paper route, but you had time to go to the beach? Some friend you are."

"No, Richard. Grubb ran away. I chased him down to Hermit Cove. Remember that place we went on that field trip back in third grade? Some crows had Mariam's locket. They gave it to me. I haven't seen it since she died, and inside was this coin—"

"Crows?" Richard said, leaning forward to meet Angela's eye. "Do you believe any of this?"

"Nope," Angela said.

"Just look at it!"

Richard sighed and took the coin. His expression went blank like he was in a trance.

"Richard?" Micah said, nudging his friend, but he remained unresponsive long enough to catch Angela's attention. "I hope you're happy. You broke my brother," Angela said, ignoring the two.

Richard exhaled. When he looked at Micah, he looked pale. "Did you show this to your mom?"

"I showed her the locket when I found it, and she thought I was making it up. She thinks it's just a rock. I found this coin hidden inside, and I haven't decided if I should show it to her." Micah felt vindicated that Richard and Angela could see the locket, but he wasn't sure what to do after seeing Richard's reaction to the coin.

The driver's side door swung open. Sheila had followed Lorna to the car, and they were still chatting. Micah snatched the coin and locket from Richard and put them away.

"Everyone ready to go?" Lorna said, easing into the car.

"Mrs. Fennly, look what Micah did," Angela said, showing the wet spot on her shirt.

Lorna looked at the stain and glared at Micah. "Well? Tell her you're sorry."

Micah didn't care. "I'm sorry," he said with as little sincerity as he knew his mother would allow. Unsatisfied with Micah's punishment, Angela threw herself back into the seat and folded her arms.

Sheila tightened her black hair into a bun as she bent over to look into the car window. She was wearing gray scrubs and had a stethoscope around her neck. "Sorry about tonight," she said, jingling her car keys. "It's only a half shift. I'll swing by the Fennlys' to pick you up after. Don't give Lorna any trouble, you hear?" She leaned in to kiss her children goodbye. She gave Angela a stern face and added, "And no fighting, young lady."

"Pfft," Angela frowned, rejecting her mother's kiss.

Lorna pulled away, heading to the highway. "So, your mother tells me she's going back to school to finish her nursing degree. That's so exciting!"

"More school," Angela said, frowning.

"You should be proud, honey. Your mother's making a better life for you kids."

Angela ignored Richard's disapproving frown and continued to look out the window. Lorna switched the radio on and began to hum to an old fifties tune coming from the worn-out speakers.

Micah noticed a nasty scrape on Richard's arm. "How'd that happen?"

"I crashed my bike with all those extra papers, thanks to you."

"Sorry about that."

"It doesn't matter. Let's hear about this nightmare. It better be a good one this time."

"They're getting worse. I dreamed I was on a big pirate ship—"

"They're called galleons," Angela said, pretending not to listen.

"Excuse me. I was on a *galleon* with a bunch of kids I didn't know, except for Wren."

"Wren Kingsley?" Richard asked.

Micah nodded. "We were on the bottom deck, standing at the railing. We saw an island, and that's when the shark came. It was bigger than any I've ever seen. The fin reached up as high as we were. Everyone was scared and crying. Wren kept saying over and over he wanted to go home. The shark attacked the ship, and I fell over the railing. When I landed, I fell on my bed, floating in the sea alone. The shark came up and swallowed me and my bed! The last thing I remember was hanging down its throat and holding onto its giant teeth."

The car veered onto the shoulder and Lorna hit a pothole, causing the three in the back to bounce up.

"Mom!"

The kids snickered as Lorna corrected. She began muttering to herself, using names Micah had never heard before.

"Who's Penelope and Twitch?" Micah asked.

"Never mind. Just words I use when I feel angry."

"That dream was so stupid," Angela said, still laughing at Micah's mom. "You made that whole thing up because you didn't help Richard with the paper route today."

"I did not!"

"Sounded scary to me," Richard said.

They talked about Micah's nightmares until they reached Stonehelm, and then the conversation turned to the boys' plans for their last weekend before school started up. The highway took them through a section of town called Fisherman's Point. It was packed with tourists attracted by the ocean view and the many shops.

Richard leaned to look out the window.

"What's the matter, Richard dear?" Lorna asked.

"Watch out for the little boy with a green shirt. His dad isn't paying attention," Richard said, scanning the tourists walking the sidewalk.

Angela rolled her eyes. Richard often had premonitions. That was how he and Micah had become friends in the first grade. Micah had been playing on the monkey bars with Wren Kingsley when Richard came along and warned him that he would fall because of that "fat kid." Moments later, Wren stepped on Micah's fingers, and he fell.

Lorna idled the car along when suddenly, a small child wearing a red jacket wandered into the road. "Oh, dear!" she said, honking the horn.

Everyone in the car watched helplessly as the toddler went straight into the path of an oncoming truck hauling logs. White smoke erupted from the truck's tires when its brakes locked. The panicked father chased after his son, receiving a horn blast from the angry truck driver.

"I still don't know how you do that," Micah said as they drove past.

"I just get impressions. Mom says we got it from our dad. Angela can do it better than me when she tries."

Glancing at Micah, Angela looked embarrassed. "No, I can't! Besides, that kid was wearing a *red coat*, not a green shirt. Richard wasn't even right. All my friends think my brother's a freak."

"Angela," Lorna reproved. "There's no reason to be embarrassed. It's a gift that's part of your family. Who cares what your friends think?"

Angela looked out the window, folding her arms. "It's just what my friends say."

"Well, he was close enough, weren't you, Richard?"

Lorna turned the car down a side street with a road sign that read *Quentin Avenue*. Taped under the sign was a colorful poster announcing the back-to-school night.

The recently paved road snaked its way into the mature forest. The shoulders had been mowed and the limbs of encroaching leafy trees had been cut back.

"I've never been on this road before," Micah said.

"This road's been here a long time. All that's down here is the school," Lorna said.

"This is a lot closer than our old school. What are they doing with that building?"

"They changed the boundaries. From now on, the kids from Seaside will use Palmer Elementary, and students south of Stone-helm will use Quentin."

"We've heard our new school is haunted," Richard said.

"Haunted? Pfft. It's just old. It's been completely renovated now. You wouldn't even recognize it if you saw it from before."

A grand building came into view as the road curved, towering above the lush evergreen forest. Piles of rough-cut logs lined the shoulders of the road, cleared from the forest to make room for the school's parking lot.

A distinguished gray stone monument adorned with brass lettering greeted visitors with the name *Alfred B. Quentin Elementary*. A large medallion, which featured the school's mascot of a gold miner with a pickax over his shoulder, topped off the monument.

"This is way bigger than our old school," Richard said.

"It used to be an academy for adults," Lorna said. "That was a long time ago, even before I was born."

"Where's the haunted mansion?" Micah asked.

Lorna shook her head. "It's just the old house built by Alfred Quentin when he was the school's director. It was abandoned years ago, so it's falling apart. The city is tearing it down later this year. You kids just stay away from it."

They arrived late, and Lorna pulled into one of the few remaining parking spots. Angela was first out, slamming the door. Sneering, Micah reopened the door and stiffened at the cool breeze. The smell of pine, mingled with sea air, triggered the peculiar thought that the school wasn't used to visitors.

The school was made of salt-and-pepper gray granite, built in Renaissance architecture with high-arched windows. Two three-story wings flanked the courtyard. A three-arched portico with a high domed roof connected the wings at the far end.

Isolated for so many years from the public, Mother Nature had adopted the old building. Creeper vines grew around windows and along prominent features. Lower walls were covered by a stubborn green moss that permanently darkened the stone.

The courtyard was overflowing with parents and children milling about and seated in folding chairs as they waited for the back-to-school night to begin.

A young girl raced from the crowd, squealing with excitement to see Angela.

"Mrs. Fennly, do you care if I sit with my friend?" Angela asked.

"Do you want me to go with you to your class tonight?" Lorna asked.

Angela glared at Micah. "No. I'll be fine. I'm sure Micah will need your help to find his class." She and her friend giggled as they skipped away.

"Will you two ever get long?" Lorna scoffed at Micah.

"It's too bad the princess had to leave," Micah said.

"She's a sweet girl, and you need to treat her like a lady."

"Lady?" Micah choked, pretending to throw up. Richard laughed.

Lorna tugged at Micah's ear, motioning the boys forward.

"Dad!" Micah called, spotting his father sitting on a large granite block.

Kimble stood, leaning on his black cane. Even at his advanced age, he looked intimidating with thick arms and a barrel chest. A wide grin spread on his face at the sight of the two boys. "I see you scared Angela off," Kimble said privately.

"I feel bad about it."

Kimble chuckled and prodded Richard with his cane. "And how's Richard tonight?"

"Fine, Mr. Fennly."

"You boys excited for school?"

"Yeah, I like school. Better than sitting around the house," Richard said.

"You're such a suck-up," Micah said, playfully punching Richard's arm. "Come on, let's go see the haunted mansion."

Lorna sighed. The boys ran off, leaving Lorna and Kimble alone.

Chapter 4
Penelope and Twitch

"You're late, hon," Kimble said with a peck on the cheek. "I thought you had to be here early to run some tests on the gate before they opened the school."

"Something came up at home," Lorna said, scanning the nearby trees.

"Weren't those tests important? You told me there were problems."

"I had Thomas run them. He said everything was fine."

"Thomas, your new assistant? He's just a kid."

"That *kid* knows the system better than I do. And he's hardly new. He's been working in the department for two years."

Lorna hawkishly watched Micah and Richard as they explored the school grounds. The boys stopped to peek around the back of the school. Lorna's eyes darted expectantly between the trees.

"Something on your mind, dear?" Kimble finally asked.

Lorna reached into her jacket for her cell phone. She tapped the screen and scrolled through a list until two names appeared in bold red type. She handed her phone to Kimble.

His eyes widened. "Penelope and Twitch? Did you see them?"

"No, *I did not*," Lorna said with an edge to her voice.

Kimble stabbed his cane into the grass. "After all this time…"

"They lured our son down to Hermit Cove."

"Hermit Cove? That's one of Alfred's old portals. I thought those went out of service years ago."

"They're still open, just on a private network…" Lorna gasped. "Wait. Micah mentioned he saw *Miss Darby*. They must have come over from Belmont Cavern."

"Do you think Alfred helped them?"

Lorna shrugged.

"What did Micah say?"

"He doesn't know what's going on. All he saw were a couple of crows."

"Crows, huh?" Kimble smiled distantly. "You never know what to expect from those two."

"I don't like that look, Kimble," Lorna frowned. "This is serious. I won't stand for you defending their antics again."

"I understand, hon. But you know Penelope and Twitch wouldn't hurt Micah. At least not on purpose."

"It's *never* on purpose. Trouble just follows those two."

Kimble thought for a moment. "What did Ramalah say about all this?"

Lorna put her phone away, remaining quiet.

"Lorna. You *did* report this, didn't you?"

"No," Lorna finally admitted. "If those two are alive, then it means they might know what happened to Mariam. They're going to speak to me, or so help me, I'm going to wring their tiny necks!"

Kimble coughed, trying to mask an involuntary laugh. "That's your plan, dear? You know there'll be an investigation."

"It's better than doing nothing. Besides, Ramalah will never know. I altered the log so it wouldn't look out of the ordinary."

"Oh, hon. You need to think this through. If Penelope and Twitch were aboard the *Gaspee*, it would change everything. If this gets out, it could be interpreted as treason."

"Treason? The ship was found abandoned, Kimble. I think we're entitled to find our own answers. It's not as though the council has given us parents much hope."

Kimble pursed his lips, shaking his head. "You've got to report this."

Lorna looked stunned. "And what about Mariam and the rest of the crew? We parents are important too, you know."

"Yes, dear. But it's because of the *Gaspee* that the council ordered the system overhaul, remember? Listen, this is more urgent than you realize."

Lorna rolled her eyes. "We're all tired of waiting for the council! All they do is talk, talk, talk. I promise, if it were one of their children that went missing, they would have done something about it. They've done nothing to discover what happened. I've talked to the other mothers, and they're just as fed up as I am."

Kimble glanced around to make sure they were alone. "Keep it down. This isn't the place to start this all up again."

"Don't tell me to be quiet! We've been quiet long enough—"

Kimble cracked his cane on the sidewalk. "Enough, dear! What I'm going to tell you is classified, understand? A week ago, a Rashaar scouting party was captured. They were passing through the Klamath mountains heading west."

Stunned, Lorna's blustery countenance fell. "The Rashaar? Here?"

Kimble nodded. "Now that you've got us both breaking the rules, just listen. One of the scout leaders was Montu, from the Nondi tribe. A big fellow, nine feet tall. He was their guide. They attempted to cross Glendale Pass, where our lookouts captured them."

"Glendale Pass? That's close to Fort Somar."

Kimble nodded. "I haven't heard anything for a couple of days now. But there's a rumor the Montu had some personal belongings from Captain Frost. They've been shipped off to New Massan to be interrogated."

Lorna's eyes widened. "Captain Frost was from Fort Somar. Oh, Kimble. Our poor Mariam! What if the Rashaar captured the *Gaspee*?"

"Now, you understand why this must be reported. Mariam told me Captain Frost discovered Penelope and Twitch. He made them honorary crew members."

"I knew that. Mariam talked to me, too, you know."

"Then don't you think their return should be reported? It's now a military concern, after all," Kimble said.

"Do you think Penelope and Twitch could have joined the Rashaar?"

Kimble laughed. "Could you imagine? Those two are many things, but they aren't traitors."

"Well, Kimble, they're trapped here for now. You know how they feel about me. You have the best chance of contacting them."

"It's been a long time," Kimble said.

"So what do you think we should do?"

"Well, dear, you've made your intentions clear. Let's just hope they resurface soon."

Chapter 5
Crows!

Superintendent Humphrey Arnold's footsteps echoed down the hall of Quentin Elementary School. His wife, Marjorie, had insisted on buying him a fancy pair of Italian shoes for the back-to-school night. The constant clacking of the hard soles on the gray-and-white terrazzo flooring had grown tiresome as he inspected classrooms and pestered teachers to get their rooms in order.

The building, built in 1906 as a private academy, was over a century old. It was from an era before mass production and cheap materials. Granite, marble, and slate were used throughout. Doors and other wooden fixtures were made from dark, old-forest hardwood.

Climbing the marble stairway, Humphrey stood on the second floor overlooking the foyer. He had a grand view out of the five high-arched windows.

Outside in the courtyard, parents and students were arriving. Beyond was the parking lot and the Pacific Ocean, with the sun descending in the late afternoon.

Swiping his handkerchief along the railing, Humphrey stuffed it away without checking. With the last two years of renovation completed, the school was ready...he hoped. He had gambled his reputation on tonight. But the rumors of the school grounds being haunted still nagged him.

Humphrey didn't believe in the paranormal, ghost stories, or other such nonsense. Pragmatic and levelheaded, his gift of logic and critical thinking made him perfect for standing up to the town's superstitious residents who opposed the school's renovation—even to that awful Cornelia Moon, who gave him so much grief.

Now, he wasn't so sure.

He looked at his wristwatch. 5:30.

"Almost there," he whispered.

For a fleeting moment, he dared take pride in his accomplishment. This day should have been a celebration in every way, but it wasn't.

He was hiding a secret.

How can I explain what I saw? he thought, sliding his fingers through his thinning gray hair. He took in a deep breath and exhaled. The air was thick with heady odors of fresh paint and floor wax.

"Humphrey?" a quiet voice called from behind.

Startled, Humphrey slipped, thanks to his new shoes on the freshly waxed floors.

"Lamptor's fire! Trying to kill yourself?" Bassam Amun, the school's janitor, exclaimed. He shuffled over, straightening the bill on his red ball cap. "Maybe I should get a pair of clackers like yours so you can hear me comin', no?"

The two old men burst into hearty laughter.

"The school's come a long way since we brought you aboard, Bassam," Humphrey said. "I'm sure ol' Alfred would be proud if he could see it tonight."

"Yes, he is," Bassam said, leaning on his broom.

Humphrey considered correcting this innocent slip. Alfred Quentin had died back in 1927. Bassam just didn't have a good handle on his English yet. His accent was one of those mysteries Humphrey wondered about. He guessed it was Middle Eastern. When he asked Bassam where he was from, the old man laughed and said, "From across the sea."

"Did I ever tell you my father attended the old academy?" Humphrey asked.

"Before the junk and dust, no?" Bassam winked.

Humphrey nodded. "Dad graduated from the academy in 1926 and was killed in a car accident when I was young. The stories he told me about this school…"

His voice trailed off as he motioned to one of the wide supporting pillars. Carved in the column was a fantastic horned creature with claws and a long wrapping tail. Colorful Egyptian hieroglyphs wrapped around the base and capital of the pillar.

"Anyway, Dad could tell some amazing stories. These walls and floors have sat unchanged for a century. For some reason, knowing that makes me miss him."

"Great memories are the reward of a life well spent, no? The simple things remind us of what's important."

Humphrey studied Bassam. Sometimes, the old janitor said things that seemed above his humble appearance. "Well said. So, you've poked around this old school. What do you think of her?"

"The school can handle the little ones. There be a few dusty corners left, but I'll take care of those."

"That's not what I meant. What do you think of these carvings?" Humphrey asked, motioning to the pillar.

Bassam looked thoughtful. "She's got a bit of mystery. But don't worry, she'll keep the little ones safe."

Little ones safe? Humphrey usually understood Bassam's misplaced words, but he wasn't sure what he meant. "So these alterations to the school don't strike you as strange or...crazy?"

"Should they?"

"I'm told that Alfred spent the last of his fortune on these alterations to the school before he died. Some say they're proof he went crazy in the end."

"Really? He went to a lot of effort to show it."

"That's just what some have said. Remember those boxes you dropped off in my office last week?"

"The ones from the third floor?"

"Yes. Did you look through them?"

"No, I saw books. You told me not to touch books from the old school and take them to your office."

Humphrey nodded. "You know what I found? Alfred's private journal."

"Learned something new, no?"

"I finally understand what motivated Alfred to build the school in the first place: God told him to."

Bassam took his ball cap off, scratching his head. "He wrote that?"

"Well, not in those words. But he saw a vision. Kind of like Moses."

"Moses?"

"You know, Moses from the Bible."

"The Bible?" Bassam asked.

Humphrey's brow rose. "I get it. You're having fun with me?"

"No, sir. Is this Bible something…how do you say…big?"

"You're serious? A man of your age not knowing what the Bible is?" Humphrey scrutinized the old janitor, expecting an explanation, but Bassam remained quiet. "Well, no matter. Where did you say you were from again?"

"I came from across the sea. Just like I told you before."

"Yes, but what country?"

Bassam's cheerful countenance withdrew behind solemn eyes as he plopped his hat back on. Humphrey felt a sudden sense of urgency as if time were slipping away. He glanced at his watch.

"Excuse me," Bassam finally said. "I need to finish Mr. Wilson's classroom before the parents come in." He hefted his broom over his shoulder and walked to a nearby classroom, pushing the heavy door open. "Good luck tonight, Chief," he said with a salute. He stepped in, letting the door close behind him with a heavy thunk.

Who doesn't know what the Bible is? Humphrey wondered. Shrugging it off, he shuffled to the stairway leading up to the third floor. A rope barred the flight of stairs with a sign that read *Third floor under renovation. FLOOR CLOSED*. The sign was there by his orders.

Ascending to the third floor, he walked under the wide archway with the words *Astorian Wing* etched on a brass plaque. He felt his chest starting to tighten.

Ahead, it was dark. The polished floor abruptly became dull and dingy as he crossed over the edge where Bassam's floor polisher hadn't reached yet. The boxes had been removed, but the walls and closed classroom doors were still covered with ages of cobwebs and dust.

Approaching the shadowy bend, Humphrey's determination began to wane. The time had come to inspect the one place he had avoided all day. His clacking shoes only added to his anxiety, so he stopped and kicked them off. Snoopy and Woodstock peered up at him as he continued silently down the hall. His grandkids had given him the socks after he announced to his family he was retiring. But the school renovation had changed those plans.

Reaching the corner, he pressed against the dusty wall and swallowed. On the other side of the hall was a filthy picture window with a view of the playground. Beyond, obscured by the forest, was Alfred Quentin's old mansion. It peered back like a crouching tiger with broken eyes and a disheveled patchy roof.

It was that mansion that caused most of his troubles.

Thanks to a retired city employee named Cornelia Moon, the city archives had sixty years of reported hauntings around the school, most in that mansion.

Humphrey would have been happy to see all those records in the landfill, but Cornelia managed to get every scrap marked as historical documents. She had started a campaign to have the school torn down. When she learned that Humphrey proposed to renovate the school, she'd unleashed a fury that he shuddered to think about.

Crash!

Humphrey nearly parted ways with his grandkids' socks. Something heavy had fallen, sending an echoing thud throughout the school. Moments later, a roiling cloud of dust emerged from around the corner.

Regaining his wits, he peeked around into the shadows. The hall was dark as night. He could just make out the trellis gate with its angled wooden slats halfway down.

There was a creak, and light from an opening door appeared on the other side of the gate. Humphrey heard whispering.

He pulled back, his heart racing.

Somewhere in the back of his frantic mind came a scolding voice of reason: *Humphrey, you're seventy years old. There's a perfectly ordinary explanation for what's down there. Get in there and face it like a man!*

His shaking hand reached around the corner for the light switch. Locating it, he remembered it required a special key.

"Bother," he breathed, feeling along the molding.

A streak of brass flashed by as the tiny metal key struck the floor with a ringing *clink-clank*.

"Run!" voices cried in the dark.

After several attempts to recover the key, he took his cell phone from his pocket and activated the flashlight. He rushed to the gate, holding the phone up like a torch.

"Who's down here?" he demanded, shaking the gate.

He reached between the slats, using the weak light to scan over the piles of boxes and chairs. The light passed over a piano with two crows perched at the top. He thought they were stuffed, as they stood perfectly still, but when he swept his light back past, one of them blinked.

"Crows?" Humphrey exclaimed.

He reached for his keys as the two birds flew through the open door, kicking up a cloud of dust. Humphrey coughed as he worked the lock and charged after the pair into the dim classroom, where he tripped and fell into a pile of newspapers. The crows escaped out the window behind a set of blinds that were doing an excellent job of keeping the room dim.

Humphrey lay sprawled out amid the scattered papers, feeling foolish. All this fuss over some lousy birds. Struggling to his feet, he went to the window and looked past the blinds. Below was the courtyard of gathering families. What would they think of their superintendent having been spooked by a couple of crows?

He breathed a sigh of relief. At least crows made sense. The ghostly apparition that had chased him down the hall last week was another matter. His pragmatic mind had been slapped, and he was still reeling from the experience. He wasn't about to side with Cornelia Moon about the school being haunted, but the third floor would remain closed until he found a rational explanation.

Why was the window open? he wondered, slamming it shut. He would have to remind Bassam to be more mindful about securing the school.

Checking his surroundings, he found the classroom was full of desks piled with newspapers and dusty boxes of tennis shoes. A blinking green light cut through the darkness. A desk lay on its side. Beside it was an old PC with its green monochrome monitor buzzing on the floor.

Straightening up the desk, Humphrey hefted the PC and monitor back into place. The desk had a broken leg and wouldn't stand up on its own. He deduced the crashing had been this desk toppling over. He grabbed a handful of newspapers and used them as a shim to keep the desk upright.

The computer disk drive whirred and rattled. A single sentence appeared on the screen: *Hold the authorization key in front of the monitor and tap the space bar.*

"Where did this old relic come from?" he mumbled.

He hadn't seen a computer like this since the eighties. He tapped the space bar, and the computer responded with a beep and a flickering green screen. A nearby heap of newspapers fell over, causing him to jump.

"Take it easy," he whispered. He decided it was time to leave.

Bending to unplug the computer, he noticed a delicate skeleton key resting on the black-and-white tile. Picking it up, an electrical surge hit him and his muscles seized up. When it finally released him, stars filled his vision, and he slumped over in a heap.

*　　　　*　　　　*

A persistent beep sounded in Humphrey's throbbing head. He opened his eyes and saw a knocked-over heap of newspapers with the headline *MEN WALK ON MOON* and a scattering of dusty tennis shoes.

Struggling to his feet, the green text on the monitor caught his attention. He read aloud the words on the display. "Unauthorized user. Identity recorded."

He was still gripping the skeleton key and saw his hand bleeding where his fingernails had dug into his palm. Relaxing, he wiped the blood off with his handkerchief.

The beeping caught his attention again. It was his wristwatch, reading 6:05. Clamoring to the window, he saw the courtyard bustling with waiting families.

"The program!" he exclaimed and dashed off.

Chapter 6
The Protest

Humphrey burst through the foyer door to find the school staff waiting in their seats before the crowd of parents. A collective sigh of relief came as Principal Lorraine Stokes stood to greet him.

"It's about time you showed up," she scolded. "Where have you been? We were getting worried."

"Inspection. Just lost track of time, sorry."

"What have you been rolling in?" she asked, smacking the dust off Humphrey's tweed jacket, stopping when she noticed he wasn't wearing shoes.

"Don't ask," Humphrey coughed. Catching his breath, he fumbled for his reading glasses and notes as he approached the podium to address the audience. His pockets were stuffed and tangled. He removed everything and laid the contents on the podium. When a breeze picked up his notes, he used the skeleton key as a paperweight.

"Parents and students, we'd like to get started. Please get to your seats."

A van from a local church pulled up in the parking lot. Humphrey hardly gave it a second notice as he leaned into the microphone and said, "I want to welcome everyone to the first year of operation of Alfred B. Quentin Elementary. I'm Superintendent Humphrey Arnold."

The audience applauded. That was when he noticed the van was discharging more passengers than seemed possible. A group of women emerged wearing their Sunday dresses, carrying professionally printed protest signs. The leader of the protesters wore a lemon-yellow dress and had a scowl etched on her face. Even with Humphrey's imperfect eyesight, he instantly recognized Cornelia Moon.

He turned to his faculty. In other circumstances, he might have been amused by their catatonic expressions, but Cornelia's presence was no laughing matter. He cleared his throat and made eye contact with Principal Stokes. "Call the police!" he mouthed.

Humphrey eyed Cornelia in silence. The first time he'd met Cornelia was at a town council meeting. She accused the council of being "a good ol' boys club" where the only way anything got done was if one were male and friends with the councilmen. She had become so belligerent that she had to be escorted away in handcuffs.

Cornelia and her cohorts prepared for battle, spreading out behind the crowd with their signs held high. They remained silent as Humprey scanned the signs. He loosened his tie when he saw Cornelia's sign, which read *Humphrey Arnold, RETIRE NOW!*

Sharon Leak, the school's nurse, whispered, "Humphrey, you alright?"

Ignoring her, Humphrey pulled the microphone to his lips. "Today is a historic occasion. We are at the beginning of a new chapter in Stonehelm's history. Many young families have recently found our gem of a town. We are delighted to have so many new faces with us this evening."

His confidence grew after seeing smiles and nods in the audience. To his relief, Cornelia remained unnoticed and silent.

"Many of you parents were students of mine back when I was a second-grade teacher. Times have changed, haven't they? Look around at your new school. It's four times bigger than Palmer Elementary, with plenty of room to grow in the years to come."

Humphrey's speech changed, and he spoke in a voice that charmed the children. "Children, we have this building thanks to a man who lived a long time ago named Alfred Quentin. Alfred was a teacher, and he believed the best place to learn was a place that inspired the imagin—"

"Our children won't be brainwashed in the halls of Alfred's asylum, Mr. Arnold," Cornelia Moon's amplified voice boomed. She dropped the megaphone to her side and climbed onto a chair. Strands of her thin, gray hair danced on her solemn face.

Humphrey entertained rebuking Cornelia over the podium but thought it better to avoid confrontation with a martyr. Besides, the police were coming. Murmurs spread quickly as the audience realized they were boxed in by the standoff.

Cornelia lifted the megaphone to her curled lips. "Alfred Quentin was nothing more than a charlatan. This building is a memorial of his insanity."

Her words incited a swell in the crowd. Cornelia motioned, and her dozen cohorts marched in a circle as they shouted and waved their picket signs. Some children became frightened. Cornelia's indifference to the effect she was having made Humphrey furious.

"Children, there's nothing to be afraid of," he said. "We've notified the police, and this will be sorted out shortly."

Cornelia and her protesters continued on, ignoring Humphrey's warning. Humphrey reminded himself that Cornelia's presence wasn't entirely unexpected. The city had warned him that a petition to protest had been requested, and an area on the road leading to the parking lot had been set aside for the picketers. Clearly, Cornelia had no regard for rules.

Parents gathered in groups and talked among themselves as Cornelia's megaphone protest echoed in the courtyard. Those closest to the front were talking with the teachers. A frazzled-looking woman named Marie Hill stood nearby, rocking her fussy baby. She was trying to speak to Humphrey as her three older children pawed at her.

Humphrey became distracted when he heard clattering from above and saw that the window he had closed earlier on the third floor was open again. The blinds blew in the wind.

"...well, do you?" Marie asked.

"Do what?"

"Think the school is haunted?"

"Of course not, Marie."

She waited for a stronger response. Her brow furrowed when Humphrey muttered something about a window and crows.

Fortunately for Humphrey, Marie's children drew her attention away.

"Cornelia is a horrible neighbor," Marie blathered on. "She'll call the police if one of my kids gets near her cats."

Cawing caught Humphrey's attention. The two crows had returned, peering scornfully at him from the window. This was his last thread of inner calm. His typically ordered world was spinning out of control: the apparition in the school, Cornelia Moon, and now the crows. He felt a migraine coming on.

*   *   *

Micah and Richard talked about video games, indifferent to the tumult around them. Only particularly rude comments caught their attention.

"Humphrey is an incompetent idiot!" Cornelia shouted.

The boys laughed.

Lorna yanked Micah's ear.

"Ow!"

"That's not funny! Cornelia Moon should be ashamed of herself," Lorna said, shaking the open house program at the boys.

Micah couldn't contain himself. He smirked, and he and Richard burst into a fit of laughter.

"Oh, pishposh," Lorna breathed, tossing the evening's program at the two.

Micah dismissed his mother's paper assault. But Richard was curious. On the cover, the boys saw two poorly reproduced photographs. The first was of the school, with a meager first class of graduates lined up at the foyer doors. The other picture showed a man with a long, thin mustache curled at the ends.

"What's it say?" Micah asked, stifling his grin from his mother.

Under the pictures was a paragraph that read:

QUENTIN ELEMENTARY WELCOMES YOU
*Alfred B. Quentin was an educator and inventor who founded the academy on
April 19, 1906, one day after the great San Francisco earthquake. The photo
of Alfred above was the last known photo of the electrical theory pioneer. The
school was closed in 1927. Later, it served as Stonehelm's courthouse, an ob-
servatory (during WWII), a shoe factory, Stonehelm's storage facility, and now,
Quentin Elementary School!*

Seeing the boys had settled, Lorna innocently asked, "Richard,
dear, did your mom decide what she's doing about your school
clothes this year?"

Richard unzipped his yellow fleece jacket, revealing a brown
denim shirt sewn with white thread. It was a size too large, and the
breast pocket was sewn on crooked.

"Yep. She bought a used sewing machine and fabric at a yard
sale. She just finished this shirt."

Kimble leaned forward to look. He and Lorna tightened their
lips to avoid smiling. Richard's parents were divorced, and money
was always tight. Richard was the usual victim of his mother's
scrimping. She was a great mom but a lousy seamstress.

"I think Micah's outgrown some of his clothes. When you come
over, let's see what we can come up with," Lorna winked.

"Mom, can Richard sleep over after my birthday party?" Micah
asked.

"Of course. Richard, I'm making lasagna."

"Oh, I love your cooking, Mrs. Fennly," Richard said, smacking
his lips. The boys soon were caught up in talking about video
games again.

Lorna and Kimble looked forward, waiting patiently. Finally,

Lorna leaned over to Kimble and said, "I wonder where Tricia and Geoffrey are tonight? I talked to her earlier, and she told me they planned to come tonight. I have some things I wanted to give her for Max."

"What grade is Max in this year?" Kimble asked.

"Really," Lorna said, "he's your only grandson..." She paused. "Oh, dear, I forgot about the package. Just before we left tonight, a priority came. I'm sure Geoffrey got one too. Maybe that's what kept them."

"A priority? Why didn't you tell me?"

"Micah told me about it after we left. I knew I should have turned around and got it. This whole Penelope and Twitch business has got me out of sorts."

"Alfred was a pagan worshipper!" Cornelia shouted from behind.

Lorna sighed. "I can't stand that woman. I didn't care for her in the first grade, and I still don't like her."

"Really? I find her quite pleasant," Kimble said sarcastically. He looked back at the protest and dug his cane in the grass.

Cornelia was satisfied with her protest except for one stubby woman named Nellie Wilkerson who marched with little enthusiasm. The Fennlys were friends with Nellie and knew she was a tender-hearted widow. She looked apologetic as she passed the scorning crowd. Noticing Kimble, Nellie pulled her sign down to hide her face. Cornelia marched behind her and tried to force her movements like a sculptor would a fat piece of stubborn clay.

Kimble winked at Cornelia as she passed by. She was not amused. "They're among us even now!" she shouted, pointing directly at Kimble. "They're your neighbors and your co-workers. Don't be fooled!"

Lorna elbowed Kimble. "For goodness' sake, Kimble, don't

aggravate the woman!"

"Yes, dear." Kimble grinned and asked quietly, "So, what happened at the cove?"

Lorna checked to make sure Micah wasn't listening. "He claims they gave him Mariam's locket."

Kimble's brow rose. "Did you see it?"

Lorna shook her head. She took out her phone and showed him the pictures of the black pebble. "This is what he claims they gave him."

Kimble zoomed in to examine the smooth black surface. "It could be hidden. It's about the size of a locket."

"My phone has the latest detection software. It would have to be hidden with something new."

As they looked at Lorna's phone, a message popped up.

NOTICE: An unauthorized user attempted to activate Gate 2 at 17:40 Oregon Time on Terminal 12. Do you want to override?

"What does that mean?" Kimble asked.

"I thought something like this might happen," Lorna said, "so I put a lock on all the emergency exits and the old mansion just in case."

"It said it was an unauthorized user. Who could that be?"

Lorna shrugged. "If I hadn't put this lock in place, they would have gone through."

"Can you find out?"

"I know you boys in the corps have little confidence in us lowly gate managers," Lorna said, taking back her phone, "but we know our jobs." She tapped on an app with an image of a gate and a giant clock in the middle. After several taps and swipes, she finally said, "It's not one of our people, so I can't tell you who without being at the office. The request came from one of the old PCs they used in the courthouse. That explains why the notice was delayed. We had them all moved into storage, which would mean…"

"What?"

"The terminal's in the school."

*   *   *

Distant sirens stirred excitement back into the crowd.

Humphrey leaned into the microphone. "Folks, if I could have your attention…parents, please…"

It was of no use. The crowd volume increased as the sirens grew louder.

The two crows sat perched on the third-floor window. Humphrey frowned at them and hoped no one saw how they had opened the window. Crows weren't supposed to open windows. These two, however, were not ordinary crows.

"Penelope, how are we supposed to get back home now? You lost the key," Twitch cawed.

Penelope's crown of pink feathers flared at Twitch's accusing tone. "It's not my fault. Humphrey surprised me!"

"So what do we do now?"

"We find it," she said, ducking under the window blinds.

She soared into the classroom to the computer on the desk, where she settled in front of the keyboard. She ruffled her feathers and let out a caw.

At this typical behavior for a crow, her black feathers pulled back as limbs changed and twisted into human arms and legs with dainty hands and feet.

Her body straightened, forming into the shape of a curvy woman in a purple snapdragon dress. Black eyes turned white with blue irises as the crow's beak formed into pouty red lips. Her nose popped out last.

Penelope was tiny, less than a foot tall. She slipped the long pink shock of hair that hung before her eyes behind her ear.

Twitch poked his head back into the classroom. "What are you doing?"

"I'm thinking!" Penelope said, scanning the room. Finally, she jumped down to the floor. "Humphrey set the desk and computer back up. I had that key around here somewhere."

She stomped next to a pile of dusty newspapers. In a fit of rage, she kicked one of the piles and leaped back when it nearly came down on her.

"Eww, is this blood?" she said, wiping the coagulated crimson from her foot onto a newspaper.

"Blood? Are you hurt?"

"It's not from me. It had to come from Humphrey. We'd be home by now if it hadn't been for this stupid desk," she said, kicking the broken leg across the floor.

She climbed back up onto the desk and stood before the computer. She knelt and tapped out the word *status*. The cursor blinked, and the disk drive whirred to life. The sentence *Security Protocol 431* flashed on the screen.

"Oh, no," Penelope said, smacking the return key several times.

"What is it?" Twitch said, flying next to her.

"We're locked out."

"So what do we do now?"

"There's another portal in the mansion. It's in bad shape, but we don't have much of a choice."

"If that doesn't work, then what?"

"We go for the main gate when they open it for the kids."

Twitch cawed furiously, flapping his wings.

"I know, it's risky. If we can't find that key, we have no other choice." She chewed her lip as she thought. Then she suddenly said, "Of course!" Closing her eyes, she spoke in a commanding voice, "Locate!"

An unseen force possessed Penelope's feet. With great determination, she leaped off the table, rushed to the window, and jumped up. She would have gone over the edge if it hadn't been for the blinds' pull string.

"Stop! Stop! Stop!" Penelope cried, clutching onto the string as she swung back and forth.

She cracked open her eyes and saw Humphrey staring back with his mouth agape. On the podium, she saw the gate key.

"I found it!" she said.

Twitch fluttered back to the window. "What do we do now? He won't just hand it over to a couple of crows. If only we had a diversion."

Four blaring police cruisers pulled into the parking lot behind the crowd. Penelope leaped back through the window and changed back into her former crow self.

"Let's go," Penelope said and dove through the window.

*   *   *

Humphrey and the staff stepped forward to watch the police cruisers arrive. Penelope glided silently down and landed on the podium. She snatched up the key with her bill. Humphrey spun around, surprising her.

"Shoo!" he shouted, flailing his arms at her.

Twitch dove straight at Humphrey, claws forward. "Caaaaw!" he cried, darting past.

The teachers looked back at the commotion behind them. All they saw was Humphrey ducked down as his speech notes scattered in the wind. Penelope and Twitch sailed over the crowd to a tree that overlooked Cornelia's protest. They landed on a branch and watched four police officers exit their cruisers.

"Thanks," Penelope said, dropping the key on the branch. "He tried to grab me!"

"Big people don't grab birds—at least not when we have these," Twitch said, demonstrating his claws.

A rusty van with the words *Stonehelm Reader* printed on its side screeched to a halt behind the cruisers. Matthew Hundley, the *Reader*'s nineteen-year-old amateur photographer, leaped out.

"I forget how loud it is here," Twitch said as the cruiser sirens wound down. "Those men sure look angry. They're as big as the guards back on Neitah Island."

Penelope flitted her wing in Twitch's face. "Shh, he's saying something."

"Cornelia Moon?" Police Chief Tommy Richins called.

Cornelia pushed her way to the front of the protest, patting her hair and straightening her corsage. She posed for a photograph as her fellow protesters crowded behind her. "You can't make us leave, Tommy," she said sternly. "This is a legal protest. Signed the paperwork myself."

There was silence, broken by Matthew as he enthusiastically bound about Cornelia taking snapshots.

"Calm down, Cornelia. We're not saying you have to leave."

"So, is the entire Stonehelm police force here to cheer us on? Or do you plan on hauling us off like criminals?"

"Now, Cornelia, I think you can appreciate that we have a whole crowd of children here, and we don't want this situation to get out of hand."

"So you mean everything will be fine if we move along like good little sheep? I'd sooner be dragged off to jail!" Cornelia shouted. She jerked her protest sign and shouted, "Boo! Shame on the police for protecting the lies! They will never silence us!"

Her protesters followed as she marched around the police cruisers.

"Close the school!" one protester shouted.

"Alfred's school is evil!" Cornelia added.

"Cornelia," Chief Richins said, his voice terse. "You *will* vacate to the protest area, or you give us no choice but to arrest you."

His threat only caused Cornelia to behave more cantankerously. Chief Richins was in a bind. With all the camera phones and young eyes watching, it was a delicate situation to deal with a belligerent seventy-year-old woman.

When Chief Richins unhooked his cuffs, Cornelia recoiled and held her picket sign like a baseball bat. "Tommy, you lay your hands on me, so help me, you'll regret it!"

Cornelia looked wildly at the other officers and then calmed herself. A warm, grandmotherly smile spread across her face as she eased her grip on the sign. "Tommy, I'm just a tired old woman. It's my heart, you see. My last wish before I leave this earth is that this school be torn down and that horrible Alfred Quentin be forgotten."

Penelope and Twitch, watching Cornelia with great interest, began to screech and caw. Cornelia glanced at the two angry crows and smiled back at Chief Richins. "See, even the crows agree."

"Oh, I'll show you how a crow agrees," Penelope hissed.

"Stop, Penelope!" Twitch shouted.

It was too late. Penelope dove with her sharp claws cocked. She snatched Cornelia by the hair, expecting to get tangled. Instead, Cornelia's wig popped off, and Penelope soared over the cheering crowd.

Matthew snapped a picture at the exact moment Penelope snagged Cornelia's wig—a photo for which he would later get a

100-dollar bonus.

Cornelia shrieked, throwing her protest sign. It smashed into the windshield of Chief Richin's new cruiser as she grabbed her bald head. Shortly after, she hyperventilated and passed out.

Kimble hobbled to the front and saw Cornelia lying spread-eagle on the grass. He suppressed his grin when Lorna, Micah, and Richard stepped beside him.

"Oh, my," Lorna gasped.

Penelope flew over the school and dropped the wig on the roof. She flapped back around to the tree, where she found Twitch eyeing Cornelia's lifeless body.

"Um, Penelope..." Twitch said timidly. "I think you killed her."

"I did not. Anyway, she was asking for it—talking about Alfred that way." She froze when she saw Micah's parents. Focusing on Lorna, she said, "Oh, look who's shown up now. Let's get out of here before she lectures us to death."

Penelope snatched up the key, and the two flew off to the back of the school.

*　　　　*　　　　*

Cornelia was awake but delirious when the ambulance blared into the parking lot. The paramedics lifted her onto a gurney. "Nellie, Nellie!" she said, sitting up abruptly.

Nellie stood at her side, trying to block the gawkers from taking pictures. "I'm here. What is it, dear?"

"Promise me. You will take care of my children, won't you?"

"Of course."

Relieved, Cornelia laid back on the gurney. "Has he shown up?" she asked.

"Who?" Nellie frowned.

"Alfred."

The paramedics smiled as they loaded Cornelia into the back of the ambulance.

"Sweetie, you're talking nonsense," Nellie said. "Alfred died a long time ago."

Cornelia smiled thinly. "Don't be so sure. I want you to pass a message along."

Nellie sighed. "And what would you have me say?"

"Tell him my mother never forgave him."

Nellie stood nearby, pained by her friend's suffering. The excitement disappeared as the ambulance and protesters exited the parking lot.

Humphrey returned to the podium, offering consoling words for Cornelia that sounded more like a victory speech.

"With that," he said, cinching up his tie, "a great deal of effort has been spent preparing the school for this upcoming year. We invite you to join us for a tour and to meet your new teachers."

Chapter 7
Registration

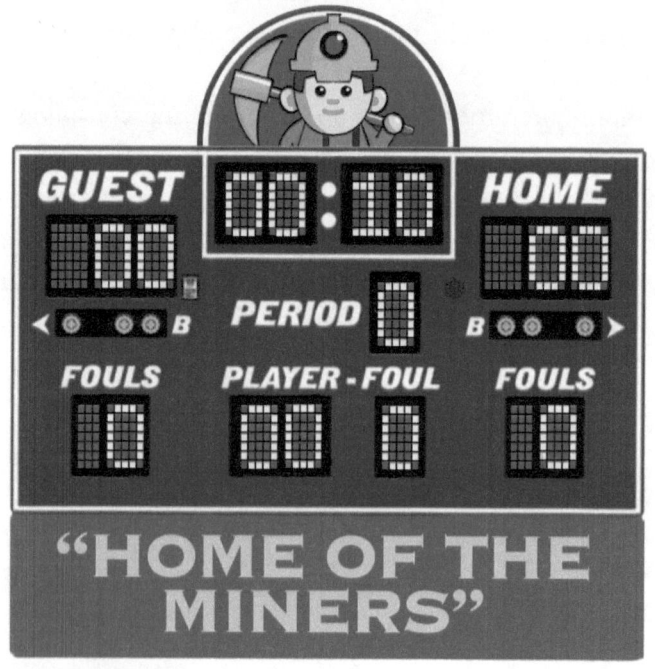

Families lined up to enter the school as Bassam hastily propped the five high-arched main doors open.

"Bassam…Bassam Amun!" Lorna called above the rabble.

Wiping his forehead with his ball cap, the janitor searched over the crowd until he spotted Lorna waving. She threaded her way to him and met him with a hug.

"Good to finally see a familiar face. But I think people might talk," Bassam said.

"Oh, let them talk. It's been ages since we've seen you."

Lorna looked over her shoulder for Kimble and the boys. The three had gotten tangled in the crowd. Bassam spotted Kimble and called out, "Is that poor old man the great Kimble Fennly?"

Kimble straightened up and cracked his cane on the sidewalk, announcing his intention to come through. The crowd divided as he boorishly made his way.

"Look at Gramps go!" a mocking voice yelled.

Micah and Richard stopped, recognizing Jack Farnsworth's voice. Jack leaned against the school wall, surrounded by his brother Ben, Kamran Higbee, and Tony Clark. Seeing Jack and Kamran together made Micah feel uneasy. Micah had been friends with Kamran when they were younger. After the Farnsworths moved in, Kamran and Jack became best friends. Micah hadn't had much to do with Kamran since.

"Geez, Micah, your dad's older than my grandpa," Kamran said, his voice cracking. Kamran had hit a growth spurt and was now notably taller than Jack.

Not to be outdone, Jack added, "Yeah, where's your real parents? If my grandparents raised me, I'd die. Oh, wait. That's what happened to your sister."

There was silence between the boys. Had Jack gone too far? Moments later, Kamran and Tony howled with laughter. Ben laughed like it was the funniest joke he'd ever heard.

Micah didn't react. He had heard this line before from Jack and was callous to it. But watching the others laugh started to get to him.

"That's cold," Tony said, punching Jack's shoulder.

"Ben said you hit him today," Jack said, stepping forward and shoving Richard aside.

Kamran and Tony surrounded Micah. Ben poked his head out from behind Jack with a taunting grin.

"I didn't hit him," Micah said, glowering at Ben. "He climbed in our yard and let Grubb out. I told him, and I'm telling you, to stay out of our yard."

"Sounds like a threat to me," Kamran said.

"What are you afraid of? Afraid they'll mow your lawn?" Tony added.

The boys laughed.

Jack's lazy eyes looked over to Richard and back to Micah. "We don't like your stupid dog or your friends. My parents talk about you guys all the time. We're sick of your dog, your yard, and your parents. You guys live like trash. My dad's a lawyer, and he said he's calling the city to make you clean up your yard. Do you think we care about what happened to your sister? You mean nothing to us. One less Fennly, the better."

Micah gritted his teeth as a red hue spread across his face. Clenching his fists, he felt his restraint slipping.

"Do it, Fennly. Hit me, I dare you," Jack said, the grin disappearing from his face.

Kamran and Tony stepped back, anticipating a fight. Ben smiled, his eyes wide. The confrontation caught the attention of passing parents.

Richard stepped between the boys and grabbed Micah by the arm. "Let's just go."

"Get lost, Richard, or you're next. You're a bigger loser than Micah. Where did you get those clothes? From the garbage?"

Richard remained unfazed. "Come on. He won't do anything with all these parents here."

The boys laughed as Richard pulled Micah into the crowd.

"Losers!" Ben yelled, sticking his tongue out.

Lorna called to Micah, but he pretended not to hear. He and Richard entered the foyer through the breezeway and surveyed their surroundings.

"Look at this place! It's way better than our old school," Richard exclaimed.

Still furious, Micah looked back to see where Jack was.

"Just forget about them. Look at this place!"

"Big deal, it's just a school."

"Really? Our old school didn't have a statue," Richard said, trying to cheer him up. He climbed the blocks of granite that depicted a mountainous bluff. Mounted on the rock was a nine-foot bronze statue of a man holding a pickax over his shoulder. In his outstretched hand, he held a gold nugget.

"Alfred Quentin, 1890," Richard read from the bronze plaque at the foot of the statue. "Do you know anything about him?"

"No. My parents mentioned his name a few times when they talked about the school."

Richard read the description under the title. "It says here he was a gold miner, and after his dad died in an accident, he became a teacher. He spent his own money building the school."

Micah didn't care. He stood off to the side as parents and students flooded the foyer. Teachers directed parents to classes, with the sixth-grade teachers standing at the entrance to the gymnasium. One of those teachers was an exceptionally tall woman Micah and Richard had never seen before. She wore a name tag that read *Miss Sorenson*. Even standing on the granite rock, Richard was still below her shoulders.

"Richard Sommers, get down from there this instant!" came an angry voice.

The boys knew this voice well. A red-haired woman stepped out from the nearby office. Knowing the statue to be a temptation to climb, she had been waiting like a spider to catch her prey.

"Sorry, Mrs. Ireland," Richard said, climbing down.

"This isn't here for kids to climb on," Mrs. Ireland said, pointing to the heap of granite. "Do I make myself clear?"

"Yes, ma'am."

"Starting this year, I'm expecting a more respectful—"

She broke off when Micah's mother called. "Micah! Richard! Come here. I want you to meet someone."

Mrs. Ireland's blustery presence sank. She had a well-rehearsed lecture and had been eager to give it. "Move along," she sighed, shuffling back into her glass lair.

"Boys, this is Bassam," Lorna said. "He's a good friend of the family."

"This must be Micah," Bassam said, greeting Micah with a firm handshake. The janitor's hands were rough. "You, young man, look much like your brother Blake when he was your age. Got the same eyes as your father, no?" he added, giving Kimble a nod of approval.

Micah struggled to understand Bassam through his thick accent. "Uh. You knew my brother Blake?"

Bassam nodded. "I know both your brothers, Blake and Kellan. They were students of mine when they were your age."

"Bassam was a teacher before he retired," Lorna said proudly. "He moved back here and is now the custodian."

Blake and Kellan were much older than Micah. Both brothers grew up in Stonehelm but moved away long before Micah was born. He rarely saw the two, who ran a business together in

Southern California. The last time he had seen them was at Mariam's funeral.

"And who is this?" Bassam said, looking Richard over.

Richard was always uncomfortable around strangers. He stared at Bassam with a bewildered expression.

"This is Richard. He's my best friend," Micah finally said.

"Ahh, best friends are something special. Richard, where you from?"

Micah finally nudged Richard to say something.

"Um. From around here, I guess."

Bassam grinned and said he was excited to get to know them. He talked to Lorna and Kimble for several minutes. They caught up on Micah's sister Tricia and her young family, who lived across town. Talk of Mariam was brief, and Bassam seemed familiar with what had happened. Richard stood aloof nearby, lost in thought.

"What's the matter?" Micah whispered.

Richard, noticing he had Bassam's attention again, didn't respond. Instead, he bent over and pretended to tie his shoe. Micah rolled his eyes. When Richard was uncomfortable, he always found interesting ways to look busy. Why would he have an issue with Bassam? Bassam was certainly more likable than the grumpy janitor at Palmer Elementary.

Humphrey came into the breezeway and entered the foyer. Spotting Bassam, he approached, looking disheveled. Some of the children tittered, noticing Humphrey was missing his shoes. He met the Fennlys with a greeting that sounded rehearsed and asked how they were holding up since their loss of Mariam. This was all a formality, as he was eager to get on with the evening.

"Bassam, I need you to get those chairs down. And, oh. One more thing. A window's open on the third floor again. The latch must be broken..." Humphrey stopped short, looking like he had more to say, but instead waved Bassam off.

"Yessir," Bassam said, tilting his red ball cap.

"Sixth graders are meeting in the gym," Humphrey said, motioning to Micah and Richard.

*   *   *

Sixth-grader families entered the gymnasium, gathering into groups of friends and neighbors. The gymnasium was three stories high, with two full-court basketball standards next to each other. It also doubled as the school cafeteria. The refinished maple floor shined with a fresh coat of floor wax. The wax odor was strong, so the three tall windows on the back wall were wide open to let fresh air in.

Micah and Richard stood at the middle window, taking in the view. Outside, an iron fence formed the perimeter of the vast, grassy playground. Straight across and behind a sizable arched gate was the Quentin Mansion. Discarded cuts of granite lay strewn about. Games like four square, kickball, and hopscotch were painted white along the black stretch of asphalt near the school. The centerpiece was a sandpit containing brightly colored jungle bars.

"Wow, I can't wait to get out there!" exclaimed Richard.

"Oh, so now you're back to normal. What was up with you back there?"

Richard hesitated. "You'll just make fun of me."

"No, I won't," Micah said.

"There's more to that janitor than he's letting on."

"Like what?"

"You know how he said he was your brother's teacher?"

"Yeah."

"Well...he was your dad's teacher too."

"That's impossible," Micah said.

The boys looked back to the exit where Kimble and Bassam were still talking. It wasn't easy to judge age beyond a certain point. Bassam seemed older, but truthfully, there was no way to tell. Micah's father was seventy-seven, so how old was Bassam?

Micah did the math. "If he's twenty years older than Dad, he'd be ninety-seven. It's not unheard of for people to live to be a hundred."

"No, that's not what I mean. Bassam looked the same when he was your dad's teacher as he does now."

"How could you possibly know that?"

Richard shrugged. "I knew you wouldn't believe me."

"It's not that. But think about it, does that make any sense?"

The sixth-grade teachers filed in, catching the attention of the crowd. The last teacher in was Miss Sorenson. Shuffling along at her side was a short, hunched-over man in a fedora and a leather jacket. Some rushed to greet the leather-jacketed man. When he reached Bassam and Kimble, it was as if three long-lost friends had finally reunited after being apart. The men hugged and laughed.

The scene went on unnoticed until Micah's mother spotted the leather-jacketed man. She rushed from a circle of parents and let out a squeal, bringing a great deal of attention that hushed the crowd. She hugged the man, making the most embarrassing fuss Micah could have imagined.

Richard laughed. "Jeez, your mom..."

"Look, more old people!" Jack shouted from across the gym, throwing his hands in the air. He mocked Micah's mother by running to Kamran with outstretched arms. When the two met, they hugged with a spin, bringing on a fit of laughter from kids standing nearby. Micah pretended to yawn.

Richard looked around the gym's rafters, perplexed, finally settling on the giant new scoreboard above the doors. The scoreboard was counting down and had just reached five minutes.

"What's the matter?" Micah asked.

"That weird sound. Can you hear it?"

Micah listened but heard nothing. "I don't hear anything."

"It sounds like…mosquitoes."

"Hiya, fellas!" a voice said. Wren Kingsley wedged himself between the two friends. Wren was shorter and had a baby face. He was often mistaken for being younger than he was. Despite his youthful appearance, he always had a sharp tongue and perfectly combed hair. Tonight was no exception. "Are you guys excited to be starting the sixth grade?"

Micah and Richard let out an indifferent "Yeah."

"Oh, come on!" Wren said, spinning the pair around to look out the window. "Just look at that old mansion over there! Do you know what I heard? That place is haunted."

"Yeah, Wren, we've all heard that," Micah said dully.

"I bet you never heard this. You know Ronny Pilner?"

"Yeah, his older brother Eric dated my sister, remember?" Micah said. The few times Eric had talked to Micah, he'd shared ghost stories about the old mansion. It was the only redeeming quality Micah could remember about Mariam's old boyfriend.

"Ronny told me there were some trucks back there, you see, and his dad was getting them running again. The gate is always locked. But that day, it was open. He heard noises coming from the old mansion. You know what he found?"

"I don't know. Unicorns?" Micah said, mocking Wren's enthusiasm.

"Unicorns? No. He caught a bunch of kids in there."

"So?"

"He could see through 'em like they were ghosts! They ran off screaming and went straight through the walls!"

A sharp sting struck Micah's neck. Laughter erupted from boys standing nearby as he removed a wet wad of paper stuck to his skin. Jack had a straw to his lips, holding his fists up triumphantly.

Wren got hit by flecks of spit. "What's your problem?" Wren said, shooting a scowl at Jack and Kamran. Wren was not one for confrontation, but sometimes his mouth got ahead of him. When Jack's smile went dark, Wren slinked behind Micah and Richard.

Micah could feel his temper rising.

"Just ignore them," Richard said.

A buzz came from the scoreboard, indicating the one-minute mark. This sound brought on a stir in the parents.

Wren's mother, Olivia, walked with Lorna to the back of the gym. "Wren, let's move up front," Olivia said, reaching for his hand.

"Mom, that's embarrassing," Wren complained.

"Micah, Richard. Come along," Lorna said.

Jack and Kamran watched with smug grins as the three boys were escorted away.

"Mama's boys," Jack mouthed.

"Jerks," Micah shot back as he brushed past.

"I hope you choke on that straw," Wren added, but not too loudly.

Jack stuffed another piece of paper in his mouth and started chewing. He nearly swallowed it when Kamran's mother and father came along. Kamran's mom said they needed to be together up front as a family.

"No!" Kamran said, jerking his hand away. "I'm staying back here with Jack!"

"Kamran," his father said, clearing his throat, "listen to your mother."

Kamran rolled his eyes but acquiesced. He was soon up by Micah and Wren, avoiding eye contact.

The countdown timer on the scoreboard was down to the last few seconds: *10... 9... 8...*

Richard looked around thoughtfully and said to Micah, "I heard there'll be five sixth-grade classes this year. I wonder which class Jack and Kamran will be in."

"Close your eyes, son," Lorna whispered.

"What?" Micah asked, looking up at his mother. She looked back with a blank expression.

3... 2... 1...

With absolute silence, the world suddenly disappeared before Micah's eyes.

Chapter 8
The Other Side

B rilliant light filled Micah's vision. He shielded his eyes, shocked to see his hand glowed like fire. There was no pain or heat—just pure, intense light. Squeals of panic rose as a deep rumble came and ended abruptly with a heavy *clunk!* Silence fell over the gym as the light gradually returned to normal.

Micah felt his mother's hand give him a reassuring squeeze, "Everything's okay, son," she softly said.

"What happened?" Micah whispered.

Lorna tittered. "It's time to register for school."

Micah immediately noticed differences in the gym. The stone pillars were now older and chipped. The wooden floor was dull and worn, and a musty odor had replaced the smell of floor wax.

Wren thrummed his comb in his pocket, catching Micah's attention. The moment their eyes met, the sound stopped.

Kamran leaned forward, his eyes wide with shock. Seeing Micah, he calmed and let out an indifferent sniff. This unexpected detour of the evening had changed nothing between them.

Micah realized Richard was gone. He surveyed the gym. Many kids and their parents were missing—including Jack and Tony.

"Where's Richard?" Micah whispered to his mother.

"He's fine, son. He's just on the other side. We'll be back soon."

"The other side?"

A feverish rabble broke out as parents explained what just happened. Wren fired off questions to his mother and was bordering on hysteria. Lorna stepped over to help.

Just as the room settled, the gym started to rumble again. There was a flash of light, and small pockets of families appeared. Several girls suddenly appeared right in front of Micah. They ducked behind their parents when they saw the gym full of strangers. The gym roared to life two more times, bringing in more bewildered children and their parents.

Micah fidgeted nervously with the coin in his pocket. The clacking of his father's walking stick caught his attention. Kimble had been talking to Bassam and the man with the leather jacket.

Leaning on his cane, he put his enormous hand on Micah's shoulder. "We have some explaining to do," Kimble said with a reserved grin.

Micah looked puzzled. Had his father caused this?

"Believe it or not, son, your brothers and sisters went through this when they were your age. Don't worry, we're old hats at this," Kimble winked.

Wren had calmed enough that Lorna could give her attention back to Micah. She disagreed with Kimble's light treatment. "What your father means is we're here to help you get through this."

At the front of the gym, Miss Sorenson stepped forward, her imposing presence towering over the crowd. "If I could have everyone's attention, please," she said, her voice cutting through the commotion.

Several teachers who had appeared during the mayhem went about calming the crowd.

"Students," she continued, "there's no need to be alarmed. Your parents are here, and I assure you that you are safe. You may have noticed that some of your friends are absent. This was necessary for us to conduct our business tonight. Rest assured, they are safe, and when you return home, everything will be back to normal. I'm Miss Yamina Sorenson, one of the new sixth-grade teachers at Quentin Elementary this year. Director Karnak has entrusted me with overseeing tonight's enrollment process. We have a lot to cover and only one hour before the arrival of the next group of students."

A sudden buzz sounded from above, catching everyone's attention. The scoreboard was different from before. It wasn't electronic and modern. This one used spinning wheels adorned with black painted digits, now spinning down from an hour.

"Children, there are moments in life when change comes

unexpectedly. Tonight is one of those moments." Miss Sorenson's voice resonated through the gym, her tone measured. "Tonight, your eyes will be opened to a grand secret. It may be difficult to grasp initially, but with time, understanding will come. Parents, as is our tradition, we entrust you to address the questions that will arise in the coming weeks."

Confusion flickered across the faces of the students, but Miss Sorenson pressed on. "The foundation program enrollment coincides with the start of school registration. I just got word that over three thousand new students are entering the program this year, beating last year's record by two hundred students."

Parents applauded.

"In two weeks, classes commence at Boshii Campus. Tonight, our objective is to finalize enrollment. With the recent renovations to the school completed, we have invited a special guest to inaugurate the class of 2025. Children, please welcome Alfred Quentin."

Cheers erupted from parents. Children clapped but remained confused.

Miss Sorenson put her lanky arm around the old man wearing the leather jacket and fedora. The audience parted as the odd pair walked to the back of the gym, where a well-worn wooden stage awaited. The old man chuckled when Miss Sorenson effortlessly hefted him up.

"Much better," Alfred said. Even with the benefit of the podium, he was still a head shorter than Miss Sorenson.

Micah thought that if the man was Alfred Quentin, he didn't look like the statue out in the foyer. This man was feeble and hunched over.

"Children, step up. That's it," Alfred said in his gentle Southern voice. He removed his hat and directed families to spread out. "No need to crowd. You'll have a perfect view wherever you stand. We have a little time before we get started. Do any of you have questions?"

There was an uncomfortable silence that lasted until finally, one shy hand raised.

"Yes, dear?"

"Are you really *the* Alfred Quentin?" a boorish young girl named Marly asked.

"I am, little lady. My full name is Alfred Belmont Quentin. Belmont was my father's name. I was born in Norfolk, Virginia, on April 9th, 1871."

Marly thought for a moment, then blurted out, "You're more than a hundred years old!"

"Correct. I'm 148 this year."

There was a swell of surprise from the students.

More questions came, but Micah got distracted when his mother took out her cell phone. The screen glowed that same ominous red he had seen down at Hermit Cove. She showed her phone to Kimble, and he motioned her away from the others.

"What's the matter with Mom?" Micah whispered.

"It's nothing," Kimble said, gesturing for Micah to pay attention.

Lorna walked to the gym exit, where she met Bassam leaning on his broom. She showed him her cell phone. Micah overheard bits and pieces of their conversation. The one word he made out was "crows."

One of Micah and Richard's friends, Bradley Merc, said to Alfred, "Miss Sorenson said there were over three thousand new students. Where are they?"

Alfred grinned. "That's a keen observation, young man. You see, this is the old gymnasium from the 1927 academy. It's our largest facility whenever we need to move a large group or equipment. Over the next few nights, we'll be repeating this evening's events with other students who live along the coast."

"Is it true what those protesters said about you and magic?"

Alfred chuckled heartily. "Oh, heavens no! Everything you've witnessed tonight and will witness is not magic. It's just laws of nature you young'uns aren't familiar with."

A curious voice piped up from the crowd. "Where do you live?"

"Now you've asked the one question I can finally *show* you," Alfred said. Looking confused, he reached into his pocket and felt the top of his head. "Where did I put my hat?"

"It's in your hand!" Marly exclaimed.

Pretending to search frantically, Alfred swapped his fedora between his hands, feigning confusion. Finally, he plopped the hat back on his head and showed his empty hands to Marly.

"Listen, little lady. There's no hat in my hand."

"That's because it's now on your head," Marly retorted with a grin.

By then, Micah felt sure that Alfred was having fun with everyone, but the old man genuinely seemed confused. With a start, Alfred suddenly discovered his hat atop his head. His antics brought on guffaws from the kids.

"Well, I've got my hat and my jacket. I guess I'll be on my way."

"But you said you'd show us where you live," Marly protested.

Alfred pointed over his shoulder with a playful grin. "Oh, that's easy. I live right over there," he said, gesturing behind him.

"In the haunted mansion?" someone asked.

"No, no. That's my former residence. I live right over there," Alfred said, pointing more forcefully behind him.

Micah and the others stretched to look out the dark windows.

"Mr. Quentin, there's nothing to see," one of the students finally said.

"Oh?" Alfred said, spinning around.

The instant he turned his back on his young audience, the wall of the gymnasium began to glow and liquefy like lava. The children fled back, anticipating danger. But to their astonishment, there was no heat, and within moments, the wall collapsed and vanished, revealing a gaping hole that led to a field outside. A collective gasp escaped the crowd as a rush of warm, floral-laced sea air swept into the gymnasium. The children stared in stunned silence, their eyes wide as they listened to the peculiar chirps and croaks emanating from the nearby forest.

Alfred was no longer standing on a worn wooden platform. The platform was now a large natural outcropping of stone cut flat at the top. A bell hung from a pole mounted on the rock.

Miss Sorenson let out a gleeful chuckle when everyone clapped and cheered.

Lorna rejoined Micah and Kimble, who both were awed by the sight before them. Kimble had a wide grin on his face. "Alfred always makes a show of things. I've never seen the new hardware in operation before. That's much more impressive than the old system."

Lorna agreed. "They've been testing it over the summer."

Micah was dumbfounded, remaining quiet.

Beyond the gymnasium stretched a vast field that extended to a towering wall of enormous trees and lush ferns. Gone was the school's playground. Nestled in the trees was a two-story plantation-style home with a garden of many colorful flowers. The mansion was no run-down monstrosity like Micah had seen before. It was a well-kept white home with a high tan peaked roof. A covered porch with stately pillars surrounded the bottom floor. The pillars stretched from the ground up through the second-story deck, supporting the awning above. Glowing pale orbs were affixed to each pillar, casting a gentle radiance that bathed the mansion in comforting warmth.

The night was approaching, with the last rays of sun painting the clouds overhead a deep shade of purple. Miles beyond, in the sea, were four impossibly tall towers obscured in fog. The towers pierced the evening sky. Three of them spewed plumes of black smoke. The fourth was aflame, appearing to set the clouds on fire with its brilliant orange glow.

"What are those towers?" Micah asked.

"They're watchtowers. They inform passing ships of the safety of the island. They can be seen for hundreds of miles," Lorna said.

"Curious," Kimble whispered to Lorna, pointing with his cane. "There's an alert in the area. They were all lit up when I left work earlier. It may be a precaution with the extra activity at the gate today."

As the excitement wore off, Alfred continued. "My young friends, what you see here is my front yard at Promontory Point. This bell marks the exact spot where the first travelers stepped out of this world and into the world you young'uns are familiar with. You might think this has nothing to do with you, but you'd be wrong. This is where your family originated from a century ago. Everything you've experienced 'til now is just the beginning."

Reaching for the chain attached to the bell, Alfred whipped the chain, causing the bell to clang out a resonant note.

"Here is your destiny," he declared solemnly. "It's time for you to learn the truth of your origins, to understand who you are and where you come from."

At this, Alfred removed his hat and nodded politely to the audience. The parents applauded. Six soldiers emerged from the mansion. They crossed the field and climbed up to the gymnasium floor. They wore backpacks and began unloading small wooden boxes. Micah studied the khaki-uniformed men and women. He judged they were young, maybe even teenagers.

Alfred walked back into the crowd. Parents patted him on the back and shook his hand. To Micah's surprise, he was coming straight toward him.

"It's good to catch up, Alfred. It's been a long time," Kimble said.

Alfred shook hands with Kimble and hugged Lorna. Looking at Micah and Wren, he said, "Micah, Wren, I'll be seeing you boys soon. I look forward to getting to know you." Then he stepped between them and met up with Bassam. The two men exited the gym and disappeared into the foyer.

"That's a weird thing to say," Wren said, and Micah agreed.

"Shh, you two pay attention," Wren's mother said.

The soldiers finished unloading their backpacks and organized the boxes into piles. When finished, the company gathered around Miss Sorenson.

"Children, this is Junior Officer Quinn Higgins. Please give him your attention as we finalize the enrollment process," Miss Sorenson announced.

Quinn leaped onto the rock. He was tall and athletic, with a black, stubbly beard. His intensity commanded attention. With a swift motion, he motioned to his fellow officers to gather in front of him.

"Thank you, Miss Sorenson," Quinn began, his voice firm and authoritative. "As the captain of the Blazing Sun's junior officers, it's my responsibility to oversee the registration process. Each of you was assigned a class months ago, and you will come together in due time. But for tonight, we need to gather some essential information. This is a simple process."

Micah became distracted when an attractive female officer

handed Quinn a fist-sized container. "Thank you, Pearl," Quinn said, opening the box. He removed a ball of clay and held it up for the audience to see. "This material is called bio clay. We've used this technology for the last few years for enrollment. The process is painless. All you do is this," he demonstrated by squeezing the clay in his palm. "Once you've done this for five seconds, simply place it back in the box. And remember, after you've handled the clay, don't let anyone else touch your sample. Understood?"

Quinn's companions each gathered a few boxes at a time and fanned out into the audience. They were well-organized and addressed students by their names.

Micah and Wren were approached by an officer who was the opposite of Quinn: thin and gangly with a lazy eye that looked off in another direction. "Micah and Wren, it's good to finally meet you," the officer said with a thin-lipped smile. "I'm Junior Officer Armin Broom."

He handed each boy a container, instructing them to remove the clay. Micah examined his box. It was made of light-colored wood with his name and an emblem of a blazing sun branded on the lid. He and Wren removed their clay and did as Quinn instructed. Meanwhile, Armin was preoccupied sorting other boxes in his backpack, unaware of Micah and Wren stealing glances at his peculiar eye.

"What's the clay for?" Micah asked, noticing his hand was getting warmer.

"Good question, Micah," Armin said. He explained that the hands were like the antennae of the mind. "The clay absorbs biometric information that is used to customize equipment you will receive later. Also, it helps identify your natural talents so teachers can plan out the curriculum for the new year."

When Wren was finished with his clay, he attempted to hand it back to Armin. Armin pulled back. "In the box first, please. It's just a precaution. We've had cases where samples get cross-contaminated, and it's caused issues." He took back the boxes and stuffed them into his backpack. "So, have you boys heard?"

"Heard what?" Micah and Wren said together.

"That you two will be joining us, the Blazing Suns," Armin said, pointing to the insignia on his shoulder.

"What are the Blazing Suns?" Wren asked.

"Only the best class ever!" Armin said enthusiastically. He side-stepped away and rummaged in his backpack. "Oh, Mr. and Mrs. Fennly, Alfred was able to get that item you asked about," Armin said, giving Micah a sly grin. He removed a dull-green animal-skin pouch and passed it to Lorna.

"It seems awfully big for just the one item," Lorna said.

"I thought I could save you some trouble by including everything else he'll need in there."

"What is that?" Micah asked, reaching for the pouch.

Lorna pulled it away and handed it off to Kimble. "It's stuff you'll need for school."

"I'll run it out to the car," Kimble said and headed out of the gym with his cane thumping as he went.

"I heard what happened to your husband, Mrs. Fennly," Armin said. "Glad to see he's doing better."

Lorna gave Micah an uncomfortable glance. "It was nothing. He should be back to his old self in a couple of weeks."

Armin snickered. "Nothing? I don't know many people who survived an attack by a Horned Rakish."

Micah and Wren's eyes lit up. "I thought you said he had an accident in the garage," Micah said. "What's a Horned Rakish?"

"Never mind. That's enough, Mr. Broom," Lorna said, ignoring Micah's dubious look. "He'll be fine. That's all that matters."

"Armin!" Quinn called. "Let's move it, we're on a time schedule."

"Yes, sir!" Armin said, shouldering his backpack. He slapped the boys' shoulders and headed off. Turning back, he pointed at Micah. "Hey, happy birthday tomorrow!"

Micah smiled. He didn't know Armin, but he liked him. He reminded him of Mariam.

Minutes passed. Micah and Wren joined the children peering outside the gym. Lorna and Olivia chatted with other parents as Quinn and his officers went about their business. A commotion broke out in the foyer. Penelope and Twitch soared into the gymnasium, landing in the rafters. The two crows brought laughter from the children.

Kimble came huffing back into the gym. Lorna met him, pointing to where the crows were hiding. The birds cawed as they dove off the rafters. Lorna snatched out her cell phone, fingers tapping urgently across the screen. In an instant, a shrill fire alarm pierced the air, and a shimmering wall of red light materialized, sealing off the gaping hole that led outside. The startled crows veered upward, back into the safety of the rafters.

Miss Sorenson and the other teachers had the students back away from the glowing red wall. Lorna silenced the alarm with her phone and approached Miss Sorenson. As they talked privately, Micah retreated back to his father.

"Dad, what's happening?"

"Those two are fugitives," Kimble said, pointing to the crows. "Your mother just locked everyone in the gym so they couldn't escape."

"Really? They're just crows." Micah moved to get a better look. The crows were agitated and cawed furiously. One had the same pink crown of feathers he had seen down at Hermit Cove. "Those are the same crows I saw earlier. They gave me Mariam's locket."

"Are you sure, son? Your mother showed me the photos…"
Kimble cut off when a distant air raid siren began wailing.

Across the night sky outside, a streak of light tore through the darkness. A meteor exploded into a shower of glinting embers, brightening the night sky like noonday. More meteors shot over, scarring the night sky with white contrails of smoke.

Suddenly, a deafening explosion reverberated through the air, shaking the school's foundations. The surrounding forest rocked in the compression shockwave. The trees bent and swayed as if caught in a powerful tempest. The red wall popped and sizzled from the debris striking the barrier. Inside the gymnasium, panic ensued as everyone cowered, and screams filled the air.

"Are we under attack?" someone shouted, trembling with fear.

"It's the Rashaar!" others cried out in terror, their voices rising in a chorus of panic.

The crowd regained their feet and surged to the shimmering wall, desperate for a better view within the confines of the gym. Some got too close and were repelled backward.

"Parents! Parents! Please, don't panic!" Miss Sorenson shouted.

Amid the commotion, the flame atop the fourth tower sputtered and went dark. With its demise, it joined its three companions, spewing out black smoke.

Quinn pushed his way through the crowd, careful not to get too close to the shimmering wall. "The gate's closing!"

Kimble scanned the four towers. "Lorna, are you closing the gate?"

Lorna scoffed. "Of course not! I don't have the authority to close the gate. I just locked everyone in—"

The gymnasium began to rumble, and there was a flash of light. The last group of parents and students that had arrived at the gym suddenly disappeared. A second siren blared to life just outside. It was much louder, adding to the confusion.

"Gather everything together now!" Quinn ordered his fellow officers, his words barely heard over the strident wailing.

"Lorna, stop the gate from closing. They need more time!" Kimble shouted.

"I don't have control over the gate closing. It's shutting down on its own! There's nothing I can do!"

"You've got to release the lock, then, or the soldiers will be taken back with us through the gate!" Kimble shouted, motioning to Quinn and his officers.

"Penelope and Twitch! I demand you come down here!" Lorna cried. She ran under the crows, frantically waving her arms.

Quinn and his companions hastily gathered the scattered boxes by the armfuls and stuffed them into their packs.

"But we're not done!" Armin protested. Just then, the gym rumbled back to life and another group of families disappeared.

"There's no time. Just make sure we get every last box and be ready to go," Quinn said with a coolness that defused the panic.

More meteors came. Distant shockwaves thundered, causing swells of panic.

Miss Sorenson and her fellow teachers directed everyone back to the foyer end of the gym. The old building was an impervious fortress to the chaos outside.

"Stay here, son," Kimble ordered Micah. He rushed over to Lorna. "Lorna, you've got to let these soldiers out, now!"

Quinn and the other officers finished up and joined behind Kimble, hefting their packs. Quinn eyed Lorna's phone with annoyance.

"No! Penelope and Twitch will get away!" Lorna cried, ignoring the pandemonium around her. "It's our daughter, Kimble. This could be our only chance."

Another rumble came from under the gym floor.

Quinn stepped forward, anxious. "Better hurry. One more, and we're going with you."

Kimble held him back with his cane. "There will be another time, dear," he said, taking Lorna into his arms. She began to cry. After several tense moments, she tapped the screen of her cell phone. The shimmering red wall disappeared, letting back in the breeze from outside.

"Let's go!" Quinn shouted.

Packs bounced as the officers raced out of the gym. Quinn did one last inspection. Satisfied, he looked back at Kimble and threw a salute before diving into the field.

For a brief moment, there was calm. The soldiers cautiously backed away into the field, gazing into the sky as embers rained down. The sound of gravel pelting the roof came. Dust poured down from the ceiling.

The floor vibrated below Micah's feet. He cowered as bright light filled his vision, and briefly, there was silence. Nearby in the light, he heard a voice—Richard's voice.

Richard was once again talking in Micah's ear about Jack and Kamran as if he hadn't noticed Micah's disappearance and reappearance. He finally stopped when he saw Micah searching his surroundings.

Micah was back in the gym as it had been before, with its shiny floor and the strong odor of floor wax. It was calm, and Jack and Tony Clark stood behind him, making faces. He heard sobbing and noticed his mother next to him wiping tears from her eyes.

"Micah, snap out of it!" Richard said, shaking him.

Hardly more than a few seconds passed before Micah began to feel tugging at the memories he'd just experienced. It was like waking up from a dream, except he was certain he hadn't been dreaming. The memories of Alfred, the gate, and the meteor shower were fading.

He stared dumbly at Richard, who was incessantly tugging his arm.

Did I black out? he wondered.

The scoreboard over the gym exit buzzed as the timer hit zero. Miss Sorenson, standing at the front of the gym, called everyone to attention.

Micah took one more long look around the gym, trying to force his mind to remember. Dazed expressions were seen in the faces of other children nearby, including Wren. The last fragments of Micah's memory were of the crows in the rafters. He looked up. The crows were gone.

Moments later, the memories of the past hour were entirely erased.

*   *   *

Micah, Richard, and Angela sat in the back of the Lincoln as Kimble sped off from the parking lot of Quentin Elementary. Kimble and Lorna were putting out suggestions for supper.

The back-to-school night had been just as boring as Micah knew it would be. They were organized and escorted to their new classrooms on the second floor. Micah and Richard were glad they had Miss Sorenson as their teacher. Wren was even in his class. But none of this seemed worth wasting their last Friday night of summer over. However, watching Cornelia Moon being hauled off in an ambulance made the evening not a total loss.

"What did you think of the new school?" Lorna asked.

"You should see my classroom," Angela said. "There's

94

monsters on the wall."

"Oh?"

"Uh-huh. I think I got your grandson in my class. Max Taggart? He wasn't there, but I saw his name on one of the desks."

"Yup, that's our grandson."

Richard sat quietly, staring out the window.

"We haven't heard much from you tonight, Richard," Lorna said. "You feeling alright?"

"Just tired, that's all."

"Too tired for a cheeseburger and fries?" Kimble asked.

Perking up, Richard said, "I'm never too tired for a cheeseburger!"

Chapter 9
The Package

K imble pulled the Lincoln into the garage as the last rays of sunshine filtered through the great pines fencing Albatross Avenue. The boys ran upstairs to Micah's bedroom, with Grubb leading the charge. They switched on the TV and game console. Micah opened a drawer, revealing his sizable collection of video games. Resting at the top, in its unopened package, was a game called Brewster's Fortune.

"When did you get this?" Richard asked, eyes glittering. He looked over the illustration on the box with a wide grin. It depicted a wizard wearing pajamas holding a lantern up to a sleeping dragon. "I thought this didn't come out 'til next week."

"I ordered it a month ago. We can play while we wait for your mom."

Richard was way ahead of Micah. He plopped down on the floor and tore into the package. Micah cleared away day-old snacks and spent soda cans with his foot. As the game started up, he reached under his bed and grabbed a stash of candy bars.

A knock at the door sounded, and Lorna stuck her head in. "Where's that package from earlier?"

"It's on the fireplace," Micah said, noticing Angela standing in the hallway.

Kimble called for Lorna, and she walked off. Angela remained, shaking her head. "This room's disgusting. You're such a slob."

"Can you do something about her?" Micah said, nudging Richard.

"Angela, leave," Richard said, waving his hand. Time was precious. He bit his tongue between his lips as he tapped at the controller, then unwrapped a chocolate bar and stuffed it in his mouth.

Angela began flicking the light on and off obnoxiously.

"Beat it!" Micah yelled, jumping to his feet.

"Oh, you wanna hit me?" Angela teased, pushing her chin out.

Micah charged, sending her squealing down the hall. She raced into the bathroom and slammed the door shut.

Standing at the railing, Micah saw his father on the couch

below. The red-star package was torn open, and two small gray tablets rested on the coffee table. Ducking, Micah peeked over the edge as his mother walked to the table.

"What is it?" she asked.

Kimble looked up to be sure they were alone. He slid one of the tablets to Lorna. She picked it up and looked around the room in a way Micah thought was strange.

"Is this Fort Somar? I see the mines on the mountainside," Lorna said, taking a step back abruptly as if something had startled her. "It's overrun with maws. Where is everyone?"

"That was recorded over thirty-six hours ago," Kimble said, double-checking that they were alone. "The camouflage walls hiding the city are down. They are vulnerable to every creature that roams the Klamath plains."

Lorna looked puzzled. "Those walls can't come down unless…unless they were sabotaged. Do you think this has something to do with what happened at the school tonight?"

Kimble shrugged. "There's more." He handed Lorna the second tablet. She walked to the center of the room, her gaze fixed ahead.

"It's dark here. Where am I?" she asked.

"Twenty miles east of Fort Somar. Look across the valley. That's Glendale Pass, where the Rashaar scouts were captured a week ago."

Micah watched his mother with growing confusion. It was as if she were navigating a virtual reality system without a headset.

Lorna pressed her lips together. "There's a lake and a herd of animals. They have harnesses."

Micah watched his mother move around the furniture as if she were searching for something. Suddenly, she froze, a look of terror crossing her face. "I see an encampment…there are soldiers here…their uniforms…Rashaanites! Oh, Kimble!"

Lorna staggered back, dropping the tablet, which shattered on the floor. Micah's heart jolted with alarm. He had never seen his mother look so frightened.

"It *was* an attack at the school."

"Now, dear. Let's not jump to conclusions," Kimble said, picking up the shards. "You know meteor showers are common this time of year, and Glendale Pass is far from Promontory Point. It's deep in the Klamath mountains."

Lorna's patience snapped. "Oh, never mind your cautious attitude! What's being done?"

"You know as much as I—"

Lorna grabbed her cell phone and tapped frantically. "A blackout's in effect. All travel's restricted."

"Calm down, dear. It's just a precaution. We don't know anything for certain yet. An emergency assembly has been called at midnight. Top ranks will be there, and we've been ordered to attend."

Defeated, Lorna sighed, "What about Micah? It's his birthday tomorrow."

Kimble smoothed his gray hair thoughtfully. "Tricia should be able to look after him tonight."

"Won't she be required to attend?"

"No, it's on the other side of the gate. The baby, remember? But Geoffrey will."

Angela cracked the bathroom door to find Micah lying on his stomach. "Micah, are you spying on your parents?" she said gleefully, slamming the door shut again.

Micah hastily retreated into his bedroom. "Your sister's such a brat," he grumbled, expecting to find Richard sitting on the floor. Instead, he found several open candy wrappers and Richard's unattended controller.

"Richard?" Micah stepped back out into the hall. In the shadows at the end stood Richard and Grubb, peering into Mariam's dark bedroom.

"What are you doing?" No response came. Micah flicked the hall light on and walked up behind. "Why are you looking in Mariam's bedroom?"

Richard remained silent. Micah poked him, and Richard jumped with surprise, startling Micah. He was about to lay into Richard but stopped when he saw dribbles of chocolate on his chin. His face looked pale and troubled.

"What's the matter?" Micah asked.

Richard gulped, wiping his chin. "I heard screaming."

The pair looked into the darkness of Mariam's bedroom and flicked the light on. The room remained untouched since her funeral. Her room was painted light pink with a neatly made twin-sized bed. There were two dressers with photos on top. A cabinet full of books and other knickknacks were on the opposite wall.

Micah frowned. "I'm sure it was just Angela messing with you. She's such a pain."

"Yeah, Angela," Richard said and laughed nervously.

They went back to Micah's bedroom and continued to play the game. Richard refused to talk about the coin, the janitor, or the screaming he heard. All he wanted to do was play the game, and Micah was happy to comply.

Sheila arrived later, thanking the Fennlys for watching her children. As they sped away, Richard leaned out the window of the car. "Don't forget about the paper route tomorrow!" he called out.

Micah waved goodbye, yawning. Moths fluttered in a frenzy around the hot porch light above him. Crickets chirped in rhythmic waves from the nearby forest.

"Micah," Kimble called from inside.

In the kitchen, Micah found his parents sitting at the table, his mother's eyes puffy from crying.

"Son, your mother and I have some urgent business to take care of and need to leave immediately. You'll be staying at Tricia's tonight," Kimble said.

"This late? What happened?" Micah asked innocently, thinking it better to let his father volunteer information rather than blurting out what he had overheard.

"I'm sorry. We can't discuss it," Kimble said, shifting his eyes to Lorna.

Micah did not find his father's reluctance unusual. His father was always tight-lipped about his work. Micah wasn't even sure what his dad did. He'd once asked about his job and was told he "protected people."

His mother's work wasn't as mysterious, though he knew few details. She had stayed home with him until he turned five, at which point Grandma Hazel started watching him. All Micah knew about his mother's job was that she was an operator for a communications company, and sometimes she went to work with his father.

"What about my birthday?"

"I know, dear," Lorna said, her eyes moistening. "We should be back by then. Tricia will get your party ready for tomorrow."

"Will Richard still be able to sleep over?"

Micah could tell his mother had something deeper on her mind. She smiled bleakly. "Of course. Richard's always welcome." It was rare for Micah to see his mother cry.

"I'll pack my things, It'll be alright, Mom," Micah said, hugging his mother.

"I love you, son," Lorna whispered back.

*   *   *

Lorna stood on the enclosed porch of her daughter's home across town. The strong wind rushed through the streets and trees. The wind chimes clanged wind-spun melodies.

Micah leaned against the railing, one arm clutching a bundle of belongings he had hastily thrown into the car and the other cradling Grubb like a pampered sausage.

The door swung open, and Micah's pregnant sister, Tricia, emerged.

"Mom," Tricia wept, her eyes red. The two embraced, exchanging sentiments about friends Micah had never heard of.

"I'll take my things to the bedroom," Micah said, brushing past his sister.

He stepped into the dim living room. Tricia's house was decorated sparingly, with a few paintings on the walls and pictures of her young family. Grubb leaped down and sniffed over to the foot of the stairway, where he began to growl.

"What's the matter, boy? Smell something?" Micah said with quiet enthusiasm.

At the top of the steps, two eyes peered down from a crouched figure. Its lazy tail swayed back and forth.

"Oh, no," Micah moaned, rushing to retrieve Grubb. It was too late. Grubb pounced onto the stairway and barked up at the figure. There was a loud hiss and a yelp. Micah winced, watching his reckless friend tumble back down the stairs.

The light at the top of the stairs flicked on. "Ramsey!" Micah's niece, Emily, yelled as she appeared above, dressed in purple pajamas. Ramsey, Emily's cream-colored Siamese cat, stood beside her, puffed up and hissing.

"Sorry, Uncle," Emily apologized, sweeping up her cat. Calling

Micah "Uncle" was a hint of the family joke. Micah's niece was a year older than he was. "I'll keep her in my room tonight."

"What's the fuss in here?" Kimble asked, stepping into the house.

"Grubb attacked Ramsey and lost," Micah said, nuzzling Grubb's belly. Grubb's white-tipped tail wagged nervously as he licked Micah's face.

The family looked at each other. "It would be best to separate those two," Kimble said.

"Um, yes," Tricia said. "Micah, keep him in the room with the door closed tonight."

"What's the big deal?" Micah asked, scratching Grubb's ears. He was exhausted and didn't care why his family acted strangely about the pets.

Tricia's husband, Geoffrey, entered the room carrying a duffel bag. "Sorry I'm late," he said.

The scent of shampoo and aftershave filled the room. Geoffrey was husky, and his black hair glistened with gel. He wore dress pants and a white pinstriped shirt. Noticing Micah, he rushed over.

"Hey, Mr. Brown. It's your birthday tomorrow," Geoffrey said, ruffling Micah's hair.

It always bugged Micah when Geoffrey called him by the nickname his grandmother had given him. She told him he got the nickname because when he was a baby he looked like Charlie Brown from the Peanuts cartoon. When Geoffrey used the nickname, it just didn't sound right.

Micah turned sideways and shoved his stomach out. "Gee, Geoffrey. I think you've gained thirty pounds since I last saw you," he said, slapping his stomach.

"Micah! You apologize this instant," Lorna scolded.

"Yeah, that was so rude," Geoffrey laughed.

"Sorry."

Kimble glanced at the wall clock. "We need to go."

Micah hugged his parents.

"Love ya, hon," Geoffrey said, kissing Tricia. He bent over, patting her belly. "And I love you too, little one."

The three left the house together, leaving Micah and Tricia alone. He watched as she straightened up the already tidy front room. He sometimes found it hard to believe Tricia was his sister. She was old enough to be his mother.

"Where's Max? I was hoping to see him at the school tonight," Micah said.

"Max went to bed hours ago," Tricia said, running her hand over her belly. "We didn't go because I wasn't feeling up to it. The baby's been quiet today, so I thought I should take it easy. Max didn't mind. He's not all that excited about school."

Micah huffed. "I know how he feels. So, where's everyone going? They sure were in a hurry to leave."

Tricia was reluctant but finally answered. "Out of town."

"I know, but where?"

Tricia looked uncomfortably at Micah and answered, "Lincoln City."

Micah frowned. "There. Was that hard? Why does everyone in this family keep so many secrets?"

"Like what?"

"Like Fort Somar. Where's that? Until tonight, I never heard of it."

Tricia looked mildly surprised. "Maybe you hear more because you're getting older."

Micah rolled his eyes. "I've heard things for years. I just want to know what's going on."

Tricia looked squarely at Micah. "What's it matter if you haven't heard of Fort Somar?"

"It doesn't matter. So why's it secret? They said it's in trouble."

"Mom and Dad told you that?" Tricia said sharply.

Her reaction caught Micah off guard. Not five minutes ago, his mother and Tricia had gone on about people and places he'd never heard of. Did his sister think he was deaf?

"I overheard Mom and Dad talking at home," he admitted, retracting his attitude. "They had these…tablets. They said something about an army."

Tricia's face went pale. "It's time to go to bed."

"What's a Rashaanite?"

"Bed!" Tricia exclaimed, clutching her belly. She leaned against the railing, calming herself.

Micah marched up the stairs without saying a word. Entering the last bedroom at the end of the hall, he slammed the door shut, nearly catching Grubb's tail in the door. He tossed everything in his arms onto the bed.

Among his belongings, a green pouch flew across the room, bouncing off the bed and hitting the wall with a thud. Tired and frustrated, Micah ignored it.

Secrets.

How many times had he walked in on a family conversation only to have the room fall silent? Or how many times had he found something curious sitting out in the open, and when he left and came back, that thing would be gone? Maybe Tricia was right. Was he starting to notice more?

He looked over Tricia's hobby room. Against the wall was the daybed with a bare mattress resting on a brass frame. There was a small nightstand with a lamp. At the other end was a sewing machine on a card table. Stacked on the floor were square pieces of cloth. Tricia was making a quilt.

Micah cooled off as he put on his pajamas. He unrolled his sleeping bag over the mattress and sat down. Picking up the dull-green pouch, he frowned. He must have grabbed it from the car by accident.

There was a soft knock at the door. He jumped into the sleeping bag and hid the pouch. Tricia peeked in. "I'm sorry. I'm just tired. We'll start fresh in the morning."

"It's been a long day for me, too," Micah said.

"Do you need anything?"

"No. I'm fine."

"We good, then?" Tricia said, stepping back into the hall. "It's your birthday tomorrow. You're only twelve once. It was my most memorable birthday." She turned off the light and closed the door, leaving Micah alone.

Grubb leaped into the bed and nuzzled his way down the sleeping bag, eventually curling up at Micah's toes.

Settling in the sleeping bag, Micah's body was ready for a night's rest, but his mind refused to call it a day. The unsettling wind outside caused the single-paned window to rattle nervously. He was certain another nightmare awaited him on the other side of slumber.

He turned the lamp on and grabbed the pouch. He'd hid it from Tricia because it was none of her business, and he could keep secrets, too. Inside, he found two items. The first was a linen brown sack crimped shut with a metal clip. The name *M. Fennly* was stenciled on the side with the red words *Keep out of direct sunlight* dyed in the fabric.

The other package was damaged. It was wrapped in a waxy broad leaf with a broken red wax seal. Unfolding the leaf, he discovered a palm-sized clamshell etched with a blazing sun image. There was also a note that read *Happy Birthday from the Blazing Suns*.

The note was strange to him. Who were the Blazing Suns?

Setting the bundle off the bed, he placed the shell on his pillow and pulled his head under the covers, cinching the bag until he peeked through a small hole.

Curiosity got the better of him, and he picked up the shell. Something rattled inside, delicate and metallic. He pried the shell open, and a ring fell onto the pillow. It was made of copper with a shiny amber stone. Etched into the band were the words *M. FENNLY/A. QUENTIN.*

In the shell was a picture of a left hand with an arrow pointing to the index finger. Below was writing that was much too small for his tired eyes to read.

He slipped the ring onto his index finger. It fit perfectly. As he admired the ring under the light, the copper lost its luster and went hazy. Wiping the ring, Micah realized the haze was a thin layer of frost that made the ring cold to the touch.

He tried to remove the ring, but it wouldn't budge. The harder he pulled, the more stubborn the ring became. Desperate, he licked his finger, feeling the icy chill of the copper against his tongue. After several futile attempts, he reluctantly gave up.

Maybe it'll come off with some soap, he hoped.

He caressed the ring, feeling like an adult wearing it. It was comfortable enough—as long as he didn't try to remove it.

It's just a ring. What's the harm? he thought. He would worry about it in the morning.

He'd fought sleep all day, but now his body seemed immune. His mind raced in circles: the nightmare of the shark from last night, Hermit Cove, the locket, the coin…and now, the ring. They all competed for center stage of his thoughts.

Micah tossed and turned, but sometime after midnight, he drifted off to sleep.

Chapter 10
Family Secret

Micah awoke early. For the first time in months, he slept through the night and didn't have nightmares. In the dark, the ring crystal glowed a faint amber, and his left hand was throbbing.

He turned the lamp on and was alarmed at the sight of his hand covered with spindly purple streaks that became solid around the copper ring. The streaks continued up his arm, tracing his veins. Even nudging the ring sent pain up his arm. Slinking from the sleeping bag, he stretched on the bed. Outside, the early-morning rays were breaking the hills.

Before him, where the sewing machine and card table had been, sat a menacing-looking contraption covered with spools of thread. Ignoring the pain, he arose for a closer look. A web of string converged at a central arm where needles were threaded and poised at different heights.

"How did this get in here?" he whispered.

An oval plaque reading *Kippler & Sons* was fixed at the top, with fancy gold curlicues decorating large inset amber crystals. Micah inspected the polished redwood machine and found no bolts or obvious fasteners holding it together. Some parts even floated in the air with no apparent support.

He was startled to find ten human hands hooked under the table. Where a forearm was expected, the end was rounded with a redwood hook. The hands hung ordered by size. The smallest was as tiny as a doll's hand. The largest were as big as dinner plates. He reached under and touched one, and it snapped to attention like a five-legged spider.

"This isn't a toy, young man," a terse woman's voice spoke from within the machine.

"Who said that?" Micah said, falling back onto his behind.

Befuddled, he was careful not to disturb the neatly stacked pieces of olive-colored material surrounding him. He picked up a piece and found it curious. It felt like rubber, but on closer examination, he saw it was some kind of skin with a scaly texture.

A series of diagrams with dimensions and specifications of

different cuts of material hung on the wall. The final illustration depicted how all the pieces came together into a rain slicker.

He placed the piece on the floor without returning it to the stack. When he looked away, he heard a whoosh and a clunk. When he looked back down, the material was gone from the floor and was settling back neatly on the pile.

Weird, he thought.

Standing, scorching pain reminded him to be careful with his hand. He left the bedroom and tiptoed down the hall to the bathroom. He was horrified at his reflection in the mirror. Purple streaks traced over the contours of his lips, nose, and eyes.

Micah lathered up his hand with soap. He took a deep breath and pulled hard on the ring. The ring glow intensified as the pain rapidly spread throughout his whole body. Through clenched teeth, he wanted to cry out.

What am I going to do? What if Tricia sees this?

Abruptly, the glow of the ring ceased, and the agonizing pain began to recede. He was relieved to see the streaks fading from his face. As he huffed away the pain, something reflecting in the mirror behind him caught his attention: three fossilized trilobites. He went to the wall and ran his fingers over the perfectly defined blue-and-green exoskeletons.

"I've never noticed these before," he mumbled.

Hearing creaking out in the hall, Micah flicked the bathroom light off and hurried back to the bedroom. Burrowing back into his sleeping bag, he felt Grubb stirring.

There was writing on the shell, he remembered.

He took it from the nightstand and held it up to the light. He winced when he felt Grubb's claws dig into his thigh.

"Grubb, we need to cut your nails," Micah said, straining to read the shell. He reached into the sleeping bag and ran his hand down Grubb's back, brushing over soft, pebbly flesh and hard, bony protrusions.

Micah thought for a moment. Exactly what part of Grubb had he touched? Since when did Grubb have pebbly flesh or bone protrusions?

Zipping down the sleeping bag, he pulled the flap back. His eyes bulged at the sight of the creature resting at his waist. It had fine-pebbled dark-green skin with fiery orange stripes and bony spikes running down its back. It wasn't Grubb at all!

The creature advanced with its sharp claws digging. Micah was tense, and the animal sensed it. Its long fur-tipped tail uncoiled cautiously, with its large golden eyes focused.

Micah's mouth gaped, his voice choking off. The familiar jingle of the collar diverted his eyes to the copper tag. It read *GRUBB*. The creature's pink tongue slid over its row of sharp teeth and licked Micah's cheek.

"Ahhhhh!" Micah shrieked, crashing off the bed.

In the mayhem that ensued, the sleeping back ripped apart in a feathery burst. The lamp shattered against the wall, and the bed flipped over. Muffled grunts were heard inside the sleeping bag, which had become twisted as Micah rolled on the floor.

Stacks of the rain slicker material became scattered in the scuffle. From under the sewing contraption, the hands sprang to life. Like angry hornets, they whooshed around him, retrieving the scattered pieces.

Micah ducked to protect his face. Within seconds, the pieces were neatly restacked away. The hands retreated to the underside of the contraption and re-hooked themselves.

The bedroom door flung open. Tricia, with a cocked baseball bat, charged in. The curlers in her hair bobbed furiously as she shot looks around the room. "Lamptor's fire! What's going on?"

The fiery striped creature bolted from the room between Tricia's legs. Emily and Max emerged from their bedrooms and ran to their mother's side.

"Tricia!" Micah said. "Something happened to Grubb! He's...he's an *it*!"

Emily went from an expression of shock to hysterical laughter. Max looked panicked and clung to his mother.

"Micah," Tricia said, lowering the bat, "what are you talking about?"

"Grubb has turned into a lizard or something!"

"Uh-huh," she said, turning to Emily. "Would you please take Max downstairs so I can talk with Micah alone?"

"Yes, Mom," Emily snickered. She and Max left the bedroom. Max asked Emily what was happening and was told Micah had a nightmare.

Tricia untangled Micah from the sleeping bag. "Are you okay? No scratches or pains?"

Micah struggled to his feet, covered in feathers. "I did *not* have a nightmare. Something has happened to Grubb. And this room..." he said, shaking his finger at the sewing contraption. "This isn't right either. It's different than it was last night."

"I see," Tricia said calmly. "Well, brother, first, I want you to breathe and calm down."

"Tricia! Didn't you hear—"

"Calm down," Tricia insisted.

Micah took in a deep breath and exhaled.

"Mom and Dad didn't tell me," she said soothingly, setting the bat against the wall.

"Tell you what?" Micah asked, concealing his ring.

Tricia gave him an admiring smile. "That my kid brother's growing up."

She led him to the bathroom and filled the sink with warm water. She opened the mirror cabinet, revealing an odd assortment of containers. She removed a large vase containing gray powder.

Micah studied Tricia. She remained unfazed by what he'd told her. "Didn't you hear me? Grubb's a lizard!"

"I heard you," Tricia answered, scooping a liberal handful of gray powder from the vase. She sprinkled the powder into the water, causing it to fizz and churn, filling the bathroom with the aroma of vanilla.

"What's this?" Micah asked.

"Put your hand in. It'll feel better."

Micah hesitated, reluctant to reveal the ring. Tricia's insistence left him with little choice. He put his right hand in the water.

"Your other hand. I know it hurts. You have no secret I'm unaware of."

Micah looked at Tricia apprehensively. His hand did ache. She was right about that. He dipped his left-hand fingers into the roiling brew.

"All the way in," Tricia insisted.

Soothing warmth coursed up his arm as the liquid fizzed around his hand. He expelled a breath of relief.

"Better?" Tricia asked, and Micah nodded. "Good. Now tell me this. Where've you been since you put the ring on?"

Micah eyed the reflection of the trilobites in the mirror. "Just the bedroom and the bathroom."

"Good. Things appear different, don't they?"

"*Way* different," he said sheepishly. How did his sister know about the pain caused by the ring? Why hadn't she reacted to Grubb?

Tricia rolled her wrist in the air in a swirling motion, catching Micah's attention. This commonly would have been perceived as a nervous tic, but the moment she completed the gesture, the room changed.

One instant, he saw the assortment of jars and vials; the next, he saw familiar containers like mist sprays, lotions, and brown plastic medicine containers.

The container Tricia held was no longer a vase. It was now a bag labeled *Epsom Salt*. The fragrance of vanilla was gone, replaced by the stale smell of salt. The reflection of the trilobites in the mirror had changed to familiar paintings of ships on the ocean.

"What just happened?" Micah asked.

"Let's talk about this later. I want you to soak for a few more minutes. Then, take a shower and get dressed. By then, I'll have breakfast ready. Agreed?"

Micah scratched his head, studying the Epsom salt bag.

Tricia's smile thinned. "One more thing, brother. At breakfast, we don't talk about this around Max. This is between you and me for now. Understand?"

"Alright."

"Good," Tricia said, her smile returning. "Happy birthday." She winked.

*   *   *

After his shower, Micah returned to the bedroom. It had been tidied up, and his clothes were laid out. The hulking contraption was gone. The sewing machine was back again on the card table. He walked around the table, scrutinizing the machine. Nothing seemed out of the ordinary. When he bent over and ran his hand over the sewing machine, he had an odd moment—he forgot what he was looking for. He looked around the bedroom, confused by what he was doing.

Basking in the sunlight, he felt strong and alert. A vivid and clear memory flashed in his mind. He recalled being in the gymnasium, his hand lit up as if engulfed in flames. He tugged at the memory like pulling a loose thread from a sweater. All the events that had happened in the school gymnasium unraveled in an instant: Alfred Quentin, the meteor shower, Armin Broom, and the crows. It was all there, neatly chronicled like every other memory he'd ever had.

The aroma of cooking bacon and cinnamon filled the room. He never recalled having such a keen sense of smell. Famished, he went down to breakfast. When he arrived in the kitchen, he found Tricia, Emily, and Max discussing baby names. When he entered, they began to sing "Happy Birthday."

Max continued, adding words to the song. "…he's twelve years old, he smells like mold, if the truth—"

"Max," Emily said, irritated.

Micah bowed and went to his sister's side. Tricia stood at the stove, stirring a steaming pot of oatmeal with one hand and supporting her back with the other. He was anxious to talk about what happened at the school yesterday and about Grubb. Knowing better, all that came out was, "Smells great, Sis. I'm starving."

Tricia served up a large helping from the pot and handed it to Micah.

"Micah, sit here," Max said, patting the chair beside him.

Max could easily have been mistaken for Micah's brother. He had the same angular face and squinty eyes. His hair was brown and cut short. The two had the "Fennly look" passed on by Micah's father. Emily looked more like her dad. She had naturally curly black hair. She was looking more like a young woman every day. She studied Micah curiously.

Much to Max's delight, Micah devoured breakfast like he hadn't eaten in days.

After Micah downed his third helping of oatmeal, Max teased, "Jeez, save some for the rest of us. Since when have you liked anything but peanut butter and jelly sandwiches?"

Micah stopped mid-bite and considered. "I don't know, but I'm starving. You eating your eggs?"

Max shook his head, sliding his plate over. Micah wolfed down the two over-easy eggs in a single bite.

"You're not even tasting. Just inhaling it," Max said, sniffing his strip of bacon obnoxiously.

"Oh, I taste it, alright," Micah said. He took a long gulp of orange juice and declared, "It's the best breakfast I've ever had."

Tricia and Emily both smiled.

"I can tell," Max said. "So tell us about your nightmare."

Emily stopped eating and looked back uneasily at her mother. Tricia calmly poured herself some orange juice.

"I dreamed Grubb was a lizard. He had green skin and licked me with his tongue. Scared me to death," Micah said dramatically.

Emily looked tense, and Tricia kicked Micah's foot under the table.

Max rolled his eyes. "That's not scary. It sounded like you were tearing the room apart."

Micah saw Emily relax, and he smiled at her. He noticed she was also wearing a ring similar to his, but hers was silver. They exchanged a look like they were sharing a common secret—though Micah wasn't sure what the secret was. He barely knew more than Max.

*   *   *

After breakfast, Tricia and Micah went to the company room,

which had a door that could be shut for privacy. Max followed, but Emily detoured him to search for Grubb.

Tricia invited Micah to sit next to her on the oversized floral couch. There was a coffee table with magazines and books. Family photos hung on the walls. A large picture window provided a view of the street lined with small wood-frame homes. Tricia retrieved Micah's gray clamshell with the blazing sun emblem from her pocket.

"That's the shell the ring came in," Micah said, taking it.

From her other pocket, Tricia produced another shell with a starfish emblem. "I got this when I was twelve, before you were born." She extended her hand to show Micah her silver ring. "The important part is the amber crystal. It's called Deity Stone."

"What are these markings?" Micah asked, comparing his ring to hers.

"They tell a history. As we experience milestones, we alter them to show respect for those events. It's tradition."

"What kind of events?"

"Things like graduating from school, military service, perhaps a courageous deed, getting married—those sorts of things. See these two marks?" She tapped her nail over two black dots on the silver band. "I added those when Emily and Max were born. And see this mark?" She pointed to a third dot. "This is for the baby coming next month. Understand?"

"I guess. Why is yours made of silver and mine copper?"

"The copper ring is called the Macabre Ring. It's nicknamed the Death Ring, by some. When our children reach your age, they are given this special ring to cleanse both the mind and body of diseases. I've heard that for some, the experience can be traumatic. How did it affect you?"

"Painful."

"That's the more common experience. Eventually, you'll receive the Hem Ring. It means 'ring of the soul,' and it's more powerful because the restrictions have been removed." Tricia sat back on the couch. "So tell me how this all happened? Mom and Dad weren't supposed to give it to you for another week."

"It was an accident. We went to the back-to-school night, and a soldier gave it to Mom. Somehow, it got mixed up with my stuff when I got here. It's weird. I forgot all about what happened at the school until I woke up this morning."

"That's the way they've set it up. Until you put on the Macabre Ring, those memories are sealed. Anyone who was there last night who wasn't wearing a ring has forgotten. So what happened?"

So much had happened yesterday. Micah began from the beginning, starting with the crows at Hermit Cove.

"Mom told me Penelope and Twitch returned," Tricia began.

"Who?"

"The crows. They're not actual crows. They're friends of our family. At least I think they're our friends. Dad found them when he was a boy, and they grew up with him. After Mom and Dad got married, Mom made them leave because they caused a lot of trouble. She can't stand them. It's funny, though, they were always with us kids when we went to school. I think they looked out for us because of Dad."

"Did Mom tell you they gave me Mariam's locket?"

"What?" Tricia said, her eyes widening.

He took the locket and coin from his pocket and set them on the coffee table. To his astonishment, they were now just two plain black pebbles.

"This is what they gave you?" Tricia asked.

Micah was confused. "Something's wrong. One of these was her locket, and the other was a coin."

Tricia picked up the stones, examining them closely. She looked thoughtful for a moment and removed her ring, setting it on the table. "Lamptor's fire," she breathed, rolling the stones in her hand. "It *is* her locket!"

"Why can't I see it now?" Micah asked.

"Because it's been hidden from someone wearing Deity Stone."

"Can you see the coin?"

Tricia picked up the other stone. "I can. This is a royal coin of the Rashaar kingdom."

Micah tried to remove his ring and winced in pain.

"Oh, dear. Don't try to take off the ring. It won't come off for weeks."

"Why?"

"Because of what it's doing. It's doing *cobedra hem*. It means 'cleansing the soul.' It's purging disease and imperfections you were born with."

Micah was quiet for a long moment. "Didn't Mariam get this ring?"

Tricia nodded.

"If this makes us healthy, what happened to her? Mom's told me the real reason she died was because she was sick, not the fall from the tree."

Tricia bit her lip. She slipped her ring back on and handed Micah the stones. "I don't feel like it is my place to explain what happened to Mariam. It's complicated. You'll need to ask Mom. If she's up to it."

The two sat in silence as the finality of Tricia's words sank in. "What is the Rashaar?" Micah finally asked, breaking the silence.

"You're not making this easy for me, are you? What do you know?"

"In the gym yesterday, something happened at the end. Meteors fell from the sky. Some parents said we were under attack by the Rashaar."

"People just say things when they panic without knowing any better," Tricia said with a dismissive wave. "I've been in a meteor storm before, and it was scary. But there's no reason to believe the Rashaar caused it. They've never even been close to the school."

"But what about what Mom said? About Fort Somar and the Rashaanite soldiers? Who are they?"

Tricia gave Micah a pensive look. "Micah, they're bad. That's all you really need to know for now. Our grandparents escaped from them a long time ago, and that's why we're here. I've never even seen the Rashaar firsthand. Everything I know came from what I was taught in school. And believe me, that was scary enough."

"What was so scary?"

Tricia looked uncomfortable and folded her arms. "They killed all of our people. Only a few survived. You don't know how close we were to never being born."

Micah searched Tricia's face.

"Let's talk about something else," she said. "What did you think about Alfred being your teacher?"

Micah's curiosity ebbed with Tricia's ominous words. Her question caught him off guard. "That old geezer's my teacher?"

Tricia slapped Micah's knee with a laugh. "Old geezer? Are you sure you saw Alfred?"

"That's what he said his name was."

"Did he speak with a Southern accent?"

"Yeah."

"That's him. Mom and Dad requested him after what happened to..." She broke off and chose more careful words. "He's the best."

There was a knock at the door.

"Ah, perfect timing," Tricia breathed, working herself off the couch. "There's a friend I'd like you to meet. Hopefully, this time, without wrecking the furniture."

Emily was at the door, scratching Grubb's floppy dachshund ears. At the sight of Micah, Grubb tried to get away. Tricia took Grubb into her arms and calmed him by putting her hand over his eyes. With a mischievous grin, Emily dismissed herself and closed the door.

Tricia sat on the opposite end of the couch, careful not to let Grubb see Micah. Removing her hand, Grubb struggled, but Tricia held him firm until he settled down. Micah warily eyed Grubb, pulling his knees up to his chest.

"I want you to meet your friend as he truly is," Tricia said, stroking Grubb's back.

"After what I saw this morning, I don't trust that...thing," Micah said coldly.

"That's too bad. This *thing* will save your life someday—more likely, he will save your life many times."

Micah grimaced. "What is it?"

"He's a white-tipped wukal."

"A Wookie?"

"A wukal," Tricia tittered. "But there's a name you might be more familiar with."

"And that would be a mutant wiener dog?" Micah huffed.

"No. Grubb's a dinosaur," Tricia snickered.

Micah burst out laughing. Grubb broke free from Tricia's grip and bolted under the couch. Letting out an annoyed huff, Tricia struggled off the couch to her knees. She reached under the sofa to pull Grubb out. By the time she retrieved him, Micah had given her an earful for making up stories.

Micah's lips curled in a sneer as he stared at Grubb. Grubb

began to growl, baring his teeth. Micah had never considered wiener dogs all that threatening. He fell back to an old habit: denial. He convinced himself what happened up in the bedroom had just been his imagination.

"Micah, don't tease him! Wukals are dangerous."

"Wukals, pfft! Dinosaurs? There's no such thing anymore. He's just a stupid dog. Emily's cat nearly killed him last night."

"Grubb's still young. Ramsey's not." Grubb's fur bristled, and his growl deepened as Micah continued to scowl. "I'm serious, Micah. Stop teasing him!"

Micah lunged with his hands raised like claws. "Raaaaaa!" he shouted.

Tricia fought to keep Grubb from attacking. "Micah, knock it off!" Clenching her ring hand in a fist, she said, "Reveal."

At her command, Grubb's fur faded, and his form changed to the green-and-orange-striped monster. His barks became deep hisses and growls. His golden eyes remained the same, glaring menacingly as his long pink tongue slithered over sharp teeth. A skin membrane around his neck rose, buzzing like a rattlesnake.

Micah leaped behind the couch. Outside the door, Emily giggled.

"I warned you," Tricia said nervously. She covered Grubb's eyes with a shaking hand. Micah peeked over the top of the couch. Tricia stroked the creature and spoke soothingly. "It's okay, Grubb. Sometimes Micah is just thick-headed."

She playfully shook Grubb's toothy maw and made clicking sounds at him. Grubb relaxed, his fur-tipped tail thumping the couch. He began to chirp.

"When he makes that chirping sound, it means he's content. It's like a cat's purr."

Micah eyed Grubb suspiciously. Grubb stopped chirping.

"Don't stare at him like that! You'll set him off again. Do exactly as I say, understand?"

Humbled, Micah nodded.

"Okay, then, come here—*slowly*, no sudden moves—and sit by me."

"I don't know…"

"Come on, he won't hurt you. I won't let him. He's just a little confused after this morning. He just looks different."

Micah wrung his hands as he stepped cautiously around the couch. Making eye contact with Grubb, he diverted his eyes. Grubb continued to chirp contently.

"That's it," Tricia said, patting the couch beside her.

Sitting, Micah held his hands tightly together in his lap. Grubb lifted his head and lazily looked up.

"Let him smell your hand."

Micah hesitated, fixated on Grubb's sharp teeth. Tricia was insistent.

He closed his eyes and relinquished his hand near Grubb's toothy maw. He felt warm, moist huffs between his fingers as Grubb sniffed him.

Micah's eyes shot open when Grubb leaped onto his lap and curled up into a ball, chirping.

"You see, he bears no grudge. He wants to be respected, that's all," Tricia said softly.

Micah laughed nervously. "Can I pet him?"

"Of course."

Grubb's skin was leathery and finely pebbled but surprisingly soft. Under the surface of the skin, Micah could feel sinewy muscles flexing around the bones. Grubb's tail was as long as his body and curled contentedly at the fur tip. His rear legs were thick, elbowing down to his three-toed feet. His front legs were thinner with finger-like claws.

"Is he really a dinosaur?"

"As real as they get." Tricia grinned, watching Micah.

Grubb held Micah's fingers with his front claw. When Micah playfully rubbed his stomach, Grubb made hooting sounds.

"I can't wait to show Richard!"

Tricia shook her head. "No, Micah. Richard can't know any of this. It isn't that we don't like Richard. We love him, but he's not one of us."

Micah was crestfallen. "But how can I keep this secret from him? Even Richard would notice a difference between a wiener dog and this wuk-thingy."

"A wukal. And that's a good question." Tricia thought for a moment, resting her elbow on the arm of the couch. She tapped Micah's ring. "The Deity Stone, remember? There's a power this stone gives us. It's called the Fire. And *only* with the Fire will our secrets be discovered."

"Then how did you hide Grubb from me?"

"There are different degrees of camouflage. If you were skillful, you'd see through the illusion."

Micah grinned widely and asked, "So, is the Fire magic?"

"I've been expecting you to ask that. 'Magic' is a word used to describe a force we don't understand. The Fire isn't magic, it just changes the way we have access to those laws. There are many forces, such as gravity and magnetism, that we just accept as normal. In this world, they make machines that obey the laws of nature. With Deity Stone, it's like holding the reins of these forces directly through the will of the mind. It's not magic. We can't do anything natural law won't allow."

"So, how do you make something appear to be something else?"

"Everything we experience comes from the mind. The Fire is the power of creation and can directly change our perceptions. Understand?"

"I guess. I still don't know why I have to keep this from Richard."

"Think about what you've seen. On your lap rests a dinosaur. The Fire can unleash frightening power. If our neighbors and friends knew any of this, they'd see us as threats. That includes Richard. He's a good friend, but we have to be careful. I know you don't want to hear that, but it's our reality. All we want is to live in peace. We've managed to do that for nearly a century. So this is important, understand?" Tricia smiled at Micah, but he wasn't looking back.

"So where are we from?" he asked, scratching underneath Grubb's chin. "Where was that place I saw at the school?"

"Mom and Dad should be telling you, but…" Tricia said, taking a deep breath. "The earth is full of secrets. We are one of those secrets. Humans have walked this earth much further back than anyone here realizes. A century ago, a man from this world accidentally found his way into the time of our grandparents. That man was Alfred Quentin."

Micah studied Tricia for clues she was joking. The creature on his lap seemed real—he could feel and see it. If this was a joke, it was an elaborate one.

"Are you talking about time travel?" Micah asked, looking skeptical.

Tricia nodded. "But it's not what you think. The connection between the two worlds is fixed. Alfred didn't invent a time machine. He just found a door and walked through it."

"So when does this other world supposedly exist?"

Tricia shuffled through the books and magazines on the coffee table. She removed a thick book and placed it in front of Micah. On the cover, a boy looked up through a fossilized skeleton of a Tyrannosaurus Rex. The book's title was *DINOSAURS: A Prehistoric Journey.*

Micah searched Tricia's face. She held his gaze confidently and nodded. "Yes, brother, our grandparents came from a world that existed over sixty-five million years ago. A place we call Astoria."

Chapter 11
Birthday

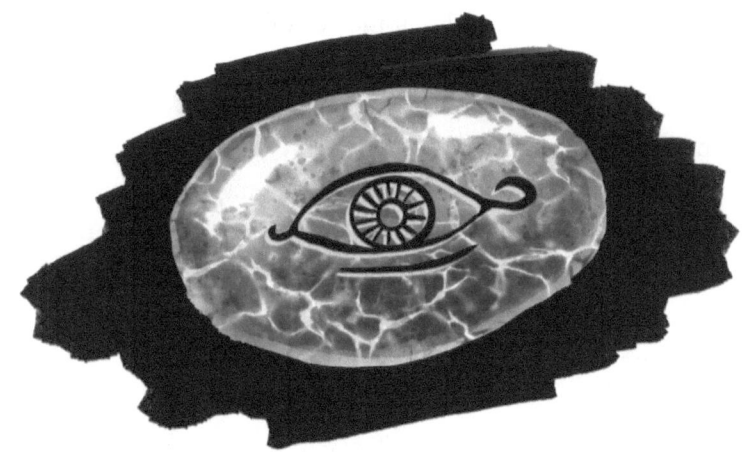

Little was spoken as Tricia drove Micah across town in her rusty pickup. Micah had hours to think about his sister's revelation, and he was still unsettled as the weight of what she told him sank in.

Tricia pulled into Richard's driveway. "You going to be alright?" she asked.

Micah scratched Grubb's head. Grubb rested his angled jaw on his knee, chirping softly. "I've been thinking, and I have more questions. I mean, why do I have a dinosaur for a pet?"

"Didn't I tell you? You were chosen to be the beast handler of your class. Every class has one. You and Emily are the only two we've ever had in our family. Wukals are difficult to train, so you got Grubb early to help you bond with him. You're going to play a vital role in your new class."

Grubb licked Micah's hand. Micah pulled away and wiped his hand on his jeans. Dejected, Grubb put his chin on the floor.

"Are you sure it's okay for Richard to see him like this?"

Tricia grinned. "Trust me, he won't know any different. Everything will be just as it's always been. Just remember, this isn't to be discussed with anyone, and that includes Richard."

Micah went to the back of the truck and removed his bike. Tricia backed out of the driveway, stopping to roll down the window. Micah looked glum.

"Cheer up, little brother," she said, giving him a sympathetic frown. "It's your birthday. I'll have everything set up later."

Micah forced a smile and spun his finger in the air sarcastically. Tricia hugged him through the window and backed out of the driveway, tooting the horn as she drove off.

Micah was numb inside. His sister's revelations had sent an earthquake through everything he knew. Nothing offered comfort except for the yearning he had to see his parents. He wanted to hear everything she told him was a lie.

If someone didn't know Richard's family, they might mistake the run-down rental they lived in for an abandoned house. The white clapboard home desperately needed a new coat of paint. The faded wood shingle roof sagged, and the few times Micah slept over, the chill of the night had blown into the drafty old house.

Inside, an out-of-tune piano was being played with surprising perfection. It was a new song recently played on the radio called "Sign of the Times."

All of Richard's family could play the piano, but Micah was sure it was Richard at the keys. His best friend had a gift for music. Richard could hear a song once or read sheet music and play as if he had practiced a hundred times. He often played when he was anxious. He practiced a lot.

Grubb rolled in the uncut lawn, snapping at fluttering white moths. The piano suddenly stopped mid-song with an angry bang. Grubb raced to the front door and peeked into Richard's house. The door burst open, sending Grubb retreating off the porch. Richard emerged, hefting two large bags full of newspapers.

"You made it!" he grunted, throwing the bags down.

Seeing Richard was the first normal thing to happen to Micah all day. He laughed at the sight of his best friend. Richard looked like a poor excuse for a hipster. His black hair was unkempt, with the back standing up like a rooster's tail. His jeans were too short and skintight.

"C'mere, Grubb. Come on," Richard called, ignoring Micah's grin.

For Micah, the sight of Grubb running upright on his hind legs was captivating. He'd seen dinosaurs in the movies before, but seeing one run in real life was an unexpected thrill.

Richard scooped Grubb up in his arms, nuzzling and kissing him. Grubb's pink tongue bathed Richard's face. Micah was spellbound by his friend's ignorance of Grubb's true reptilian form. His sister's words, "Only with the Fire can our secrets be discerned," were confirmed.

Richard saw Micah grimace when he let Grubb lick his tongue. "What the matter?"

"That's disgusting," Micah said.

Richard shrugged. "Go load your bags. I've already folded the papers."

"Where's the princess?"

"She's out shopping with Mom," Richard said, gathering a few newspapers that had fallen out of the bags.

"Figures," Micah breathed, stepping into the house. A tingling sensation crawled over his skin like he wasn't alone. He also smelled something burning.

"Happy birthday!" Sheila and Angela shouted, leaping from the kitchen. Micah jumped in surprise. On the table was a droopy cake with a single burning candle. Richard hurried into the room with a wide grin.

Sheila welcomed Micah with a hug. "We've got something special for you! I think you'll like it." She reached behind the couch and pulled out a package wrapped in the funny papers. "This is from Angela and me."

Tearing into the package, Micah feigned delight at the folded gift. It was one of Sheila's homemade shirts. The green-and-black-checkered flannel was sewn together crookedly with misaligned buttons.

"Oh, this is great. The fabric's so soft. I can't even tell it's home-made," Micah gushed, holding it to himself for Sheila to see how it fit.

"It's flannel. It'll keep you warm in the winter. It was Angela's idea," she said, hugging Angela. "She told me how much you loved Richard's new clothes. You just can't beat the quality of something homemade these days. I'm finally getting the hang of that dang sewing machine."

Angela suppressed a grin at Micah's expressionless face. He said, "Thank you, Angela. You know, the other day, Mom was asking for ideas for your Christmas—"

"We need to be going," Richard said, slapping Micah's shoulder with a paper.

After stuffing their mouths with slices of tasteless chocolate cake, the boys loaded the papers on their bikes and headed off. Along Birch Way, the boys veered their bicycles up a backwoods path.

The worn trail was narrow as it wound into the woods. Watching Grubb run along with them raised Micah's spirits. Grubb leaped effortlessly over rocks and through the bushes. Sometimes, he would stop at the sight of a squirrel scurrying up a tree or when they surprised nesting birds. Grubb would rise and bellow a triumphant "all's clear" squawk. Richard never showed an inkling of curiosity.

"Does Grubb seem different to you in any way?" Micah asked between laden breaths.

"Grubb's always been a little odd. He runs pretty fast for a wiener dog," Richard gasped.

"Yeah."

They emerged at a paved corner of a quiet oceanside neighborhood called Timber Hook. Mature pines, maples, and hemlocks dwarfed the homes. Several sailboats were making their way up the coast. Their white triangular sails were like teeth on the serene green-and-blue sea palette.

Micah was surprised the journey had hardly affected Grubb. Richard could barely talk, catching his breath. He hand-signaled and gasped out the plan to distribute the papers. Micah nodded patiently, wondering how Richard had made it this far without ripping his tight pants.

"Whose turn is it to do the old coot?" Micah asked.

"Let's think about this. Who did the route yesterday—*by himself?*"

Micah groaned.

They rode up the opposite sides of the street. Grubb plowed through the yards, sniffing everything. Micah kept expecting someone to rush out, shouting, "A dinosaur just ran over our front lawn. Get the net!" But no one gave them a second look.

One incident did catch his attention, however. Emma Hart, a three-year-old girl, was riding her tricycle in her driveway. When they reached her, Grubb stopped to sniff the big wheel of Emma's tricycle. Satisfied, he scampered on.

Emma cried gleefully, "Momma, the running alligator is here again! Momma!"

Micah nearly crashed his bike. He had forgotten about her. She had made this same observation before.

They soon reached their final street: Hurley Street. Micah looked dismally down the road. "Are you sure you won't take Crowther's street?"

"My advice? Pedal fast," Richard said, jumping off his bike. He set it against the tree and laid back in the grass.

"Thanks for nothing."

* * *

Micah pedaled down Crowther's street, delivering papers back and forth between the two sides in a way that would confuse the untrained eye. This curious pattern came after months of perfecting the "Crowther sneak." He and Richard used the trees and shrubs to minimize their exposure from a direct line of sight of Morty Crowther's front porch.

Four houses away, Micah stopped to prepare for the final delivery. He removed a paper and had it in hand. There would be no risk that the delivery would be botched because he couldn't get the paper out of the bag. Pressing hard on the pedal, he quickly gathered speed.

Grubb charged past like he was standing still.

Morty Crowther poked his head over the hedge.

"Ah, crap, he's waiting for me," Micah grumbled, throwing the paper blindly over the bushes.

Morty Crowther was kind, but he had a habit of telling the same stories over and over. He was a foreigner—from Austria, Micah recalled, or was it Poland? It didn't matter. Crowther had told him and Richard so much that Micah had trouble keeping anything straight anymore.

When they'd first met him at the start of their paper route job, they had made the mistake of accepting a cold glass of lemonade. This innocent offering was bait for a two-hour ramble about a subject Crowther often talked about: the Great War.

Micah's dad knew Morty Crowther and told Micah he was a good man who had seen much in his lifetime. His dad was right about that. It was just too bad the old coot insisted on telling his life story every time they met.

Racing past at terminal velocity, Micah hoped his speed would communicate a sense of urgency—but just as he passed, he heard the dreaded words, "Micah, wait!"

Old coot! Micah screamed in his mind. He skidded to a halt, leaving a ten-foot skid mark. Throwing his bike down, he walked back, admiring the many skid marks he and Richard had left over the summer.

Crowther whistled to Grubb, removing a bag of hamburger from his pocket. He tossed morsels of food, and Grubb gobbled them up. Micah snuck up behind and picked up the paper he'd thrown. He waved it violently at Grubb to shoo him away, but Grubb didn't budge.

"Micah, what you doing?" Crowther said, catching Micah mid-swipe with the paper.

"Um…er," Micah stammered. "Grubb's been a pest all day,

and, well, here's your paper."

When Micah and Richard first met Crowther, he was larger. Through the summer, the weight seemed to melt off him, leaving his skin like an oversized coat. When he spoke, his jowl jiggled like a bulldog. He had a high hairline and bushy gray eyebrows. He wore a light-blue one-piece jumpsuit with work rags stuffed in the pockets.

Crowther laughed. "Grubb never is a bother. I missed you yesterday."

"I wasn't feeling well."

"That's what Richard told me. You know, I like Richard. He's a hard worker. He told me today's your birthday, no?"

"I turned twelve today."

"Twelve," Crowther repeated like he'd been told a priceless secret. "What an important age. I have something for you." He retrieved a wrapped rag from his pocket. "Richard told me you've been having bad dreams lately."

This bugged Micah. That's all he needed was for Crowther to have one more subject he could ramble on about. "Um. Yeah."

"Bad dreams can sometimes be a sign of trouble, but they can also bring many truths. I think this could help." With a wide, droopy grin, Crowther presented the rag bundle and motioned for Micah to take it.

"You didn't have to get me anything."

"It's not much. Made it myself."

"Thank you." Micah took the gift warily. He unwrapped it, revealing a gray oval stone the size of an egg. The flattened rock had an eye carved into the rough surface. The opposite side was smooth with a shiny finish.

Wondering what it was, Micah felt it wiggle in his hand. With a second glance, he saw that the smooth side now had the words

Urmin Stone inscribed on the surface. *Was that there before?* he wondered. The words changed into a single word that read *no*. Micah raised his brow, thinking it was his imagination playing tricks on him.

"Urmin Stone. I think I've seen these in gift shops. Thank you."

Crowther chortled merrily, his jowl flapping as he shook his head. "Gift shop? Micah, don't make me laugh." He went on to explain how difficult it was to find the perfect cut of stone to make an Urmin Stone and that no such item was ever found in a gift shop.

As Micah listened, a thought struck him. Crowther's accent was similar to the janitor at school. This curiosity lasted about one second before the only question that mattered hit him: *How much longer is this going to take?*

The stone wiggled in his hand again, causing him to drop it.

Crowther didn't notice. "...one time, I was in the Rocky Mountains of Utah and happened across a fabulous slab of blue agate," he rambled on, oblivious to Micah retrieving the stone.

The Urmin Stone now read *One more minute.* Embarrassed, Micah stuffed it in his pocket.

"Enough about rocks. I just wanted to wish you a happy birthday and thank you for delivering my paper. I always look forward to our visits. I see Richard's up there waiting for you, so I won't keep you. I'm sure you have more important things to do on your twelfth birthday than talk to an old coot."

"Thanks for the rock."

"Urmin Stone," Crowther corrected.

Micah climbed onto his bike and pedaled back up the street. Grubb's tail wagged expectantly when Crowther bent over to pet him.

"Grubb!" Micah yelled over his shoulder.

Crowther waved with a broad smile as Grubb leaped away.

$$*\qquad*\qquad*$$

"That was quick. What'd he say?" Richard asked, sitting up on the grass.

"Nothing, he just told me happy birthday and gave me this," Micah said, showing Richard the Urmin Stone.

"A rock, really?" Richard said, annoyed. "After all that fuss yesterday, I would have thought he was going to give you a million dollars."

"It's an Urmin Stone," Micah corrected, polishing it on his shirt. "Pretty cool, huh?"

Richard looked at him sideways. "There's something different about you today. When did you get that ring?"

"It was a birthday gift. Why do you ask?"

"You look like the others now."

Micah was caught off guard by Richard's off-the-cuff comment. "What do you mean? What others?"

"A lot of people that live around here. I don't think it's a bad thing. It's just that you sort of…glow now."

"I glow?" Micah asked, examining his hands and arms. He didn't see any glowing, but he did feel good—like he could climb a mountain.

"I see that same light in your family, especially in your mom," Richard said, redistributing papers between his and Micah's bike. "I also see it in young children. It's bright with babies."

"What do you think causes it?" Micah asked.

Richard looked over his palm and the back of his hand. "I don't know. I've seen it for so long that I stopped asking that question. But I've always seen the glow in me, too."

Grubb sniffed the air and let out a curious bleating sound.

Richard took out their route map from his pouch and looked it over. "Mr. Higgins from the paper called yesterday. He asked if we'd take another street. I told him we could do it."

"Why would you do that?" Micah said, letting out an annoyed groan. "We already have the biggest route."

"It's just one street. Mr. Higgins said we were his best delivery boys and he'd give us an extra twenty every month."

"Sounds like a setup to me."

Grubb sniffed and began scampering back and forth. Micah and Richard laughed at his odd behavior.

Suddenly, Grubb took off at a dead run.

"What's with him?" Micah asked.

"I don't know, but he's heading in the right direction. C'mon."

The two pedaled down Billington Street, taking opposite sides to deliver the papers. Consulting his map, Richard pointed out which houses Micah was to deliver to. Grubb was nowhere to be seen. They stopped when they heard a woman screeching obscenities a few houses farther.

"Grubb," they said together.

Laughing children looked over a hedge into the yard where the commotion was coming from. Micah knew the kids—they were the Hills. The oldest daughter, Delcy, saw Micah and Richard approaching and asked, "Is that your dog?"

They skidded to a halt. Twenty cats were crammed together on a low branch, hissing and meowing like a chorus of crying babies. Grubb pranced proudly around the black cottonwood, hooting at his treed prisoners.

Richard fell over on his bike, laughing. Micah laughed, looking around the immaculate yard. Yellow flowers were arranged in perfectly symmetrical patterns in the garden. The house wasn't large but looked fancy, painted bright yellow with white trim.

The screen door crashed open, and Cornelia Moon rushed from the house, a broom clenched in her fists.

"Hey, that's the lady from yesterday," Richard continued to laugh.

Cornelia was shoeless, wearing a yellow paisley duster and a yellow turban covering her bald head. Grubb bolted when she rushed at him, flailing the broom. She was furious.

"Shoo, you mutt! I've called the dog catcher. Shoo!"

Grubb retreated behind Micah.

"Is this your dog?" Cornelia said, rushing up to the two boys.

Micah scooped up Grubb. "Yes, ma'am, I'm sorry. He has a thing for cats."

"Well, I have a thing for little boys who show up unwelcome. I'll have that beast put to sleep!" Cornelia said. Grubb became agitated when she stepped near, waving her broom. "Who are you two? I'm on neighborhood watch. I know everyone that belongs here."

"Cornelia, they're your paper boys," a gentle voice said from the house. Nellie Wilkerson stepped down the porch and stood by Micah. "I'm sure they meant no harm, did you?"

"No, ma'am," Micah said.

"You're Lorna Fennly's boy, aren't you?" Nellie smiled.

"Yes, and this is Richard—"

"Kimble Fennly's boy?" Cornelia shouted, her voice filled with disdain. "Get off my property! I'll have nothing to do with you lot of wizards!"

Giggles erupted from behind the hedge. Richard nearly choked with laughter.

"Oh, you think that's funny, do you? I can prove it," Cornelia said.

She grabbed Micah's hand. Grubb broke loose, landing between them, growling. The membrane around his neck buzzed.

"Get back, you beast!" Cornelia shouted, jabbing the broom to defend herself.

Grubb held his ground. The bristles shredded when Cornelia got the broom too close to his toothy maw.

"He's eating my broom!" she cried.

"Cornelia, stop this nonsense! You are working yourself up over nothing," Nellie said, twisting the broom away.

Richard rushed from the hedge and snatched up Grubb, retreating back to the laughing Hill children.

"Let me be clear, *son of Kimble*," Cornelia scowled. "I know all about your secret. It's been a plague in this town for too long. One day, the truth will come out, and then everyone will see you people for what you are: wolves in sheep's clothing! If I ever see you on my property again, I'll see you in jail for trespassing." She poked her crooked finger into Micah's chest and hissed, "Do I make myself clear?"

"Cornelia…" Nellie pleaded.

Micah nodded. He slowly backed away, dragging his and Richard's bikes with him.

Cornelia stepped near and snatched a paper from his bag. "Nellie! Get me the phone. I need a new paper boy!"

*　　　　*　　　　*

After completing the paper route, Micah pedaled home alone.

"*Son of Kimble?* Who does she think she is?" Micah grumbled to Grubb, who jogged at his side. "Who owns that many cats, anyway? Old Betty…"

Unlatching the gate, he rolled his bike into the backyard. Grubb sniffed in circles, finally catching sight of a squirrel scavenging for acorns, and darted after it. Micah tossed his bike down and stepped into the kitchen, where he paused.

At first, he thought he'd entered the wrong house. A rock-encrusted fish mounted over the kitchen table caught his eye. The kitchen table had always been made of dark wood with a single pillar. Now, its top was fashioned from crystal, with spindly veins of gold under the surface. A single bulged pillar supported the top, carved from polished marble.

The vase of fake flowers on a shelf above the kitchen table was now a beautiful arrangement of fresh magnolias. Micah felt the flower's pedals—they were real and smelled sweet.

The living room was starkly different. Only the tan carpet and family photos on the mantel remained the same. The couches were covered in dull blue leather.

The curio cabinet contained glowing stones and figurines carved from exotic woods and polished stone. Limestone frescoes of prehistoric beasts replaced art Micah had known his whole life.

The tropic fish in the shimmering fish tank were gone. Strange-colored fish with long, transparent spiked teeth schooled together. Each had some menacing feature or looked oddly out of proportion.

"I can change things back if it would make it easier," a quiet voice spoke.

"Mom," Micah said, relieved. He spun around and froze. The woman standing before him only hinted that she was his mother. The wrinkles were gone. She was young, looking in her early thirties, with dark chestnut hair. Micah knew this woman from black-and-white photographs taken decades ago. She was slender and beautiful.

"Micah, we didn't mean for you to find out this way," Lorna

began.

"What happened to you? You're so *young*."

Lorna presented her hand wearing a silver Hem Ring. "I am seventy. The Fire prolongs our lives. This is the way I truly am, son. Tricia told me you found the ring. It wasn't supposed to happen this way."

"Is Dad young too?"

Lorna nodded.

"I woke up this morning, and everything's different. I don't know what's real anymore."

"I know this is hard. Your brothers and sisters all went through this. I still don't have the words to make it easy. Just know that we love you, and everything is the same in our eyes. Acceptance will come in time. I only wish your father was here. It's been thrilling for us to see you children learn who we are. There's so much more to come."

Micah embraced his mother. "I don't know if I can take any more."

*   *   *

Micah's birthday party was overshadowed by everything that had happened that day. Richard, Wren, and Dylan Buckley were there, as were Angela, Emily, and Max. They ate lasagna and watched a movie. Micah was distant, finding himself distracted by his mother's appearance.

Most of the gifts he received were ordinary. Richard gave him a music player, which irritated Micah. He knew Richard must have spent weeks of his paper route money on him. Dylan gave him a new video game.

Wren's gift was different—a rugged blue backpack marked with symbols that Micah now recognized as Astorian. Wren apologized for giving such a lame gift, explaining that it had been his mother's idea.

Micah didn't mind. He was curious about the strange differences around him, and the backpack was something new to examine. He filled the pack with several heavy books to give it a test. He found it unexpectedly light. His interest piqued, he filled it with other heavy items only to discover the pack weighed practically nothing. He passed the pack around to the others before his mother confiscated it. She whispered into his ear that the pack was special and that she would put it away for later.

Tricia gave Micah a pair of boots. They were made of black reptilian skin with Astorian symbols in the soles. A note read *Micah, these are for "school." Love, Tricia, Geoffrey, and family.*

His mother gave him a new wardrobe of clothing—an assortment of loose fabrics, khaki denim pants, loose-fitting shirts, a dark-brown reptilian jacket, and a rain slicker. Dylan secretly teased him about his new stylish clothing.

For the last gift, Lorna had all the kids go into the backyard, where they promptly climbed up to the tree house. It wasn't long before Jack and Ben appeared in their backyard, peering curiously over the fence.

Lorna and Tricia emerged from the shed, wheeling along a brand-new bicycle. Micah and his friends gathered around his new bike and found they had two new additions: Jack and Ben.

"This is a nice bike," Jack said. He and Ben were surprisingly polite with grown-ups nearby.

The new bicycle was a step up from Micah's old one. It had adult-sized tires and was painted white with black skulls. There were levers to change gears and hand brakes.

The parents went back into the house with Emily and Angela.

The boys wheeled the bike around to the front. Micah rode up and down the street, passing his friends, who cheered him on. He turned the bike over to Richard to let him try. In the end, everyone got a chance.

"Can I try it?" Jack asked.

Micah didn't want Jack to ride his new bike, but Jack and Ben begged. Finally, he passed over the handlebars and said, "Just one time."

Jack jumped on and pedaled way down the street. He turned around and raced back at full speed. He pretended he was losing control of the steering and rode by erratically. Ben laughed at his brother's antics.

"Be careful!" Micah shouted.

Jack laughed and rode on. He turned around and came back on the sidewalk. As he approached, he took his hands off the handlebars and folded his arms. The sidewalk was buckled from years of tree roots growing underneath. Hitting a high spot, Jack crashed the bike spectacularly.

"My bike!" Micah yelled.

Jack stood and dusted himself off. He shoved the bike into Micah's hands.

"You okay, bro?" Ben asked.

"My bike's way better," Jack said. "I do that all the time, and it never made me crash. Come on, Ben, let's go home."

Micah looked over the bike for damage. The paint was scuffed and the handgrip had been ripped, but otherwise, it was fine. He was angry at himself for letting Jack ride his new bike, but his friends made him feel better by telling him that all bikes eventually get that kind of damage.

At the end of the party, everyone went home except for Richard, who slept over. He and Micah stayed up playing video games and eating junk food—something they'd regularly done this summer and in the past.

Micah had a dull ache he tried to ignore. The ache came every time he caught a glimpse of the ring on his finger or whenever he laughed with Richard. Something told him that his simple life was about to change, and he feared his best friend wouldn't be there. This made his last realization even more poignant.

Summer was over.

Chapter 12
Shina Shedets

October 31, 1974

A ll day Sunday, Micah and his mother talked. From the basement, she brought up three boxes labeled *yarn*. Micah had seen these boxes a hundred times growing up and never gave them a second thought. She removed neatly organized containers of photographs and mementos, each labeled with the names of his siblings and the year of the content.

As Micah rummaged through the containers, among the letters, photos, and mementos, he found blue coin collection books. Opening the first book labeled *Blake, 1974*, he was disappointed to see the coins were nothing more than small gray slate discs, each the size of a quarter, with a date written in marker. He was about to dismiss them.

"I think you'll find those the most interesting of everything you've seen here," Lorna said, taking the book from Micah. "They anciently called these discs *shina shedets*. A literal translation would be *the eye of the past* or *memoirs*. We just call them shedets for short." She thumbed through the thick cardboard pages, extracting one of the shedets labeled *Halloween, October 31, 1974*. She handed it to Micah and showed him how to use it.

Micah palmed the slate disc and closed his fingers. The living room disappeared around him. He was outside, walking along a crowded street at dusk. At his side were several boys and girls Micah's age wearing the most authentic Halloween costumes he had ever seen. They were dressed like pirates, superheroes, and hippies.

The vision felt like he was actually walking in this foreign place. He could smell food cooking and saw fireworks bursting in the sky. Ahead, there was a decorated plaza with lights and hundreds of kids dancing and partying. The song "Kung Fu Fighting" was blaring in the streets.

"Mom, Dad. It's Halloween, and they let us out of class early today. We're heading to the party," Blake's young voice said.

Micah opened his hand and was once again sitting next to his mother. "What is this?" he asked.

"That's your brother Blake when he was your age. He was a brightling at Boshii Campus then."

"A brightling?"

"Yes. That's what we call first-year students."

Micah was hooked. He spent the afternoon watching his siblings' memories recorded on the shedets. Immersed in those memories, he learned more about his older siblings than he had gathered in his whole lifetime.

One of the more curious memories was catching sight of a pair of talking orange birds. On a few occasions, he saw them transform into tiny humans. Before he could get a good look, the vision would cut off. He pleaded with his mother to tell him more about the two until, finally, she became annoyed.

"That's Penelope and Twitch," she said, irritated. "I told your brothers and sisters this, and I'm telling you. Stay away from those two. They're nothing but trouble."

Micah was especially captivated when he found discs where his siblings encountered dinosaurs. Each brought on a thrill. These weren't Hollywood productions. These were memories. He could hear and see the great beasts. On a few occasions, his siblings even touched the animals. What he saw had actually happened, and he wanted to know more.

Watching the shedets was more than just a passive viewing of a hyperrealistic movie. The shedets were like plugging a USB drive into his mind. Once he was immersed in the memory, he could search for specific moments or subjects. He would pause and rewatch the parts with the dinosaurs.

His mother became dismayed by Micah's enthusiasm for the great beasts. At the back of Blake's book, she extracted one particular disc tagged with a red marker. When Micah viewed this memory, he found himself in a great deal of pain, lying in a hospital bed bandaged with his leg raised in a splint. He was surprised to see Bassam, the janitor he'd met at the back-to-school night, with his red baseball cap, standing at the side of the bed, holding his hand. Beside Bassam were several adults and kids who were look-ing apologetic.

"You feeling...okay?" Bassam asked in an accent much thicker than Micah remembered from school.

"Sore," Blake moaned. Micah agreed. He felt every pain and twitch of his muscles.

"Lorna and Kimble," Bassam said, looking abashedly into Blake's eyes. "It's sorry for me to report, but Blake has been hurt. He got away in the night with his classmates and decided to chase a herd of Criken. They stomped on him," Bassam said, slapping Blake's hand gently. "Blake is strong. So don't you worry..."

Lorna snatched the disc from Micah's hand. "You see, it's not all fun and games," she said sternly.

Micah insisted on watching the rest of the disc. The part his mother didn't want him to see was Blake admitting it was the best time of his life and he'd do it all again if he had the chance.

The last collection of shedets was from his sister Mariam. The set was incomplete, only having her first year. When he asked his mother about the rest of the records, she reluctantly admitted she hadn't organized them yet.

As with his older siblings, the recordings were short, usually only a few minutes long. As he watched Mariam's shedets, a story unfolded. Micah experienced his sister transform from a shy, quiet girl to a confident, respected leader of her friends. He learned that Mariam's class was called the Tridents.

In one of the first recordings, she was aboard a ship called the *Gaspee*. They were out at sea and the water was rough. Micah could feel himself growing queasy as the horizon pitched and rolled. The recording began with Mariam approaching the captain of the ship. He was a stern-looking man with a weathered, kind face. He wore a black sea coat with a high collar. Tufts of gray hair sprouted from under his peaked cap. He was introduced as Captain Harrison Frost.

"Good afternoon, Mr. and Mrs. Fennly," Captain Frost said, looking up from a chart he was consulting. "Mariam has been in good spirits. She's got a talent for lifting everyone's morale and has been studying hard. You've raised a wonderful young woman that you should be proud of." Looking back down to his chart, he grinned and added, "Although her classmates say she needs to learn to clean up after herself."

"Who said that? Was it Missy?" Mariam exclaimed, and the recording suddenly went dark.

A moment later, Mariam was walking about the ship, greeting her crewmates. One by one, Mariam had each of her classmates introduce themselves and report what they were up to. Mariam seemed to have a strange effect on the boys, as they all were embarrassed to talk to her.

Micah was surprised when a blond-haired girl appeared in front of him. It was Camille George. Camille was Mariam's best friend and had often come over to their house to play when she was younger. From the recording, it was clear Camille was still a good friend to Mariam. The two giggled as they searched over the ship. They were discussing someone named Reynold, who they spotted a few yards away gathering rope. Reynold was older. He looked like he was probably in his late teens. Noticing the girls spying on him, the young man whipped the rope in their direction. Mariam and Camille fled in a fit of laughter before the recording concluded.

This shedet made Micah wonder. If Camille was a Massanite, it was too much of a coincidence. Camille had died in her home from a pandemic that swept through the west coast of Oregon last year shortly after Mariam's death.

When Micah asked his mother for an explanation, Lorna

packed up the containers, telling him he had seen enough for the day. She dug in, refusing to discuss Mariam or her classmates any further. Micah knew how stubborn his mother was and decided there was no sense in pressing her.

Later, they talked about what happened now that he had the ring. She told him he would soon join Alfred's Blazing Suns in Astoria, where he would learn about the Fire, survival skills, history, and more.

"You've seen some of what your brothers and sisters went through. Boshii Campus will be tough, but one day you'll look back and remember it as some of the best days of your life."

Micah asked how so many kids could attend school in Astoria without raising suspicions. She assured him there was a way, and told him to be patient.

Chapter 13
The Fire

I t was Monday morning, the first day of school.

Lorna prepared a breakfast fit for a young prince. Micah still found it difficult to believe this young woman was his mom. She danced around the kitchen, whipping up eggs, reaching for bowls, and bending over for pans—all without a single groan or complaint.

After breakfast, Micah loaded his school supplies in the backpack Wren had given him for his birthday.

"Don't use that pack for elementary school. Use a different one, please."

"But it was a gift from Wren. It's just a backpack."

"Absolutely not," Lorna insisted. "It's too easy for you kids to talk, especially if there's an excuse. This isn't a game we're playing."

Micah groaned. "You told me that all day yesterday. I'm not to discuss the ring or Grubb or anything."

"That's right. Use one of your old packs. Oh, there's something else. We need to hide your ring."

"But it won't come off!"

"I didn't say you had to remove it, silly. We just need to hide it." Lorna took his hand in hers and brushed over the ring. It disappeared.

Micah tried to feel the ring on his finger, but there was no trace of it. "How do I use the Fire?" he asked.

"Would you like to try?"

Micah was elated. "I'd love to…unless it gets you into trouble."

"No, *I* won't get into trouble," Lorna laughed. "You're sure you want to try this now? It may not work yet."

"Why not?" Micah said, disappointed.

"You've only worn the ring for a couple of days. I don't know if you've had time to heal yet."

"Heal?"

Lorna tapped Micah's head. "Deity Stone alters a part of the brain called the *barsa*. It's the part of the mind that connects the Fire. Let's see how you're doing."

Sitting beside Micah, Lorna removed an ice cube from his

orange juice and placed it on the table next to his spoon.

"With these two items, how would you cool the spoon?"

"I'd pick up the ice with the spoon."

Lorna nodded.

"We call that transference. With Deity Stone, your mind becomes the conduit to move energy. The Fire becomes an appendage of your body, just like your hands and feet. There are simple exercises you can do to practice."

"Like what?" Micah asked, anxious to get started.

"Your grandma showed me this when I was your age. Close your eyes and imagine picking up that ice and putting it on the spoon, just like you would with your fingers."

Micah closed his eyes. Staring into the blackness, he concentrated. Mentally, he reached out, picked up the ice cube, and placed it on the spoon. It was all very deliberate and mechanical. He repeated the task in his mind over and over. As he did so, the motion became more familiar and fluid. A stabbing pain began to grow from the center of his head.

After several moments of watching Micah grimace, his mother sighed. "Well, it's just not ready yet. Give it another—"

"Something's happening," Micah said, squeezing his eyes tightly.

Lorna jumped from her chair and stood behind him. "Keep trying, I know you can do it," she whispered.

Micah pushed through the pain. He pushed and pushed, and then…the black veil in his mind's eye burst into a brilliant world of vivid color. All around, showers of light streamed down like rain. The kitchen was a vibrating wonder. Electrical currents flowed as rivers back and forth on wiring hidden in the walls. A shimmering wall of heat poured from the oven like an upside-down waterfall that pooled and churned on the ceiling.

"I can see it!" Micah exclaimed.

"Oh, I knew you could! Now, concentrate on that ice."

The ice cube was a dark smudge bathed in burbling mist. Micah went through the mental motions of picking up the cube. The mist began to rise up in his mental container. It wasn't exactly like using his hand. The mist obeyed his will and collected into a small cloud above the table. He thought of the spoon, and the mist drifted down.

"I feel cold," Micah said.

"You're getting it! It's melting," Lorna said gleefully.

At that moment, he got distracted by a finger of black smoke curling toward him. Curiosity led his eye back to the oven. In the waterfall of shimmering heat, a blackness spewed out in a billowing curtain. Micah got confused and began siphoning heat toward the spoon.

"Something's burning."

"My cookies!" Lorna cried.

The experiment abruptly ended. His mother rushed to the oven and removed a tray of smoldering chocolate chip cookies.

"Ohhh, these were for your father! I was going to surprise him when he returned home today."

Micah picked up the spoon and instantly tossed it away. "It's hot!"

"Well, that's a good start," Lorna said, opening the kitchen window. "That's enough for today. Oh, I should warn you. If your experience is anything like what I went through, there may be side effects."

"Side effects? Like what?"

"This is going to sound crazy, but shortly after I got my ring when I was your age, I discovered I had a talent for understanding plants. I was out on the porch reading a book when I heard crying.

I found a small rosebush that appeared sick. It begged me for water. After that, we became friends."

"A rosebush talked to you?" Micah said, rolling his eyes.

Lorna laughed. "I told you it was crazy. But that's what happened to me. You've met Bernina. She's that rosebush I moved to the back fence. She was complaining it was too hot in the front. So I put her in the backyard for the shade. Funny, she's not been doing well lately. All of her flowers dropped off."

To Micah, the whole conversation was ridiculous, but there was no questioning that his mother loved plants. Their yard was a jungle.

"Enough talk for now. It's time for school."

Chapter 14
The Football Incident

Micah leisurely walked down Albatross Avenue to the bus stop. The air was cooler that morning, hinting at the approaching fall. The intrigue of the shedets he had watched the previous day captured his imagination. Then there was the ring and its power. Going to school—especially the first day of school—couldn't have come at a more unwelcome time. Each step forward felt like a spear was at his back. Ahead, kids were lined up at the bus stop.

Grubb rooted past through the Dickersons' yard. "Go home!" Micah shouted.

Up the street, the school bus labored up the hill. Red lights began flashing as the bus shuddered to a stop before the children.

Micah ran.

"The bus arrives promptly at 8:15 every morning," Miss Coburn said, stabbing her wristwatch with her bony finger. "You almost missed the bus, young man. I'm not going to put up with this again this year."

He apologized and stepped past her.

"Is that your dog?" she asked.

Grubb peered up over the bottom stair, whimpering.

"Yes, ma'am. Go home, Grubb."

Miss Coburn slammed the door shut, and the bus lunged forward.

"He's the one whose sister died last year," someone whispered as Micah found a seat. Kids were cheering as Grubb raced alongside the bus. That lasted until Miss Coburn yelled for silence.

"What's your dog's name?" a girl sitting nearby asked.

"Grubb," Micah said. He had never seen the dark-haired girl before.

"I love dogs. I'm Jolyn, but my friends call me Jo," she said with a grin. "I'm in the sixth grade this year. What's your name?"

"I'm Micah. I'm in sixth grade this year too. Who's your teacher?"

"Miss Sorenson."

"Mine too," Micah said.

A strong impression came to him as he looked into Jo's hazel eyes. From his experience with his mom that morning, Micah wondered if the Fire was doing something. He decided to take his mother's advice and blanked his mind. As he calmed, he noticed traces of swirling yellow light appearing around Jo's face.

"What's the matter?" she asked as Micah's stare grew uncomfortable.

Embarrassed, he broke eye contact. The light disappeared. "Nothing, you seem nervous."

"I am! We missed the back-to-school night, and I don't know anyone at this school. I'm worried I won't remember how to get home."

"Where do you live?"

"My parents bought the Holdmans' house. I don't know the street name."

"That's a couple of houses down from the Farnsworths. They live behind me. Have you met Jack or Ben?"

"No."

"I'll help you find it after school."

"Thanks. This is all new to me. I've lived in New Mexico my whole life."

It was a new experience for Micah to talk to a girl. Usually, the only girl he talked to was Angela. Those conversations typically ended with a punch in the stomach or a wet finger jammed in his ear.

The bus reached the next stop. Micah looked forward to this stop because it was where Richard got on. Angela climbed aboard first, giggling with her friends.

Richard was last on the bus. "Hey buddy," he said, plopping onto the seat.

Micah was glad to see Richard wearing the hand-me-down clothes his mother had given him, and he'd even combed his hair. The three talked about the back-to-school night and about where Jo had lived previously.

A tossed piece of paper landed on Micah's lap. Jack and Ben were turned around in their seat, looking back with mischievous grins. The note read *Is that your new girlfriend?*

Micah scowled at the brothers. Jack had a football, which he threatened to throw. The brothers laughed when Micah crumpled up the note and threw it back at them.

"Who are they?" Jo whispered.

"Jack and Ben," Micah sighed and looked out the window.

*   *   *

As Micah, Richard, and Jo entered the school foyer, they were greeted by the imposing statue of Alfred Quentin and a throng of excited students. Micah spotted Mrs. Ireland. As the self-proclaimed defender of silence, her forehead glistened from sweat as she went about squelching pockets of noisy students.

The three ducked to the opposite end of the foyer near a wall covered with hundreds of carved hieroglyphs. The previous day, Micah's mother had shown him Astorian books. He recognized the hieroglyphs as Massanite—more precisely, what his mother called Proshen.

"What are you looking at?" Richard asked.

Jo stood nearby with her backpack at her knees. Micah stared back with a blank expression. The words his mother had drilled into his head about keeping "the secret" tied his tongue. He didn't know if the two could see the writing.

"What language is that on the wall?" Richard finally asked.

"What writing?" Micah said dumbly.

"Look around, goofball. It's everywhere."

Micah said nothing.

Richard slapped the back of Micah's head as he stepped to the wall. "*This* writing," he said, tracing his finger in a deep-cut character resembling a lizard with horns. He traced other figures, making sarcastic remarks about Micah's eyesight.

Jo ran her fingers over the intricate characters. "I think it's Egyptian hieroglyphs. My dad has been to Egypt many times. He studies languages. He has books I always look through."

Micah liked Jo the more he got to know her. "Isn't Egyptian art amazing? I think it's really interesting."

Jo agreed. "If this is real, I'm sure my dad could read it."

Richard gave Micah a bemused smile. This prompted a question in Micah's mind: Why wasn't the writing hidden? And why were the other carvings on the walls visible? Surely, those would raise suspicion. He would have to ask his mother about it later.

Richard focused on a string of dots that ran along the bottom of the wall. He began to hum a song that was familiar to Micah. At the end of the movement, both Micah and Jo hummed along with the last few notes.

"Those are notes," Richard said. "I've never heard that song before. How did you guys know it?"

Micah and Jo both shrugged. "Mom sometimes sings to that song," Micah said. He'd never bothered to ask about it.

"Mine too," Jo said, nodding at Micah.

The bell rang, and the foyer began to empty.

"Why are you three just standing around?" a stern voice came.

Startled, the boys jumped, making Jo laugh.

"Is this a joke to you, young lady?" Mrs. Ireland said, squaring off on the three.

"I wasn't laughing—"

"Save it. You're new here, so I'll let it by this time. But if I see the same from you as I have from these two, you won't see a single recess, understand?"

Waving them off, Mrs. Ireland hurried away to catch boys playing tag around Alfred's statue. Defiantly, Micah sprinted up the stairs, leaving Richard and Jo behind.

"No running! That's your first warning!" Mrs. Ireland shouted.

Micah didn't care and kept running until he reached the second floor.

Miss Sorenson stood outside her classroom, greeting students. She was just a few inches shorter than the eight-foot-tall door. She eagerly invited the trio into her room with a wave of her enormous hand.

"Micah and Richard. I've heard all about you two." Miss Sorenson looked down at them like she had an eye for mischief and was double-checking for anything she might have missed. They tried to get by with a simple nod. "Where's your manners, boys? Who's your friend?"

They halted, looking back at Jo, who was spellbound by Miss Sorenson towering over her. "I…I'm Jo."

"Joylyn Tomkins?" Miss Sorenson finished. "We missed you at the back-to-school night. I understand you moved here from New Mexico."

"Yeah," Jo smiled.

"Welcome to my class. Go straight in and find your seats."

Micah and Richard were disappointed—though not surprised—to find their assigned seats were at opposite corners of the classroom. The boys had a long history of focusing on anything but their schoolwork when they sat together. Micah counted twenty-five desks, all arranged facing three large chalkboards mounted on the wall. At the back, cabinets were stocked with supplies and books surrounding a connecting door to an adjacent classroom. On the wall that had the exit to the main hall, five new computer stations were set up displaying bouncing screen savers of the school's miner mascot. Micah sat at the opposite corner from the exit next to one of the three high-arched windows with a view of the playground.

"Hey, buddy," Wren said from two desks back.

Micah and Wren rolled their eyes at each other when Paisley Cooper sat at the desk between them. The blond-haired girl with thick glasses and braces had the reputation of being a tattletale. Micah was sure the abrasive girl was taking lessons from Mrs. Ireland.

Others in his class, Micah remembered seeing at the gate on Friday night. Tricia had told him no one would remember because they hadn't yet received their rings.

Miss Sorenson closed the door and walked to the front of the classroom. She greeted her new class with a warm but reserved smile. She knew better than to be too light with twelve-year-olds. Scrawled on the brown chalkboard behind her were the rules of her class and business items.

"Did everyone have a good summer?" she asked.

There was a rousing response to the affirmative. She rolled her chair to the center of the room and sat down.

"Let's hear about it, then."

They spent the first hour reviewing everyone's summer. Micah was one of the last to report. Video games weren't that interesting, so he talked about his adventures with Grubb. The class snickered at his encounter with Cornelia's cats on his birthday.

During Wren's report, everyone laughed as he related the practical jokes he and his younger sister, Jenna, played on each other. His story about hiding under a tarp with an airsoft pistol to surprise her brought on an eruption of laughter when he explained he'd accidentally shot his mother instead.

Micah always found Wren amusing. But after watching Mariam's memories on the shedets the previous day, he missed his sister. It still bothered him how Mariam could have been in Astoria while at the same time home in Stonehelm. The only reality he understood was that Mariam would have been a tenth grader this year.

On the first day of school, it had been a tradition that their mother would line them up at the front door to take pictures. His mother had forgotten to do that with him today. Perhaps, with all that had happened, this was excusable. What bothered him most, though, was that he was starting to forget Mariam.

Micah felt tears coming on. He thought about something else. He fidgeted with his finger, wondering about the ring. He closed his eyes and imagined silence. The Fire came quickly this time.

The stone classroom wall appeared as a vibrating gray clumpy light. He followed the wall to Miss Sorenson's desk. A billowing waterfall of mist surrounded her oversized mug of ice water. Pulses of yellow light burst from her cell phone and purse. He imagined picking up the cell phone. The bursts of light bent in a beam and became more intense. A strange, warped buzz emitted from her phone.

Suddenly, a cracking whip sound broke Micah's concentration.

Miss Sorenson towered over him, looking over the class. No one else had heard the crack, as everyone was quietly listening to the last girl in the class give her summer report. Though Miss Sorenson didn't say anything, he suspected she knew what he was trying to do. It wouldn't have surprised him to find out his mother had called her about his ring.

"Good," Miss Sorenson said, walking back to her desk. "Since you've had three months to work out the wiggles, it's time to get back to work. The first order of business is the class rules. Inside your desk is a piece of paper. I want you to write these down…"

Micah's mind wandered again. He looked out the window and saw the mansion. He wondered about Alfred.

"Pay attention, Micah," Miss Sorenson said, rapping his desk with her knuckle. "These last rules are especially important. The third floor is off-limits to all students. In addition, no one is to play on the fencing. The old mansion is especially dangerous, and there is absolutely no excuse for anyone to go near it."

The morning was spent reviewing materials for the new school year. The typical lineup included English, math, and geography. It wasn't long before Micah wished he was home playing video games.

Later that morning, the first recess bell rang. Richard grabbed a red rubber ball from the sports rack and waited in the hall.

Micah was the last out of Miss Sorenson's classroom and was dismayed to find Mrs. Ireland scolding Richard. He tried to walk past, but Mrs. Ireland grabbed him by the arm and began reciting a litany of hall rules.

Micah could see Richard's impatience growing as other students walked by. The minutes of their recess were being wasted. Over Mrs. Ireland's shoulder, he noticed creatures carved on the wall with Proshen writing. One creature stood out to him—a squatty figure with a long tail tipped with fur. It was a wukal, just like Grubb.

"Are you listening, Mr. Fennly?" Mrs. Ireland said, moving to catch his eye.

"Yes, ma'am," he lied.

Shouting came from the stairwell at the end of the hall. Mrs. Ireland rolled her eyes and thrust the ball back into Richard's hands. Stomping off, she muttered to herself that she was the most overworked employee at the school. Micah and Richard grinned as they recognized the voice shouting from the first floor.

Hundreds of kids ran about the playground. Micah looked for Jack and Kamran. Being the tallest kids in the school, they were quickly spotted. Jack and his friends were playing football at the far end of the yard, with Ben obnoxiously running around begging for the ball to be thrown to him.

"Micah, Richard, over here!" Wren called.

The two met up with Wren, Jo, and Dylan Buckley on a four-square court.

"What did you think of our diversion?" Wren said proudly, running his fingers through his thick black hair.

"I knew it was you," Micah grinned.

"It was Jo's idea."

"What's her problem, anyway?" Jo asked, taking the ball from Richard and setting up to serve.

"Should I tell her, or you?" Richard said to Micah.

"Mm," Micah mumbled. He was preoccupied with watching Jack and Kamran. He was bothered that they were getting closer, throwing the football back and forth.

Jo served the ball and the game was underway.

"A couple of summers ago," Richard grunted, hitting the ball back, "we were riding our bikes through a neighborhood near my house. We saw a little boy, maybe three years old, crying, sitting on a curb. We stopped to see if he was hurt—"

Richard chased the ball and batted it into Dylan's space, catching Dylan off guard. Dylan was out. Micah took Dylan's place, and Richard served the ball.

"So?" Jo asked.

"That little boy was Mrs. Ireland's oldest son, Danny," Micah said, continuing the story. "She came out and assumed we hurt him. She ran us off before we could explain."

"That's not right!" Jo said.

"We know. Try telling that to her," Micah said, smacking the ball hard into Richard's square.

"Thanks, pal," Richard grunted, struggling to recover the ball, and hit it to Wren.

Just then, a football bounced into their game. They stopped playing, and Micah retrieved the ball. Written with black marker was the name of its owner, *Farnsworth*. Micah threw it back to Jack. Jack and his friends laughed. They were now playing close by.

"I'm glad we had to stop. I'm getting sweaty," Wren panted.

Dylan swapped places with Wren, and Dylan served the ball. Jack, Kamran, and their friends were no longer playing football but were huddled together, pointing in Micah's direction.

As the game was shaping up, Kamran ran straight into the four-square court and caught Jack's football. He smacked Micah's head with the ball and ran back to his friends. Jack and the others cheered.

"Let's go somewhere else," Richard said.

"Where? This is the only court left," Micah snapped back.

A sickening, fleshy thud was heard, and Jo let out a piercing scream. She jumped up and down, clutching her face as blood gushed from her nose. Jack's football settling nearby said it all.

Jack and Kamran stifled their grins until Micah ran for the football.

"Micah!" Richard shouted.

Jack sprinted for the ball, but Micah got it first. He snatched it up and ran out into the grassy playground. Kids gathered around Jo as Mrs. Ireland forced her way into the crowd. Nobody noticed Micah being chased by the eight boys.

Micah raced to the rusted gate in front of the abandoned mansion. Out of options, he kicked the football over the fence. The ball crashed through one of the mansion's windows, causing a report of shattering glass.

"That's my dad's ball!" Jack shouted, tackling Micah.

Micah's eyes widened at the red light radiating from Jack's face. It was similar to the light he had seen in Jo's face that morning on the bus, only much more intense. He looked at the others and saw that they, too, had the same red light.

Micah curled into a ball as Jack, Kamran, and the others began pummeling and kicking him. They cursed and tore at his shirt. Ben spit on him.

Richard approached cautiously, ducking into bushes surrounding a large granite rock.

Overwhelmed, something primal snapped in Micah. In his mind's eye, he became keenly aware of the life in the forest behind him. He sensed hundreds of insects, birds, and small animals. And then something large and lumbering was felt among the trees perhaps a hundred yards away.

"Help me!" Micah cried as fists flew.

Suddenly, the trees rustled with a torrent of wind, whistling over the old mansion. Birds erupted from the trees as if an explosion had gone off, and the forest came alive with a chorus of insects, birds, and chattering squirrels.

At this, Jack and his friends released Micah. The forest seemed angry, and they backed away from the fence when they heard rustling and twigs snapping. Something large was making its way toward them.

"What's happening?" Ben asked.

The boys scanned the trees warily. Micah saw the light in their faces change from intense red to waves of cautious yellow.

The snapping grew louder, and soon leaves shook in a thicket of bushes. A massive bull elk thundered out of the woods. The great beast snorted and dug its hooves in the dirt.

Ben ran off in a screaming panic. The others stepped back, leaving Micah alone at the gate. The elk towered over Micah, its rack of antlers higher than the fence. Calming, the creature sniffed at Micah through the fence.

"It's biting him!" Kamran exclaimed.

Micah felt connected to the elk and could sense complex emotions. The beast thought it was helping one of its own in distress. Flashes of thought came from the elk—memories of past encounters with humans—and it knew to be cautious. It felt vulnerable out in the open.

Micah patted the animal's muzzle, and it let out a soft huff, nuzzling him back.

Jack pretended he had a rifle and took an imaginary shot. "Bam!" he shouted. His friends laughed.

The elk raised its head and bellowed. Micah felt the connection break off as the boys rushed the fence. The beast swiftly rushed back into the trees. The forest fell silent.

"I've never seen anything like that," Kamran said. He and the other boys looked into the forest, bewildered.

Ben returned to his brother's side. "What about Dad's football?"

Attention was again focused on Micah.

"Go get my ball!" Jack demanded, stabbing his finger into Micah's chest.

Micah spat blood on Jack's shirt. Rage returned in Jack's eyes. He snapped his fingers and pointed to the top of the fence. Kamran and Tony climbed to the top, where they straddled the crossbar. Jack and the other boys grabbed Micah and tried to heft him up the fence. Micah stubbornly gripped the bars.

"Let go!" Ben demanded, kicking Micah's hands.

They rolled him over the fence onto the other side like a bag of trash. Micah landed hard on the eroded cement walkway.

"You better go get it, or I'll…" Jack began.

A whistle blew. "Boys, get away from that gate!" Mrs. Ireland shouted across the playground. "Get over here right now!"

Jack and his friends reluctantly left, shouting threats as they walked off.

Richard snuck out from behind the rock and ran to his friend. "You okay?"

"How's Jo?" Micah moaned as he stood.

"I don't know. I chased after you. What happened in the forest? How did you get that elk to come to the fence?"

"I didn't do that. I don't know why that happened."

Richard looked unconvinced. The recess bell rang. Kids on the playground began filing into the school.

"Help me back over," Micah said, reaching up to pull himself up the metal bars.

"What about Jack's football? I think you should go get it."

"Are you serious? Let him go get it."

Richard shoved his hands in his pockets, scuffing his worn sneaker in the grass.

"What?" Micah asked, dropping back down.

"You know Jack and Kamran are going to cause trouble over this. If you get his ball and tell him you're sorry, maybe this will blow over."

"Why should I be sorry? What about Jo? Whose side are you on?" Micah grumbled.

"I'm on your side. It's just…it's the first day of school. I don't want trouble from those guys."

Micah gritted his teeth, kicking the gate. Why did Richard always have to be such a pacifist? "Alright," Micah hissed. "I'll get his stupid ball. But I don't like it!"

Richard gave Micah a crooked smile. "I'll say you're in the bathroom or something. It'll buy you some time."

"Get out of here before I change my mind." Micah kicked the gate, still thinking about climbing back over. His shoulders sank when he saw Richard looking back at him across the grounds. Defeated, he turned toward the old mansion and stepped into the underbrush.

Chapter 15
The Mansion

The front door and lower windows of the mansion had been boarded up. Finding a way in proved difficult, leading Micah to eventually find the back door behind an overgrown bush. The porch was made of wood covered with soft, spongy moss. It took some effort, but the warped door finally sprung open. A dank, mildewed odor wafted out. Inside, vandals had defaced the walls with graffiti, and the floor was strewn with dingy clothing and numerous old water-soaked newspapers. Furniture lay overturned, and in the middle of the room, there was a charred patch where a fire had been started.

Micah wasn't afraid. He was angry. But as he searched the first floor, the ghost stories told by Mariam's old boyfriend, Eric, whispered in his ears.

"Stupid Eric," Micah said out loud.

Eric's stories suddenly took on new life as he searched the dark recesses of the mansion. There were more signs of recent activity, and when a giant rat darted across the floor into the lath and plaster wall, Micah felt his courage crumbling. He decided to hurry.

Climbing a creaky flight of stairs, he found Jack's football on the second floor among many mold-covered books. He considered leaving it and telling Jack he couldn't find it, but that wasn't good enough. The shattered windowpane gave him an idea. He grabbed the ball and pretended Jack was in the room with him.

"Oh, you want your football back?" he shouted.

Micah stabbed the ball into the jagged windowpane, and it popped.

"Oh, I'm sorry, Jack!"

He raked the ball over the sharp glass until it shredded apart.

Micah's adrenaline was charged up as he surveyed the dim room. He guessed it had been a library with its many empty shelves. On the floor, he perceived tiny glowing footprints. He also saw precisely where the football had bounced around and finally rested. Calming, this perception began to fade and eventually disappeared.

He wondered what caused the footprints to glow. Had his aggression brought on something new from the Fire?

With little more than simple curiosity, he felt his mind reaching out. The footprints began to glow again, revealing recent activity in the room. The more he willed it, the brighter they became. His own footprints glowed white-hot, as they were the most recent disturbances, but there were other signs of activity. Rat trails snaked around the room, and bird tracks were scattered. That was when he noticed a glowing skeleton key nestled among the books. Micah lost focus, and the light disappeared.

He picked up the key. A deep grumbling like bad plumbing groaned under the mansion. Moments later, there was a click, and the room fell silent again. Micah stuffed the key into his pocket.

Nearby, an old desk lay on its side with missing drawers. Micah searched the desk and found nothing of interest. He was about to walk off when he noticed a sliver of white sticking out at the back of a drawer. Excitement hit him to discover a secret compartment that spilled out several letters and a black-and-white photograph.

In the photo, several figures were standing on a ship. At the center of the picture was a man with dark hair and a long, thin mustache. Micah presumed it was Alfred, as his distinctive appearance looked just like the statue in the school. Hanging off Alfred was a beautiful woman looking up at him, laughing. Standing with them were four stoic-looking men.

Micah recognized one of the four as Bassam, with his ball cap, looking just as he did at the back-to-school night. On the back of the photograph were the words *My new friends, June 14, 1924.* After watching his older brother's shedets, Micah felt like he almost knew Bassam. He was surprised to see that even in 1924, Bassam hadn't looked any younger—

A door creaked downstairs. He slipped the picture and letters into his pocket and grabbed the football.

Someone was coming up the stairs.

Creaks grew louder, and then came the scent of perfume. He

felt the hairs on his neck stand up when a shadow appeared at the door and a face peeked in.

"Micah Fennly! You're in big trouble!" Mrs. Ireland shouted, rushing into the room like an enraged red-haired witch. She grabbed Micah by the ear, pulling him back down the stairs.

*   *   *

Micah sat on the office bench, rubbing his ear. Looking down at the football remnants, he regretted shredding it.

Penny Morris, the school's barely-out-of-high-school secretary, sat behind a half wall, clacking away at a keyboard, and stopped when a door opened behind her. Jo emerged, holding an ice pack to her nose. Behind her followed Sharon Leak, the school nurse.

Micah stood, looking apologetic. "You alright?"

"Is that Jack's football?" Jo asked, removing the ice pack.

Micah nodded, his eyes widening at her swollen and bruised face.

"It isn't broken. The swelling will go down in a few days."

Mrs. Leak led Jo out of the office.

"So, Micah, any cuts or bruises I need to tend to?" Mrs. Leak asked, looking him over.

"No, I'm fine."

The principal's door opened. Kamran, Tony, and Ben emerged along with the other boys who had chased Micah. Notably missing was Jack. The boys did double takes when they saw the football. Micah overheard Ben confiding with Kamran that his dad was going to be angry because they weren't supposed to take the football to school.

Richard and Wren shuffled out next. "We're in so much trouble," Richard said, looking pale. Wren disagreed with Richard and gave Micah a reassuring "don't worry about it" nod as the two left.

Principal Stokes poked her head out the door and noticed Micah. "Micah, Superintendent Arnold wants to talk with you. Penny, I need you to type up a memo." She stepped back into her office, followed by Penny carrying a notebook and pen.

"Good luck," Penny whispered and closed the door.

Shortly after, Humphrey Arnold's door opened. Jack walked out with a smug grin. This made Micah angry, and it felt good to present him with the football.

"I found your ball. Something's wrong with it."

An intense red light burst from Jack's glowering face. "You're going to pay," he seethed, refusing the scraps, and stalked off.

"Come in, Micah," Humphrey Arnold called from his office.

Humphrey stood with his back to the door, looking out the high-arched window toward the ocean. His desk was made of golden-stained oak, with a sheet of glass protecting the surface. On his desk were several clocks and trinkets that Humphrey called icebreakers.

"Take a seat," Humphrey said without looking back.

Micah sat uncomfortably at the edge of the chair. Humphrey turned around. Purple light swirled around his concerned face. The novelty of the light was beginning to annoy Micah, and it suddenly disappeared.

"So, let's hear your side of the story," Humphrey said, sitting down.

He listened like a patient grandfather as Micah related the incident. Humphrey nodded sympathetically but, in the end, stated the school's policy about fighting. He detailed the punishment that all the boys would face. Micah didn't complain. He was just grateful worse punishments weren't imposed—like calling his mother.

Humphrey stood, and Micah thought he was excused, but

Humphrey motioned for Micah to sit back down. He stood with his arms behind his back and looked out the window. "I have one more item to discuss with you. Micah, I've been in education for thirty years," Humphrey began. He went into the history of the school, explaining how much trouble the mansion had caused him, and that he wanted to keep the incident quiet.

Micah's eyes wandered around the trinkets on Humphrey's desk, eventually settling on an open manilla folder containing a stack of yellowed news clippings. One of them was set off to the side. At the top of the stack was an article entitled "The Pacific Flu." Micah had seen this article before in a book his mother kept. It detailed the epidemic that had swept through the northwest last year. The sickness had claimed the lives of fifteen teenagers who were all Mariam's age—including Camille George, Mariam's best friend. His mother had told him Mariam came down with the same sickness before she had the accident.

The other clipping was more interesting, and he slid it near. It was titled "Protester Strikes Out." It featured several black-and-white photographs of the protest at the school. Micah smiled at the most prominent photo of the crow snatching Cornelia Moon's wig. One photo was circled in red marker: a close-up of two crows in a tree. Micah was certain the crows were Penelope and Twitch, as one of the crows had a light crown of feathers. The article read:

Protester Cornelia Moon gets a surprise from a pesky crow at the Quentin Elementary open house last Friday. Moon has been charged with four counts of assault on Stonehelm's police officers. When asked for comment, Moon replied, "It's not my fault those half-wits parked where they did. Look, one day, you ignoramuses will listen to me. This town is full of wizards, and that school is a time machine. This town needs to wake up before it's too late." Cornelia Moon is the daughter of Harold and Darby Moon. The late Harold R. Moon was mayor of Stonehelm from 1962 until his death in 1968.

She knows about us, Micah thought, sliding the news clipping away.

"...that mansion is dangerous. I can't have children climbing the fence, especially you older kids who set examples for the younger..." Humphrey blathered on, unaware that Micah had stopped listening two seconds into his lecture.

Micah realized something was different about Humphrey's office. There was no Proshen writing. The upper walls were overlaid with copper mesh. It reminded him more of a cage. Deity Stone was mounted in recesses where the brick had been cut. Some of the stones were the familiar amber, but others appeared to be made of pure gold.

Chapter 16
Hard Weeks

Two weeks passed. Micah's father hadn't returned home, and neither had his brother-in-law Geoffrey.

As Tricia's due date approached, she often came over to spend time with their mother after Emily and Max went off to school. Micah would only see his sister in passing as he left the house for the bus stop.

Both his mother and Tricia refused to discuss anything more about the gate closure. He gathered it had been sealed the night of his birthday party and was confident more had happened than just a meteor shower. He even went so far as to call his niece Emily, hoping he could use a "favorite uncle" angle to get more information. Emily confided that she was worried about her dad, but she didn't know anything more than he did.

As the days passed, the anticipation of something big coming was forgotten by what was happening at school. After the football incident, the boys had their recess suspended for a week. This reduced school to a boring day of paperwork and staring at four walls.

At home, Jack and Ben started a full-on war. Micah and Grubb couldn't go into the backyard without facing a barrage of threats, pine cones, and a few times, even rocks. Micah especially hated the bus stop. Every day, Jack would try to pick a fight, which escalated until some of the younger children refused to go to the stop without their mothers.

The real trouble began the second week after the recess punishment was lifted. While most kids played carefree on the playground, Micah, Richard, and Wren spent their recess being chased and bullied by Jack and Kamran's growing gang. Kamran, in particular, was a master at recruitment through intimidation. He managed to get some of Micah's fair-weather friends to join in the chase.

Mrs. Ireland, who had a nose for the tiniest infraction, acted blissfully unaware of Micah's problems. He caught her more than once looking the other way when he got cornered on the playground. As long as Jack and Kamran didn't attract too much attention, she wouldn't say anything.

Micah grew so desperate he even tried to use the Fire to fight back. Strangely, whenever he imagined harm to the boys, the Fire would stop working for several hours.

By the third week, Jack and Kamran had the chase down to a science. On Monday morning, just as Micah, Wren, and Richard arrived at school, Kamran and Tony led a band of boys to trap the three in the foyer bathroom. Like mob bosses, Jack and Ben followed at their leisure from the bus.

Ben, being the sadistic lackey he was, kept throwing ideas out for the day's punishment. "Put their heads in the toilet and flush it!" he suggested gleefully.

"We're Americans, we have rights!" Wren shouted. As was typical, he stayed behind Micah and Richard.

"I'll show you a right," Kamran said. He yanked Wren out and punched him repeatedly on the arm.

The boys laughed when Micah tried to defend his friend. Jack and Kamran shoved Micah up against a bathroom stall. Ben cheered them on until the boys guarding the door told them to keep it down.

Jack and Kamran slapped Micah's face and punched his stomach, threatening worse if he didn't stop resisting. When Micah stopped struggling, they released him.

"I got yelled at by my dad last night. Do you know why?" Jack said, his face pulsating with red light.

"Because you have an ugly sister?" Micah retorted.

Ben protested when all the boys laughed, except for Jack.

"All of you shut up!" Jack shouted. "Micah," he hissed, kicking Micah's foot, "you just don't know when to keep your mouth shut! I got in trouble with my dad for losing his football." Jack pulled his shirt down over his shoulder, revealing a large purple bruise where his father had hit him.

"Did you tell him why?" Micah said.

"Yeah!" Wren and Richard chorused. Tony clunked their heads together, and the pair fell silent.

Jack glared at Micah. "You owe me a football! If I have to put up with my dad yelling at me, I want your new bike as interest!"

"Are you kidding? It's your fault this all happened in the first place!" Micah said.

"Tell him about his dog," Ben said.

"Shut up, Ben!" Jack snapped.

"I wonder what they brought us today?" Kamran said. He grabbed Richard's backpack and dumped it out on the floor. Everyone stared at the meager contents. There was a single thin sandwich and an apple that was past its prime.

"So, this is what it's like to be poor?" Jack said, grabbing the apple. He threw it against the wall, where it disintegrated into pulpy bits. He picked up the sandwich and unwrapped it. "You guys want to know what it tastes like to be poor?"

Jack took a huge bite of the sandwich. He chewed thoughtfully then spat it out, throwing the remainder at Richard. Richard looked embarrassed.

"That's disgusting! It's just two pieces of bread—and they're stale!"

Micah had had enough. He cocked his arm and punched Jack in the eye as hard as he could.

Everyone gasped. Jack recoiled, grabbing his face with a groan. His stunned expression went fierce as the initial shock wore off. "You're dead, Fennly!"

Micah retreated to the wall, protecting himself when Jack began taking swings. Kamran rushed over and tackled Micah to the floor.

Frantic knocking came at the door, and everyone froze. Moments later, Mrs. Ireland poked her head in. "What's going on, boys? Do I hear fighting? Micah, why are you on the floor?"

Richard started to say something, but Ben kicked him with the heel of his shoe.

"He fell," Kamran said, offering a hand to pull Micah up. Micah stood without any help, slapping Kamran's hand out of his face.

"I think you boys need to come out of there right now."

"Sure, Mrs. Ireland, whatever you want us to do," Jack said with his best suck-up voice. "We're just trying to help."

Micah was angry. He wanted to attack, to lash out and scream. Being the last to leave, Mrs. Ireland held him at the door. "Trouble seems to find you wherever you go, Mr. Fennly. Do we need another visit with the principal?"

"No, ma'am," Micah said coolly and walked off.

*   *   *

Micah had given Jack a black eye. It didn't go unnoticed by Jack's mother. Margot was so upset that she marched over to Micah's house to talk to Lorna. Their conversation was brief and curt.

"Your son's a bully. He deserved what he got," Lorna insisted. Micah stood behind her, chewing his thumb.

Margot would hear none of it, insisting that Jack was just protecting Ben. When Margot tried to directly yell at Micah, Lorna slammed the door in her face.

"That woman!" Lorna breathed, giving Micah a reassuring hug.

The next morning, Margot raced her boys to the bus stop just as the bus arrived. Her black SUV skidded to a halt. Like an angry mother grizzly, she charged Micah and got in his face.

"You even so much as look my sons with a frown, and I'm calling the police!" she shouted and raised her hand like she was going to slap him.

Micah braced himself. Both he and Margot ducked with surprise when the bus horn honked. Inside the bus, Miss Coburn shook her head at Margot.

Margot composed herself, straightening her hair and smoothing her hands over her blouse. She glanced over at Ben and Jack, whose eyes were as wide as saucers. "I don't know what your problem is, young man, but you better fix it!" she said to Micah, turning to leave.

Micah attempted to explain, but Margot just threw him a dismissive gesture. She returned to her car and yanked the door shut. Nearly colliding with the bus, the tires of her SUV squealed as she sped off.

Once their mother was out of sight, Jack and Ben gave each other a high five and climbed aboard. Stunned, Micah and Miss Coburn stared at each other through the bus windshield.

*   *   *

Jack's black eye had done more than upset his mother. It was a message—a message that the school's biggest bully wasn't invincible.

Jack doubled down on threatening anyone who teased him about his black eye or attempted to stand up for Micah and his friends. No one wanted to get tangled in Micah's troubles. The only friends who remained true were Jo, Wren, and Richard.

Wren and Richard suffered every bit as much as Micah did. Jo, however, had a unique way of dividing Jack's group. While even Jack wouldn't hurt a girl, he didn't hesitate to tease her. If it got too severe, Kamran would step in and stop the others from picking on her.

There were a few recesses where Bassam was outside doing

maintenance. Micah, Wren, and Richard would gather around the friendly janitor, offering their company. In return, they would have immunity from the constant chasing and fight-picking.

Bassam turned out to be good company. He had a wealth of experiences to share about his time as a teacher that brought laughter to the boys. Of the three, Bassam was particularly taken by Richard.

It was these days that Micah missed Mariam the most. He had spent countless hours with her. One of his favorite memories was whenever they went on their adventure hikes, they had to stop first at the gas station for supplies. This usually was just a can of pop and some chips. She always made sure Micah got what he wanted. He remembered the time when some older kids tried to pick on him while his sister was inside paying for the snacks. Without hesitation, Mariam raced out of the store and ran the boys off. She was just that kind of sister, always looking out for him. He longed so desperately to have her back. He was certain she would have known what to do about Jack.

*   *   *

It was Friday, and the recess bell rang. Richard, Wren, and Micah sat at their desks as the rest of the class filed out. They were in no hurry to face what awaited them outside.

As they were about to leave, the connecting door between classrooms opened. Mr. Wilson, another sixth-grade teacher, stood at the door. He was a plump man wearing a tight tan jacket and blue jeans. He was also Jack and Kamran's teacher.

"Yamina, may I speak with Micah?"

Miss Sorenson looked up from the papers she was grading. "Good morning, Greg. He's sitting right there."

"Do you mind if I talk to him alone, please?"

"Why, sure. Richard, Wren, you boys go on out to recess. Micah will be out shortly."

Micah followed Mr. Wilson into the classroom. Alone, Mr. Wilson closed the door. There was a table with several computers and shelves filled with games, models, and various statues. Micah knew from his mother that Mr. Wilson wasn't a Massanite, but after looking over his room, he concluded that Jack and Kamran's teacher was cooler than Miss Sorenson.

They walked to Mr. Wilson's desk, where there was a statue of Albert Einstein with one of the arms broken off. Wilson stared at Micah, waiting for a response. When none came, he asked, "Well?" Mr. Wilson's stone face was hard to read, leaving Micah confused.

Every day since the first day of school, Micah's mother had done small exercises to help him learn more about the Fire. The nuances were usually subtle. The light had become a tool he could interpret to better understand the state of mind of others.

Through observation, Micah had developed a sense of the meaning of the light he saw in faces. While colors varied slightly from person to person, there were some typical traits. Yellow was common. It meant worry or concern. He often saw this color in Richard's face. Red meant anger. White meant peace and contentment. Colors shifted rapidly as emotion was affected by the many factors the senses presented. Purple was one he had seen a few times. It was a cross between anger and worry. The more intense the color, the more deeply the emotion was felt. Everyone presented a different countenance that took time to become familiar with.

As he dialed up his perception of Mr. Wilson, Micah discovered an unhealthy shade of blue. This was one of the rare colors. There was something else on Wilson's mind besides the statue. Digging deeper, a complex web of light rays appeared emanating from Wilson's head. While a few rays of red were directed at Micah, there was a stronger connection of yellow light connected to photographs on Wilson's desk. In the photos was a woman hugging Mr. Wilson. Was she his wife? A girlfriend?

An angry expression crossed Wilson's face as the silence lingered. The light in his face coalesced into pulsing pink hues aimed straight at Micah.

"I don't know what you're asking," Micah finally answered.

"The statue. You broke it. I want to know why you were in my classroom this morning."

"I wasn't in here. I didn't break it."

The red light in Wilson's face deepened. "Don't tell me you didn't break it! You were in here goofing off, and I want to know why."

"I've never even been in your room before," Micah protested.

"I have a whole classroom of kids that saw you do it. So don't you dare stand there and lie to me."

"They're lying!" Micah said.

Mr. Wilson took Micah by the shoulder and led him to a desk, where he demanded he sit. "You're going to sit right here until recess is over and think about how you're going to make this right."

Grabbing his coffee cup, Mr. Wilson marched out of the room. Micah looked over the statue, shaking his head with disbelief. He had nothing to do with what happened, and the accusation stung. But at least he didn't have to go out to recess.

*   *   *

Brakes protested as the bus shuddered to a stop on Albatross Avenue. Micah and Jo were already standing at the front of the bus, waiting to get off. When the door swung open, they said their goodbyes and hurried off. Jack and Ben followed, shouting threats as Micah sprinted home. Jo scolded the two, which brought on a profanity-laced verbal assault.

Micah was relieved to see the end of the worst week of his life. He was looking forward to the weekend.

Reaching home, he went into the kitchen and set his backpack on the counter. He saw traces of blood on the floor. "Mom!" he called, but she wasn't home.

Taking a deep breath, Micah closed his eyes. One of the exercises his mother had taught him was how to read his surroundings. He'd found this skill handy on several occasions when Jack and Kamran chased him.

Opening his eyes, he saw glowing footprints. Judging from their brightness, he knew they were made several hours prior. Mingled with the sneaker prints, he also found Grubb's distinct three-toed prints. There had been a confrontation at the back door, which led into the kitchen. The prints went round and round in a frantic pattern.

Whimpering came from the pantry. Micah opened the door and Grubb ran out, covered in spaghetti sauce and potato chips.

"What the heck are you doing in there?"

The pantry was a disaster. Grubb had indulged in multiple feasts and had chewed up everything below the second shelf. Mingled among the ripped-open bags and punctured cans, Micah was horrified to find a shoe covered in blood. Picking it up, he was relieved to discover the blood was actually spaghetti sauce.

"Where'd this come from?"

Micah's mother had the gift of communicating with plants. This was a skill Micah could not duplicate, no matter how hard his mother worked with him. But the one talent they discovered he

Karl Loveridge

did have was a connection with animals—as primitive as it was. This had opened up a whole new world between Micah and Grubb. While Grubb wasn't the most eloquent communicator, Micah could piece together scraps from Grubb's erratic mind.

Micah dangled the shoe in front of Grubb's blunt snout. Grubb sniffed at the shoe and made odd hoots and clicks. Concentrating, a rudimentary sentence formed in Micah's mind: *bad... hurt... bit... mine!*

Micah focused as Grubb kept repeating the same sounds with different intonations. *Someone bad tried to hurt Grubb? He bit them? He took something?*

Lorna and Tricia had gone to a doctor's appointment in Portland that day, leaving Grubb home alone. Grubb had been left in the backyard when Micah went to school, leaving the house empty all day. Micah did a quick search throughout but found the glowing footprints were isolated to the front room and kitchen.

As he was cleaning up the pantry, the phone rang. Micah picked up the receiver, and Richard was already talking. "Micah! You said you were coming right over. The papers just got dropped off."

"I know, I know," Micah said, trying not to touch anything with his sticky hands. "I'll be there as soon as I can. Bye!"

Micah washed up and went to the back door. He was in no mood to confront Jack and Ben. He thought through the steps to get to his bike as quickly as possible and slid the door open. Hurrying out, he found that the cable he used to lock up his bike had been cut.

His bike was gone.

He searched the yard, hoping he had just forgotten to lock it up. He tried to follow the glowing footprints but found they were lost in a peppering of glowing splatters from the recent rainstorm. His bike had been stolen. He looked over to Jack and Ben's yard,

188

expecting to find them laughing at him. The pair were nowhere to be seen.

Whoever had been in the house hadn't been there to rob it. They'd just had to get Grubb out of the backyard. Although he had no proof, Micah was sure Jack and Ben were behind this.

Feeling sick to his stomach, he gathered his empty paper bags and retrieved his old bike from the storage shed. He rode down the back trail to Richard's. Grubb, elated to be out of confinement, led the way through the woods. Fifteen minutes later, Micah arrived at Richard's house.

"Where's your new bike?" Richard asked. He had finished folding the papers by himself and had his bike ready to go.

"It was stolen," Micah said, trying to hide his tears.

Richard's face went red as he helped Micah load his bags. There wasn't much to say.

"Sorry. Who do you think did it?"

"I'll give you two guesses."

The boys delivered the papers in silence. Their usual laughter and antics were replaced by introspection and tears brought on by self-pity. Reaching near the end of their route, they stopped under the tree at the top of Hurley Street. Neither wanted to face Morty Crowther. Grubb knew the route as well as the boys. He started down the street but returned when Micah and Richard didn't follow.

"No sense putting it off any longer," Richard finally said.

"Yup... Wait," Micah said, noticing the smoke-belching orange Beetle pulling out of the driveway. It was Crowther's car. "He's leaving. Maybe this won't be so bad after all."

As the car sped off, the boys' spirits lifted.

"Let's go!" Richard said.

They leisurely delivered papers down Crowther's street. It was a great feeling to toss the last paper onto Crowther's porch with the certainty they wouldn't get sucked into another hour-long ramble. Richard stopped alongside Micah.

"So what are you going to do about your bike?"

"Report it, I guess. Whoever did it had trouble with Grubb. They got into the house and trapped him in the pantry. You wouldn't believe how much of a mess he made," Micah said with a quiet chuckle.

"Trouble with Grubb? Who could have any trouble with a little wiener dog?" Richard said, petting Grubb. Grubb loved the attention and lapped at Richard's hand. Richard was blissfully unaware of the razor teeth and claws that must have awaited the intruder.

The brassy putter of a car winding up came from behind. The boys looked back to see Crowther's orange Beetle racing toward them, flashing its lights and tooting its horn.

"Oh, great," they moaned. They considered scattering but decided it would look too obvious.

Crowther pulled up next to them, dragging along a cloud of blue smoke. "Micah, Richard! I was hoping to find you. I have something for you."

The boys looked disappointed but lit up when Crowther presented them each with an ice cream shake. From a bag, he produced a couple of hamburgers. He unwrapped the burgers and tossed one to Grubb.

"Micah, what happened to your new bike?" Crowther asked.

"It was stolen," Richard said, licking a drip from the side of the cup.

"Ohh," Crowther moaned, leaning out the Beetle's window. "I'm so sorry to hear this bad news."

He took a bite of his burger, chewing thoughtfully. The boys exchanged an amused grin that Crowther was unaware of the ketchup blot off the side of his mouth.

"When I was a boy, someone broke in where I lived…" Crowther began. He went on to relate an overly detailed account from his childhood that could have been summarized in one sentence. Five minutes later, he was still rambling.

You should dust off the Urmin Stone I gave you, a voice whispered.

Micah choked on his last slurp of shake as he looked around for the source of the voice. Richard was several feet away and was preoccupied with his treat. Crowther tapped his hand on the driver's window, not skipping a word as he blathered on.

For the first time, Micah noticed the Hem Ring on Crowther's finger. It was made of gold with an amber crystal. It was unmistakable. Crowther was a Massanite! Why hadn't he noticed before?

Micah thought through the endless dronings he had endured from Crowther that summer. The clues were there. Crowther often referred to the "Great War," which Micah assumed referred to World War II. But since when did soldiers have the power to create earthquakes, summon tornadoes, and erupt volcanoes?

Crowther's stories were often peppered with those kinds of outrageous details. Micah and Richard usually went away snickering at the crazy old coot, but if Crowther was a Massanite, could his far-fetched stories be true?

His thoughts turned to the Urmin Stone. When Crowther first gave Micah the stone, he experimented with it a few times. He asked it simple questions about himself. It always responded correctly. At the time, he dismissed it like it was just a clever toy, like a Magic 8 Ball or the game of twenty questions. He soon grew bored and forgot about it. But with Crowther being a Massanite, a renewed interest hit Micah. He knew right where he'd left it.

"I just remembered something," Micah said. "I need to go home."

Chapter 17
The Coin

"I can't believe that worked," Richard said for the third time as the boys arrived back at his home. Shortly after Micah's declaration, Crowther wished the boys a good night and drove off.

Angela was waiting on the porch, waving a box of macaroni as Richard dismounted his bike. "Mom called from work. She said you'd make dinner."

"Alright," Richard said, taking the box.

Angela noticed Micah's old bike. "Sorry your bike was stolen," she said.

Micah's brow rose. "How did you know it was stolen?"

Angela swung the screen door open and stepped inside. "Richard told me," she said, letting the door slam behind her.

Richard flashed his crooked smile. "Hey, you said you remembered something. What was it?"

"I don't know, I just made that up."

"Well, that was a good one. Let me know what you find out about your bike."

Micah pedaled home to find his mom wasn't back yet. Up in his bedroom, he shoved his mattress over, revealing the box spring covered with hundreds of small treasures he had found since he was a little boy. His mother once told him about a princess who slept on a pile of mattresses and could feel a single pea at the bottom. If that princess had lain on his bed, she would have suffered back problems. There were marbles, baseball cards, bullet casings, and many other odd bits he'd collected.

He took the Urmin Stone resting next to the two black pebbles. A week prior, the Macabre Ring had finally allowed itself to be removed. The moment he took it off, the two black stones had changed to the locket and coin.

Outside his open bedroom window, he heard laughter. He peeked out the window, where he saw Jack and Ben throwing a baseball back and forth in their backyard.

Ben was not as coordinated and kept missing the ball with his glove. Patiently, Jack worked with Ben, giving him pointers on how to catch. Jack always was a good big brother to Ben. An unexpected wave of jealousy hit Micah. With all the pent-up resentment he felt, he struggled to believe those two tyrants had an ounce of kindness in them. Why did they insist on turning his world upside down?

Micah slammed the window shut. Looking down at the coin and locket, he felt anger. All he had were memories. He stuffed them in his pocket and held the Urmin Stone in his palm, trying to remember how to use it.

"All-powerful eye, where is my bike?" he said out loud in a monotone voice.

The etched eye stared back, but nothing happened.

"How is this supposed to help me find my bike?" Micah asked.

The stone remained still.

Crazy ol' coot. Where's my bike? he thought.

The instant the thought crossed his mind, the stone wiggled. An arrow appeared, pointing in a constant direction like a compass.

Walking out the front door, Micah followed the stone's direction up Albatross Avenue with Grubb at his side. They walked for several blocks, eventually turning down a side road not far from the trail that led to Hermit Cove.

Micah stopped at a ledge overlooking the Stonehelm bluffs. The arrow on the stone pointed forward. Looking down the vertical cliff, he saw the mangled remains of his new bicycle scattered among a pile of boulders.

He wondered who had stolen his bike, and the stone revealed the name: Dylan Buckley. Dylan's betrayal was especially difficult for Micah. He had been a friend to Richard and Micah since they were little. After the football incident, Dylan had distanced himself from Micah—especially once the bullying began. Micah remembered Ben saying they had a big surprise for him that morning. It all made sense now.

Looking out at the sunset, Micah wondered how everything had gone so wrong. No, he shouldn't have destroyed Jack's ball. If he had followed Richard's advice, perhaps all of this could have been avoided. But the amount of retribution he'd endured far exceeded the price of the football.

Jack and his friends had made his life miserable. With his father gone and his mom as she had been lately, Micah felt alone and helpless. He took out the coin and locket. All of his troubles began the day these showed up in his life. He resented his mother. What was she hiding, and why had she refused to believe him about Mariam's locket in the beginning?

With a sudden indifference to everything, he palmed the Urmin Stone, the locket, and the coin together, stretching back to throw them over the cliff.

The instant he closed his palm, a vision burst into his mind.

Mariam appeared before him. She peered back expressionless, bathed in red light. Micah staggered backward. The coin and stone lost contact, and the vision disappeared.

"Mariam!" he cried out.

He closed his hand around the coin and Urmin Stone again, and the vision reappeared. It was the same experience he had with the shedets and his siblings' memories. Mariam stared forward, her face gaunt and bruised. Her once-long chestnut-brown hair had been shaved to stubble.

"Micah, I'm alive," Mariam whispered.

A loud *clank* sent panic across her face as she nervously looked over her shoulder. Micah followed her gaze and saw a closed door down a shadowy corridor.

Mariam was alone in a cell surrounded by bars and rock. The smell was disgusting, a cross between vomit and rot. The only source of light emanated from a massive, deep purple glass window with a red crystal ankh embedded in the glass. The window cast stark, ominous shadows across Mariam's face. Amid the silence, distant cries and moans echoed, hinting at the chamber's expansive size concealed in darkness.

Mariam's shaking voice continued. "The Rashaar captured our ship. I don't know how long it's been—weeks, months? We were sailing up the Ivory Strait when the attack came. They knew we were coming. There were so many of them, and there was nothing we could do. They killed Captain Frost right in front of us..."

Mariam struggled to say the last words, weeping bitterly. Suddenly, everything disappeared, plunging Micah into darkness.

Moments later, Mariam reappeared composed. "They've taken us to a place called Venuba. I've had no contact with any of the others since arriving here, but Penelope and Twitch tell me they are alive. I don't want you to be angry with Mom and Dad when you discover the truth of what happened. Penelope and Twitch promised they would somehow get this message back to our families. All I can do is hope for a miracle." Mariam smiled as tears flowed. "Tell Mom and Dad I love—"

The door beyond the cell crashed open. Two shadowy figures appeared, shouting in a harsh, angry-sounding language as they rushed toward Mariam's cell.

Mariam shrieked.

There was a squeak, and whatever was recording the shedet scurried through the bars into the darkness. The vision ended abruptly.

Micah sank to his knees, overcome. He stared at the coin with disbelief. *How could Mariam still be alive? I saw her die!*

"The truth is a heavy burden to carry, my young friend," Morty Crowther said, walking up from behind. He leaned against a large boulder, looking back at Micah with weary eyes.

"My sister's alive?"

"Yes. The fate of the *Gaspee* is now certain. There's no sense keeping that from you now. When the *Gaspee* disappeared, it was a shock. To learn they fell into the hands of our old enemy was devastating. In the years since Alfred has been among our people, nothing like this has ever happened."

"Why would they take my sister?"

"There's a great deal you don't know about our people, Micah. To our enemy, the children of their lost slaves are of great value," Crowther said. He unzipped his jumpsuit to his chest, revealing a tattoo over his heart. It was a faded black image of an eye surrounded by scrollwork. The pupil of the eye had been burned out, leaving a lump of scar tissue. Crowther explained that all of the old ones bore the marking of a slave.

"The Rashaar have absolute power over every living thing in their kingdom," Crowther said with a distant look in his eye. "They rule by stone and blood. When I was born, our people had been in bondage for generations. I never knew what freedom was. None of our people did. It took a miracle to deliver us from our enemy. We were led by the hand of our maker to a new land where we met Alfred. We've been lost to our enemy ever since. But now, with the capture of the *Gaspee*, the dread of the former times has returned."

"Will I ever see Mariam again?" Micah asked quietly.

"I cannot see the answer to that, Micah. The Rashaar now have all they need to find us. Your sister and the crew of the *Gaspee*...well, the Rashaar have their ways. I've warned the council for years that our growing numbers and expansion would draw attention and that Alfred should retire. He's become too much of a liability. What happened to the *Gaspee* was inevitable. The council wouldn't hear it. The young ones know nothing of the cruelty of being slaves, especially under the stone of the Rashaar. Too many of our people have forgotten the God of our fathers in this new world. Only by putting our trust in our maker can we remain free."

Crowther rubbed his tired eyes.

"I once held the highest position among our ranks. They sent me here because I was upsetting too many of our young people. My advice, my friend, is don't grow old. No one listens anymore."

Micah was silent, ashamed he had thought so little of Crowther. He was more than just a lonely man needing someone to talk to. Since Mariam's death, Micah knew what it felt like to be alone and an outcast. Crowther's words stung.

"Well..." Micah hesitated. "I believe in the God of our fathers. I don't know anything about the Rashaar, but I loved my sister. If you say God delivered our people from the Rashaar, I believe he can deliver my sister."

"Your heart is so pure, young one. Don't ever let those who doubt take away your hope." Crowther smiled. "I have some news that might brighten your spirits," he finally said.

"What news?"

"I want you to pass along a message to your mother. Tell her to be happy again. Your father will be home soon."

"Are you sure?"

"Heard it myself. Tell her the old coot Crowther told you. She'll know."

A broad smile appeared on Micah's face. "I need to be going, then. She might be home now," he said, starting back for home.

"What about your bike?"

"Who cares?" Micah said, running.

Grubb held back, wagging his tail, expecting his usual free meal.

"Time to go home, Grubb," Crowther said, motioning him

away. Grubb reluctantly left, chasing after Micah.

Crowther looked out into the sunset, feeling pleased with himself. The moment lasted until he tried to remember where he'd parked his car.

*   *   *

When Micah arrived home, things didn't go as he hoped. He found his mother cleaning up Grubb's mess in the pantry. She lashed out at Micah for being lazy and neglecting Grubb.

This infuriated Micah, so he accused her of lying about Mariam.

"I don't want to discuss her, Micah! Not until your father returns!" Lorna shot back as she pummeled the floor with a mop.

Micah removed the coin and waved it at her. "Remember this?"

Lorna scoffed and pushed past him. Weeks before, Lorna had spent hours trying to discover anything meaningful from the coin to no avail. She'd concluded if there was anything to it, Penelope and Twitch had botched it up like they did everything else.

"There was a message from Mariam!"

Lorna plunked the mop into the bucket with a splash. "A message?"

Micah showed his mother the Urmin Stone. She became incensed, ranting on about who was irresponsible enough to give an Urmin Stone to a twelve-year-old. Learning it was a gift from Morty Crowther, she went ballistic.

Micah forcefully made his mother take the stone and coin into her hand. Lorna suddenly fell silent, her eyes widening in astonishment.

"Oh, Mariam! Mariam!" she cried. As she watched the memory, tears began. At the end, she cried out, "It's true, it's all true!" Weeping bitterly, Lorna ran to her bedroom and locked herself in.

That night, lying in bed, Micah puzzled over Mariam's message. He thought back to when he and his mother had that day-long talk—the day he'd watched all his siblings' memories. It bothered him that two years of Mariam's shedets were missing. His mother's excuse that she hadn't had time to organize Mariam's things didn't seem truthful. She never left anything unorganized. Micah was sure she was keeping them from him.

He snuck down to the basement, determined to find answers. He closed his eyes while holding the Urmin Stone and thought, *Where are Mariam's shedets?*

An arrow appeared, pointing at the three boxes he had looked through previously.

Are there others?

The arrow spun around, pointing behind him. He followed it until he stood at the corner of the basement. Above, tucked in a nook, was a box. He stretched to grab it and it came tumbling down. Two booklets with Mariam's name and dozens of news clippings scattered on the floor.

A shadow appeared as Micah knelt down to clean up the mess. His mother stood over him, her eyes red from crying.

"I'm sorry, son. You deserve to know the truth," she said, kneeling beside him. "Mariam was finishing up her fourth year when the crew of the *Gaspee* disappeared," Lorna said softly as she organized the news articles and obituaries scattered on the floor. "We call fourth-year students Archeologists. Kids only attend Boshii Campus for two years. After that, school changes. Students learn more through apprenticeships and travel further from home.

"Archaeologists learn history. Thanks to your sister Mariam and her friend Camille, the two convinced the Tridents and three other classes to make their final project a study of the Ivory Strait. It's a chain of islands where modern-day Florida is located. It's the first place our people landed after they escaped the Rashaar."

"Florida? That's really far from here," Micah said.

Lorna agreed. "The continents and sea are different in Astoria. Much of the northern hemisphere is underwater. It's about a month's journey by ship to the Ivory Strait. Some of us parents objected, but we were overruled. They headed out on their journey in January of last year. It was the last semester before the summer break.

"It's a rule among the captains that ships never sail alone. They made it to the Ivory Straight and spent two months doing their studies. But on their return home, Captain Frost reported the *Gaspee* was having difficulty. He fell behind by half a day. When the Tridents didn't show up at the rendezvous point, the other ships' captains turned back to look for them. They found the *Gaspee* run aground on one of the islands. There were signs that the crew survived, but after they searched for a week, they had to start for home. The crew of the *Gaspee* had disappeared."

Fifteen obituaries were neatly placed in front of Micah. Lorna laid Mariam's obituary next to the others.

"All of these young ones were the children of the *Gaspee*. A cover story was invented to explain their sudden deaths here in Oregon. Remember the Pacific Flu? If you read through these obituaries, it's reported these kids died from a mysterious sickness. But this isn't the truth..."

Lorna handed a final familiar clipping to Micah. The headline read *The Pacific Flu*. Lorna waved her hand over the article. The headline now read *GASPEE CREW VANISHES*. The obituaries had changed as well. Each were now articles about the missing.

"If you read through these now, you'll learn everything we knew about Mariam and the other crew up until recently. For the longest time, we held out hope they were hiding somewhere amongst the

Ivory Straight islands. Now we know better," she said grimly.

Micah was confused. "But she died. I saw Mariam fall. We went to Mariam's funeral, remember?"

His mother went to a nearby shelf and removed the familiar brown linen sack he'd last seen the night he put on the Macabre Ring. It was still crimped shut with a staple. She broke the staple and removed a pouch that contained a shedet. She handed the gray disc to Micah, motioning for him to watch it.

Micah palmed the disc and closed his hand.

"Greetings, parents! I am Director Karnak. I have been director of Boshii Campus for the past sixteen years," the cheerful man said, standing before Micah. He was dressed in a formal uniform, leaning against a neatly set desk. "From all the staff at Boshii Campus, we are excited about your child's enrollment. Years have been devoted to creating a place where your young ones will begin their journey into the world of their ancestors. Today, we are discussing preparations that you as parents must make before your students start school. I'd like you to meet someone."

A young girl walked into view and stood next to Director Karnak. She wore a khaki uniform with loose trousers, similar to the clothes Micah had received on his birthday. "Hi, my name is Jenny. I live in Astoria," the young girl said with a wide grin.

A twin girl walked in from the other side. She wore blue jeans and a T-shirt. "Hi, my name is Jenny. I live in Oregon," she said with the same wide grin. The two were identical twins.

"Jenny here, wearing our school uniform, is a second-year student at Boshii Campus," Director Karnak continued. "While away in Astoria, her twin remains in Oregon, where she continues living the life Jenny left behind. It is important that we maintain continuity between Astoria and Oregon. Thanks to the cooperation of parents like yourselves, we are able to remain anonymous among our friends in Oregon."

Jenny, dressed in the khaki uniform, took a clay brick resting on the desk and presented it to Director Karnak.

"Thank you, Jenny. This is called Atuma clay. Every enrolled child receives this prized material. Before we came to Oregon, only kings possessed this valuable substance…"

Lorna snatched away the shedet disc. "I hate these presentations," she said, stuffing the shedet back into the sack. "No matter how they try to explain it, it sounds like an infomercial."

"So the Mariam I saw fall from the tree was a clone?" Micah asked.

"We don't think of them as clones, dear. We call them *Ba Rey Hems*, meaning *servant of the soul*. They are twins that share a common mind."

"So my real sister was in Astoria while her twin lived here, home with us?"

"That's right, dear."

"So why did all the twins die?"

Lorna sighed. "Unlike pure Atuma clay, ours have a flaw. If the twin doesn't make contact with their progenitor, they eventually lose their borrowed life force."

"You mean die?"

Lorna nodded.

"So how long can they be separated?"

"Six months at the most, usually less. If they don't make contact, they age prematurely. Eventually, they succumb to the effects of old age. That's what happened to the children of the *Gaspee*. They never returned home, so their twins expired."

There it was.

As Micah processed his mother's revelation, the final piece of the puzzle dropped into place and everything became clear. He felt

203

the guilt he had carried so long lift from his shoulders. The guilt transformed into a deep sense of yearning and hope.

"I miss Mariam so much," Micah said, tears streaming down his face.

Lorna took Micah into her arms and wept. "I do, too, son."

*   *   *

Later that day, Micah finally got the chance to tell his mother Crowther's news about his father. Micah hadn't seen his mother that happy for weeks. He never mentioned what happened in the kitchen or his stolen new bike.

Chapter 18
The Boots

Monday morning.

Lorna sang as she went about the kitchen preparing breakfast. She had spent all day Saturday cleaning the house. She even got Micah to clean his room. She told stories about how she met his father when they were young—before video games and color televisions. She talked about Grandma Hazel.

This conversation prompted a question in Micah's mind: Where was his Grandma Hazel? He had attended her funeral in the second grade. She had still been young by Astorian standards. Micah was about to pose this question when the front door swung open.

"Lovely morning," Tricia said, bounding into the kitchen. She hugged Micah and sat with their mother. Soon, they were lost in planning their day.

While the three were eating breakfast, an unfamiliar chime came from the large box mounted to the wall. For the past three weeks, it had sat quietly. Before the Macabre Ring, it had been a cuckoo clock. Spindles spun to life, followed by a series of green blinking lights.

"The gate. It's reopening," Tricia said.

A few minutes later, the door from the garage opened, and Geoffrey and a man Micah barely recognized walked in. There were hints that the man was his father—but this man was in his prime, tall and confident. Gone was the cane.

Tricia cried as she rushed to hug Geoffrey. The two embraced, and Geoffrey went to his knees, thankful Tricia hadn't had the baby yet. Lorna and Kimble embraced, inviting Micah to join.

Micah held back, unsure of the man who seemed so different.

"Son, what's the matter?" Kimble said, looking confused.

Geoffrey stood and looked Micah over, his eyes locked on the Macabre Ring. "Charlie Brown, welcome to the club!" he said, lifting Micah in a bear hug.

"When did that happen?" Kimble asked.

"Next time we get a surprise gift for Micah, dear, I'll be the one who hides it," Lorna said quietly.

"I missed it," Kimble said, disappointed, hugging Micah.

A chime came from the strange clock. A pleasant woman's voice said, "Stand by for an announcement to parents of children entering the foundation program." This repeated three times. Finally, a last chime came, and the announcement: "The commencement ceremony will be held Saturday, September 22, starting at 7:00 a.m. Astoria Gate Time. Parents, to prepare for the event, we ask that you take the steps detailed in the enrollment materials provided. If you have further questions, please contact your local charters. Thank you."

"Micah, you need to be getting off to school," Lorna said.

"Mom, do I have to go today? I'm going to miss the bus anyway."

Lorna looked down at her watch. "You won't if you hurry."

"We'll catch up later, sport," Kimble said.

Micah went to his bedroom to get his backpack, sure he would miss the bus. He removed the Urmin Stone from his pocket. After it helped him find his bike, he decided it was worth keeping close by.

How am I going to make it to the bus now? he thought.

The stone revealed the words: *Birthday boots.*

The black boots he'd got from Tricia on his birthday were buried in his closet. He had forgotten all about them. He never bothered to try them on and was curious about what to expect. It didn't take him long to think of an excuse: *Oops, I guess that's what happens when I put my shoes on in a hurry!*

Micah said his goodbyes to his father and Geoffrey. With his father home, everything seemed right again. Something told him it was going to be a better day.

He stepped onto the front porch and saw yellow flashing lights up the street. Grubb bolted out of the bushes, greeting Micah.

"How did you get out of the backyard? Get in the house," Micah said, opening the door.

Grubb refused.

Leaning into the house, Micah called his mother. "Mom, Grubb's out, and I don't have time to get him."

"It's okay, dear, we'll take care of it," she yelled back.

Closing the door, he looked back at the now red flashing lights of the bus. He knew it was a waste of time, but he started to run anyway.

Except he wasn't just running. He was *really* running!

Houses flew past like he was in a car. Micah shot past Grubb as he ran up the street. He laughed, looking down at his feet as they pounded the pavement in a blur. His sprint was so unexpected that he overshot the bus and had to turn around.

He made it just as the last kid climbed aboard. His feet tingled in the seemingly innocent-looking boots, but he wasn't even breathing hard.

Miss Coburn looked over Micah, her mouth agape. Micah looked for Grubb, but he was nowhere to be seen. Shrugging, he climbed aboard and sat behind Jo, where he tucked his pack under the seat.

Jo turned around as the bus lurched forward and whispered, "They're up to something."

Jack and Ben were talking feverishly at the back of the bus as they looked out the window. Ben shot a glimpse at Micah. When their eyes met, Micah got a clear impression of what the brothers were up to.

"They're after Grubb!" Micah shouted.

Shock crossed Ben's face. "Ben! I told you to keep your fat mouth shut!" Jack said.

"I didn't say anything, I swear."

Micah searched out the window as they passed a truck with the words *Animal Control*. Margot Farnsworth stood next to a uniformed man holding a net.

"I've got to get off," Micah yelled, running up the aisle.

"Micah Fennly, when this bus moves, you will remain in your seat!" Miss Coburn said angrily. Usually, anyone would have withered at her acid rebuke, but Jack and Ben's laughter spurred him on.

"Stop the bus now!"

In the tense silence, the bus gears wound up as it slowed and finally stopped. Red-faced Miss Coburn slammed the door open, and Micah jumped off.

*   *   *

The uniformed man was as wide as he was tall. His stubby legs bound like springs as he stepped in Grubb's path, waving his steel-poled net.

Grubb rose on one foot, sniffing curiously at the man who barred his way.

"What are you waiting for?" Margot said impatiently.

"Shhh. You'll scare 'im off. He's got tags. C'mere, boy. C'mere."

Grubb retreated, his tail swaying cautiously.

"Oh, it's just a stupid dog! Throw the net already. I'm late for work!"

"Come here, little fella," the dog catcher said. He reached into his pocket and produced a handful of dog food. He threw pieces to Grubb, dropping the rest at his feet. "This'll get 'im," he said.

Grubb sniffed at the brown morsels and chomped them up.

"That's it, just a little closer…gotcha!"

Micah plowed into the dog catcher, causing Margot to holler with surprise. Sprawled over the man, Micah saw the man's name was Smith, according to the plastic name tag pressed against his nose.

Smith's face was as red as an apple, baring teeth that had never seen a toothbrush. Smith didn't speak. He flailed and snorted like a barking seal, trying to regain his feet.

Micah rolled off, chased down Grubb, and scooped him up.

"Micah Fennly! You…redneck!" Margot shouted, stomping her foot.

Jogging home, Micah dropped Grubb into the backyard. "No more bus stops for you," he said, double-checking the back gate. Contemplating his situation, he thought about asking his mother for a ride to school. She would be furious.

Wait, I forgot my pack! I left it on the bus! What am I going to do?

The Urmin Stone wiggled in his pocket. On the stone, it read *The back trail.*

Dismissing the advice, Micah watched Grubb hunker down among a bed of petunias. He considered riding his bicycle to school, discarding the idea that it would take too long. Could he run to school with his new boots? Even if it were possible, he wouldn't go unnoticed, and his mother would surely find out. Besides, he needed his pack off the bus.

Of course! The next bus stop!

"The back trail!" Micah said triumphantly. He hurried back down Albatross Avenue. He saw Smith and Margot arguing furiously. Smith had regained his legs and was using the net to keep Margot back.

If only he could haul her off, Micah mused, heading through the grove of trees down a gentle slope.

The foot trail wound through the forest. It took fifteen minutes to get to Richard's house by bike. He figured he had about five minutes. He hoped the new boots were up to the task and that Miss Coburn would let him back on the bus.

At first, it was tricky. He couldn't maintain control and nearly collided with the trees and boulders. But his boots gripped the ground and obeyed his every command.

Superglue boots, he thought.

Micah hit the bottom of the hill and poured on the speed. It took skill to maintain it. He'd run off the path if he didn't focus on a curve or think ahead. Something about the experience reminded him of a video game, and when he did it right, he was taking turns at fantastic speed.

Around a blind bend, his eyes bulged when he saw Tanner Creek. He had forgotten about it and had no time to stop. He jumped with all his strength, flying over the boulder-strewn, burbling stream.

"I jumped the river!" Micah cheered.

He looked back over the distance. He estimated he must have jumped over thirty feet. He looked down at the boots with amazement and noticed something odd. He was standing in wet sand, but there were no footprints. He stomped his foot, and it left no impression.

Strange, he thought. He pressed his hand into the sand and left a perfect print. But the boot left no impression.

No time to be screwing around, he thought and started running again.

He reached Hollow Meadow, now very close to Birch Way. He was tired. His legs ached, and he had a cramp in his side. Micah had sprinted two miles over treacherous terrain in minutes.

Five deer grazing off the trail took his mind off the discomfort. They hadn't noticed him yet. This struck Micah odd because deer always heard him coming, no matter how quiet he tried to be.

"Coming through!" he shouted.

The deer bolted, and Micah kept up. He got so close that he grabbed for one of the deer's flicking tails, causing the deer to scatter into the woods.

Emerging onto Birch Way, he hunched over to catch his breath. A ways off, he saw the bus stop with the kids waiting. Down the opposite way, he heard the bus coming. He had beaten it with time to spare.

"Why aren't you on the bus?" Richard yelled.

"I missed it," Micah said, breathing hard.

Angela rolled her eyes.

"You ran here?" Richard said, shaking his head.

The bus pulled up, and the door crashed open. "Micah! How'd you get here?" Miss Coburn shouted, both irritated and surprised. Micah shrugged. "Sit down and hold your tongue!" She eyed Micah curiously as the other kids climbed aboard. Slamming the door shut, she ground the bus into gear and turned back for Stonehelm.

Chapter 19
Making Amends

"Not again, Micah. What's he in for this time?" Penny asked.

"Backtalking the bus driver," Mrs. Ireland said, using her sympathetic voice. She always used that voice when she brought him into the office.

213

"Oh, dear," Penny said, frowning at Micah.

"Where should I put him?"

"Well, you've already got two others waiting in Principal Stokes' office. I guess Superintendent Arnold will need to take him."

Mrs. Ireland did a poor job of hiding her delight. The superintendent's punishments were harsher.

"It'll serve you right, young man," Mrs. Ireland said with a pouty face. "Maybe next time you'll think before you let that tongue of yours lead you into trouble."

Micah sighed when he detected a skip in Mrs. Ireland as she stepped out of the office.

Penny shook her head and whispered, "She loves her job a little too much. Superintendent Arnold is off on an errand. You know the way. He'll be back shortly."

Micah sat in the usual high-back chair facing the desk, admiring the deep purple sky out the high window. He had grown more comfortable sitting in the superintendent's office.

He heard voices. Nearby in the corner of the office, two workers were hunched over, methodically inspecting the fist-sized amber stones mounted along the wall. They stopped to inspect one of the fractured stones, which had gold veins that appeared to be growing out of the crystal. Trimming the gold away with wire cutters, the worker inspected the crystal through a monocle.

"Stone position 2 is good for three more months," he declared.

The other worker made a note, and they went on to the next one.

"Seven months."

They passed over several stones with no apparent defects, finally arriving at the one Micah was most curious about. This one had completely lost all traces of the Deity Stone and looked like a lump of gold.

"Stone 5 needs to be replaced," said the man with the monocle.

"This was my office years ago," a quiet Southern voice said.

Micah spun around. Standing over him was Alfred, beaming down at him.

"Alfred!" Micah said.

Alfred plopped down in the chair next to Micah.

"I've been away for a spell. I apologize for not catching up sooner. Things didn't go as expected. I thought we'd better check in on the gate this morning. I was surprised when you walked in here."

Micah didn't say anything. He was mesmerized by the calm white light that swirled around Alfred's face. This was his fourth visit to the office since school started. Something about Alfred's gentle demeanor calmed him.

With all the secrets he had pent up and everything that had happened at school, Micah thought he'd burst.

Alfred smiled and said, "I've seen that look from plenty of young faces. What's on your mind?"

"Oh, Mr. Quentin, it's been rough."

"Call me Alfred, please."

"Alfred...there's these bullies, you see. I got in a fight with my next-door neighbors, the Farnsworths, and their friends. Since then, everything's been terrible."

"Ah, bullies. Bullying goes with teaching like peanut butter and jelly."

"Well, if I hadn't kicked Jack's football over the fence, none of this would have ever happened."

"It doesn't matter who started what. Bullying is bullying, by my reckoning. I've seen this too many times, and I think folks should find a better way to spend their time. This reminds me. I saw Wren in the hall, and he looked pretty beat up. Is he tangled up in all this?"

"Well, um, yes. Wren's one of my best friends. There's also Richard and Jo. They had nothing to do with what happened…well, Jo did. Since they're my friends, they got picked on too," Micah said, noticing the white light around Alfred's face tinging red.

"I get the picture. How long have you had the ring?"

Micah hesitated. "I put it on the night of the open house."

"You weren't supposed to put it on until you were instructed. Does it hurt?"

"Not anymore."

Alfred looked down at Micah's feet. "Not supposed to be wearing spelunking boots yet, either."

"Well, I was in a hurry, you see…"

"Uh-huh. You thought you could outrun this Farnsworth gang, did ya? Don't get any bright ideas. We can't have you kids running around here in spelunking boots. It would draw too much attention."

This thought hadn't occurred to Micah. "I was late for the bus. I didn't even know there was anything special about the boots until I ran to the bus stop."

Alfred looked concerned. "Did anybody see you running in those boots?"

"Well, uh…" Micah stammered, "I think my bus driver might have seen me."

"Miss Coburn?" Relief swept over Alfred. "Well, she's seen stranger things in her life. I suppose no harm's done. Just take them off when you get home. What gave you the mind to put them on in the first place?"

Micah removed the Urmin Stone from his pocket and showed it to Alfred.

Alfred looked at the stone and frowned. "My, my. You're looking for all kinds of trouble. Who gave you that?"

"This old man I know. He knows all about you."

"This wouldn't be Morty Crowther, by chance?"

Micah nodded. "You know him?"

"Know him? We go way back. Back to the beginning of all this," Alfred said, waving his hands around the room. "I am surprised about one thing, though."

"About what?"

"That you're not still standing at his doorstep. He's a bit of a talker."

Micah agreed.

"So what did he say?"

"He said the Rashaar were after you."

Alfred laughed so loudly that the two workers looked up from their inspection.

"What's so funny?" Micah asked.

"And he worries *I'm* a security risk? Old Morty has quite the tongue, doesn't he? If he had his way, he'd taken care of me long ago."

"You mean killed?"

Alfred snorted. "You've seen too many gangster movies. No, he wanted me to teach in a classroom here in Oregon, someplace like this, where it's safe and boring. I told him to forget it. Astoria's my home, and I'd have it no other way. Besides, I'm too young to retire."

Micah's brow rose. Alfred was not young. He was the oldest man Micah had ever seen. "So when do we get to go to Astoria?"

"The announcement went out today for the parents to start preparations. Boshii Campus opens in a week. There's also a little matter of the commencement on Saturday. I don't suppose you've heard about any of this?"

"I heard something this morning, but don't know anything about the commencement."

"Not surprising. It's all very hush-hush. You little ones can't open your mouths about something you don't know about—"

Superintendent Arnold walked into the room. "Who are you talking to?" he asked Micah, looking around the office.

Micah glanced at Alfred. Alfred put his finger to his lips. "Um…myself?" Micah said.

Humphrey looked tired this morning. "Micah, we can't keep this up. If you don't stop having problems, I will have to call your parents." He sat in his chair, ignoring Alfred and the two men working at the wall.

"When I was a young boy, they expelled children," Humphrey said as he filed away several loose papers scattered on his desk. When finished, he stood up and looked out the window with his back to Micah, continuing his lecture.

Micah glanced over to Alfred. "He can't see me," Alfred whispered. He listened to Humphrey's ramblings for a few moments. "He certainly likes to talk, doesn't he? Just like his father, Merrill."

Alfred got up from his chair and went to the window. He stood next to Humphrey, sizing him up.

"Yup, looks like his father, too, the way I remember him before he died. Speaking of bullies, Humphrey here was a notorious bully when he was a young man. Your father had a few run-ins with him when he was your age. Something to do with your mother, I seem to recall."

"My father?" Micah asked.

Both Humphrey and Alfred looked at Micah.

"What did you say?" Humphrey asked.

Micah slunk back into the chair. Humphrey turned back

around, continuing his lecture. Alfred remained transfixed on something behind Micah.

"What?" Micah mouthed.

"Who's that fetching young lady?" Alfred asked, shuffling to the doorway.

Micah and the two men working on the wall stopped and looked out the office door. Standing outside was Sheila, Richard's mother. She was holding two brown bag lunches and talking to Penny.

"That's Sheila, my friend Richard's mom," Micah whispered.

"Is she hitched?"

"You're *way* too old for her," Micah said, forgetting Humphrey was still talking.

Humphrey spun around and gave Micah a stern look.

Alfred patted Micah's head. "Good luck," he said, shuffling out of the office.

Humphrey sat down in his chair and slipped on his glasses. "Let's talk about the consequences…"

*   *   *

Miss Sorenson taught geography during class that morning, which Micah usually enjoyed. Between the return of his father, Alfred, and the thrill of the sprint to Richard's bus stop, he found it difficult to focus on schoolwork.

When the recess bell rang, Richard waited at the door with his backpack in hand. Micah noticed something different about him. Usually, Richard's countenance shone with yellow swirling light. He was always worried about something. But this morning, he was calm, and his face beamed a steady white glow.

Motioning to Richard's backpack, Micah asked, "You going

home? You sick?"

"No, I just had an idea how to solve our problem on the playground," Richard said, patting his backpack.

"Let me guess. It's full of rocks, and you plan on beating Jack and Kamran with it?" Wren said.

"You'll see."

The three boys descended the stairs to the main floor without noticing Mrs. Ireland following behind. Arriving on the first floor, they walked into the bustling crowd of children heading out to recess. Just as the three were about to exit the building, Mrs. Ireland blew her ear-piercing whistle, causing everyone to cringe and cover their ears.

"Stop right there! I thought you might try something like this. Let me see what's in your backpack, Mr. Sommers. You know the rules. No backpacks on the playground."

"That's not a rule," Micah said.

"It is when I think there'll be trouble," she said, motioning for Richard to hand it over.

"Jeez, what do you think he's got in there, a gun?" Wren said. He thought for a moment and turned to Richard. "Wait, you don't have a gun in there, do you?"

Mrs. Ireland unzipped Richard's pack and removed a brown paper sack lunch and a brand-new football, still in its packaging.

"I wanted it to be a surprise. I didn't mean to cause trouble."

Richard broke Mrs. Ireland, as she had nothing to say for the first time ever. Several teachers hurried down the hall to investigate the whistle.

Bassam swung the door open from the playground and saw the boys with Mrs. Ireland and the football. "Well, Loretta, I see you found another good excuse to use your whistle. Obviously, those boys are up to no good."

Mrs. Ireland shoved the football back into Richard's pack, glaring at the janitor as she stalked off.

Bassam walked with the boys to the playground. "I've been watching you boys dealing with your problem. It takes a great deal of courage to face a bully."

"I can't believe you bought a football for that loser," Wren said, combing his hair.

"And what do you think, Mr. Fennly?" Bassam asked.

Micah shrugged. He felt terrible because Richard had done nothing to bring on the bullying and could have turned his back on his friend. But Richard was loyal, and being a peacemaker was in his nature.

"I guess...I'll help pay for the ball. I got us into this mess in the first place."

"Oh, great, now you're making me feel like I have to help pay for the ball," Wren moaned.

Bassam was pleased. "It makes me happy to see you working this out. Restitution is a good start, and it shows your hearts are in the right place. What happens from here on," he said, gesturing to Jack's gang waiting for them across the playground, "may be out of your hands. I'm proud of you boys."

Squeezing Richard's shoulder, Bassam wished the three good luck and returned to sweeping.

Micah saw Jo playing with some girl classmates and motioned her over. "This ends today," he said.

They made their way to the four-square game area where all their troubles had begun. Jack and his gang ran up, eager for the daily chase to begin. This standoff on the playground quickly attracted attention, bringing in a sizable crowd.

"Holy cow," Wren moaned. "The entire school is going to watch us get pounded!"

Richard and Wren grew nervous at all the attention. Micah looked over his shoulder for Bassam and found he had climbed the stairs to get a better look. Another figure emerged from the school. It was Alfred. He leaned against the school wall and adjusted his fedora.

"Look, guys. The four idiots," Jack said.

Kamran and the others snickered.

"Four idiots," Ben repeated with a giggle.

Between Jack's black eye and flattop haircut, he looked ready for a fight. He kept punching his fist like he couldn't wait for the day's pounding to begin.

"Leave my brother alone!" It was Angela. Her entire third-grade class followed her, including Max, Micah's nephew.

Though the children were small, their numbers brought a measure of intimidation. Angela forced her way between Micah and Jack, kicking furiously at Jack's shins with her rubber-tipped shoes.

"Angela, stay out of this!" Richard shouted.

Jack laughed. With his index finger, he pushed Angela far enough away that her kicks missed. "I guess I was wrong, guys. Here are the *five* idiots."

"Five idiots," Ben cackled.

Angela was worked up. When Jack looked back at his friends, she chomped down on his finger.

"*Yeow!*" Jack cried, yanking his hand away.

Angela had a good bite and was jerked along like a trout caught on a five-fingered fishing lure. Rabid, she bared her buck teeth to find another place to bite.

Seeing Angela's courage emboldened her classmates. Max jumped on Kamran's back while two other third graders grabbed his legs. The others swarmed in, causing a great deal of confusion.

"I know where your weak spot is!" Angela shouted, kicking at

Jack until Jo stepped in and dragged her off.

Ben stuck out his tongue. Angela broke free and walloped him in the stomach. Ben collapsed like an empty sack, causing the crowd to explode with laughter.

Mrs. Ireland blew her whistle as she waded into the crowd, causing a mayhem of children to flee in every direction. She grabbed Angela and Ben by the neck.

"Angela, how many times do I have to tell you not to punch boys!" Mrs. Ireland scolded as she struggled to keep Ben on his feet. "Everyone, go about your business! If I see any of you standing around here when I get back, I'll send every last one of you to the principal's office!"

As Mrs. Ireland escorted Angela and Ben away, Richard reached into his backpack. "Jack," he said timidly.

Jack's stern expression softened when Richard produced the football from his backpack and handed it to him.

"It's not as good as your old one, but it's the best we could find," Richard said.

"I'm sorry I ruined your football, and for everything else," Micah added.

The smile that spread across Jack's face was encouraging. Kamran and Tony had been shaking off third graders when they saw what was happening.

Kamran shouted, "Don't take it, Jack!"

Jack looked the ball over and back to Micah and Richard. His smile disappeared.

Micah and Richard knew they were in trouble when the football dropped to the ground. With a prodding finger to Micah's chest, Jack charged, "Do you think this changes anything, Fennly? You made my mom cry when she saw this," he said, rubbing his black eye. "You're just lucky she told my dad I got hurt from a baseball.

223

You would have really known what trouble was if he knew I got it from you."

Micah was confused. Did Jack really not understand that he had been the aggressor and that Micah was only defending his friends? "I…I think you're getting it wrong."

Kamran snuck behind the three and got down on his hands and knees.

"Here's what I think of your apology *and* your football!" Jack roared. He shoved the boys, sending them tumbling over Kamran. Micah yowled with pain as his elbow cracked on the asphalt.

Everything was hazy after that.

Jack seized Micah by the foot. The others grabbed Richard and Wren by their shirt collars. The three hollered as they were dragged to a nearby dumpster and tossed in.

"My hair, my hair!" Wren cried when he landed headfirst in a pile of discarded mashed potatoes. Micah and Richard were fortunate to have their falls cushioned by hundreds of art projects constructed of cotton balls.

Lastly, there was a thump, and the popped football landed nearby.

The boys sat silent as they considered their situation. Finally, Wren exclaimed, "I'm not paying for that football now!"

Chapter 20
Justice Served

Every day for lunch, the gymnasium was converted into the school's cafeteria. Today's hot topic was what had happened at recess that morning. The excitement on the playground had produced an unlikely group of heroes: Angela and

Max's third-grade class. Their bravery in taking on the school's biggest bullies overshadowed everything.

Richard and Wren sat across from Micah and Jo as they ate their lunches alone, ignoring the occasional finger-pointing from the other tables.

"It's embarrassing that the third grade tried to protect us. Now we really look like a bunch of wimps," Wren said, running his comb through his hair for the tenth time. His shoulders were covered with flecks of potato like he had a bad case of dandruff. "I don't think we'll ever live that down."

"You should thank Angela," Jo said. "Thanks to her, hardly anyone even noticed what happened to you. She was just trying to help."

Micah picked at his food. "Yeah, being thrown in a dumpster is loads of fun. Last week, they destroyed my new bike. This morning, they tried to get Grubb sent to the dog pound."

Richard had been thinking quietly the whole time. He finally said, "I thought that football would work. Can you believe I got in trouble over that backpack?"

"You got in trouble?" Micah asked.

"Yeah, Angela told Mrs. Ireland what happened with Jack. So Mrs. Ireland went to Principal Stokes and said everything that happened this morning started because I took a backpack on the playground."

"Figures," Micah said, shaking his head.

"Well, your sister's my new hero. I don't think Ben will ever live down what she did to him," Jo said.

The four laughed as they searched the cafeteria for Ben. He was nowhere to be found.

"All I know is those harebrains need to be stopped," Micah said.

"What about my hair?" Wren asked, whipping out his comb again.

"Wren? Enough with combing your hair," Jo said.

"It's important to me, okay?" Wren swiped the comb through his hair and put it away like a gunfighter. "Look, I say we all go out and hang around the janitor for a few days. They always leave us alone when we're around him."

"Shut up, Wren," Micah said, ruffling Wren's hair.

"Man, I had it just the way I liked it!"

"Wren, you take out that comb one more time and you'll never see it again. I hate it!" Jo said.

Defiantly, Wren took out his comb and slowly dragged it through his hair with a daring sneer. Jo swiped it away. "Hey!" he shouted, catching Mrs. Ireland's attention. She walked by with her finger pressed to her lips. "Give it back or I'll...I'll..."

"Or you'll what? I'm putting this *exactly* where it belongs."

Jo stood up, taking her tray. She weaved a leisurely course through the cafeteria. Wren followed like a fool until they reached the exit, where Jo threw the comb into the garbage, dumping her tray on top.

"Aww, man," Wren groaned. He tried to goalie the garbage from Micah and Richard. He failed. "I hope you all feel better."

"We do," the three chorused.

Wren considered leaving his comb, but after catching sight of his messed-up hair, he took a deep breath and reached into the trash. "Now I've gotta clean it," he moaned.

They hadn't noticed Richard standing at the cafeteria exit looking in the foyer to the third floor. "Micah, I hear that sound like I heard at the back-to-school night again. It's coming from the third floor."

"Who's responsible for this mess?" Mrs. Ireland said, charging up behind Richard. She pointed to the trash littered around the garbage cans.

The four shrugged.

"Every year, you kids return to school and treat it like your mother works here. Well, she doesn't! Micah, why are you still here? You're in detention."

Micah had forgotten all about that. His punishment from the bus that morning was to go to the office right after lunch.

"Wren, what did you do to your hair? For heaven's sake, comb it. And you two," she said, grabbing Jo and Richard by the necks, "come with me."

*   *   *

Micah and Wren walked through the foyer, heading for the bathroom. The foyer was empty.

"I heard a rumor that Mrs. Ireland's quitting," Wren said.

"Really?"

"No. But wouldn't it be great if she did?"

The boys laughed as they pushed open the bathroom door and went to the sinks. Micah washed his hands as Wren cleaned his comb. With the benefit of a mirror, Wren took extra time to get his hair just right.

"So, what are you supposed to do in detention?" Wren asked.

"I'm not sure. I overheard Superintendent Arnold telling Miss Morris something about mailing newsletters."

The bathroom door creaked open, and Ben poked his head in. He grinned and called over his shoulder, "They're in here."

Hurried footsteps came, and Jack, Kamran, and Tony slipped in. Ben was the last to enter, staying safely in the back.

"Hello, guys," Jack said. "Bring us any more *gifts*?"

"Don't you ever get sick of picking on us?" Wren asked, stepping behind Micah.

"How could we? You make it so much fun," Jack sniffed. His mischievous, lazy eyes swept pompously over the boys.

"Yeah, and don't think the third grade will come to your rescue this time," Kamran added.

Ben laughed.

"Why don't you shut up, Ben, or I'll send Angela after you," Wren said.

Ben frowned when the boys all laughed at him. Jack wasn't amused, as he had been a victim of Angela's vicious bite. He pounded his fist against the wall to stop the laughter.

Micah could feel his adrenaline rising. He saw something unexpected in Jack's face—patchy yellow light mingled with the intense angry red. Something was making Jack uneasy.

Looking about, Micah noticed a single bee circling above. He wondered about the bee and got an odd impression: *Who are these intruders, and are they dangerous?*

Micah knew little about bees, but he did understand fear and danger. Not sure what he was doing, he tried to mentally project to the bee that the tall intruder in the middle of the room was hunting for bees. He realized his idea was working when two more bees emerged from the ceiling grate.

Seeing more bees, the red light on Jack's face shifted to full-on yellow.

"What's the matter?" Tony asked, seeing his friend had become hesitant.

"There's bees in here," Jack said, stepping back. "I hate bees."

Micah glanced at Wren and smiled. Mentally, he communicated to the bees that all the intruders in the bathroom were a threat and were there to kill the queen.

The sound of a hundred bees buzzed to life in the ceiling.

"Run!" Micah yelled, grabbing Wren's arm.

Micah and Wren rushed the boys, who now were flaying their arms at the swarm of bees pouring out of the grate. The two promptly exited the bathroom and pulled the door shut behind them. When the other boys realized Micah and Wren were holding the door shut, they began to holler and shout. Jack was screaming like he was being murdered.

"Now what do we do?" Wren said as they fought to keep the door closed. They had about five seconds to decide before the boys overpowered them.

"Up here!" a voice called.

They looked up. Alfred was standing atop the third floor, waving them up.

"Who's that?" Wren cried.

Micah released the door, leaving Wren alone. Without Micah's help, the door ripped out of Wren's grip, and Jack's gang fell back in a heap, desperately swatting to protect themselves from the angry swarm.

When Wren looked back, Micah was already at the top of the stairs, thanks to his spelunking boots. "How the heck did you get up there so fast!" Wren cried, chasing after him.

"Hurry and get up here!" Micah hollered.

Wren raced up the stairs, jumping over Humphrey Arnold's sign barring students from the third floor. When he reached the top, they looked down to see Jack and his friends running in circles below, fighting off the bees.

"Ha! That's what you get!" Wren yelled.

The boys looked up, and Jack yelled, "Get 'em!"

Micah grabbed Wren, and the pair raced down the hall.

"Slow down, you're running too fast!" Wren shouted.

They reached the corner and peered down the dark corridor. Micah discerned Alfred's glowing footprints leading into the dark.

"Where did he go? What's down there?" Wren asked, looking nervously back at the way they came. Footsteps pounded up the stairway.

"I don't know, I've never been up here before. C'mon," Micah said, following the prints. They started down the dim hall, slowing as the darkness enveloped them.

"I can't see a thing," Wren whispered.

"This way," Micah said, following the glowing footprints until they abruptly ended.

"Wait, something's blocking the way. There's a gate here!"

Micah and Wren frantically shook and pulled at the angled bars of the trellis gate. It wouldn't budge. When they heard approaching footfalls, they pressed up against the fence.

"What do we do?" Wren whispered.

"If they come down here, we run for it."

Four heads poked around the corner.

"Are you sure they went this way? They might have gone into one of the classrooms," Jack whispered.

"I checked the doors. They're all locked," Ben said.

Kamran ran his hand up the wall. "Where's the light switch?"

"If they're down here, we'll find them," Jack said, leading them into the darkness.

Wren strummed his comb in his pocket and whispered, "It's been good knowing you, buddy."

From the other side of the fence came a sudden breeze and the smell of fresh air.

"What do we do? I'm too young to die," Wren whispered.

There was a buzz of electricity, and the fluorescent lights shimmered briefly.

"There they are!" Jack shouted and led the charge down the hall.

The lights suddenly brightened to a white-hot intensity as a buzz of electricity surged. One of the bulbs burst, raining down a shower of sparks on Jack's gang.

A terrible roar came from behind the gate.

The boys slid to a halt. "Jack, what was that?" Ben asked in a shaky voice.

Pandemonium ensued as the gate flew apart in a wind storm, sending dust and newspapers back up the hall. Standing in the center of the chaos, backed by a shimmering wall looking into Astoria, was Alfred, saddled to a creature the size of a horse. It stood erect on its two muscular legs, balanced by its long, swaying tail.

Seeing the boys, the creature leaned forward and let out a terrifying hiss. Everyone, including Micah and Wren, screamed.

The boys all scrambled to retreat. Micah tripped over Wren, attempting to run. They cowered when Alfred shouted, *"Yah!"* and leaped over them.

Jack and the others were screaming as they raced up the corridor.

"Stop!" Alfred commanded, thrusting his hand at the boys. Thunder cracked as the Astorian corridor burst into brilliant light. Everyone froze like statues.

Alfred dismounted the creature and bent over Micah, who was crouching nearby.

"It's me, Micah," Alfred said in his disarmingly calm voice.

Micah stood and saw Alfred, the creature, and himself glowing like fire. With the protection of his Macabre Ring, he was somehow immune to the effects of Alfred's command. Wren was in a crouched stance, frozen like the other boys.

The creature's enormous feet thumped as it stepped close to

Micah, its legs thick as tree stumps. It sniffed curiously. Its long, swaying tail brushed the dusty floor. It made a throaty growl as its snout came within inches of Micah's face.

Micah closed his eyes, sure he was about to become a snack for the terrifying beast.

"Bert," Alfred said. "Be nice, Micah's our friend."

One of Micah's eyes popped open. "His name is Bert?"

"*Her* name is Bert," Alfred corrected.

Bert let out a huff, and a putrid stench filled Micah's nostrils.

"I think Bert needs some mouthwash," Micah said, fanning his nose.

Alfred laughed. "Well, Mr. Fennly. After I saw what happened on the playground this morning, it got me thinking. You know, every problem has a solution. Sometimes, it can be subtle. But I think in your situation, we need to nip this whole thing in the bud before it gets any worse. What do you say?"

Micah looked at Bert, then back at Alfred. "What did you have in mind?"

Alfred mounted Bert's saddle and pulled on the reins. Bert lifted her head high, making a throaty snort. With the brush of his knee, Alfred turned the great horned beast back down the corridor and reached for Micah.

Micah grinned. As frail as Alfred appeared, Micah was surprised when Alfred yanked him up and sat him down on the saddle.

"Hold tight!"

Bert charged past Jack and the others with a flick of the reins. It was a comical sight. The four boys had expressions of terror, frozen in a dead run. Each boy's face and arms were pocked with red welts from bee stings. Alfred stopped at the bend and turned back to head off the retreating boys. He raised his arm and brought it down in a sweeping motion.

Jack, Kamran, Tony, and Ben suddenly sprang back to life. Racing toward the business end of Bert, they skidded to a halt and crashed over each other. Ben screamed.

Bert leaned forward and hissed at the boys. Jack panicked, struggling to his feet. When he tried to run, Alfred kicked Bert's sides, tugging the reins. Bert lunged forward and hooked Jack by his belt with her teeth, lifting him into the air.

The scream that came from Jack was almost as terrifying as Bert's hiss.

Micah peeked around the beast's thick neck and saw Jack's wide eyes peering back at him.

"Boys, I want your attention for a moment," Alfred said nonchalantly, flicking the reigns.

Bert dropped Jack back down to the floor. The boys cowered up against the wall and began to cry.

"Now, now. There's no need for tears. I just thought we might have us a little chat. You see, I know you all are big-shots around these parts. But nobody gave you permission to treat others as unkindly as you have Micah and his friends.

"Here's the way I see it. Sometimes, you young'uns get confused about how to spend all that pent-up energy. There's a big ol' world out there and plenty of unkind folks without you four adding your brand of misery. My advice to you young pups is this: Don't underestimate the underdog, because one day, there will be a reckoning."

Alfred yanked the reins, and Bert snapped at the boys. Hands and feet pulled back as Bert strained to sniff at the four.

"I think you get the point. Any questions?"

Sobs came from the boys. Finally, Jack whimpered, "I'm sorry."

"What was that?" Alfred said, leaning forward.

"We're sorry," the boys repeated together.

"Well, you young'uns are learning already. Micah, do you have anything you'd like to add?"

Micah shook his head.

"Fine, then. Hopefully, this is all settled. Well, boys, we've managed to have ourselves a little adventure here. I want you to think about what I said and go have yourselves a pleasant afternoon."

The boys remained hunched over like their spines were made of jelly. They winced when Alfred pulled the reins and Bert gave a final hiss. Bert ambled back down the hall where Wren kept a healthy distance with his back against the wall.

"Mr. Kingsley," Alfred said, tipping his hat.

Micah slipped off Bert and stood next to Wren. Alfred nudged the reins and proceeded down the hall with heavy thumps that abruptly ended when he entered the portal. The shimmering wall disappeared, plunging the corridor back into darkness.

"Was this a dream?" Wren moaned.

Beyond the slatted fence at the end of the hall, the double doors crashed open, bathing the corridor with sunlight from the stairwell. Bassam rushed in with his broom. "Micah? Wren?"

The two boys stared back at Bassam, stunned.

Bassam surveyed the mess, shaking his head. "I didn't think this was a good idea. That's Alfred—act first, think later. He's as wild as the day I first met him. You two will learn his way soon enough. Off with you both, quickly. I've got a bit of tidying up to do."

Chapter 21
The Omen

The official explanation for what happened at school was less than sensational: A power surge overloaded a circuit breaker. Hardly newsworthy. The ridiculous story that Jack, Kamran, Tony, and Ben insisted happened was dismissed by Humphrey. When he investigated the third floor, it was just as he remembered at the back-to-school night. The four boys were punished for causing mischief and breaking the third-floor rule.

This event was not insignificant for them, however. For the rest of their lives, they would remember what happened on the third floor of Quentin Elementary School. They also wouldn't forget that Micah and Wren had been there too, despite Humphrey's findings. Micah and Wren had a witness placing them in their classroom during the entire incident. No one would dare call Bassam Amun a liar.

The next few days at school were heaven for Micah and his friends. Not only had Jack and his friends left them alone, but they ran when they saw them coming.

Everything was right again…almost.

Since the first day Micah put on the Macabre Ring, he hadn't had a nightmare. He couldn't even recall having had a dream. This changed the night after his father returned home.

Micah had a nightmare unlike any he had ever experienced. In the dream, he and Richard set out on their paper route. They left late, and it was getting dark. Wisps of fog boiled behind Micah as he pedaled hard up a hill, unaware he had outpaced Richard. When he reached the fork where they normally departed into the woods, he found himself alone.

"Richard!" he called.

Crickets chorused in the dark forest that surrounded him. He coasted back down the hill, where he found Richard's bicycle lying off the side of the road.

"Richard, where are you?" Micah called.

"Shhh!"

Micah followed the hush into the forest and found Richard sitting on a stump, wearing his ragged yellow fleece jacket.

"How did you get here?" Richard whispered, looking surprised.

"I don't know. What are you doing?"

Richard motioned for Micah to be quiet. "Keep your voice down or you'll scare her off."

"Scare who off?"

"Mariam. Ever since you let me touch that coin, she's appeared in my dreams. She told me what happened and all about the place they're keeping her. She says she's risking her life to talk to me…"

A rustling came, and out stepped Mariam from the trees. Her appearance shocked Micah. She was clean, wearing a golden skirt and a cream-pleated blouse adorned with a wide, colorful necklace. Bracelets and anklets made of gold clinked as she walked toward him.

Seeing Micah, Mariam gasped with a wide grin. She quickly covered her mouth to stifle the outburst.

"Mariam, is it you?" Micah called, rushing toward her.

"Stop, Micah!" Richard cried.

Mariam's expression changed to horror as she looked back into the trees. A terrifying roar came from deep within the forest.

"Run, hide! You can't let him see you!" Mariam cried.

The ground shook as something enormous crashed toward them. The pounding of the earth grew louder and louder, and then a violent force pulled Mariam back into the forest.

Then there was silence.

From the trees emerged a man adorned in a gold headdress and a long black robe. Golden hieroglyphic symbols traced the wide hems of his robe with a large eye over his right breast. Inside the pupil of the eye was a glowing deep-red stone. The man's face was tight and gaunt, with sunken eyes and high cheekbones. His ears were gauged with large, jeweled discs.

The robed man swept a stony look over Micah and settled on Richard. Finally, he revealed a long staff from under his robe, which he pointed at the boys.

"What have I stumbled on?" the man said in a raspy voice.

He spoke in a language Micah couldn't understand with his ears, but somehow the thought behind the words was understood perfectly.

Pointing to Richard, the man said, "Child of mystery, I have been watching you. You've been meeting secretly with my little pet well past your bedtime, haven't you? Naughty, naughty." He shook his finger.

Sweeping his eyes over Micah, a blackness spread over the robed man's face.

"But you. I can smell the stench of a Massanite above the corpse of a rotting Carcharian. Kneel, boy! No slave child will ever stand in my presence!"

A powerful force buckled Micah's knees, and he fell to the ground.

"What is your relation to the girl?" the robed man demanded.

When Micah refused to talk, the man stretched out his staff and touched the crown of Micah's head. Thoughts and images were forcefully snatched from Micah's mind. He tried to resist, but it was no use. Micah stole a glance at Richard, who peered back with horror.

"The brother," the robed man hissed with disdain. "It seems the lost children of Pometh are returning home. Pathetic slave-bloods."

Dismissing Micah, the man's eyes swept back to Richard.

"But you. I've never encountered your bloodline."

The robed man ran his thin fingers through Richard's black hair. Richard shuddered. Suddenly, the man raised his staff like he was going to strike.

"Help! Help!" Richard cried.

A bright light burst from above. The man stepped back, shielding his eyes. A woman wearing a glowing white dress descended in the light. She held a drawn sword bathed in fire. Shocked, the man eyed the flaming blade cautiously.

"Away with you!" the woman demanded.

The robed man's overpowering presence shrank to a timid, frail old man. He retreated hastily into the trees, his robe fluttering behind him like bat wings. He stopped and glanced back at the boys. The woman lunged at him, and the dark stranger disappeared into the forest.

The woman in white lowered her sword and turned back to the boys. "Stand, child," she said to Micah.

"Who are you?"

"Brother, who I am does not matter. I have been sent to warn you of the great reaping about to be unleashed on the world of your fathers. Even now, the hosts beyond the veil cry night and day for the end of Astoria. Your generation will be the last before Astoria's fate is recorded in the Book of Life."

The angel looked down at Richard and smiled.

"And you, son of Adam. Much will be required of you. You have been prepared from the foundation of the world to be a guide to those who face the fate of Astoria."

"Who was that man?" Richard asked.

The woman's gentle smile disappeared. "Setehk is one of many that have walked the earth, sowing misery and suffering among the human family. His nature has been seen in every world that has rolled forth from the eternities. But don't fear. His bounds are set. From his ashes, the heirs of eternity shall spring forth. In the end, the humble shall inherit the earth."

The woman smiled back at Micah. She reached out and pressed her palm to his chest.

"Brother, the prayers of your fathers have been heard in the heavens. I have been tasked to give you the gift of discernment."

A warmth began to grow in Micah's chest when the woman touched him. It spread until it consumed him from head to toe, radiating like fire. Looking into the eyes of the angel, he felt her great compassion and love.

"Now, I have other business I must attend to. Before I leave, I am to show you the sign." The woman pointed into the sky and said, "Behold the heavens of Astoria."

Night had taken hold, and the stars glittered more brightly than Micah and Richard had ever known. The waning moon gazed down like an evil eye.

Suddenly, two intensely bright meteors streaked in from the horizon. When they were directly overhead, they exploded into a shower of fire that rained down.

"When the sisters of Apophis fall, know this: The gathering of the House of Massan will begin, and soon the end comes."

The woman ascended into the fire. A powerful shockwave thundered down. The forest erupted into consuming flames.

Micah awoke screaming.

Lorna and Kimble rushed into his bedroom to find him squirming in his bed, drenched in sweat. Calming him, they assured him it was just a dream.

The crown of Micah's head where Setehk's staff had touched him ached. Micah was sure this wasn't a dream. It was an omen—a prophetic vision of what lay ahead—and a certainty came that nothing would stop it.

That day at school, Micah pressed Richard about the dream. Richard denied knowing anything, but Micah could see in Richard's eyes he was lying. But no amount of coercion could get him to talk about it.

The second night, the nightmare came again. Richard was there, but Mariam and Setehk didn't return. But the sign of the sisters of Apophis returned. Awakening from the dream, Micah spent another night afraid of the shadows in his bedroom.

That Friday night, his mother made him drink a sleeping elixir, and the nightmare didn't return.

Chapter 22
Atuma Clay

"Wake up, son. It's time," Kimble whispered in the dark.

Micah woke groggy from the sleeping elixir his mother had given.

"What? What time is it?" Micah yawned, wiping the sleep out of his eyes.

"It's a big day—*your* big day. Hurry, everyone's waiting. Mom's laid your clothes out."

"Everyone? Who's everyone?"

"Get dressed. We'll talk on the way."

In the hall light, Micah saw his father wearing a dress uniform with a long-sleeved khaki shirt and drab olive trousers. White oversized buttons neatly complemented the uniform, accentuating his father's chiseled physique. Crimson stripes encircled the cuffs with a matching red sash cinched at his waist. Adorning his left breast were numerous distinguished pins and badges, including the unmistakable emblem of the blazing sun. Modest rank insignia were pinned over his shoulder. Micah had learned that his father was a colonel in special forces, but he still knew few details.

Micah put on the dark trousers and button-up khaki shirt with its blazing sun emblem. He tightened the wide red belt around his waist and slipped on the spelunking boots. The clothes were comfortable and were probably fashionable sometime in history. They made him feel like he was dressing up for Halloween.

Downstairs, the usual signs of breakfast were absent. Lorna walked into the kitchen and hugged him. She was dressed in an elegant but simple royal violet skirt with a yellow belt. The form-fitting, long-sleeved yellow jacket was intricately pleated and embellished with buttons in a complementing violet hue. A loose, gracefully draped head wrap cascaded along her side. Embroidered over her left breast was a white flaming meteor.

"What are you wearing?" Micah asked, looking her over.

Lorna laughed. "Never mind. Where's Grubb?"

"I let him out to go."

"Get him. He's an important part of this too. As of today, he's more than just a pet. He's part of your new class. The others will want to meet him. It's dangerous in Astoria, and wukals help protect—"

Micah exhaled, shaking his head. "Jeez, Mom, you've told me a thousand times. I should be scared of everything."

Lorna looked dismayed. "Micah, this isn't a vacation. Surely you understand that now. Alfred can't protect you all the time. I want you safe."

"I know," Micah sighed.

"Get Grubb, we're in a hurry."

Micah went into the backyard. The mornings were chilly now, and Grubb had an aversion to the cold. He was found shivering by the house under the steaming clothes dryer vent.

The many pine cones thrown by Jack and Ben throughout the summer were strewn about. Knowing better, Micah grabbed an armful and approached the back fence. He threw his arsenal at Ben and Jack's windows. When the lights came on, Micah scooped up Grubb and ran into the house. His parents were waiting in the kitchen. Kimble held the brown linen sack from the basement.

"Son, we need to prepare a couple of things before your first day of school," Kimble said. From the sack, he removed two blocks of clay wrapped in parchment paper. One of the blocks was the size of a tissue box, and the other size of a baseball. On the block, he saw an impression of a left hand pressed on the surface. Stamped under the hand was the sentence *Place hand in the imprint and say full name clearly. Keep in place until released.*

"So this is Atuma clay?"

"It is," Kimble said, unwrapping the smaller cube on the floor. Instinctively, Grubb sniffed, thinking it was food. A snap of electricity zapped his snout, sending him yelping from the kitchen. Micah complained until he noticed the clay began to move.

"What the…"

A head ballooned from one end of the clay and a long, slender tail from the other. Bulges appeared at the sides, forming hind legs that grew downward and forward, ending in clawed appendages. Two tiny arms grew out of the chest. The smooth charcoal-gray clay pebbled with green and orange splotches. The entire

245

transformation was completed when white fur blossomed from the tip of the tail.

The lifeless form convulsed and then took in a gulp of air. It lay there breathing for several seconds before its golden eye opened and its iris focused on its surroundings.

Lorna removed Grubb's spare collar from a kitchen drawer and fastened it around the creature's neck. Resting her hand on its head, she spoke a few quiet words, and the wukal transformed into a perfect twin of Grubb as a dachshund.

It hopped up and dashed to a bowl of water in the corner. It drank and drank. Satisfied, it trotted off to the front room. There was a commotion, and then Grubb—the real Grubb—scurried back into the kitchen.

"That's the strangest thing I've ever seen," Micah said, his brow raising as he examined the other block of clay.

"You won't see that every day…at least not here," Kimble said, patting Micah's shoulder.

Micah had had days to think about this moment. He knew deep down that if he ever was to be reunited with his sister, this step was unavoidable. He was more curious than worried. He examined the clay brick resting on the table. It had a pungent, earthy smell. Subtle hues of grainy crystals and dust were mixed in the gray material.

"So what do I do? Will it hurt?"

"There's nothing to it," Kimble said.

Micah pressed his hand on the cold, hard surface.

"That's it. Now say your full name."

"Micah Onitah Fennly," Micah said, feeling a bit silly. The clay softened, and his hand sank. "It's getting warm," he said, squishing the fleshlike material between his fingers.

There was a prick, and he tried to yank his hand out, but it remained stuck.

"Ouch! It poked me."

"It's alright. It's almost finished."

Micah relaxed as memories flashed in his mind. He saw things he had long forgotten, like his parents looking down at him in his crib. The face of his Grandma Hazel. The first time he met Wren and Richard—everything from his past to the present. He saw Mariam's fall and how, afterward, life had withered. The only life he saw after Mariam was his friendship with Richard.

Then it was over. The clay melted away from his hand, forming into a twitching lump.

"This takes longer with people. We'll be back tonight, and you'll meet him then. Let's be going," Lorna said.

Micah picked up Grubb, following his parents into the front room.

"Ready?" Kimble asked, checking his pockets one last time.

"Don't we need to go to the school?" Micah asked.

"No. The gate at the school is for when we need to move big stuff. We still have a private connection to the old system. It's a bit more jarring, but it works the same."

The house phone began to ring.

"Who could be calling this early in the morning?" Lorna asked.

Before Micah could stop his mother, she picked up the receiver. She held the phone away as shouting came from the other end of the line.

"Pine cones?" Lorna said, confused. She looked over to Micah and frowned.

Kimble took the receiver from Lorna and hung up. He removed his cell phone and said, "To the cabin." He tucked it away and took Micah's hand.

The phone rang impetuously again. The sound became a fading tone as everything around Micah disappeared into darkness.

Chapter 23
Nikola Seaport

A dot of light appeared. It approached rapidly until Micah found himself standing at a picture window, looking out into a forest with the morning sun cresting the treetops.

His parents stood nearby, beaming at him in the sparsely furnished room. There was a couch, a table, and a couple of chairs. Decorations were similar to those back home. There were painted frescoes on rock slabs and a cabinet filled with rifles in the corner. Three doors exited the small room, including one that led outside with a large telescope leaning near the door.

"Are we there?" Micah asked, anxiously looking out the window.

"First stop, Astoria!" Kimble said, squeezing Micah's shoulder.

His mother leaned over to kiss his forehead. She stopped and ran her fingers through Micah's hair.

"Mom," Micah protested.

"What have you done here?" Lorna said, feeling the top of Micah's head. "Take a look at this, Kimble."

Kimble examined the crown of Micah's head. "His hair has turned white at the top."

"Could that be from the gate?" Lorna asked.

"I've never seen that happen before."

Micah examined his hair in a mirror. A tuft of white hair sprouted in the exact spot Setehk had struck him in the nightmare with his staff. Fearing his mother would overreact, he pleaded ignorance to what had happened.

Lorna quickly forgot about the shock of white hair when she scanned the room. "Kimble Fennly, is this how you and Geoffrey lived while away?" She pointed to clothes scattered on the floor.

"We stayed here for an entire month, hon."

Lorna squealed with surprise when a long centipede with hundreds of spindly legs uncoiled from a stack of plates covered with food scraps. The creature rippled down the table and quickly escaped through a crack in the wall. Kimble got the hint from Lorna's annoyed face and began picking up the room.

Micah stepped over to the front door and pulled the latch. He tingled with anticipation when he took his first step onto the gravel path.

Outside, it was muggy, smelling earthy and fresh. Albatross Avenue was gone. His neighborhood was gone. The cabin was a lone structure built under a rock overhang. Vines and lush green shrubs cascaded down, cloaking the cabin in natural camouflage.

The forest seemed safe enough. The trees were as wide as cars, rising perhaps a hundred feet. They reminded Micah of the redwoods in Northern California. The forest was alive with strange chirps and guttural calls from high above, with occasional odd clicking sounds.

Grubb sniffed the ground, pushing aside undergrowth with his muzzle.

"What'cha found, boy?"

A beetle the size of Micah's fist hobbled along in the thick grass. It was black with a grooved shell and inch-long mandibles. Micah prodded it with a stick, which caused the bug to stop and aim its hind end directly at him. Having seen this same behavior from stink bugs back home, he stepped aside just in time to avoid a squirt of liquid that smelled like rotting meat. Catching a whiff, Micah put his sleeve to his nose.

Lorna came to the door and gagged, bunching her scarf to her nose. "Oh, Micah. You haven't been here five minutes and you've already found trouble," she said, annoyed. "That's a death beetle. It's a horrible bug. The stink will attract scavengers for miles." She took Micah's hand, walking him away from the putrid odor.

"You mean it'll attract dinosaurs?"

"Of course—except we don't call them dinosaurs here."

"What do you call them?"

"We call them maws. Well, that's the general name. Depending on how dangerous they are, they have more specific names."

"Maws? So what do you call a Tyrannosaurus Rex?"

"That's one of the dangerous ones. They're called Hellbar Rakish. You'll learn more about this world in an hour than paleontologists who spent their lifetimes digging in the earth. They were close about some things, but about others, they were way off.

Hellbars are frightening, but they're scavengers. Usually, they will avoid confrontation unless they're hungry. There are much worse creatures here. The worst ones aren't that big, either."

Micah hung onto every word.

"Of course no maws are on the outer islands. Oh, there may be a few little ones."

"We're on an island?" Micah said, looking around. All he saw was the forest.

"Yes. It's a sentry post called Oshar. We're located where the western shore of Oregon is in the future. In Astoria, the coasts of the western states of North America are covered by ocean."

"Really?"

Lorna nodded. "Many fascinating changes happen over the next sixty-five million years."

"So where are we going?"

"Nikola Seaport. It's one of the larger islands about ten miles away."

"How do we get there?" Micah asked, looking around the forest. There was only a foot trail that looked rarely used.

"We'll fly."

"Fly?"

"Well, it would be a long way to walk and swim, wouldn't it? Here comes your father now."

Kimble emerged from a hidden cavern covered over with vines. He turned around, gesturing back toward the cave. Silently, a curved hull vehicle emerged with two round thruster pods at its flanks. It was smaller than the Lincoln.

"We call it a skeeter," Kimble said, anticipating Micah's question. With another gesture, the skeeter settled to the ground.

"That can fly?" Micah asked, walking around the antique-looking vehicle. It resembled a boat more than a plane. The name

Seaworthy was carved on its stern.

"Antigravity is a natural phenomenon of the stone and the kind of wood used," Kimble explained, helping Lorna aboard. "It's made of redwood, one of the most valuable materials in Astoria, next to Deity Stone. You'll find the *Seaworthy* a bit more interesting than the Lincoln."

Kimble motioned Micah aboard and inspected the skeeter's flaps and rudder. Micah ran his hands over the polished surface. It had the same antique feel as that strange sewing machine in Tricia's hobby room.

Intricately carved in the deep-red wood were scaly patterns with inlaid rope. Glass beads outlined the runners on the side and the contours of the cockpit walls. The seats were made of animal hide and were padded. Micah sat down, and the seat cushioned his weight. He looked under the seat for a mechanism, but all he saw was air.

"Where's the steering wheel? The speedometer and the gas pedal?"

"No need," Kimble said, climbing aboard.

"What about seat belts?"

"Unnecessary."

Micah looked surprised.

Kimble sat next to Lorna. He clapped his hands, commanding, "Off with you, now, to Nikola."

The *Seaworthy* lifted gently off the ground. Silently, it drifted forward a few miles per hour.

"Pretty slow, huh?" Micah said, unimpressed.

Kimble and Lorna laughed.

"We're in a hurry. Step on it," Kimble said.

With a whoosh, the *Seaworthy* surged forward.

"Whoa!" Micah breathed, grabbing the seat.

Soon, the cabin was far behind. They banked around trees and rocks. It was a comfortable ride, but one that was unfamiliar. If it weren't for the whooshing sound from the thruster pods, they would have traveled in silence, and there was no wind, either.

Micah stretched his arms over his head. Just a few feet above, he felt his hand pass through an invisible barrier where he felt the wind rushing through his fingers.

"These are fairly recent additions," Kimble said, motioning to the pods. "In the old days, we used wind and sail. We couldn't travel at these speeds, but it worked. These pods work like jet engines—with the help of the Fire, of course. You'll be surprised at how advanced some things are here and how backward others are. Our people in Oregon have been working for decades to adapt technologies to Deity Stone."

"In Oregon?"

"That's what we call the future here. It's a funny story about how that came about. When Alfred first met our parents, he told them he was from Oregon. So, the name stuck. They've called the future Oregon ever since. Your mother and I were the first generation raised in the future."

"Really?" Micah said, curiously examining the pods.

"Many things changed for our people after the gate was discovered," Kimble continued. "One of the first things they did was to learn English and change their names to fit in. It was thought it might make it more difficult for our enemies."

"Kimble, I don't want to discuss that now. At least not today."

"The boy needs to learn sometime."

Micah agreed. He wanted to know everything.

"I understand. But today is a special day. There'll be plenty of time for that later."

"Alright, dear," Kimble said, patting Lorna's hand.

Micah searched the passing forest, thinking how ordinary everything seemed. There were many varieties of trees, ferns, and flowers. If he didn't know better, he would have guessed he was on the back trail that led to Richard's house.

He looked into the pod droning to his right. The chamber appeared empty. He could feel the air being sucked past him. Kimble snapped off a leaf from a passing tree and tossed it into the pod. It spun around violently and shot out the back.

"So, how does this work?" Micah asked.

"There's actually a small tornado inside there," Kimble said.

He opened a compartment in the dash. Inside a protective case was a Deity Stone mounted on a circuit board. Kimble removed his smartphone from his vest and showed it to Micah. The screen prominently warned they had no cell service.

"The phone obviously doesn't work here. There are no cell towers or satellites in Astoria. But the underlying science of technology works here just as it does in the future."

He swiped through his apps and found one with the icon of an airplane and tapped it. A graphic appeared resembling the skeeter looking down from the top. It showed several statistics, like the speed they traveled (which was thirty miles per hour), the amount of thrust being produced by each pod, and how much energy remained in the crystal.

"The stone is doing all the real work here. The computer directs the power regulation to the pods and monitors the system. It all can be seen here on my phone. Since the introduction of computers, especially the miniaturization of circuits, a new realm has opened up with Deity Stone. You kids really took off with these computers. Many of our young families living in Oregon have tech jobs these days. What they've learned has changed everything."

"So, how fast will it go?"

"The civilian models like the *Seaworthy* here do about a hundred. The military versions are much faster. We've clocked them as high as six hundred. A full squadron of howlers can affect the weather," Kimble said proudly.

"The weather?"

"Oh, yes. Whenever a great amount of Deity Stone is discharged, it affects the weather. Great swelling storm clouds. Real soakers, too."

The whooshing grew louder. Micah looked down at the phone and saw they were picking up speed as they headed down a steep incline toward a landing. There, the trail ended at the edge of a rocky cliff. Beyond was the blue ocean.

"We're going over!" Micah shouted. Instinctively, he ducked, pulling Grubb tight. As the cliff edge came up, the whooshing intensified, and the skeeter shot over the edge.

Kimble tucked away his phone as Lorna calmly touched up her lipstick. Instead of plummeting as Micah's instincts feared, the skeeter gracefully nosed upward, banking to the right.

Micah looked back at Oshar and saw two contrails of thin white mist streaming out of the pods.

"This is incredible!" Micah said, peering over the edge.

They followed the shoreline and soon were heading out over the open sea. As the skeeter settled its climb, Micah saw a chain of islands richly covered with green blankets of foliage.

Lorna turned back and smiled. Micah recognized his mother's look. She had something on her mind. "Micah, your father and I have some news. We've had to keep so many things secret...like Mariam. It's a burden we all share who live in Oregon. Some of those secrets are going to be hard for you."

"Like what?"

"Grandma Hazel. We told you she died. But today, you'll see

she lives."

"We went to her funeral. Why would she pretend to die?" Micah said. Nothing surprised him anymore, but this news made him feel irritated.

"You need to understand, son. When our people first came to Oregon, they made mistakes. The idea that they had discovered a new world blinded them to the consequences. Grandma Hazel fell victim to this. When she arrived in Oregon, she was thirty-four. That was the year I was born. After ten years, she had established many friendships. People started to notice she wasn't aging."

"So she had to pretend to get old so no one would notice?"

"That's right. And when she began to get all that newspaper press about her being the oldest citizen in Stonehelm, she decided her time had come to return home for good."

"So why didn't she just pretend to be someone else? She could have still visited me."

"No. The lesson we've learned is that we must fit into the natural order. People are smart, Micah. They notice more than you realize. Now that you are entering the program, your father and I are considering leaving Oregon for good."

"We can't move! What about Richard?" Micah said.

"We know how much Richard means to you. We plan to get you through the foundation program before making any changes. You've got a few years left. But you know we can't stay forever. At our ages, we've already brought too much attention with you as our young son."

Micah was relieved they wouldn't be moving soon, but he wasn't sure how to feel about his grandma. He had overcome the grief he had for her loss long ago.

"Are Dad's parents still alive?"

"No, son, Grandpa Fennly died a long time ago. And I never

knew my mother," Kimble said.

Micah set his chin on the edge of the skeeter, looking out over the sea. Below, the ocean was covered with a white cotton fog. Black specks peppered the clouds, which Micah realized were other skeeters, all heading in the same general direction. He started counting but gave up when a thinning in the clouds revealed many more below, skimming the sea.

The *Seaworthy* nosed down into the cloud. There was a flash of light that repeated every few seconds. They passed by a red-and-white striped lighthouse with a spinning light at the top. Tips of pines passed underneath, and then a familiar building appeared.

"This is Alfred's Island, called Promontory Point. It's the place where the back-to-school night took place," Kimble said. They flew over a building that looked like Quentin Elementary School, with one major difference. The wings of the school stretched out, only to end abruptly in a tangled maze of girders and stone pillars that hung out over the cliff edge of the island.

"What happened to it?" Micah asked.

"You've seen the carvings in the school. The gate was constructed back in the thirties. At the time, they had many workers going back and forth between Astoria and Oregon, and they feared they'd attract too much attention. So, they engineered the gate here in Astoria to match the exact dimensions of the old academy. In a single night, they swapped the two sections. They added the carvings in Oregon to throw off the residents to what they were up to. It's not a school here. This is the actual gate—the part where the portal is attached. The other half we call the antenna. That's in the elementary school back in Oregon."

"Can we see it?"

"Not today. But Monday, this is where we'll drop you off. I'm sure Alfred will give you kids a tour."

The skeeter cleared the island and plunged downward with a droning whine. Micah held his breath as he couldn't see more than a few feet ahead in the soupy fog.

"Relax, son," Lorna said, patting Micah's anxious hand.

They passed through the fog and skimmed the sea surface. They were fast approaching the four great watchtowers. They rose like enormous candles from the water, each tower base fifty feet wide with roiling flame licking the clouds high above. Beyond the towers, a vast, conical-shaped island rose up with a great steaming pillar of mist that formed a cloud high above.

Skeeters of different shapes and sizes were converging on the island. Some were small, like cars, and others as large as buses.

"That's Nikola Seaport. It's where we all lived in the beginning. Back then, there were only a few thousand of us. We've grown since then. Now we're a nation of over three hundred thousand and have colonized the northwestern region of Biblios—that's North America in the future," Lorna said.

"Three hundred thousand people are living here?" Micah asked.

Lorna chuckled. "Of course not. We outgrew Nikola long ago. Now it's just a lookout post. We still hold special events here, like the commencement ceremony. The rest of the time, it has a small contingent of soldiers."

"Why doesn't anyone live there anymore?"

"Most of the islands in this area are sparsely populated now," Kimble said. "We can't risk the Rashaar stumbling into a populated region this close to the time gate."

"Kimble!" Lorna snapped.

"Sorry."

Micah sat up straight. "Hey, that reminds me. What happened at the back-to-school night with those meteors?"

Lorna gave Kimble a hard stare.

"It's still under investigation, sport," Kimble said, looking back at Lorna. She gave an approving nod.

Grubb had been resting on Micah's lap. His ears suddenly perked.

A pod of enormous fat blue creatures with slender flippers and blunt snouts broke the surface of the water, swimming along with the *Seaworthy*. They made strange barks as they snapped at the boat.

"Those are kilts," Kimble said. "I'm told they're the distant relatives to dolphins."

The island loomed ahead. Many galleons had dropped anchor near the island. There was no visible landing, so those in boats had to tender in. Kimble had the *Seaworthy* veer to the left, and a giant vessel resting on the water came into view.

At first, Micah thought it was part of the island, with many tangled trees and odd structures growing out of its massive hull. It rested on the sea like an island unto itself. There was a natural beauty and order about it. The ship dwarfed the galleons docked at its waterline with its twenty masts; the greatest were as tall as skyscrapers. Skeeters buzzed in and out of the ship through gaping holes in its hull.

"That's the *Majesty*," Kimble said proudly. "It's the largest ship in the Massanite Navy. It's a floating city with a crew of twenty thousand. She's a mile long."

Micah was amazed. He craned his neck to look up at the hull.

A sweeping light suddenly appeared from the sky.

"Halt your vessel! Power down and hit the deck!" a stern voice boomed.

The *Seaworthy* glided to a stop and sat in the water, bobbing on the surface. The light shimmered, and a sleek craft appeared above them.

"Where did that come from?" Micah asked. "It wasn't there

before."

"That's a howler. It's military," Kimble said.

The howler descended rapidly until it circled the *Seaworthy* a few meters away.

"This area's restricted," an amplified gruff voice said. Micah saw two uniformed men sitting one behind the other in the ship's cockpit, wearing maw-skin helmets and goggles. The one in front pointed at Micah. "No children allowed here!"

Micah shielded his eyes from the intense beam of light they shined in his face. Two more howlers approached, their engines winding down.

"You'll follow us into Nikola, where you'll be detained for questioning. Make no attempts to deviate your course, or you will be destroyed."

At this, Lorna shook her head, giving Kimble a stern look. Kimble shrugged.

The first howler took the lead. The other two took up the flanks of the *Seaworthy*, waiting. The *Seaworthy* accelerated, and the two patrollers shot ahead. Their motors howled with a deep, droning growl. Thirty-foot water roosts formed from the vehicles, creating a watery corridor for the *Seaworthy*.

"Are we in trouble?" Micah asked.

"Oh, Micah…" Lorna said.

"They're just uneasy when we get too close to the *Majesty*, that's all," Kimble said.

Lorna looked back to Micah, shaking her head.

The patrollers slowed as they neared Nikola. They passed many anchored galleons that bobbed and swept in the tide. Most appeared devoid of crew. Those that had crew were preoccupied with unloading cargo onto wide floating platforms. Fully laden platforms had broken away into the main channel churning slowly toward the rocky face of the island with a burbling wake. The *Seaworthy* passed over one of the freighters. It was covered with hundreds of wooden crates and barrels. The freighters appeared to operate without a crew.

"What are all these ships doing here?" Micah asked.

"Supply ships. Everything has to be shipped in for the gathering. It's been a busy week," Kimble said.

Micah was growing concerned. The lead howler was speeding straight for the cliff face ahead. The craggy cliff rose perhaps a thousand feet, hostile and majestic. A jungle forest draped over the top like a curtain of vines and daring tropical fauna. The sea crashed against enormous rocks that formed almost a toothy expression at the foot of the cliff.

They approached between two particularly tall pointed outcroppings. Micah's eyes widened when the lead howler showed no signs of slowing as it raced forward.

"We're going to crash!" Micah cried, bracing for impact.

The lead howler plunged into the cliff face and disappeared, followed by the *Seaworthy* and the other two howlers.

"Calm down, dear," Lorna said, patting Micah's anxious hands.

The *Seaworthy* passed into an expansive cavern with hundreds of docked galleons, each unique in size and design. Some ships were utilitarian with simple rigging, while others were grand and majestic. Each ship bore two flags—a royal blue flag and a more prominent flag that was unique to each ship. The cavern was a flurry of activity, with a bustling city surrounding the docks. Enormous cranes were busy moving pallets of cargo, while damaged ships were being dry-docked for repairs.

"This is Nikola Seaport," Kimble said. "All of these ships are for the different classes that will be heading off to Boshii Campus on Monday. Everyone will meet here before they depart."

One galleon in particular caught Micah's eye. It was the largest of any in the port. The black ship had a massive stern with four masts supported by a complex web of rigging. The high stern living quarters were ornately carved with fantastic creatures that appeared to continue up the sides. Of all the ships, this one even had cannons on its deck. The name *Maximillian* was carved into the stern.

"The *Maximillian*?" Micah asked.

"That's Proud Shipley's rig," Kimble said. "He's the captain over the Raptors. He's one of the most famous captains in the fleet."

"You mean the one with the biggest ego," Lorna corrected under her breath.

"Oh, dear. I know you've had your spats with him. But he's one of the best. I bet he'd give ol' Alfred a run for his money."

Lorna shook her head, giving Kimble a dismissive wave.

"Wait, I thought I was going to Alfred's island on Monday?" Micah said.

"You will be, along with all your classmates. Alfred has his own private lagoon where he launches from."

The patrollers passed over the crowd below and entered one of a dozen natural fissures connecting the seaport to the interior of the island. The fissure was wide enough that the three howlers could easily fit side-by-side. The ceiling was gnarled and twisted with sharp spikes. The water glowed a deep sapphire blue, sending swimming light up the magma walls.

Roaring grew louder as they went deeper into the cavern. The cave widened where adjacent caves joined together. The water became smooth like glass as they approached a giant mouth of stalactites and stalagmites.

The cavern was miles across. Waterfalls raged around the

perimeter wall, plummeting into the steaming depths below. Mist rose upward, where it exited through the opening high above. In the middle of the great expanse was a city like no other Micah had ever imagined.

Nikola was carved from the ancient, solidified magma floor. A network of roads interconnected the castle-like spires and towers. Bridges joined several isolated sections, spanning over deep, mist-filled chasms. Much of the city was covered with jungle growth. In the middle of the city was a vast courtyard with a great coliseum.

"This is where we all lived in the beginning," Kimble said proudly.

"It's incredible," Micah breathed out in wonder.

Skeeters flew around the city like bees over a hive. Some came very near the *Seaworthy*, carrying passengers and cargo. Occasionally, large-winged birds were also spotted. They appeared to be carrying passengers, though Micah never got a close look.

The three howlers changed formation. One took the lead. The others took the stern of the *Seaworthy*. They entered the city above the crowds and threaded their way through the network of streets and walkways. Crossing over a bridge, they descended upon a crowd gathered near a Parthenon-like structure.

The engines of the *Seaworthy* wound down as they landed. The howlers settled nearby. Micah's attention wasn't on their escorts, however. The world before him was wondrous and dangerous. They were below sea level. A monstrous waterfall showered down just beyond the Parthenon. He felt small and vulnerable in the face of the watery giant.

Ten-foot-wide ornate pillars surrounded the Parthenon. A circular stairway led up to the arched entrance, flanked by six great bowls of fire. At the top of the stairs was a gathering of men and women wearing cloaks.

Micah glanced over the three patrollers. From each, a man leaped off, leaving one aboard. Their cloaks danced in the wind the instant they stepped away. Their faces were hidden under the helmets and goggles. The shortest of them approached.

"I don't recognize this vehicle's markings. Where are you from?" the man said in a tone Micah didn't like.

"We're from Oshar Island. I'm Colonel Fennly. This is my wife, Lorna, and my son, Micah."

"Fennlys? I've heard of your clan. Troublemakers! This boy doesn't look old enough to be here. Nine, ten at most. We'll need proof of his age."

"I'm twelve!" Micah snapped, his face reddening.

The uniformed man leaned on the hood of the *Seaworthy*. The other two men stood behind. Grubb growled.

"Was I talking to you, runt?"

Micah snorted. "Don't call me a runt."

"Micah!" Lorna snapped.

"Listen, I don't want any of your lip…Charlie Brown!"

Micah took a deep breath, about to fire off. He stopped, seeing a grin spread under the man's reflective goggles.

"Geoffrey!" Micah shouted.

The two soldiers behind Geoffrey burst into laughter as they removed their gear.

"Kellan! Blake!" Micah said when he saw the faces of his brothers.

"Micah, you take things far too seriously," Blake said, straightening his cloak.

"Quite the hothead. You do that with a real colony guard, and you'll be sorry," Kellan added.

"Hey, I am a colony guard," Geoffrey said. He gestured back to the men sitting in the patrollers. The three men saluted and then lifted off the ground, speeding away.

"You *were* a colony guard. Now you're a captain," Kellan said proudly.

"Yes, Geoffrey. What was that nonsense back there about destroying us? Really," Lorna said, annoyed. "It wouldn't hurt for you guards to…"

Micah ignored his mother's lecture and climbed out of the *Seaworthy* carrying Grubb. He surveyed the crowd around the plaza. Some on the periphery waved up to him, and he waved back. Micah's family came up behind him.

"Do you know who these people are?" Kimble asked.

Micah shook his head.

"These are relatives—cousins, uncles, aunts, great-grandparents. Many generations. Actually, this isn't all the family. Not everyone has children entering the program this year. The entire family probably wouldn't fit in this city these days."

Grubb became increasingly restless in Micah's arms. "Stop it, Grubb!" Micah exclaimed, finally letting him drop to the ground. Grubb backed away from Micah, hissing.

There was a deep bellowing roar that sounded like a giant cow clearing its throat. Micah looked up, and his eyes bulged.

Two monstrous heads were coming down to him, suspended by necks that arched over the platform out of sight. The animals were brown with green mottled patterns around their necks.

Micah panicked, scrambling backward. "What—what are they doing?" His shirt and pants puffed in and out as the two creatures took enormous sniffs.

"They smell something," Kellan said, patting the cheek of the giant beast.

"They smell the death beetle Micah ran into earlier. These two are harmless, Micah. Just curious," Lorna said.

Micah presented his hands to the two gentle giants. "What are they called?"

"Bullmonks. They bring them every year because they're so impressive. They're one of the few animals the paleontologists got right," Kimble said. "Today, they'll be used for the ceremony."

The gentle brown eyes of the creatures looked over Micah curiously. He rubbed their burly foreheads. The skin was clammy and cool from the mist hanging in the air. The bullmonk conceded Micah posed no threat, letting out a throaty huff.

"Charlie Brown!"

Micah spun around to the familiar woman's voice.

"Grandma!"

The bullmonks lifted their enormous heads high, watching the woman rush to Micah with outstretched arms. Micah grinned widely. His grandmother looked like his mother's twin—both young and vibrant.

"How I've missed you," Grandma Hazel moaned, hugging Micah.

Micah was overwhelmed. All around him were loved ones standing in this foreign world that seemed impossible to exist.

Lorna and Kimble hugged Micah, and the tears flowed.

Micah was finally home.

Chapter 24
The Blazing Suns

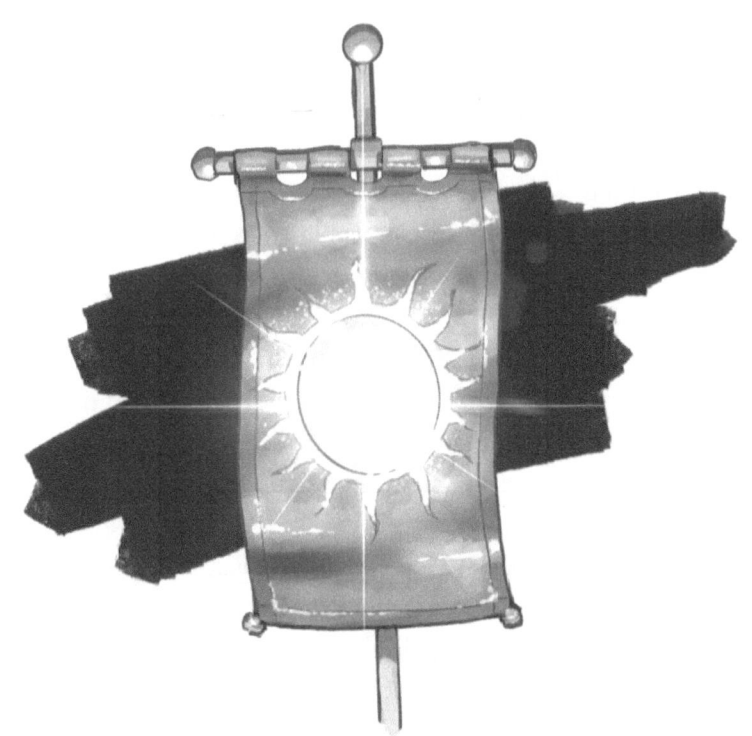

For the first hour after Micah's arrival at Nikola, he was introduced to many strangers. After so many names and family connections were given, he stopped trying to keep track of the complex web of genealogy surrounding him.

Throughout the morning, he discerned two distinct groups in the family. Older family members, mostly grandmothers and great-aunts, spoke with thick accents that sounded like Morty Crowther and Bassam Amun. The younger families spoke English with perfect American accents.

It occurred to Micah that he hadn't met any grandfathers. When he asked why, Grandma Hazel told him most of the older men, including his Grandpa Onitah, had been killed in the Great War.

Among the many strangers were a few familiar faces. Bassam and his wife, Fiona, greeted Micah's family. Bassam wore a deep purple uniform trimmed in yellow with a meteor emblem. It was the same style of uniform Micah's mother wore. Fiona stood next to him, beaming, greeting Micah with a kiss. Micah's family lavished the Amuns with endless praise, recounting stories from the past. Listening, it became clear to Micah that the two had lived extraordinary lives.

Miss Sorenson made a brief appearance. She commended Micah's parents for raising such a "strong-willed son," and that even though Micah had a knack for finding trouble, he had a good heart. She excused herself, saying she had twenty other students to meet before the commencement.

Breakfast was served under the old Parthenon. Families ate at tables arranged in a half circle around a raised platform at one end. On the platform was the head table. Ten frail women dressed in white spoke lively as they ate and laughed with those close by.

Throughout the meal, Micah was curious about his surroundings. Vines hung down from the sections of the roof that were missing. With the heavy humidity, moss had grown on everything. Giant bowls of fire provided heat from the chill that hung in the air. Wide gold ribbons and banners with the family crest were suspended between the pillars. The crest depicted a soldier behind a shield, staving off sweeping fire. The words *Fight for Liberty* were stitched boldly at the bottom.

It wasn't long until the neatly ordered tables were in disarray. The serving plates and bowls, earlier heaped with pancakes, sausage, bacon, and every conceivable fruit, were empty. With breakfast out of the way, the Parthenon was filled with laughter and conversation.

Micah's family sat at a long table conversing with Bassam and Fiona. Micah sat quietly next to his grandmother in the shadow of the conversation. He picked over his barely touched plate of food.

"What's the matter, son?" Lorna asked.

"I'm not hungry," he replied quietly, seeing his family focus on him.

"It's a long day. Eat something for your strength," Lorna said, stuffing an apple into his pocket.

"Oh, Mom," Blake chided. "Leave him alone. This is all so much for him."

Kellan and Geoffrey nodded sympathetically.

"Don't you remember what happened at my commencement?" Blake said.

Kimble snorted. "Gadfrey, you got sick."

"Right," Blake grinned. "Micah, I threw up right when Bassam called me before the entire family. It was so embarrassing."

"You always had the weak stomach," Bassam mused. "I remember you received a nickname for this. What was it the kids called you?"

"The barf king."

"The barf king?" Lorna laughed. "You never told me that."

"For the first month at sea, I was sure he wouldn't make it," Bassam said. "Couldn't even hold down the biscuits. Nearly had to send him back home."

Everyone laughed. Even Micah cracked a smile. The outburst at the table caused inquisitive hoots nearby. Grubb and four other wukals were chained to a massive pillar off to the side. They lay in strewn hay, gnawing contentedly on giant bones.

A horrendous cough came from a boy down the table. All through breakfast, this boy had fits of sneezing and coughing. Micah caught himself meeting eyes with him all morning.

"Micah, look up there," Grandma Hazel said, pointing to the ten women seated at the head table.

"That's the widows' table. They are the oldest generation still living in the family. See the woman in the center—the one in the tall chair? That's your Grandma Pometh. She's the matriarch of the family. She's your great-great..." Grandma Hazel started counting on her fingers. "Anyway, she's seven great-grandmothers back. She might not look it, but she's as sharp as a whip."

More coughing came from down the table. This time, it was so severe that it caught the attention of other tables. Micah noticed the boy was wearing the same uniform he was. He leaned over to his grandmother and whispered, "Who's that boy?"

Grandma Hazel looked excited. "That's your second cousin, Stu Fennly. You don't remember him? I watched you boys when you were babies. You two were a handful. And that young lady at the end there is Sariah Thorup. She's your third cousin. Do you know what you three have in common?"

Two giant bells rang out at the front of the hall.

"You'll find out soon enough," Grandma Hazel whispered.

Two women rose at the widows' table and pulled Pometh back from the table. This made Micah think the great-matriarch was feeble. But Pometh stubbornly shooed away her two helpers. With a wave of her gnarled hand, she floated into the air with her chair under her. From her vantage, she could see the entire family.

The hall fell silent, leaving only the thundering waterfall filling the great hall. Pometh waved her arm, and the roar of the waterfall faded away.

"My dear family," she said in her aged, raspy voice. "It's a great blessing to be with all of you on this wonderful morning. It fills my heart with such joy to see this family grow."

Her voice quivered. Her two daughters floated up, giving her their handkerchiefs.

"Oh, my sweet daughters," Pometh said, waving the handkerchiefs. "These tears are tears of joy. For seven hundred years, I have watched this family endure. But we have remained strong! I look into your faces and I see so much love for your children. How I worry and pray for your welfare, you young ones. There's nothing in this world I cherish more."

She paused and looked lovingly around her family.

"Could the new generation come and stand with me?"

Lorna and Kimble motioned for Micah to go to the front. They beamed proudly as he stood with the others.

Among the family, twenty-two boys and girls Micah's age went before Matriarch Pometh. Some knew each other, but to Micah, they were all strangers. The one common trait they shared was the style and cut of their uniforms, though the colors were different.

As they congregated before Pometh, those with matching colored uniforms grouped together. Micah stood between Stu and Sariah, each wearing the same khaki uniform with the blazing sun emblem.

Pometh floated back down before the children. She beckoned each child one by one to her. They talked briefly and she kissed their foreheads. Each child went to her with reluctance but walked away spellbound.

Sariah went up. She talked with Pometh the longest of any of the grandchildren. When she finished, the matriarch kissed Sariah on the forehead. She removed a necklace from her neck and placed it on Sariah. When Sariah returned, she stepped off by herself, wiping tears away.

It was Micah's turn next.

"My dearest Micah," Pometh said so tenderly that Micah couldn't hold back his own tears. They embraced for a long moment. Beams of pure white light shone in Pometh's face as Micah looked into her tired eyes.

My heart has been so heavy over Mariam. Pometh's voice pierced Micah's mind. Her dark eyes sparkled as Micah looked at her with wonder. *But by the name of our eternal maker, you shall see her again. How exalted we shall be from the pillars of sacrifice! You will bring hope to our captured brothers and sisters from the days of King Ninevah. Your life is destined for hardship—how great, I dare not speak. But trust our dear friend Alfred and rise above your afflictions. In your darkest hour, remember the sunrise soon follows. Be brave and merciful. Above all, remember the weak and outcasts will be your greatest allies. I love you more than words can express.*

At this, Pometh kissed Micah's forehead and fell back in her chair, taking an exhausted breath. Her daughters rushed to her side, but she insisted they stop fretting over her.

Micah couldn't look away from Pometh. Though she appeared old on the outside, she radiated like the sun inside. Never had he felt such intense feelings of love.

Finishing with the last grandchild, Pometh floated back into the air. "These little ones are the greatest treasures of my life. Parents, remember the sacrifice you make today will ensure there will be a tomorrow for your children. Little ones, know you are from a noble heritage. Much has been sacrificed to give you good lives. I love you. Now the time has come."

She waved her hands, and the two giant bells rang again.

At the back of the hall, a dark-green striped wukal appeared. It rooted back and forth in a curious manner as if restrained. Seeing the large crowd, the creature rose up on one foot, letting out an inquisitive barking hoot.

Grubb and the other wukals perked up. They responded with the same hoot and throaty barks. Micah and the others grinned at the strange echoing sounds.

A towering figure ascended the steps, coming to a halt beside the creature. Clad in a gray uniform adorned with two gold star medallions, he stood tall and commanding. His crimson cloak billowed in the brisk winds outside the hall. With a wave of his hand, he directed his attention to those following him. Micah noticed a prominent shield and a spiny-ridged tooth intricately embroidered on his robe.

Behind this man came two uniformed officers, a woman and a man. Their clothing matched that of the captain, but instead of stars, they bore wide gold bars on their uniforms.

Bringing up the rear was a group of five individuals with a timid, bright-eyed boy positioned in the center, holding the leash of the wukal. Micah immediately recognized him. It was Marty Tuttle, a classmate from Mrs. Hall's sixth-grade class.

"Captain Pensky," Pometh said ceremoniously. "What is your business here?"

Captain Pensky bowed low. "I am here to accompany two of your children home."

"And what have you brought as a covenant for this great request?"

The two senior officers walked up the aisle bearing two small chests. They placed them next to the widows' table and stepped back. Pometh's two daughters stepped forward and tied a golden bow around the chests.

Pometh floated down to Captain Pensky, looking earnestly into his eyes. "Do you promise to guard these children?"

"With my life, this is my oath, Matriarch Pometh," Captain Pensky said, bowing low, and kissed her outstretched hand.

"Who has come to take my children?" she said.

"I present Chief George Moxly and Counselor Esther Crow," Pensky said, stepping back.

The two senior officers stepped up together. Esther was a husky woman with bright-red cheeks and a youthful face. George was a short, middle-aged, balding man. They were an odd twosome, Micah thought. But they conducted themselves with great confidence.

Esther searched over the children. In a high-pitched voice, she announced loudly, "Matriarch Pometh, we request the honor of taking brightling Connie Thorup, your precious daughter."

Pometh nodded her approval.

Slipping between the children, Esther stopped next to a long-haired blonde girl. When Esther took her by the hand, Connie burst into tears. She followed reluctantly, looking back to her parents.

"There, there, darling. You're among friends," Esther said delicately. She took the weeping child to her side and walked her to Captain Pensky. There were audible sobs from Connie's parents from the back of the hall.

Chief Moxly went through a similar ceremony, calling for Dugan Simpson.

"Very well, then," Pometh said, pleased.

Captain Pensky clapped his hands, and the giant bells rang. The entourage marched out of the hall to the family's applause.

Shortly after, another class arrived with more brightlings in tow. And so it continued for the next half hour. One by one, the captains came and took Matriarch Pometh's grandchildren, each repeating the same ceremony. Some took one child, and others took as many as four.

Micah knew some kids entering the hall that morning—some he had grown up with through elementary school.

He was delighted when Jo stepped into the hall. Her leader was Captain Proud Shipley. He was a short, broad-chested man who wore a ridiculously large orange feather in his hat. His crew colors were black and orange, with the symbol of a running raptor embroidered on their velvet robes. Captain Shipley had a large class already and took only one of Pometh's granddaughters.

When Jo noticed Micah, she waved excitedly. Micah waved back with a wide grin—until he saw Kamran among their ranks. When their eyes met, scowls were exchanged.

After the Raptors' departure, the hall's excitement fell away. All that remained were Micah, Stu, and Sariah. Rabble broke out from the family as they waited.

Micah leaned against a pillar near his brother Blake. His feet were tired from standing on the marble floor. Stu teetered next to him, on the verge of falling asleep. His only signs of life were the occasional sniffs from his allergies. Sariah stood aloof from the two boys, preoccupied with the necklace Pometh gave her. Though she was the same age, she carried herself with the dignity the boys lacked.

Pometh rapped her knuckles on her chair, her patience spent. Finally, she rang the bells again.

A gentle clucking sound, like two pieces of wood being clapped together, caught Micah's attention. He searched behind him, trying to spot the source of the clucking. Eventually, he found two orange birds waddling through an arrangement of flowers. The birds settled among a vibrant array of orange marigolds, perfectly blending in. The birds were slightly smaller than crows, with orange wings and mottled yellow chests. They would have appeared natural in Oregon except for their elongated toothy snouts and curved horns. The horn of the smaller bird was pink. Micah was sure they were Penelope and Twitch. He had seen them many times in his siblings' shedets.

Blake and Kellan discreetly tossed a couple of apple slices near the pair. The two birds plucked up the slices, gobbling them up in a single bite.

"Have you met Penelope and Twitch?" Blake whispered. He and Kellan glanced back to be sure their mother hadn't noticed. Lorna was busy chatting with her mother.

Micah nodded and whispered back, "They were crows when I first met them."

Kellan chuckled, "Those are hornbill ravens. Those two tend to blend in wherever they go."

Outside the Parthenon, there came a horrible screech. Grubb, the last wukal in the hall, let out a bark-like cry and burrowed down into the hay. Micah had never heard Grubb make the startled noise before. He followed the large shadows that glided outside the Parthenon pillars. Two immense creatures touched down just out of his view. Craning his neck, he caught glimpses of wings flapping, and then a gust of wind blew into the hall.

"Step down now! That's it, watch your step," a gruff man said.

"Come, come, this is no time to dawdle," an agitated woman said. "Wren, pick up your shoe. Hurry along."

Four brightlings climbed the stairs at the back of the hall. There came snickers from the family when they saw unkempt hair and clothing. The only boy in the group was Wren. His jacket hung off him oddly, as only one of his arms was in the sleeve. He had a blank expression and was cuddling his shoe to his chest. Micah had to bite his tongue not to laugh.

A stout, bearded man walked to the head of the brightlings. From his belt, he removed a whistle. He blew two short toots. The creatures outside screeched a deafening cry, causing the disheveled brightlings to jump. The fantastic creatures flapped, sending a swirling mist over the family. Micah tried to get a good look, but they dove away too quickly.

The man tucked away his whistle, speaking with a cheerful grumble to his companions. He patted Wren on the head. "There, you see? We got you here in one piece."

"Chief Sterling Hawkins!" Pometh demanded. "Where's Alfred?"

Hawkins' white cloak fluttered as he hustled up the aisle. As thick as he was, he moved with surprising grace. He wore a formal khaki uniform with a glinting gold bar insignia over his breast pocket. He looked back and motioned for the class to follow, revealing the yellow blazing sun embroidered on his cloak.

Keeping pace with Hawkins came a stern-looking woman with tied-back hair. She wore the same formal uniform, except hers had distinct feminine touches like a skirt instead of trousers. Immediately behind the senior staff came three junior officers wearing the same drab uniforms but no cloaks. Micah recognized these three from the back-to-school night.

The first junior officer was Quinn. He was agitated and muttering as he marched up the aisle. Next came the young woman Micah remembered well. Quinn had called her Pearl. She was lively and animated. Her curled shoulder-length hair bobbed as she passed by. She turned back to the others with a bright smile, beckoning them to catch up.

Armin held back with the four brightling students. He walked with his arm around Wren, talking him out of his daze.

"Many apologies," Hawkins said, greeting Pometh's hand. "There was a delay at the Kingsley family on the other side of the city, and we had an accident on the way over." He stepped back, looking merrily over Stu, Sariah, and Micah.

"Where's Alfred?" Pometh demanded.

"He's not here? He should've been back by now."

There was a commotion at the back of the hall when a ghostly apparition appeared. The luminous being came in and out of focus like a television not properly receiving the signal. Penelope and Twitch gave away their hiding place when they began to squawk.

"You see, here he is," Chief Hawkins said proudly.

Alfred Quentin appeared, bringing on delighted gasps from the family. He fidgeted with what appeared to be a phone. Satisfied, he tucked it away, removed a pair of boots roped under his belt, and tossed them to Wren.

After seeing the other captains that morning, Micah was struck by how old and frail Alfred was. Alfred walked to the front of the hall taking short, careful steps.

"It's good to see you, Alfred," Pometh said, her eyes twinkling.

"I beg your pardon for keeping you waiting, my lady," Alfred said in his quaint Southern accent. He kissed Pometh's hand. Micah swore he heard a tiny giggle come from the matriarch.

"Alfred, you've never been conventional, have you?" Pometh said.

"Conventional?"

"You know," she said, pinching her wrinkled cheek.

"Oh, that. There was a matter to attend to in Oregon—forgetting the proper boots. We didn't realize that until it was almost too late. That was a good catch, Hawkins!"

Hawkins swept a smile at Micah, Stu, and Sariah. "The ride may not always be easy, but we always deliver," he said a little too proudly. He and Alfred stopped chuckling when Pometh gave them a stern look.

"Let's get on with it, then," Pometh said, frowning at Alfred. "Oh, take off that disguise. It isn't flattering at all!"

Alfred gave a feigned look of hurt. He removed his hat and rolled his hand in the air.

Micah and his cousins watched as the hunchbacked man went through an amazing metamorphosis. His arched back straightened, adding two feet to his height. His gray, thinning hair turned thick and chestnut brown. His age spots disappeared as his skin tightened.

Twisting his mustache to sharp points, Alfred rounded on his three new pupils, grinning proudly. He was a powerful-looking man, rivaling even Micah's own father. He wore the same khaki uniform with the blazing sun robe. Over his right breast were five gold stars and four ship wheel medallions hung from colorful ribbons.

Hawkins stood next to Alfred, sizing up the three. Compared to Hawkins, Alfred was a young man.

Sariah straightened her outfit, running her fingers through her hair. She threw Micah and Stu an icy look when she noticed them staring at her.

"Much better," Matriarch Pometh swooned. "Captain Quentin, what's your business here?"

With a commanding voice, Alfred replied, "I am here to accompany three of your children home, my dearest lady."

Three chests were presented to Pometh. By now, there was a heap of chests collected. The stern woman in Alfred's staff was introduced as Counselor Grace Mulgrew. With her junior officer companion at her side, the two took Sariah by the hand. The junior officer was introduced as Pearl Gypson.

Chief Hawkins stepped over to Micah and Stu. The two other junior officers stood nearby and were introduced to the family. Armin, who had been helping Wren with his boots, was introduced as the company's beast master trainer.

Quinn led Stu to the other brightlings, with Hawkins following. Hawkins clapped his large hand on Stu's shoulder, welcoming him to the class.

Armin shoulder-hugged Micah. Micah found himself staring again at Armin's odd, bulging eye.

"This way, my new friend," Armin said, leading Micah to Grubb.

Seeing his acceptance, Micah's parents and siblings cheered.

"Way to go, Charlie Brown!" shouted Geoffrey.

"Charlie Brown?" Armin mouthed, slugging Micah's arm playfully.

Micah threw an irritated look back at Geoffrey as they unchained Grubb. Lorna and Grandma Hazel stood as Micah passed past his family's table.

"We're so proud of you, son," Lorna said. She hugged Micah, who went bright red.

"Mom, you're embarrassing me," he protested.

"Oh, fiddlesticks," Grandma Hazel said, doing the same.

Alfred gathered his company. Micah and Grubb became the center of interest. Unlike Micah, his peers had never seen a wukal before that morning. Wren was jealous. So many secrets, even among friends.

"Look sharp, ya whelps!" Master Hawkins bellowed with a hearty laugh. His enthusiasm brought cheers from the family.

Outside, bells were ringing.

"So the yoke is taken up by another generation!" cried Matriarch Pometh. She clapped her hands, and the two great bells rang, adding to those outside.

The family stood as Alfred's class departed. They shouted, "Blessed be the name of our eternal creator!"

Chapter 25
Lost and Found

Alfred, with his senior officers, Chief Hawkins and Counselor Grace, led the Blazing Suns into the city. The junior officers had been tasked to keep the brightlings together. Micah struggled to keep a grip on the leash as Grubb sniffed back and forth, curious about his new surroundings. Wren moaned at how horrible his morning had been. Stu, being the only other boy, walked with Armin. The four girls walked with Pearl.

"Everybody, stay close. The city is jam-packed," Quinn said, nodding to Armin and Pearl.

Alfred entered the outskirts of the city onto the main street. Hundreds of travelers and friends of the families were already milling about. Royal blue Massanite flags hung from every shop and vendor that had taken temporary residence before the celebration.

"When your ancestors first arrived here, this island was the most active volcano in this region. This whole city was a lake of lava," Alfred said, addressing the class as he walked backward.

"My parents told me they used the Fire to change the volcano."

"That's right, Sariah. Fire is the pure power of creation and tames the elements. When your grandparents chose to live here, they went to work and made this wonderful place their new home," Alfred said, continuing on.

Armin picked up several black lumps of rock and distributed them to the kids. "Notice this black rock that's everywhere. This is the remnants of the magma. They had to bring in mountains of different materials to make Nikola habitable. Otherwise, it would have been like living in an oven here."

Armin's recount of Nikola's history continued as they passed by smaller merchants selling equipment and clothing out of wheelbarrows and repurposed crates. When they reached the open-air market, they stepped into chaos. Thousands filled the plaza, where vendors offered food and drink. Crowds of onlookers cheered and danced as they watched street performers and musicians. Alfred's class spread out as they threaded through the crowd.

Quinn stopped to check on the others. Armin was still droning on about the city. "Armin!" he shouted over a flood of passing onlookers. "Enough with the history lesson already! We've got to get through this mess."

Continuing on, Quinn was shoved back by a large, pot-bellied man who stepped in his way. "Watcha where you're going. Ya made me spill my drink, ya young pup," the pot-bellied man slurred, lifting a mug of golden liquid to his lips.

Quinn tried to step past, but the drunk blocked his way. Finally, Pearl stepped up. "Excuse us, sir, we are going to the coliseum. Would you let us pass, please?"

"What have we here?" the pot-bellied man said, looking Pearl over and licking his lips.

By now, Micah and the other brightlings had caught up and were standing behind Armin. Quinn's face was flush, and he was ready to fight. He balled his hands into fists and lunged at the man. The two went down, and a scuffle ensued.

"Quinn!" Pearl cried.

Chief Hawkins, who was intimidating in his own right, saw the entire exchange. He grabbed Quinn and lifted him to his feet. "Step back, Mr. Higgins. That's all we need is to get tangled up with the law."

Quinn tossed the empty mug onto the stomach of the pot-bellied man and stepped away.

"Is that you, Sterling?" the pot-bellied man said to Chief Hawkins, struggling to stand back up. "It is! It is! My long-lost friend!"

"Pugmire, who let a drunk like you in?" Hawkins said with a hearty laugh. He helped Pugmire to his feet, and the two men hugged.

"I just stopped for a pint while they repaired my ship. There's a storm coming, and I barely got out alive."

"Is there, now?" Hawkins said, more interested in keeping his drunkard friend from falling over.

"It's a real doozy comin', Sterling, be ya sure of it! It's heading up from the southeast, probably be here by tonight."

The scuffle had alerted the city police. Four officers surrounded Pugmire and Hawkins with their distinctive black uniforms and batons. "I thought I told you to go sleep it off," one of the officers said, poking Pugmire's chest with his baton.

Pugmire staggered back. "I got thirsty again."

"Well, how 'bout we take you to the tank and make sure you stay put this time?"

The four officers took Pugmire by his enormous arms. As he was escorted away, he winked at Pearl and gave Quinn a scowl. "You owe me a pint!" he growled before they disappeared into the crowd.

"Don't judge him too harshly, Mr. Higgins. He's rough around the edges but a good man," Hawkins said.

Quinn snorted. "He's a drunk."

Hawkins ignored Quinn's assessment and pointed forward. "Ever onward!"

Armin looked like he had something on his mind.

"Do you have something to say, Armin?" Quinn said, irritated.

"Probably nothing. He said there was a big storm coming from the southeast. Big storms don't come from the southeast in these parts. That's on the Biblios side. Major storms always blow in from the Endless Sea from the southwest."

"You believe anything that crazy drunk says? Forget about it, and let's get going." Quinn slammed his fist against a garbage bin and followed Hawkins into the crowd.

"You'll get used to Quinn. He's always like that," Armin said with an awkward smile to the brightlings. He nodded forward, and the class continued on.

Micah and Wren fell behind as Grubb kept getting tangled in the crowds. Fortunately, Alfred couldn't make it far without attracting attention. He was a celebrity, and everyone wanted to meet him. They congratulated him on his new class. It had been years since Alfred had attended a commencement—six, to be exact, back when Armin and Pearl were two of his fresh-faced brightlings.

"We'll never get to the coliseum at this rate," Alfred said to his senior officers. He decided they needed to make up for lost time and changed into his old-man disguise, topped off with his fedora. His class started making headway again.

For the tenth time, Micah and Wren had to stop to pull Grubb out of the shrubbery planted along the way. He insisted on sniffing everything. There was much to see. The plaza had been decorated for the occasion. Enormous bowls of colorful plants with long, draping vines hovered overhead, suspended in redwood bowls. As the wind shifted, they drifted about, providing shade over the crowd. The smell of spices and meat cooking filled the air.

At the center of the plaza was a stage. A strangely out-of-place band was setting up with a drum set, synthesizer, and guitars. They were dressed in light cotton clothing, which contrasted against the more subdued palette of drab worn by onlookers. A squeal of feedback came, and at the signal of the vocalist, the band started playing with the tapping of a snare and the swelling of the synthesizer. They were playing a cover of "Every Little Thing She Does is Magic" by The Police.

"So why were you late this morning?" Micah shouted to Wren over the blaring music.

"It was my mom's fault. When Alfred showed up, she wanted everyone in the family to shake his hand. I'm the oldest in my family, so all my aunts and uncles were there."

Micah understood. He knew Wren's mother was the youngest of thirteen children.

"What were those giant birds that flew you here?"

Wren shuddered. "Chief Hawkins called them Pysons. Those are really scary. They've got teeth! When I got too close, one of 'em bit me!" Wren showed Micah a red welt on his forearm. "When they told me we were flying those across the city, I said no way, I'm afraid of heights! But my dad made me do it. He told me I needed to start being a man."

Micah laughed.

"Yeah, real hilarious. One of those flying cars nearly hit us when we were over the city, and that Pyson made a flippity loop. That's when I fell out!" Wren said, explaining with hands. "The girls in our class grabbed me by my jacket, but I slipped out. Chief Hawkins caught me by my foot at the last second. I could've died, can you believe it? Died! That's it! I'm staying put on the ground—no more flying birds. No more climbing trees. Nothin'!"

The two passed through an audience that was dancing and singing to the music. Two gray-haired women, who'd had too much to drink, grabbed Micah and Wren.

"Oh, Winney, aren't these two just adorable?" one gray-haired woman said, pinching Micah's cheek. Her friend grabbed Wren and gave him a bear hug. She ran her fingers through Wren's thick, dark hair and wished him well.

"They sure are friendly here," Micah said, yanking Wren away from the clutches of the overly handsy woman.

Wren looked himself over in a shop window reflection. Scoffing, he took out his comb to fix his hair.

"Where did they go?" Micah asked, looking over the crowd.

"Isn't that Quinn over there? Boy, he sure was angry when I fell off that bird—"

Grubb yelped when a passerby stepped on his tail. "Sorry, son," the squatty man said, moving along quickly to avoid Grubb taking a bite of him. Micah picked up Grubb to calm him.

"I can't believe Grubb's a dinosaur. How long have you known?" Wren said, running his hand down Grubb's back to his long, slender tail.

"Only a month."

Grubb stretched to sniff Wren's hand. "He's so cool," Wren said, pulling his hand back. After the Pyson incident, he wasn't too keen on exposing anything to toothy creatures.

"Alright, I've lost everyone," Micah finally said, stopping. They searched over the sea of strangers. Micah climbed a flight of stairs to get a better look over the crowd.

"Well?" Wren asked, hopeful, sidestepping over to the foot of the stairs.

Micah shook his head. "I don't see 'em."

"That's great!" Wren said, frustrated. "My first day. I nearly get eaten, fall to my death, and get mauled by an old lady, and now we're lost."

"Don't panic. They're here somewhere."

Micah scanned the sea of celebrators, his eye snagging on a gaunt uniformed man leaning anonymously against a shop with his arms folded. The dark blot was dressed like the police—except he was easily three feet taller than anyone around him. Slinking back and forth on his shoulders was a mangy, short-legged creature with a narrow nose, sniffing everyone that passed by.

Curios, Micah dialed up his powers of perception and saw the light around the scowling officer's face emitting a steady blue light. The moment he used his power on the officer, the light shifted to a shade of yellow and settled on a black pulsing wave. The officer uncoiled his arms and stood at attention. Searching over the crowd, his eyes quickly zeroed in on Micah.

Micah ducked.

"Found them?" Wren asked hopefully,

Micah shook his head. He peeked over the stone railing and saw the officer was now making his way toward them. A feeling began to well up in his chest. It was a warm, stirring sensation radiating from his heart. It reminded him of the nightmare when the angel had touched his chest.

Two hornbill ravens fluttered down, landing on the railing. "Here you two are!" the raven with the pink horn cawed.

The ravens surprised Micah, and he was momentarily distracted from the officer. "Penelope? Twitch?"

The bird with the pink horn ruffled her feathers. "We've met before. Remember the beach? I'm Penelope, and this is my brother, Twitch."

Grubb sniffed and suddenly had a great interest in the two birds. Twitch hissed and flapped furiously at Grubb when he got too close.

"We're lost," Micah said.

"We know. Alfred sent us to find you."

"Who are you talking to?" Wren said, stepping up the stairs. Seeing the two birds, he was confused.

"You're lost too," Twitch said in his chirpy voice.

Wren's eyes widened. "What's this, talking birds? They've got everything here!"

"You haven't met Penelope and Twitch?" Micah asked.

Wren shook his head.

Penelope hopped over to Wren. "Nice to meet you, Wren. Any friend of Micah's is a friend of ours."

Micah glanced back up the plaza. The officer was closer now, and the creature on his shoulder was sniffing in their direction. The warmth in his chest began to flutter. "Penelope, who's that coming this way?"

"Lamptor's grave! It's Pantera! He's a Montu guard we've had trouble with before," Penelope said, flapping her wings to catch Twitch's attention.

"Stop that!" Twitch snapped.

"Look!"

"Pantera!" Twitch cried, leaping into the air. "Hide!"

"What's a Montu guard?" Micah shouted as Penelope and Twitch flew around the corner.

Wren was already down the stairs chasing after the two birds. Micah followed, double-stepping down. They dodged through the crowd, eventually ducking into a narrow side street.

Micah and Wren peeked out of the alley. Pantera strode to the stairway, and the creature on his shoulder leaped off. It sniffed the railing exactly where Penelope and Twitch had been previously.

"Why'd you two run?" Penelope asked, looking down from a stove pipe above.

"You said to hide," Wren said.

"Not you two! I meant us!"

Twitch landed on Wren's head, and the pair continued to spy on Pantera.

"It's too late now. If Pantera finds you with us, you'll be detained for sure. He's been looking for us."

"What did you do?" Micah asked.

"Does that matter now? We need to get out of here," Penelope cawed and flew down the alley.

Pantera summoned back his four-legged companion and plodded forward.

Twitch became frantic. "We better think of something quick, he's coming this way!"

Penelope squawked, motioning for Micah and Wren to follow. They ran through a maze of alleys overgrown with weeds and rubble.

Twitch dove down from above. "Hurry. He's running now!"

Penelope shot down a flight of stairs leading into the dark. "Quick, down here!"

Micah and Wren ran past an old rusty door. "Lock the door," Twitch cried, darting past.

The tunnel was dim with streaming rays of sunshine from grates above. They hurried down the misty tunnel where it split into side passages.

"Where are we?" Micah asked. He sniffed and scrunched his nose. The air smelled like an outhouse.

"It's the sewers…" Twitch said.

"Oh, seriously!" Wren shouted, putting his sleeve up to his nose.

"Oh, calm down. The sewers are hardly used anymore. It can't be that bad. The last time we came down here, the rain washed everything out."

"And when would that have been?" Wren said, breathing through his mouth.

"Twenty years ago?"

"Oh. I'm sure everything's fine, then," Wren said, rolling his eyes.

"Listen, the Montu don't like us—especially that one. They're one of the few living things able to find us if we're not careful," Twitch said.

"So, what do we do?" Micah asked.

"Stay here and don't move."

Penelope and Twitch flew out of the tunnel through a grate in the ceiling.

Micah and Wren surveyed their surroundings. Hearing running water, they went farther down the corridor to investigate. They found a pipe gushing out a steady stream of murky brown water at a junction that split five ways.

"That's disgusting," Wren said. He paced as the minutes passed. "I think they've abandoned us."

The warmth in Micah's chest intensified when a loud explosion was heard up the tunnel from where they'd come. The two made a hasty decision and ducked down the closest tunnel.

Penelope and Twitch flew over them.

"Why did you go this way? You're going the wrong way!" Penelope said.

"Seriously, Penelope? Do you think we know where we're going?" Micah huffed as he jumped over muddy puddles reeking of feces.

"Listen. If Pantera catches you two, you never saw us. Tell him you got separated from your class and panicked. That's not far from the truth." Twitch said.

"You can't leave us here!" Micah cried.

Penelope landed on a broken tree branch wedged in the floor while Twitch flew back the way they came. "Look. I promise Pantera has no interest in you. I need to show you how to find Alfred if we get separated."

Wren glanced around nervously.

"Wren, look at me," Penelope said, transforming into her natural tiny self. She climbed the tree branch until she was at eye level with Wren.

"Wow! You're pretty," Wren said.

"I know, so pay attention. I need you to focus on Alfred. Think of his name, his face. Everything you can remember."

"How old are you?" Wren asked.

"Wren, focus! Did your parents teach you anything about the Fire?"

"They showed me a few things, why?"

"Did they teach you anything about using a trigger?"

"A trigger? I don't know what you mean."

"It's simple. The Fire can help you when you're in trouble. But you need to make it clear you want help."

"Oh, I get it. Like if we were led down into a sewer while being chased by a maniac?" Wren said.

"Exactly. Some twist their wrists, some wiggle their noses. It doesn't matter. You just need to use that trigger once you've thought of what you need."

"Would this work?" Wren asked, giving Penelope a wink.

"Cute! Now, think of Alfred and repeat after me."

Wren did his best to think hard.

"Say 'locate,' " Penelope said.

"Locate!" Wren shouted.

The instant he winked at Penelope, he took off at a dead run down the corridor.

"Hey! What's happening?" Wren shouted.

"That's it, Wren, keep going!"

Micah cradled Grubb in his arms, grinning, as he watched Wren sprint away.

"What are you waiting for?" she said to Micah. "Follow him!"

Twitch returned, anxiously squawking. "He's coming!"

Micah slung Grubb over his shoulder and raced after Wren. His boots blurred as he splashed his way through the corridors. Wren was wearing his spelunking boots, maintaining a good lead. Reaching a long straightaway, Micah finally spotted him turn down a passage.

There was a loud *clunk!*

Micah rounded the bend to find Wren sprawled out in a heap of wet garbage, rubbing his head. The two had reached an impasse at a metal grate that blocked the way outside. Wren had run smack into it.

Penelope and Twitch flew around the corner and saw their predicament.

Micah shook the grate. He could tell it was designed to open, but in his panicked state, he was unsure how. The warmth in his chest lurched.

"Listen, I know Alfred's got to be close," Penelope said, breathing hard. Twitch nervously hopped back and forth on the bars. "We'll find him and be back."

"Hurry!" Micah said, dropping Grubb to the ground.

Penelope and Twitch flew through the grate and disappeared.

"Man, this is the strangest day of my life," Wren moaned, shaking the leaves out of his hair. "But all things considered, that was pretty cool."

Grubb began rooting through the pile of debris collected by the grate.

"Get out of that," Micah said, yanking Grubb's leash.

Grubb began to growl as he fought the leash. He stretched, sniffing a particularly icky piece of refuse.

Just then, the pile moved, startling the boys.

"What is it?" Wren asked, leaning over to look. A gray blur shot out, heading straight for Wren. "Rat!" he shrieked, bolting back up the tunnel.

Seeing its prey elude it, the rat screeched and dove into a pile of garbage. It hunkered down with only a gray plume of fur visible. Micah held Grubb back to get a closer look. The skittish creature stared back with its beady black eyes. When Micah got too close, it sprung at him, snapping its long, gopher-like teeth.

Grubb broke free, snatching up the creature. He shook it violently, and it died with a horrible tiny shriek.

"What was that?" Wren shouted from up the tunnel.

Micah's chest burned hot, bordering on intolerable. Just when he thought he could no longer stand the pain, it abruptly went away. "I don't know. But I don't think it's a rat," he said, nudging the twitching creature with his toe.

Wren stood a ways off at the junction where they'd detoured down the side passage. He looked back and forth. Suddenly, he turned on his heel, sprinting back with a horrified expression. "It's got friends!" he shouted.

Screeching came. Hundreds of the rat-like creatures emerged at the junction. Teeth snapped and claws scraped as they swarmed down the tunnel, heading straight for Micah and Wren. Grubb fearlessly ran forward, picking off the first few leading the charge, but he was quickly overwhelmed and made a hasty retreat, where Micah swept him up in his arms.

Micah and Wren tried frantically to open the grate. "Help!" they shouted.

A thunderous explosion erupted from behind them. The two spun with their backs to the grate just in time to see a huge fireball sweep past the junction. The creatures scattered but were channeled in the tunnel. They had no choice but to flee straight for Micah and Wren.

Pantera emerged, dark and foreboding, standing at the junction. A sword sprang from his back, which he caught with a quick flick of his wrist. The creature on his shoulder puffed up and let out a terrifying hiss.

"We're gonna die!" Wren shouted.

The Montu made a grand sweeping gesture with his sword, and a blast of wind rushed in from outside the sewer through the grate. Micah and Wren clung to the bars, their feet flailing in the air.

The charging rats tumbled back as the wind picked up ferocity.

Twisting trails of mist formed, and lightning arced between metal fittings in the sewer walls. The rats spasmed to death when licks of lightning snapped through them, finally erupting into a blinding fireball.

Clenching their eyes shut, Micah and Wren fell when the wind abruptly stopped. As quickly as the pandemonium began, it was over. A putrid, twitching mound of smoldering fur and flesh separated the boys from the Montu guard.

"Micah, Wren!" came a voice from behind.

The boys looked over their shoulders to see Alfred and their class peering from a bridge above.

Chief Hawkins came down the angled canal wall to meet them at the grate. "Looks like you two have found some mischief," he said, reaching the grate. With a simple tug upward, it lifted open.

"Pew," Hawkins said, fanning his nose. "Gompums. Foul creatures—where there's one, there are a thousand."

"We got lost," Wren said, retreating from the tunnel.

"Hold it, you two," Pantera said, coming out of the tunnel into the light.

"Pantera," Hawkins said, stepping up to meet the intimidating Montu. "I would have thought the old sewers were out of your jurisdiction."

Pantera was not amused. He flicked tufts of fur off his golden spiky sword. Releasing the hilt, the sword hovered briefly before twisting over his shoulder and sinking into the sheath at his back.

The creature on his shoulder obediently curled up, withdrawing its presence, but its black eyes remained narrowed on Hawkins.

"I demand to know where Penelope and Twitch are. They have a great deal to answer for. These boys were just with them," Pantera said, speaking with a heavy accent.

Alfred slid down the canal wall and stood next to Hawkins. He dismissed the boys, and Pantera glowered back at him.

"Look, Pantera, we've been through this before. We don't control Penelope and Twitch. They're free citizens—"

"They're a menace and need to be sent back to the world they came from. They left me stranded on the outer islands when they tricked my boat into departing without me. I'm tired of their pranks, Alfred, and I demand justice!"

"I thought you requested a transfer," Hawkins said.

"I did, but after Fort Somar and with all the meteor showers, they denied my transfer."

Micah and Wren climbed the canal wall to be confronted by Counselor Grace. "I hope this isn't going to be regular practice with you two," she said. "Next time, you may not have a Montu to get you out of trouble."

"It's not our fault. It was Penelope and Twitch that led us down there," Wren said, sneering when he sniffed his uniform.

"Who's Penelope and Twitch?" the other brightlings asked.

*   *   *

The afternoon went more according to plan, and the Blazing Suns arrived at the coliseum without further incident.

The grand structure was the most prominent edifice in all of Nikola. It was five stories high, constructed from gray granite like Quentin Elementary.

Many of the less load-bearing sections and decorative pillars were cut directly from the black volcanic rock. Statues lined the cobbled road that led into the coliseum.

Other classes were gathering, making their way into the coliseum. Alfred and his senior officers led the Blazing Suns over the gantry that spanned a great fissure below. The girls walked ahead with Pearl. Micah and Wren walked together, with Stu close behind. At the rear came Quinn and Armin, ordered to keep their eyes on the boys.

"This is Black Rock Coliseum," Alfred said. "These statues were erected to honor those who have gone before. These are some of the old ones who sacrificed their lives so we could be together today."

"Who's this woman?" Sariah asked, stepping over to a white marble statue of a weathered woman with a basket in her arms. Clinging to her leg was the statue of a small child. When Sariah reached up to touch the smooth surface, the statue suddenly came to life and smiled at her. The child buried her face into the leg of the woman when Alfred's class gathered around.

"The statue moves!" Sariah said gleefully.

"My name is Katra," the statue said, pulling the child close. "I was one of the original forty to escape during the three days of darkness that hid our flight into the wilderness. I raised five orphaned children as we trekked across Biblios…"

Sariah took her hand off, and the statue went back to its frozen stance.

"Lilly, this should interest you," Alfred said, inviting the quiet brown-haired brightling to touch the child's statue.

Lilly touched the child's ragged hem, and the shy child statue looked up and said, "My name is Tenka."

"Tenka?" Lilly repeated. "That's the name of my great-grandmother."

"That's right," Alfred nodded. "This child was your great-grandmother when she was a child. Katra raised her."

"How long ago was this?" Lilly asked, scrutinizing the statue child, which appeared to be roughly five years old.

Alfred twisted his mustache thoughtfully. "Well, let's see. This is after Avram's vision but before the exodus out of Rashaar when your people were still in Venuba. So I'd place this depiction of her about two hundred and fifty years ago."

Another of the brightlings, Tiyana Ska, pulled a sketchpad and pencil from a pouch she was carrying. She had been making simple sketches as Alfred's class made their way through Nikola. She thumbed through the pages to an empty page and began drawing the statue with the others gathered around.

"You're really good," Lilly complimented as Tiyana captured Tenka's shy expression with surprising accuracy.

Alfred looked at her sketch, smiling proudly at Hawkins and Grace. "How long have you been practicing, Tiyana?"

"I've drawn for as long as I can remember, but it has come more naturally since I got the ring."

"That's not surprising," Counselor Grace said. "The Fire nurtures natural talent."

Alfred walked across the road to another statue. This statue was of a humble-looking man wearing primitive armor and holding a sword at his side. "Class, this gentleman should be familiar to some of you. Does anyone recognize him? How about you boys from Quentin Elementary?"

Micah studied the face. "It sorta looks like our old janitor, Bassam."

Alfred smiled. "You're correct."

He touched the statue and it came to life, gesturing with its sword as it spoke. "My name is Amun. I was a soldier in the Massanite army and helped liberate a thousand of our people from the Rashaar during the great exodus."

Alfred released his touch and said, "Amun was one of the first of your ancestors I met in Astoria. He trained me to use the Fire and survive in this wonderful world. He's a personal hero of mine."

Armin, Quinn, and Pearl trotted up to the most prominent statue near the entrance of the coliseum. This statue was of a man with a thin mustache. When Armin touched the statue, the figure raised its arm as though shielding itself from the sun. The figure wore simple attire: a pair of trousers and a button-up shirt, with a pack slung over one shoulder. A necklace with a jagged stone hung from the statue's hand.

Releasing the statue, Armin asked, "Can any of you guess who this is?"

"That's you, Mr. Quentin," a dark-haired brightling girl with curly short hair said.

"That's right, Gertie," Alfred said with a smile. He posed in the same stance as the statue. "This depicts a very significant event in my life. It's the day the Almighty called me. Long before I met any of your grandparents."

"You mean God?" Sariah asked, studying the face.

As the class waited for Alfred's answer, he looked thoughtfully into the sky. "It was a sacred moment to me. Class, if you ever wonder why I call you the Blazing Suns, remember this statue. It depicts the moment I was shown a vision of your ancestors and the great love he has for all of his creations. In each of us is great potential. You are powerful beings as bright as a blazing sun."

An amplified voice from the coliseum asked the classes to get to their seats. Tiyana made hasty last strokes on the sketch she made of Alfred. She perfectly captured the look of wonder in his eyes.

A twenty-foot Massanite flag hung from the center of the coliseum. The flag was royal blue with a white stripe. In the middle was the image of an eight-spoke ship wheel knocked out in white. At the end of each of the spokes was a star.

The coliseum was decorated with banners celebrating the commencement. The stadium seating was partitioned into sections for each class. On the center floor, there was a stage. A man with gray hair, dressed in gold and blue robes, stood on a high podium among a seated group of men and women. Montu Guards were stationed at the four corners. Micah and Wren were quick to notice one of the guards was Pantera.

Alfred pointed to the man standing at the podium and told his class, "That's Director Karnak up there in the robes. He's over Boshii Campus, where we're heading next week."

A company of eighty young soldiers came marching into the coliseum. They wore dark-blue uniforms with white caps and trousers. They spread out along the periphery of the coliseum floor, settling at parade rest.

Quinn, who had shown little emotion but fury all day, became excited to see the soldiers. The soldiers all looked about Quinn's age of nineteen.

"It's the new marines from the *Majesty*," Quinn said, looking to see if he recognized anyone. "I bet they just came out of basic training over the summer. I'd be with them if it hadn't been for my mother—"

"Well, we're glad we got you instead, Quinn," Counselor Grace said. "We could use some of your discipline around here. Things got a little lax last year, didn't they, Chief Hawkins?"

"Oh, Grace, it was the end of the year when all that happened. Besides, it was a lot of fun, wasn't it?" Hawkins said, wrapping his thick arms around Pearl and Armin.

Giant bells at the top of towers around the coliseum rang. The rabble of the coliseum fell silent.

"Good afternoon, young brightlings and leaders. I'm Director Karnak, and I welcome you to the ninety-first annual gathering."

He spoke without a microphone, his voice sounding loud and clear. He turned about with his arms raised, welcoming the audience's thunderous applause.

"If I had asked any of you brightlings a month ago to imagine where you might be today, it's certain none of you would have guessed you'd be in a world filled with dinosaurs."

Laughter filled the coliseum.

"Your home world of Astoria welcomes you with open arms. Your journey into this bold new world begins today. Over the next six years, your education will be like none other you've experienced. It will be my great privilege to be director of the Boshii Campus."

Director Karnak went on for another fifteen minutes relating the school's noble heritage. He thanked the teachers and other staff for devoting so many tireless hours to "the cause." In addition, Karnak thanked the military for their presence that day. It was the first time the military had attended the gathering in over forty years.

Micah met eyes with Pantera several times throughout the course of Karnak's speech. After their fourth eye contact, Micah concluded it wasn't just a coincidence that Pantera had been positioned so close to Alfred's class. Even Wren could sense the tension.

"That guy gives me the creeps," Wren whispered.

As Director Karnak concluded his speech, a group of soldiers appeared at the entrance. They carried armfuls of banners and flags. "Let's make the class of 2025 a red-letter year! Oh, there's one more item of business I failed to mention…"

With a sweep of his arm, Director Karnak caused a section of the coliseum to retract, widening the entrance on the opposite side of the gathered soldiers. A deep rumble came like boulders hitting the ground. Wukals throughout the coliseum began yelping.

Gasps came as the head of one of the bullmonks, which Micah had been given a preview of earlier, rose to the height of the coliseum. The enormous beast trundled in, guided by eight handlers who directed its lofty footsteps. It was paraded around the outer floor of the coliseum to the wonder-struck audience.

"This is Jaamini. She's a bullmonk over 100 years old," Karnak said. "She was one of the beasts of burden that helped build this great city long ago. She's been a part of the Gatherings ever since…"

Jaamini let out a mighty bellow. The audience fell quiet and then exploded into thundering applause.

Micah and Wren were thrilled by the site of the beast, though perhaps not as much as Stu. Stu jumped up, barely containing himself. "I've loved dinosaurs since I was just a kid!" he said, wild-eyed with a ridiculous grin.

"Me too!" Armin said with an equal amount of enthusiasm.

Their excitement wasn't an isolated case. Everyone was captivated by the tree-sized beast. But when the second bullmonk lumbered in, Micah thought Stu might pass out.

"This is Jarvis," Karnak announced. "These two will be leading our parade through the city."

The girls were more subdued but marveled at the sight before them. Tiyana was furiously sketching.

Alfred's eyes glittered at the sight of his class with their enthralled faces. "It's the moments like this that make it all worth it," Alfred said to Hawkins and Grace.

The parade was well orchestrated. Jaamini and Jarvis led the procession out of the coliseum down Statue Road.

The soldiers called out class names to take positions behind the beasts. Each class was given flags and banners with their colors and mascots prominently displayed.

When the soldiers called for the Blazing Suns, Alfred led his class to the coliseum floor. Stu and Sariah volunteered to carry the Blazing Sun flags presented by the soldiers.

The parade threaded through the festive city, with confetti cascading over and thunderous excitement. The enthusiastic crowds cheered loudly in a show of grand celebration

Micah met the parents of his fellow students as they made their way. The one who stood out was Gertie's mother. She came running out of the crowd and swept Gertie in her arms. "I'm so proud of you, sweet angel girl!"

Gertie was a twin of her mother. They were short with the same dark curly hair and walked with the rest of the parade, holding hands. After two blocks of overhearing Gertie's mother gushing, Wren finally whispered to Micah, "I think I'm going to be sick. I hope her mother doesn't plan on going with us."

The parade eventually circled back to the coliseum, where the brightlings were reunited with their parents. Micah's family took him on a tour of the city. Though unoccupied for twenty-five years, the buildings were remarkably well preserved. His parents took the family to a section of town with small apartments. They showed Micah where they'd lived for the first few years of marriage. Lorna and Kimble had moved to Oregon before their first child, Blake, was born. They'd lived in Oregon ever since.

They stopped at several street merchants to pick up last-minute items he needed. They purchased a pair of hiking gloves and a hat made of piggle skin, which looked like alligator skin.

As night came on, a great feast was served out of the coliseum. The military put on an air show like none Micah had ever seen. Swarms of howlers took to the air. In a dazzling display of precision, they reproduced the Massanite national flag out of cloud vapor filling the sky. A final howler jettisoned several glowing balls into the flag, creating a tremendous lightning storm that flared and arced between the stars. The spectators spontaneously began to sing the Massanite anthem throughout the city—a humble, melodic hymn of bravery and rising from the ashes of oppression.

"That's what this song is?" Micah yelled to his mother. This was the song she often sang back home—the same song Richard had identified carved on the school wall.

"It's the story of our people!" Lorna said enthusiastically.

At the end of the evening, Grandma Hazel, Blake, and Kellan prepared to leave. Micah learned the truth about his brothers. They lived in New Massan, three hundred miles north of Nikola. They never lived in California.

Lorna chided the two as they climbed aboard the packed air bus to head home. "When are you boys going to settle down and start thinking about having families?" she asked.

"Someday, Mom," the two said, giving their mother a peck on the cheek. They gave Micah a hug, wishing him well on his journey. They promised they'd visit him at Boshii Campus when they could.

"If it makes you feel better, dear," Grandma Hazel said, giving Micah a hug, "I have some news."

Lorna dismissed her two sons onto the bus. "Oh? What would that be, Mom?"

"I'm seeing someone," Grandma Hazel said.

"What?" Lorna said, shocked.

"All aboard!" a voice from the bus announced.

"Love you," Grandma Hazel said, stepping aboard.

"Mom, get back here this instant!" Lorna demanded.

"Can't talk now, dear. We'll catch up later."

With that, the doors closed. Moments later, the bus lifted into the sky.

"My mother!" Lorna fumed.

Geoffrey gave Micah a big hug before departing with his military unit. He told Micah how proud he was and wished Tricia could have been there. He told Micah to look for Emily when he got to Boshii Campus. Emily, being a second-year student, didn't receive the fanfare there was for first-year brightlings and had departed the day before.

The night ended with Micah and his parents flying the *Seaworthy* back to Oshar Island. He watched the city twinkle away into darkness as they headed into the clouds. A brooding storm was approaching on the horizon. In the flashes of lightning, Micah saw curtains of rain and whitecaps on the water, revealing how tumultuous the sea was becoming.

While peering into the darkness, he worried if he was ready to face what lay ahead.

Chapter 26
Journey Begins

Micah's dreams that night were processions of doom. He dreamed of flying in stormy clouds, being chased in sewers by rabid gompums, and visions of fire. At the crescendo, the dream of Micah pedaling his bicycle in the forest with Richard returned. Once again, he outpaced his friend up the hill. When he coasted back down, Richard was waiting in the middle of the road.

From under his tattered yellow jacket, Richard produced a worn cigar box and presented it to Micah. Micah instantly recognized Mariam's pencil box from elementary school, adorned with flower stickers.

"Don't forget this before you leave," Richard said.

Micah awoke. He mused over the dream before curiosity led him down to Mariam's bedroom. He looked over the many books she'd collected in elementary school. At the end of a row of Nancy Drew novels was the old cigar box.

There was nothing unusual about the box, but inside, Micah found a single chewed-over number 2 pencil resting on top of a small diary. Thumbing through the diary, he found the pages empty. He wrote his name on the first page, and nothing unusual happened.

Because the dream had been so vivid, he was determined. Attempting to erase his name, he discovered the eraser was Deity Stone painted with pink fingernail polish. He spent several minutes trying to decipher the meaning of the pencil and the diary. Finally, he resorted to using the Urmin Stone. The word *sleep* appeared. Flustered, he tossed everything into the steamer trunk his mother had got him for school. He'd think about it more later.

Sunday was hard. His mother bawled all day. Though they never discussed it, the worry over Micah going off to school clearly troubled Lorna.

Later that day, Kimble drove Micah to Richard's house for his last paper delivery. As was typical, Richard was waiting with the papers already folded, playing "Count On Me" on his off-tune piano. Kimble drove Micah and Richard on their paper route that afternoon. It was bittersweet for Micah to spend his last few hours with his best friend.

At the end of their route, Richard threw a paper a little too hard and it landed deep in a tall shrub. Richard walked around the prickly shrub with a frown. After several moments, Kimble told Micah to go help him.

Alone, the boys worked together to retrieve the paper.

"Remember that dream where we saw your sister?" Richard casually said as he finally got hold of the paper.

"I knew you were there!" Micah said.

"I *was* there. That wasn't the first time I've talked to your sister in a dream. She's told me everything about what happened to her. She said your life will be in danger if you go to Astoria."

Micah glanced back at his father in the car. "I'm not supposed to talk about this with you."

Richard nodded. "It's all a big secret, I know. But you have to go. You are going to be her only hope of seeing home again."

Micah raised a brow. "Are you really Richard? You never look for trouble."

"This is different. Some things are worth being brave for. Your sister is one of them. She had a message for you."

"What?"

Richard, who never made eye contact, looked squarely into Micah's eyes and said, "Don't be afraid."

"Hey, you boys get that paper?" Kimble called from the car.

Richard held up the paper in his hand. "It's right here, Mr. Fennly." He walked it over to the porch and placed it on the door mat that read *Home Sweet Home*.

As the boys walked back to the car, Richard said quietly, "I'll always be your best friend. You be careful."

Dropping Richard off back home, Micah fought back tears as

he waved goodbye. Standing on the porch, Richard yelled, "Hey! Don't forget about the paper route tomorrow!"

Kimble chuckled as they drove away. "I love that kid. I hope you appreciate Richard. He's a good friend."

*   *   *

It was Monday morning, 4:30 a.m. Micah awoke to the sound of a thud. He felt Grubb under the covers. Lying in the darkness, he wondered if it had been his imagination.

There was another thud, and the closet door creaked open, revealing a dark figure stirring among Micah's whisking shirts.

"Aaaaah!" Micah screamed, leaping out of his bedroom.

Kimble and Lorna met Micah running down the stairs. They were already dressed.

"There's someone in my closet!" Micah cried, ducking behind his father.

A dark-haired boy came to the railing, looking bewildered and confused. He stopped when he saw Lorna, Kimble, and Micah looking up at him.

"What's going on?" the boy said, rubbing his eyes.

"He's naked and he looks like me!" Micah cried.

"It's alright, son," Kimble chuckled, hugging Micah.

"Young man, march right back in that bedroom and put some clothes on!" Lorna said, bounding up the stairs. She followed Micah's twin back to the bedroom. "Oh, my word! Look at this mess—it will be cleaned today. Oh, shoo, you two!"

Grubb and his dachshund twin came running down the stairs and into the kitchen.

"So that's my twin that came from that clay?" Micah asked.

Kimble nodded. "You won't see him much. He'll live here while you do your schooling in Astoria. Nobody will know the better. Is your trunk ready to go?"

Micah nodded. "Mom helped me."

"After today, you're not going to have your mother to look after you."

"So I don't even come home for the weekends?" Micah asked.

"No. You're going to be far from the gate. It's a week's journey by ship to get to Boshii Campus—"

"Micah, you need to get ready," Lorna called.

Kimble motioned Micah away. Micah stepped cautiously into his bedroom. His mother was muttering to herself as she gathered a pile of laundry. Micah's twin was wearing a pair of pajamas and was preparing to go back to bed.

"Hello, my name is Micah," the twin said, extending his hand.

"Don't be rude, Micah. Shake his hand," Lorna said.

"We're supposed to shake hands whenever we meet. That's what Mom said," Micah's twin said.

When their hands touched, a flood of memories rushed into Micah's mind. His twin's memories were very odd. He had spent the entire Sunday in Micah's closet sleeping with Grubb's twin. A strong recollection of the smell of shoes filled his mind. While in the Nikola sewers, Micah had cut himself. That same scratch was now on the hand of his twin.

"Jeez, your day was way more interesting than mine," the twin yawned. "Shut off the light when you leave. I've got school in a couple of hours."

Micah's twin whistled and a moment later, Grubb's twin dashed into the bedroom. He leaped into the bed and burrowed down in the covers. Micah looked around his bedroom one last time and shut the light off.

After breakfast, Micah sat on his black steamer trunk with

Grubb. His parents joined him with rain slickers in hand.

"Put this on," Lorna said.

"Why do I need this?" Micah asked.

"It's raining in Astoria." She motioned to the strange clock on the wall. Some of the lights were blinking.

"Well, son, today is the beginning of a new life. How do you feel?" Kimble asked, admiring his son.

"Scared."

"That's a healthy attitude, for now. Are we ready?"

Micah's last memory of home was looking up to the second floor where he saw his twin crouched down, eavesdropping.

*   *   *

Steel-gray clouds loomed overhead as the *Seaworthy* set down on Promontory Point. From the air, Micah had a good view of the grounds. Broken tree limbs and shrubs were scattered everywhere. Crates and barrels were neatly stacked near Alfred's mansion. Canvas tents were set up and being inspected. Some classmates had already arrived and were unloading their things.

Armin was the first to greet Micah. "Mornin', my sewer roaming friend. Had a good night's rest, I hope?"

Micah flashed a crooked smile, "I've slept better."

Micah and his parents unloaded his trunk and bags from the *Seaworthy*. Armin and Pearl helped unload Stu and Gertie's equipment.

"Lovely morning! Put your things in the pile," Hawkins said, greeting Micah's parents with outstretched arms and a hearty laugh.

"Where's Alfred this morning?" Lorna asked.

"We've been having quite a storm. He and Quinn are down at the *Darby*, checking her over with Melbourne. They should be back anytime. We haven't seen a storm like this in years."

The remainder of the students arrived over the next half hour. By the time everyone had gathered, a drizzle was coming down.

There was an awkward silence between the brightlings. Micah and Wren had the advantage of being the only friends. Stu loosely tagged along as the odd boy but quickly warmed up when the three began chasing Grubb around the field. Occasionally, they had to stop to let Stu recover as he wheezed and coughed.

"Allergies," Stu said, catching his breath.

The girls started off a bit more rocky. Sariah and Tiyana argued over whose bags were whose. From the outset, it was clear they were both strong-willed. Lilly Marshall and Gertie Pepper clung to their parents, reluctant to mingle with the others.

Pearl and Armin organized the students into groups for chores. The brightlings moved supplies from Alfred's porch out onto the grounds. Hawkins held back chatting with parents.

Repulsive squeals came when Armin directed the boys to move cages of insects and small animals. There were beetles, cockroaches, centipedes, flies, and spiders—all larger and different from any the children had seen before. Micah was proud to explain the death beetles to his curious friends. Armin meticulously inventoried everything.

Alfred arrived and welcomed the families. He summarized the curriculum for the next three months and answered questions. In the end, he thanked the parents for coming and assured them their children would be well cared for.

When the time came for parents to depart, there wasn't a dry eye.

Kimble and Lorna embraced Micah, wished him well, and told him to mind Alfred's instructions. Lorna then went through a litany of things for Micah to remember.

"Don't wander off… Don't go looking for trouble…"

"I know, I know," Micah sighed.

"Be sure to write to us, son. We'll expect a letter once a week," Kimble said, embracing him one last time.

Gertie's parents were the last to leave. They hugged goodbye so many times that Wren started counting. With great reluctance, they left, and Wren declared the final tally as fifteen hugs.

The rain was coming down steadily, pattering the jungle of trees surrounding Alfred's home. Clouds were growing black as the minutes passed.

Alfred climbed the steps of his porch and clanged a dinner bell dangling from a chain. "Welcome to my home, young'uns!"

Twisting his mustache, he gazed confidently over his new class. The rain dribbled down the edge of his fedora.

"You're my thirteenth class I'll have the honor of leading into this wondrous world. I've gone over each of your histories, and I do believe this year could be one of our finest. I'm not much for speeches. I'm confident your parents have discussed the dangers here, so I'm not going to bore you with those details for now. But I do have three ground rules I want you all to follow.

"First, I expect you to get along. I don't like fighting. You seven are stuck together. I expect you to make the best of it. If we have problems, there are plenty of chores to take the fight out of you. Second, follow orders. You young'uns are here to learn, and we're not here to babysit. We'll encounter hard times. The sooner we establish trust, the better. I've taken classes through some mighty difficult scrapes. We got through those times because my class learned to trust.

"Lastly, no complaining. You'll be soft at first, but we'll work on that together. I believe it's good to be a little hungry, a little cold, a little afraid. You get too comfortable here and that's when

314

trouble comes along.

"We had a brief encounter last Saturday, but let's make this official. While on land, you may refer to me as Alfred. While at sea, you refer to me as Captain. You all met Chief Sterling Hawkins and Counselor Grace Mulgrew. These are my senior staff and good friends. You will address them as Chief Hawkins and Counselor Grace. Together, we plan the curriculum for the year."

Alfred jumped off the porch and wrapped his arms around his two younger staff members.

"These two were my students last year, and they graduated. This is Armin Broom, and this lovely lady is Pearl Gypsum."

The two greeted the class with enthusiastic nods.

"You met Junior Officer Quinn Higgins. He graduated last year from the Golden Monkey. I'm a good friend of his mother. He's on an errand at the moment but will be along shortly. Quinn will be over you boys, and Pearl here over you ladies."

Micah remembered Pearl well. Even wearing the long drab rain slicker with the big floppy hat, Pearl was perhaps the prettiest girl Micah had ever seen. When their eyes met, he looked away.

"And this fine young man," Alfred said, patting Armin's shoulders, "is our beast master trainer. Among his many talents, he has a great deal of insight into the animal kingdom of Astoria. He'll be your favorite uncle. I expect you all to treat my junior staff with the same courtesies you treat us. Now, this year, I have a smaller class, and I'm missing three of my junior staff. But we'll make a good run at this, and it's going to be a great year."

A crack of thunder came from the darkening sky.

"This storm has put us behind schedule. We need to get everything down to *Miss Darby* before this storm lets loose again."

Loud squawking came. Penelope and Twitch flew over Alfred's home using their orange hornbill disguises. They looped wildly around the class. Chasing the two came a large clumsy bird with enormous wings.

"Made it!" Penelope cried, transforming midair into her tiny-person self. She landed on Alfred's shoulder, using the brim of his hat to protect herself from the rain. "Keep going, Twitch! Bosco will wear out eventually!" she shouted.

"Penelope! I told you to leave him alone!" Twitch cawed as he frantically flapped into the trees with Bosco screeching after him.

"Oh, yes, and who could forget about Penelope and Twitch?" Alfred said.

The brightlings gathered around to get a better look at Penelope. They'd all heard about Wren and Micah's harrowing adventure in the Nikola sewers. To see Penelope for themselves had them spellbound.

As the rain picked up, Alfred had the class gather their things. The brightlings loaded their arms with bags, waiting for directions on where to go.

"My, this bunch has been trained real proper, Oregon style, haven't they?" Hawkins chuckled.

"They certainly have," Alfred grinned.

"Are we doing something wrong?" Sariah asked.

Alfred tapped Armin on the shoulder. Armin invited Micah over to a crate where they had the insects. He withdrew a cage containing a hairless spotted spider the size of Micah's fist. "Yes, Alice here will do."

"Do what?" Micah said, eyeing the spider warily. He wasn't particularly fond of spiders.

"This is Alice. She's a Torlean tarantula, an ancient cousin to the Oregonian variety," Armin said, opening the cage.

Micah backed away. His eyes widened at the sight of the inch-long fangs.

Armin coaxed Alice out of the cage. When the spider emerged, it revealed its long, spindly legs that gently crawled onto Armin's outstretched hand. Gerty and Wren hastily retreated behind the pile of bags while the others drew near, fascinated by the creature.

Armin motioned Micah forward. "Put your hands out. Be gentle, and move slowly."

Alice's crept onto Micah's hands. His skin crawled feeling her spiky claws.

"That's it, Micah," Alfred congratulated. "Now, class, what I am about to show you is a very old mode of travel used for centuries here. I believe you will find it entertaining." He bent over Alice and cupped his hands around her. He whispered and took in a deep breath. Holding it, he stepped to the pile of bags and exhaled.

For several moments, everyone stared at the bags like they were going to explode.

"Nothing happened," Tiyana said.

Alfred smiled, straightening his fedora.

A billowing mist rose out of the bags. Suddenly, one of them flipped over in front of Wren like popcorn. Then another, and another.

Wren and Gertie found themselves in the middle of the excitement. "They're growing legs!" they shrieked, scattering in terror. Wren ran straight into a tree, much to Penelope's amusement.

There was a grotesque crackling as Torlean tarantula legs budded out of the bags. Soon, the pile of bags were creeping about.

Grubb cautiously sniffed at one of the crawling backpacks made of maw hide. When Grubb pounced on it, the backpack scampered off.

Armin picked up a small pouch that belonged to Tiyana. It had fallen out of her mini-pack and sprouted tiny legs. He held it in his hand. The bag rose up like it was going to attack, but its lack of fangs did little more than bring a titter of laughter from Sariah and Tiyana.

"This way, class," Alfred said, leading them to the school across the field.

The bags followed. The smaller bags moved quickly, nipping at each other. The large bags and crates lumbered along with legs as thick as tree limbs.

Micah held back with Armin and Stu to get Wren to his feet. Seeing the creeping bags, he started to run away.

"Take it easy," Armin said.

It took all three to keep Wren heading in the right direction. Pearl also had to prod Gertie out of her hiding place.

The company stopped at the school's corner door. The bags and supplies gathered nearby, and some started to crawl up the three-story wall.

The door burst open, and Quinn straightened himself, out of breath. He was wearing the same drab rain slicker and holding a length of rope with a metal ball fastened at the end.

"Just in time, Quinn. Would you and Penelope mind seeing after the bags while I show the others around?" Alfred said.

Penelope squealed as she leaped off Alfred's shoulder. She bound over bushes and clambered up to Quinn's shoulder, hugging him tightly around the neck. "I love you, Quinn," she said, rubbing his cheek.

Quinn rolled his eyes and stepped down into the middle of the bags. He shook the rope and the ball began to buzz. Dropping it to the ground, he walked away from the school, pulling the rope and ball along like a strange, vibrating pet.

The bags pursued in a frenzy. The smaller ones pounced like they were catching prey. Penelope changed back into the hornbill raven and pecked at the more stubborn bags to get them moving.

The odd herd followed Quinn off into the jungle.

Alfred led the class into the school, where a deep, resonant hum greeted them. A brass plaque on the wall read *Welcome to Quentin Academy. Leave your fears at the door.*

Occasionally, a sharp buzz of electricity pierced the air, followed by a deep rumbling from beneath the earth. Alfred guided the company toward the source of the rumble, leading them to a stop at the foyer's entrance. The brightlings gazed with wonder at what lay before them.

The floor had amber stone laid in geometrical patterns. In the center of the expanse was a great spherical metal cage with a lightning storm heart. Violent tendrils of purple and blue lightning sizzled out of the cage. Embedded in the granite walls and scattered about were odd bits of junk like car tires, twisted metal, stuffed animals, and chunks of stone.

Most startling, however, were the hundreds of ghostly figures emerging from and being consumed by the lightning. Whispering and hiss-like voices echoed in the great hall. An especially bright burst of light exploded from the heart of the machine, causing a deep rumble. Briefly, the glow of the apparitions intensified.

"This is the gate," Alfred said proudly. "It's this marvel of nature that brought you and me together today. Each of you passed through this portal this morning."

The children stared with fascination at the ghostly apparitions for a long while.

"What's all the junk in here?" Stu asked.

"The gate is a force of nature and is prone to collect debris. We've got a whole museum in the next room. Occasionally, we have to shut down to clean up."

"Could you set the gate to different times besides the one we came from?" Sariah asked.

"There's a little wiggle room, perhaps an hour or so. But the more we've tried to interfere, the more unstable the time connection behaves. That's why you'll find bits of history lying around here. It's a force greater than we fully understand, and it can have a mind of its own. Sometimes, it hiccups. But like clockwork, it always has reliably connected Astoria to the modern timeline you young'uns are familiar with."

"What if it stopped working? Couldn't we get trapped here?" Gertie asked.

"Unlikely. It's been going for a hundred years."

"But how would we get home if something went wrong?" Gertie said with a hint of alarm in her voice.

"Now, now, Miss Pepper. Don't let that imagination of yours run away here. I promise no matter what happens, you'll see your mother again. Understand?"

Gertie relaxed. Alfred led the class to another room off the foyer. The walls that partitioned the adjacent classrooms had been knocked down, forming a single long room. Piles of jewelry, old computers, weapons, and thousands of other odd bits littered the floor.

Micah went to a pile of swords and withdrew a scimitar with a polished blade and brass handle. Carelessly, he slid his thumb over the sharp edge.

"Ouch!" he cried, seeing a sliver of red appear.

"It's real," Alfred said. "Got it off a Turkish soldier years ago. Pearl, could you see to his cut?"

Pearl withdrew a small pouch from around her neck. She removed a vial and poured a few drops of orange liquid onto Micah's cut.

"That stings!" Micah yelped.

"It will heal quickly," Pearl said, blowing on the cut.

Micah was mesmerized by Pearl's delicate touch. Her hair smelled of cherry vanilla, and he began to blush.

Pearl studied Micah's reddening face for a moment. She smiled back with a wide, toothy grin as she secured the vial back in her pouch. She patted Micah on the head and went back to Counselor Grace's side.

Micah ignored Wren, who was wagging his eyebrows at him.

"This brings up an important issue, class," Alfred said. "If any of you are injured, report to one of us immediately. Your immune systems will need to catch up. You young'uns will encounter sickness and disease none of your bodies are ready to deal with. Each of the staff carry medical kits and will take care of common injuries. But Counselor Grace here is our specialist as our chief medical officer."

"Do you have anything for…" Stu said, finishing with a loud sneeze. "Allergies?"

"Of course," Counselor Grace said. She rummaged in a pouch under her rain slicker. She removed a pill from a bottle and pinched it under Stu's nose. A whitish powder burst from the pill. "Breathe deeply. We'll have you take another dose later today."

The class fanned out, looking over the debris piles down the immense hall. Sariah stepped over to the wall where a series of plaques and awards hung. "What are all these awards?" she asked.

Alfred wandered behind the students who gathered with Sariah. "Oh, these are a few things my classes have picked up over the years," he said, brightening. He glanced sideways at his new class.

Chief Hawkins scoffed, stepping next to Alfred. "Don't let Alfred's modesty fool you. These represent our life's work. Every year, the top five classes are awarded for achievement. Look at the years. 1966, 1972, 1978. Every one of our classes has received top honors."

Along the wall hung many photos sealed in gold frames. The pictures reminded Micah of those taken in elementary school. The first photo was a picture of a brightling class filled with young, bewildered faces. The second was of the same class after they grew up, confident and strong. In every class, the junior staff was different. But Alfred, Chief Hawkins, and Counselor Grace were notably consistent in each picture. They hadn't aged a day, even after all the years.

Micah looked for the Fennly name. Sure enough, there were Fennlys all the way down the line until he reached the class of 1966. There was something different about this picture. There was Alfred, Counselor Grace, and Chief Hawkins…

Micah paused. That wasn't Hawkins in the picture. There was another man; an older man wearing a red baseball cap.

"Is that Bassam?"

"Yes, it is," Alfred said. "Bassam was my Chief Officer in my early years in Astoria. He later became a captain heading up his own ship. We had a mutually beneficial arrangement. He taught me how to master the Fire and I helped him learn to captain a ship. He's like a father to me."

The last class was the class of 1960. 1960 was the only year with no awards, but it did have the pictures. Micah spotted his father. He was young and easily could have been mistaken for Micah. In the graduating photo, however, there were several of the older students missing, and the rest looked like they had gone through a war. Micah's father had a head bandage and a cast on his arm. Others looked just as banged up. The photo noted that four of the twelve students were missing.

"What happened to my dad in this photo?"

Alfred and Counselor Grace exchanged a brief glance. "It's a long story, Micah. We had a few accidents—kind of kinks in the curriculum, if you will. But to be fair, it was my rookie year," Alfred said.

"Kinks in the curriculum?" chuckled Counselor Grace.

From the hall, there came a loud crash followed by the deep, throaty growl of a car engine revving up. A car horn began to blare angrily. There was a moment of confusion among the students. Alfred motioned for Armin to investigate. A few moments later, Armin returned.

"You've got to see this," Armin said.

Back in the gateway chamber, the class found a blue Bel Air convertible that had crashed into the rock wall. A stunned man in a business suit was at the wheel. Seeing the class approach, the man panicked, throwing the car into reverse, crunching into a pile of rocks and nearly hitting Counselor Grace.

"Scuse me, fella," the wobbly man said, staggering out of the car. He carried a sloshing bottle of whiskey in one hand, trying to cinch up his tie with the other.

Micah struggled to hold Grubb back on his leash as he stretched to sniff the inebriated man.

"Wow! I've never seen such an ugly dog in my life," the man slurred, balancing himself on the rear of his car. "Can any of you tell me how to get to San Francisco? I'm late for a party."

Counselor Grace scowled at the man. "You should be ashamed of yourself. You could kill someone."

"What are you, my mother?"

"If I were your mother, I would lock you in a room with a hag maw until it beat some sense in you."

"Are you a cop?" the man said with a cheesy grin.

"Sir, what year is it?" Alfred asked.

The man thought, swaying on his heels, finally blurting out, "1961. What kind of sobriety test is this, anyway?"

The man became increasingly aware of his surroundings. He looked over the brightlings, finally meeting Hawkins' gaze, who nodded with a wide grin. He looked over his shoulder and saw the apparitions passing by and through him. He spun on his heel and fell back, his mouth agape.

"Enough of this foolishness," Grace spat. She reached into the car, yanking the keys from the ignition, and tossed them to Hawkins. "Away with you!"

At this, the car began to skid toward the gate. The drunk man began to shriek as he, too, was being drawn in. A sudden burst of lightning from the cage struck the car and the two became like the other ghostly apparitions glowing an intense blue. They shot into the lightning storm and were gone.

The class mused over the incident until Alfred finally declared it was time to leave.

Chapter 27
The Chat

The rain was coming down hard. The class tightened their raincoats and quickly headed down a cobbled path that led away from the school. Along the way, they passed orchards of apples and peach trees laden with fruit.

Twitch dove down from a tree, landing on Alfred's shoulder.

He turned back into his tiny self and ducked under Alfred's fedora for cover from the rain.

"My dad told me you invented the time machine. How'd you do it?" Stu asked.

"Ha!" Chief Hawkins guffawed, surprising the brightlings. "Mark the time, Alfred—two minutes. I won the bet this year."

"The bet?" Stu asked.

"On how soon that question would come out, Mr. Fennly," Alfred said.

"Oh, is that a secret?" Stu said, now feeling foolish.

"No, it's a perfectly normal question, but let's get out of this rain first."

The company hurried along until they entered a dense jungle of tangled vines and leaves. Among the verdant foliage, vibrant purple and red flowers stood out. Somewhere hidden within the undergrowth, the burbling of a river could be heard.

Despite the relentless downpour, the jungle provided some respite from the torrential rain.

"So, where were we? Yes, the time machine. It's not entirely accurate to say I invented a time machine. It's more of a gateway. The force that connects the two time periods was already there. I just punched a hole in it and walked across. It was purely by accident I discovered it at all."

"How did you find it?"

"Back when I was younger, I had a hobby of toying with electricity. Have you young'uns ever heard of Nikola Tesla?"

"He was an inventor," Lilly said from the back. "He made inventions using electricity."

"That's right, Lilly. He was one of my idols in my younger days. I first met Nikola on a trip back east in New York back in 1910. This was after his work in Colorado Springs, you see. We had dinner together, and we started up a correspondence that went on for years. He was a man before his time. I was captivated by his work regarding the transmission of electrical energy without wires. It was Mr. Tesla who put me on the path. I built his machine—well, part of it, anyway. I even invited him out to show him my progress. That was around 1918, and he was thrilled. But he never made it. It was a complicated time, you see, with the war on as it was…"

"Was that the Great War with the Rashaar?" Micah interrupted.

"No, that was—" Alfred said, cutting off.

Counselor Grace looked sideways at Micah and then stopped abruptly. "Who told you about the Great War and the Rashaar?" she demanded.

All eyes turned on Micah.

Micah was surprised at Counselor Grace's reaction. Crowther had shared his war stories on the first day they'd met, long before Micah had the ring or ever heard of Astoria. It didn't seem like much of a secret to him.

"Well, uh. I heard it from… I thought he was crazy until I got my ring. He told me about the Rashaar—"

"Stop right there, young man," Counselor Grace said with an edge to her voice. She glanced over to Alfred with a frown. "You said *he* told you. Who's *he*? Was it your father? Was it *Twitch*?"

"Hey, it wasn't me!" Twitch spat.

Micah shook his head.

"It was Morty Crowther," Alfred said, looking thoughtfully at Micah.

"Crowther? Why, I didn't know that ol' windbag was still alive," Hawkins said.

"Isn't he the one from the paper route you and Richard are always complaining about?" Wren asked.

Micah nodded.

"I'll be sure to have the authorities have a talk with Mr. Crowther," Counselor Grace said, shaking her head.

Alfred, with Twitch smoldering on his shoulder, stepped between Counselor Grace and Micah. "You others move along while I have a chat with Micah."

Armin took Grubb's leash from Micah, leading away Wren and Stu down the path.

"What's the Rashaar?" both Gertie and Lilly asked, looking worried.

Pearl wrapped her arms around Gertie and Lilly, following Armin.

"Never mind that, now. Move along," Counselor Grace said, locking eyes with Sariah. Sariah and Tiyana refused to leave until Grace broke out her withering scowl. As they stalked away, Chief Hawkins followed with a chuckle, easing the tension.

Twitch glared at Micah.

"You too, Twitch. I need a word with Micah alone."

"Fine. But I didn't say nothin'!"

Twitch changed into the orange hornbill, cursing as he flew away.

"Micah, I want you to understand, you aren't in trouble. But let's get something straight. This creates a bit of a situation. It's a tad irresponsible that Crowther discussed these things in depth with you. What all did he tell you?"

"He told stories about when he was a soldier. We tried to avoid him because he seemed crazy."

"Who's we?"

"Me and my friend."

"Richard Sommers?"

Micah nodded.

"And what did Mr. Sommers think?"

"He was just as irritated as I was. If Crowther got us on his porch, he'd keep us for hours."

"So none of this ever sunk in with Richard?"

"No. We thought he was just crazy. I didn't even know he was a Massanite until after I realized he had a Hem Ring."

"Morty's not crazy. He's misunderstood, that's all—and very brave. It's thanks to the likes of him that you young ones aren't off in some slave camp somewhere. It's unfortunate he had to be re-located to Oregon. He was becoming a liability."

"Slave camp?"

"Now there you go. You got me talking too. It's no secret now that you kids have stumbled into something much bigger than you realize. Part of our duty as your teachers is to teach you brightlings of your history and introduce you to the realities of where you came from. Tell me, what did Crowther tell you about the Rashaar?"

"He mainly told war stories. He talked about being chased by armies that used earthquakes and tornadoes as weapons."

"My, my. You and Crowther did have a little chat, didn't you?"

"There's something else," Micah said, feeling around his neck. He pulled over his head a silver bead chain with the black pebble. He passed it to Alfred. "I got this from Penelope and Twitch."

After Micah explained that the pebble was Mariam's locket, Alfred smiled. "Those two can be taught. I showed them how to hide it." Raising his hand, he brought it down in a forceful clap onto the pebble. When he took his hand away, Mariam's locket rested in his palm.

Micah grinned. "Inside, there's a coin. My sister, Tricia, told me it's a royal coin of the Rashaar."

Alfred removed the coin and briefly glanced at it. "You know,

Micah, I know all about what happened to Mariam. I discussed with your parents if we should reconsider having you enter the program this year. But your parents, especially your father, felt it was important for you to face this." Alfred waved the coin at Micah. "I know this was hard for you."

Micah nodded. "That's an ankh, see? So are the Rashaar Egyptian?" he asked.

Alfred grinned, giving Micah an understanding nod. "Well, the Rashaar aren't Egyptian. That's a common misconception you young'uns have. It was a misconception of your grandparents, as well. I remember the discovery of Tutankhamun's tomb. That was in 1922. When your ancestors saw the treasures ol' Carter hauled out of the Valley of the Kings, your people about packed up and went home. They figured the Rashaar were in Oregon as well. That's back when I met Onitah."

"Onitah? That's my middle name," Micah said.

"Yes, it is. It's also the name of your grandfather."

"No, my grandfather's name was Ernest Fennly. Onitah was his middle name. He died when my dad was young."

"Ernest Fennly was the name he chose later. He, along with the others who settled in Oregon, decided it best to adopt English as their new language, along with new names. But your grandfather's name was Onitah."

"Really? You knew my grandpa?"

"I did. He was a great man—and strong, like all the Massanites are. They were desperate in the beginning. I don't know if I believe in fate or destiny, but they sure believed I was an answer to their prayers when I showed up. As slaves, they were mighty humble—"

"My grandpa was a slave?"

Alfred nodded. "They all were, in the beginning. They'd been running and fighting long before I showed up. That's what all that talk of the Great War was about." He handed the coin and locket back to Micah and pointed at the coin. "To the Egyptians, this symbol means eternal life. But to the Rashaar, the ankh is their symbol. To them, it means *creators of eternal life*."

Micah was astonished.

"It's troubled me for years too. To my reckoning, it has something to do with the time gate. The Egyptians didn't have Deity Stone, at least as far as we've ever discovered. But there's a connection there somehow."

Alfred removed his fedora and shook the rain off. Running his fingers through his thick chestnut-brown hair, he looked down the pathway for the class. They had disappeared in the jungle. He plopped his hat back on and thought for a moment.

"Well, shucks, Micah. This little chat has been enlightening. I don't think there's any real harm done here. You're a strong young man who I think can carry the burden. But I want you to keep these things quiet for now—from the others, that is."

"But don't they deserve to know?" Micah said.

"They do, and they will soon enough. But we have a great deal to get through over the next while. I'm going to have a boat full of homesick children. They'll be sick, tired, and afraid enough without this information."

"So what do I say when they ask?"

"You tell 'em you don't know anything."

"But I do."

"You *think* you know. But you have no idea what's waiting for us out there," Alfred said, stroking his mustache. "Come, let's move on."

Micah and Alfred jogged down the trail and caught up with the class.

"You in trouble?" Wren whispered.

Micah could feel Counselor Grace's eyes on the back of his head. He glanced back and sure enough, she was glaring at him.

"No."

Fortunately, Grubb had become the center of attention. There was rustling in the shrubs off the path that Grubb found impossible to ignore. He would pounce on the leaves, causing a fit of giggles from the brightlings—except for Gertie, who wasn't enjoying Grubb's antics at all.

"Are there dinosaurs here that can hurt us? My mom says they're very dangerous," Gertie said, wringing her hands.

Armin looked back. "None that are too dangerous. I spotted a few jak maws and spine eaters. If you ignore them, they'll ignore you. Just don't do something stupid like surprise or chase them."

"Just remember, class. You can't really say you've lived in Astoria 'til you've been chased by something twice your size. Then you'll really know what it means to live," Chief Hawkins said cheerfully.

Pearl laughed at Armin. "Like that time you ran into that nest of nettle maws. They must have chased you for miles!"

Armin burst out laughing. Gertie moaned, wringing her hands more desperately. Counselor Grace cleared her throat, and the company fell silent.

They followed the winding trail that stretched the length of the island. Eventually, the trail led them to a steep stairway that descended to the base of a rugged mountain ridge with sharp peaks. As the group descended, Alfred halted the class at the jagged entrance of a cave.

"Brightlings, this is one of my favorite moments. I want to introduce you to Belmont Cavern, named after my father." He stepped aside inviting them in proudly.

The cave went in ten feet before meeting up with a rickety

landing of wooden planks. The landing was three yards deep, following the edge of the cavern. It connected to a natural trail in the rock that zigzagged down the cavern wall. The landing bowed between thick wooden trunks driven into the wall. A series of thick ropes added additional support and served as a crude guardrail. The landing was wobbly and bounced unnervingly as the company stepped onto the wooden planking.

They looked over a natural cavern that plummeted to the sea below. Great craggy pillars of rock rose from the calm sea in the lagoon. There was a constant roar from falls formed from the rain. Long, twisty vines hung down from wide fissures in the ceiling, revealing sections of the cloudy sky.

Below, anchored in the sparkling sapphire lagoon, was a great galleon, her three masts spearing upward. A large crimson flag hung from the center mast bearing a blazing sun. The sun wasn't just stitched in the flag. The sun was a ball of fire that radiated brilliant light in the cavern. The cavern was spacious enough that the entire ship had room to maneuver and was protected from the rain. Leading out to the galleon was a dock with numerous crates and barrels stacked neatly near the ship.

Miss Darby's horn blew, echoing up the great cavern.

The sound of the horn brought a smile to Micah. He recognized the sound from that day at Hermit Cove.

Micah, Stu, Lilly, and Sariah all bravely hung over the rope, admiring the view.

"Wren, come look. It's amazing!" Micah said.

"Micah, get away from there. You're gonna fall!" Wren cried, unwilling to even set foot on the wooden landing. Tiyana had ventured a few steps out but was being held back by Gertie, who had grabbed Tiyana by the trousers.

Chief Hawkins marched out onto the landing, causing it to bob up and down.

"Please, please stop!" Wren bawled, falling to his knees. He wrapped his arms tightly around a rock.

"It's perfectly safe, Mr. Kinglsey," Hawkins said, jumping up and down. The landing bucked and lurched violently.

Micah and Stu pretended they were going to fall, grabbing the thick rope.

Sariah rolled her eyes and went to help Tiyana pry Gertie off her leg. Gertie grabbed Sariah in a death grip and began to shriek. Wren had a complete meltdown.

"Alright, Mr. Hawkins, you've had your fun," Counselor Grace said. Both she and Pearl went to work calming the two irate children.

"I guess you two really are afraid of heights. There's always a couple, aren't there?" Hawkins said, his bellowing laugh echoing in the cavern.

Alfred led the company down the precarious way. It took a great deal of coaxing to get Wren to even step a toe on the landing.

Counselor Grace showed no sympathy to Hawkins, who was charged with the task of bringing Wren and Gertie down to the *Darby*.

After five minutes of pleading, begging, and demanding, Hawkins' patience was spent. He grabbed the two and threw them over his shoulder. The pair screamed the entire way down as he ran to the bottom.

Chapter 28
Miss Darby

The galleon loomed impressively large before the class. At the front, below the bowsprit, the name *Miss Darby* was carved in delicate script. Ropes ran in different directions between her three masts. The main mast in the center was the tallest, with ladder roping strung from the hull up to the crow's nest high above. Most of *Miss Darby*'s hull was made of redwood, with the upper portion stained light honey. There was fanciful imagery of cherubim chasing through wilderness carved along the upper edge of the hull. A figurehead of a sleek maw with sharp, powerful claws wrapped around the bowsprit. The ship gently bobbed in the clear water with a loosely tethered ramp leading up to her midsection.

"Class, I present to you my pride and joy, *Miss Darby*," Alfred said with a welcoming bow.

The brightlings gathered together, marveling at the towering ship. Wren, having recovered from the traumatic descent down the cavern, let out a whistle. "Whoa! I've had dreams about this ship."

Alfred had the class remove their rain slickers to let them dry on the railing. He helped Micah with Grubb. "Grubb won't need the leash on down here. He's been here before," Alfred winked.

A loud squawking echoed through the cavern as Bosco descended from above. He glided lazily round and round in the updraft of the cavern before diving down and landing with a flappy thud on *Miss Darby*'s bowsprit.

"Twitch! Twitch!" Bosco cawed.

"This is Last Chance Lagoon," Alfred said. "It's high tide now, so we'll spend the rest of the day loading the ship and giving orientation. We'll stay aboard *Miss Darby* tonight and set sail in the morning. The other classes are departing today from Nikola, which will put us a day behind. But the *Darby* is a fast ship. We should catch up to the convoy in a day or so."

Grubb sniffed the air. He suddenly raced down the ramp, disappearing on the dock.

"Grubb, come back!" Micah yelled.

"He'll be alright," Alfred said.

Chief Hawkins walked down the ramp and put his hands on his hips. At the bottom, he found the bags creeping on the dock. A few had retreated into the cracks in the cliff. "Why aren't these bags secured? Where's Quinn? Quinn!" he barked. His usual cheerful demeanor had been spent getting Wren and Gertie down the cavern. "Keep your eye out for the bags. There's lots of places they may have wandered off to."

"Hey, my bag's torn," Tiyana said, reaching for her duffle bag, but it retreated like a wounded animal.

"Look, somebody's clothes are floating in the water—wait, those are mine!" cried Sariah.

Armin stepped into a shed adjacent to the dock. He came back carrying a long pole with a hook. He stretched out over the water to retrieve the clothing and the duffle bag from the lapping water.

"Release!" Hawkins ordered.

All the bags plopped down instantly, their legs withering to dust.

"It's the perfume," Armin said, smelling the bag.

Alfred snapped his fingers, and his staff had his attention. "Look in the cracks and under the dock. I'm sure they're still around. Quinn, Melbourne, where are you?" Alfred shouted. "Pearl, Armin. Watch over the others. Hawkins and I will check the ship. Everyone, keep your eyes open."

"For what?" Micah asked.

"Gompums. There's been an outbreak of the little nasties this year," Armin said.

Micah and Wren looked nervously around.

"Melbourne!" Alfred shouted again. He climbed aboard the *Darby* and went below deck.

"Who's Melbourne?" Tiyana asked.

"He's the island keeper. He watches over the island while we're away—" Pearl said, cutting off when movement caught her eye.

From out of a wide crack, there came a squeal. A gompum, larger than Grubb, scampered out, running straight for the class. On its heels was Grubb.

Gertie screamed when she saw the gompum coming directly at her. Pearl leaped in the creature's path, knocking it off course with a powerful kick. She cried out in pain, grabbing her foot.

Grubb sank his teeth into the gompum's hind leg, and the two went down in a vicious fight. They broke apart, circling each other. The gompum growled, showing its jagged teeth. The membrane around Grubb's neck buzzed menacingly. The creature was now severely bleeding. It turned to run. Grubb charged, biting into its neck. The gompum flailed about but finally succumbed to Grubb's powerful bite.

Counselor Grace went to Pearl to examine her foot. When the brightlings stepped near the dying gompum, she commanded the class to stay back, motioning for Armin to take charge.

"I'm alright," Pearl winced as Grace felt Pearl's big toe. "These aren't the best shoes to go around kicking gompums with."

"You've fractured your toe, Pearl." Counselor Grace went over to a pile of bags crammed between the rocks. Rummaging through them, she withdrew a red bag with a cross on it. She quickly sifted through the content, finally removing what appeared to be a piece of black rubber.

Micah glanced in the medical bag. There was an odd assortment of vials, sticks, and rocks. There were many of the black rubber strips of different sizes and lengths.

"Sariah, come assist me. Take this maki, and don't touch the sticky side."

Grace gently removed Pearl's sock, revealing a swollen and red toe. She took the piece of maki and wrapped it around the injury.

Even though Pearl was in great pain, she remained silent. Micah was impressed.

Grace patted the loose parts of the maki flat. She laid her hand on Pearl's injured foot and closed her eyes. She muttered a few words Micah could not hear and released Pearl's foot. The brightlings watched, astonished, as the black bandage began to melt—more accurately absorbed into the foot. It completely vanished, leaving behind a perfectly healthy-looking toe.

Pearl put her socks and shoes back on. She stood and walked to test her foot. She hugged Counselor Grace.

"That may be tender, so take it easy the best you can," Grace said, zipping up the medical bag.

"C'mere, Micah. It's safe now," Armin said, motioning Micah over to Grubb and the gompum. He removed a towel and a vial of liquid from his mini-pack. He handed it to Micah. "This is niacrum. Grubb has been bitten and needs to be seen to. Take this and clean the wound. He won't like it, but these big gompums are poisonous, and their bite is fatal. In a few hours, Grubb could die if he isn't taken care of."

Grubb leaped to Micah and nuzzled into him. For as vicious as the fight had been, Grubb only had a small puncture in his leg.

Armin picked up the carcass by its scaly tail. The creature twitched, and Armin quickly tossed it into the bay, where it floated to the middle of the lagoon.

"Rakme! Rakme!" cried Bosco from the bowsprit.

The class looked out into the lagoon. From under the floating carcass swelled an enormous mouth full of teeth. It broke the surface, swallowing the gompum in a mighty chomp.

Gertie and Lilly screamed. "I want to go home! I want to go home!" cried Gertie.

Micah's heart leapt. He and the rest of the brightlings were standing on the dock near the water. The dark silhouette glided silently nearby. He ran back to the shore with Grubb in his arms.

Armin whistled. "Nice, that's a baby burly tip! Never seen one of those so close before."

The shark circled the lagoon, searching for other easy morsels. It was the largest shark Micah had ever seen.

Alfred and Hawkins appeared back on deck. Alfred jumped to the dock and followed the gliding dorsal fin. "We can't find Quinn or Melbourne. Any signs of them out here?" Alfred asked Counselor Grace.

Counselor Grace frowned. "Did you look for them like a typical man, or did you *really* look?"

Alfred flashed a less-than-amused face. "*Miss Darby*, I need to talk to you immediately."

The class looked at each other, confused. Alfred was talking to the ship.

"Look, there's a face in the wood!" cried Tiyana.

Descending the bow of the ship appeared the face of an aged woman. Her facial features extruded out of the wood like she had been carved.

"What is it, Alfred dear?" the face said softly in a lovely grandmotherly voice. *Miss Darby*'s face blended with the material her face moved over. Her eyes and facial expressions moved as naturally as if she was made of flesh.

"Have you seen Melbourne and Quinn?" Alfred asked.

"Certainly. They're lying down below in the forward hold. I think they're taking a nap."

Grace snorted with a satisfied nod.

"Is this the new class of brightlings?" *Miss Darby* said. "It's not a very large class this year, is it?"

"Never mind that now," Alfred said, running back aboard and

disappearing below.

"Why do all of you young ones look so frightened?" *Miss Darby* said, looking genuinely concerned.

The face slid across the wooden surfaces of the hull to look over the children. She grew warts and pockmarks as her face slid over knots in the wood and brass rivets. She stopped, noticing the dorsal fin gliding in the water.

"Oh, dear. Is that pesky shark bothering you? Shoo!"

A bright arc of electricity snapped out of the tip of the bowsprit, contacting the shark's fin. With a mighty splash, it thrashed out of the lagoon.

"There, there. You don't have to be afraid when Grandma Darby's around."

"She's nice," Gertie said, grinning at the others.

Soon, Chief Hawkins and Alfred emerged back on deck, helping Melbourne and Quinn off the ship.

"Oh, me head," Melbourne groaned. His gray hair hung in wet strands over his bleeding forehead.

Quinn had his arm around Hawkins, who led him to a thick post, where he sat. "Counselor, would you mind seeing to this?" Hawkins said.

Counselor Grace packed up her medical bag and examined Melbourne.

"What happened, Quinn?" Alfred said, agitated.

"The last thing I remember was Twitch coming down here upset. Penelope went off with him to calm him down. That's when I heard Melbourne aboard the ship yelling for help. He was in the hold, pinned down by a crate. I tried to get him out, but I forgot my gloves. So I had *Miss Darby* signal for help. That's when the ship got hit by something. I...I don't remember anything after that."

"The ship was hit?" Hawkins said. He ran along the deck, inspecting the timbers along the waterline. "No visible damage from here. I'll take a closer look this afternoon. The day's young, and we've already had excitement. This is shaping up to be a good day!"

"You alright, Melbourne?" Alfred asked. "Maybe we should get you back up to the house and have you lie down."

"Don'tcha be pamperin' me," Melbourne snapped, slapping Alfred's hand away. "There's work to be done, and don't you be thinkin' that poor old Melbourne has become a namby-pamby!"

"Well, class, you heard Melbourne. There's work to be done. Let's get to it."

Chapter 29
Preparations

The morning was spent loading *Miss Darby*, stowing the brightlings' things and the other cargo. The boys were tasked with loading the heavier items such as barrels of water, food provisions, and numerous anonymous crates.

The three boys were introduced to their hiking gloves, nicknamed grippers. The fingerless gloves were made of maw hide with thin wafers of redwood and shards of Deity Stone sewn into the back. The grippers enabled them to lift cargo many times heavier than they would have otherwise.

"This ship is great!" Micah told Wren as they together lugged a fifty-five-gallon barrel full of water down a flight of stairs into the lower hold. Stu followed, carrying a long crate.

The hold was the lowest floor of the *Darby*. The large room ran the ship's length, divided into sections. The cargo of barrels and crates was spread evenly between the sections to distribute the weight. Animals and living creatures were put in the middle of the hold. The walls were ribbed and covered with thick, dry tar. Rough-hewn trees served as support. The lighting was poor but made better with glowing crystals mounted on the timber. The hold smelled strongly of aged wood, tar, and earth.

"Why do we have to pack so many of these water barrels down here, anyway?" Wren asked.

"They're for ballast and drinking water," said Armin, coming down the stairs with a bundle of wooden beams. He dropped the beams and began sliding them into holes in the ceiling supports. "They stabilize the *Darby* while out at sea. How are things going with the loading?"

"Good, I guess. We put things where Chief Hawkins tells us. What's all this other stuff for?" Stu said, pointing to several crates they had previously loaded.

"Those are supplies we deliver to our destination. Rarely do ships head out to sea without cargo of one sort or another. Much of this is food."

"Oh."

"What kind of ship is this, anyway?" Micah asked.

"*Miss Darby* is a caravel-type ship. She was patterned after the *Santa Maria*, one of the three ships Christopher Columbus discovered America with: the *Santa Maria*, the *Pinta*, and the *Niña*. She's about the same size. Alfred commissioned her years ago and converted her to a spirit-class vessel."

"What's a spirit-class vehicle?"

"You've seen *Miss Darby*? She's the steward over the ship and does what she can to maintain and protect it. But most of her duties are related to navigation."

"Really?"

"Yup. She can set her sails, raise and lower the anchor, and remove the water she takes on. You know, the everyday things. If she were an ordinary ship, we'd need a crew of twenty to do those duties alone. She can also help you find your way around the ship."

"She can?" Micah asked.

"Miss Darby?" Armin called.

Miss Darby appeared on the sturdy center mast, her face clearly visible against its smooth surface. She looked thoughtfully around the hold. "May I help you, Explorer Broom? Have you finished your studies for the day?"

Armin frowned. "I'm not an explorer this year, *Miss Darby*. I graduated last year, remember? This year, I'm one of the counselors."

Miss Darby sighed. "Oh, that's right. I'm afraid my memory isn't what it once was."

"Have you met Micah, Stu, and Wren?"

"Yes, I've been watching them. Bright-eyed and cheerful, aren't you three? You've been very respectful to my timbers, which I always appreciate. And look at how well you have stowed the supplies. It's so important to secure supplies properly. Let me tell you a story that happened—"

"*Miss Darby*," Armin interrupted. "We have chores to get to. Would you be able to show the boys to their sleeping quarters?"

"Oh, of course, how thoughtless of me. Follow me." The face disappeared from the mast and reappeared near the steps. "Up this way, boys. Mind your step."

The four climbed to the middle deck of the ship. They had been passing through this room all morning, loading supplies. Compared to a house, it was small, about the width and length of a medium-sized front room. The ceiling was low. Stu, the tallest of the boys, could easily touch the ceiling.

Miss Darby appeared again on the mast that speared through all ship decks. Her face was bathed in light from outside. The large rectangular holes in the floor and ceiling allowed the loading of more oversized cargo. Once the ship was loaded, a heavy grating was put in place, letting light in but protecting the crew from accidentally falling into the hull.

"This is the great cabin, brightlings. Just remember your bearings. The front of the ship is called the bow, and the rear is the aft. Looking forward, the port side is to your left, and the starboard is to your right. You brightlings will be at the bow of the ship, and the leaders at the aft. Continue this way."

Miss Darby appeared down a narrow hallway on the forward mast. At her sides were two small doorways that entered the sleeping quarters. The boys followed and stepped into the two rooms, which were mirror copies of each other. They were cramped and sparse, curving inward as they followed the contour of the hull. There was a small nook at the narrow end. There were hooks screwed into the ceiling from which hung long bunches of netting. In both rooms, there was a small port that allowed in fresh air and sunlight.

Tiyana and Gertie happened by and saw the four boys. "What's down here?" Gertie said brightly.

"These are your bunk rooms," Armin said.

"These closets are our bedrooms?" Gertie said, shocked. "So which room will be mine?"

Miss Darby smiled at the two girls. "That's a good question, young lady. We've always had the girls stay in the port side room," she said, gesturing to the room Wren was standing in.

"We have to all *share* two rooms?" Wren and Gertie exclaimed simultaneously.

"Certainly not! You girls will be in this room and the boys in that one."

"But that's not fair. The boys only have three, and we have four girls," Tiyana said.

"Well, look on the bright side. Normally, we would have six girls and six boys. So this year, you will have plenty of room to spread out."

Gertie groaned. "My closet at home is bigger than this whole bedroom. What are we supposed to sleep on?"

"I can answer that," Armin said, stepping into the cabin. He pulled down one of the bunches of netting and hooked it between ceiling hooks, forming a hammock.

"You're joking!" the two girls cried.

"Alright!" the boys shouted. They rushed into their cabin and strung their hammocks enthusiastically. They grunted as they each tried to climb in, twisting and falling out several times, each bringing on fits of laughter.

Finally, Wren tangled himself up in the netting, swinging back and forth. "It's a piece of cake!" he said triumphantly.

Gertie and Tiyana peered in and sneered at the boys.

Quinn came up behind Armin, frowning. "Hey! We've got work

to do. If Counselor Grace sees you fooling around, she'll have you scrubbing the decks for a week. Wait. I'm the one in charge of chores. Maybe I should have you three scrub the decks for the week."

Micah and Stu both rushed out of the room. Poor Wren was hopelessly twisted up, requiring Quinn's and Armin's assistance.

"Ha!" Gertie and Tiyana shouted, squealing away.

*   *   *

The storm worsened. The wind howled through the cavern. The crashing of the waves outside sounded ominous and dangerously close. Even in the safety of Last Chance Lagoon, the *Darby* still rocked and pitched.

For lunch, sandwiches and fruit were served in the mess hall. Counselor Grace warned the young crew to go easy, as they might experience sea sickness. Disregarding her advice, the brightlings made quick work of the meal.

"We've made good progress. I'm hoping we can get everything tidied up before suppertime," Alfred said, taking a bite of an apple.

The food was delicious, Micah thought. But as he sat quietly in the corner, he began to feel queasy.

Hawkins related stories from adventures past. They were usually amusing and ended with someone falling into huge piles of dung or accidentally eating something that made them dreadfully sick.

Without warning, Sariah leaped up and ran straight for one of the open portals, where she promptly expunged her lunch.

The sound and odor of Sariah retching was all it took to cause a chain reaction. All at once, Gertie, Stu, and Lilly bound for the open portals, where they, too, lost their lunches.

Micah couldn't fight it any longer. His mouth started to water, and his stomach churned.

"This should be quite a slop week!" Hawkins roared as Micah ran past to the last open portal.

Micah leaned far out, letting the specks of rain and cool air wash over his face. He looked over his shoulder to the others. They appeared like stuffed human heads staring glassy-eyed at the churning water below. Little fish made quick work of the floating puddles of vomit drifting on the water.

"Oh, you poor dears," Pearl said, patting Micah's back. She pulled him back in, wiping his face with a towel.

"I feel terrible," Micah moaned.

"It's seasickness. It will pass in a few days."

"Days? Don't you have something we can take?"

"No, it's better to let it work its way out. But I can give you this," Pearl said, removing a knotted root from her mini-pack. "This is ginger root. It may help with the seasickness. Bite off a small piece and chew on it the best you can."

Pearl went on and helped the others. Micah bit off a chunk and grimaced. The root was strong and spicy. He wasn't sure which was worse.

Alfred stood, perusing through the pages of a book he held. On his shoulders were Penelope and Twitch. Grubb was rooting around, snapping up scraps.

"Now that some of your gullets are full, let's get organized," Alfred said, laying papers on the table before the brightlings. "You've all had a few hours aboard *Miss Darby*. From watching you young'uns, I'm sure none of you have spent much time aboard a ship. You'll adapt quickly. For the next week, *Miss Darby* will be your home. Feel free to roam her decks and ask lots of questions. She's a good, strong ship. After you get your sea legs, you'll find she's even quite hospitable.

"*Miss Darby* is capable of doing many of the difficult tasks. But some chores still require human hands. You will be given assignments that you are expected to learn and carry out. You'll be grouped in pairs with one of the staff to help you learn your duties."

Micah looked over his duty list. On the list was a schedule for feeding and watering the animals. Lilly and Armin were his partners. On everyone's list was lookout duty in the crow's nest.

"So what did you get?" Wren asked, starting on a third sandwich. He was immune to the effects of seasickness and offered a bite to Micah. The smell of the onions on Wren's breath sent Micah back to the portal, where another piece of ginger root found a watery grave.

Wren leaned against the outer wall of shelves containing bags of sugar and dried fruits. He took a huge bite from the sandwich and spoke to Micah out the portal.

"I got storage, cleanup, and cooking. I got Gertie as my partner. I think they've made a mistake. Listen to what they say I'll be doing: cooking. Good call. I tried making macaroni once. I almost caught our house on fire. Cleaning. Pfft. How easy is that? Gee, this sandwich is the most tasty thing I've ever eaten. I love the spread they used on it. Wonder what it's made of?"

"That's roast bulden," Armin said. "There are no cows here, you know."

"Do I want to know what roast bulden is?" Wren said, looking at his sandwich like it just bit him.

"It's from a bulden maw. It runs on two legs and is about the size of a goat. They eat grass and bugs. They're really hard to catch—got to sneak up on 'em. And that spread you love? It's regurgitated saliva from bong beetles."

"A beetle?" Wren said with a sour face. He scowled at the sandwich and discreetly tossed it out of the portal.

Between dry heaves, Stu leaned over to Micah. "I got maintenance," Stu managed to get out before his back arched, dry heaving.

"Maintenance, eh?" Armin said. "You'll be working with Hawkins and Quinn. Quinn's a genius when working with *Miss Darby*. His mother's the captain of the *Osprey*. You'll learn tons about *Miss Darby* from him."

Alfred cleared his throat. "Listen up, everyone. Since last year's class disbanded four months ago, *Miss Darby* hasn't left the lagoon. We plan on leaving in the morning at six thirty sharp when the tide is low. Between now and then, we've got more work to do.

"One word of caution. You with seasickness might disagree, but we're resting on calm water right now. You'll see waves taller than *Miss Darby* when we hit the high seas. When you stow your things, put them away properly. A loose barrel, even a cup of water, can be hazardous. Be cautious when in the hold of the ship. Cargo shifts. I've seen too many broken arms and legs, so be careful. Lastly, breakfast is served promptly at 5:30, lunch at noon, and dinner at 1800 hours. Turn-in is 2200 hours."

"2200 hours?" Gertie asked, puzzled.

"That's ten o'clock at night," Sariah said.

"Oh."

"For the rest of the afternoon, we'll be doing inspections and maintenance. Those assigned cooking details and inventory will work below deck. Those with repairs will meet me on deck in ten minutes."

Micah, Stu, Sariah, and Lilly spent the afternoon above deck. Micah was happy to be out of the ship. Being out in the open air relieved the seasickness.

He was directed up into the ropes, where he climbed up and down the ratlines all afternoon. It was unsettling work at first. Unlike his tree house back home, *Miss Darby*'s main mast was fifty feet tall and swayed as the ship bobbed in the water.

Micah learned how valuable his spelunking boots and grippers were. The ropes were wet and at first difficult to climb. Climbing the ratline, he slipped and fell backward. The grippers countered gravity. He fell slower than expected and was able to grab the ropes before falling far.

It was Micah's job to inspect the sail mechanisms for damage. Lilly was to help too. But she was uncomfortable higher up where the boat swayed the most. So Armin patiently spent the afternoon with her on the lower ropes.

"Ready, Micah? Watch the main topgallant sail this time!" Alfred shouted. "It's been coming down delayed. I think some of the ties need to be replaced. Ready, *Miss Darby*? Let fall!"

Everyone watched the sails unfurl with fascination. The larger sails unrolled first. Micah studied the mechanism. The boom arms, where the sails were rolled, were made of redwood. The long poles would rest on iron hooks driven into the masts when unused.

When Alfred ordered, "Let fall!" they lifted off the hooks and unrolled. Like magnets, blocks of redwood, secured to the fray of the sail with bolts, expanded outward, hooking to mating pieces fastened to the ropes. The ropes tightened the sail through a network of pulleys and wenches. Though quite elaborate, it happened very quickly and smoothly. In less than a minute, *Miss Darby* was ready to run.

Micah held tight to the crow's nest railing as a downdraft caught in the sails. Being anchored, the ship leaned and creaked in the wind.

"Micah," a voice said softly. *Miss Darby* appeared in the

topgallant sail. "You must be brave to be up so high. My sail's damaged. See how the wood has splintered on the ties?" A part of the sail unhooked from the ropes and drifted close by. "These two binders are worn. They'll need to be replaced."

Micah relayed the message down to Quinn below. The sail rolled back onto the boom arm and floated down.

Stu and Sariah stood by with their hands in their pockets. "Don't just stand there, be ready for it and grab the ends!" Quinn barked.

When the boom reached the two, *Miss Darby* released her hold, putting the total weight on Stu and Sariah. The boom arm was heavy with the sail wound on it. The two strained until, finally, they dropped it. The large sail fell hard to the deck with a mighty thud.

"Oh, dear!" cried *Miss Darby*.

Quinn's face went bright red. "I told you two to keep your grippers on, didn't I?" he barked.

"But they make my hands hurt!" Stu whined.

"That's because all you've ever done is sit around and play video games. It's time for you to man up and start doing real work for a change. And you," Quinn said, pointing at Sariah, "don't think that just because you're a girl I'm going to take it easy on you."

"Maybe next time you should warn us when something's going to be heavy!" Sariah spat.

"Everything's heavy on this ship! There, you've been warned. Put the grippers on and keep 'em on!"

Sariah glared at Quinn as she angrily pulled on the gloves.

Quinn went to the middle of the heavy sail and lifted it with ease. With grippers, it wasn't heavy but awkward. Sariah and Stu took it down to the dock where Melbourne and Hawkins were doing the repairs.

There were long breaks between the work. Micah kept himself

amused watching Penelope and Twitch zip around the masts and ropes, playing tag and hiding from each other. Bosco would dive from the tip of the main mast to snap at Twitch, much to the delight of Penelope.

At one point, Chief Hawkins disappeared into the shed.

"Chief Hawkins, what are you wearing?" Sariah laughed.

Micah looked down to see Hawkins emerge wearing an old-fashioned one-piece bathing suit with blue-and-white stripes. His attire brought the other brightlings up on deck, where they all pointed and laughed.

Hawkins played to his audience. He twirled and modeled the suit. He reached down and picked up a couple of small stones, pretending they were the heaviest weight he'd ever lifted. "This suit is the height of fashion in Astoria!" he said.

He retrieved several tools from the shed and put them in a pouch he slung over his shoulder. In one hand, he held a mask and snorkel. With the other, he grabbed a large ring with a crystal that hung on a hook at the shed's door.

Stepping barefoot to the water, he spat in the mask, rinsed it, and slipped it on. With a great leap, Hawkins jumped in the water with an amusing scream, much to the children's delight.

Micah followed the blue-and-white swimsuit as Hawkins swam along the ship's waterline. From time to time, he would stop to inspect a particular section. Removing different tools from his pouch, he would tap and scrape the hull when he was done with the inspection on the surface. He pulled the large ring from his neck and shook it. The crystal glowed brilliantly. He dove deeper, sometimes going under one side of the ship only to reappear on the other. The only hint of Hawkins' location was the warbling glow coming from the lit crystal. For as portly as Hawkins was, he was a strong swimmer and could hold his breath for a long time.

Micah guessed he had been under for four or five minutes a few times.

After an hour, Hawkins finally climbed back onto the dock.

"Anything?" shouted Alfred.

"I looked over every inch of the hull. I'm not sure what happened down here. If *Miss Darby* got hit by something, there was no damage. Not so much as a mark."

"No problems, then?"

"No, sir! She's ready to go."

"Excellent."

*   *   *

By the end of the day, all of the brightlings were exhausted. From Micah's vantage, he had a perfect view of the clouded sunset over the massive jutting rocks outside the cavern.

For dinner, they ate on deck, where the seasickness was minimal. The brightlings dined on charred biscuits, a tasteless stew, and a delightful fruit beverage called bazzleberry. It was the first meal the two young cooks, Wren and Gertie, had prepared. Wren had made the mistake of complaining about how Gertie cut vegetables, causing the two to argue all afternoon.

It was a long day. Before Micah could go to bed, he and Lilly went to the ship's hold to feed the animals. Seeing Micah, Grubb's tail thumped against the wood floor. Grubb had been confined to a five-foot-wide cage to heal from the gompum bite. Micah released Grubb from the cage and fell into the hay, where Grubb pounced on him, demanding attention.

"You can let him loose on the ship when we leave in the morning. He'll keep the pests down," Armin said. "So, what do you think of your first day?"

"I think this is like doing my paper route ten times in the same day," Micah said.

Armin laughed. "How 'bout you, Lilly?"

Lilly shrugged. She tossed a handful of grain into a cage containing ten snippy radmals. The radmals reminded Lilly of oversized chickens. The two-legged critters attacked their meal, hissing as they competed for the bits of grain.

"Hey, there's plenty for everybody," Lilly said.

"Don't get discouraged," Armin told them. "It takes time to adjust. You two did a great job today—as good as we ever did. Why don't you go up and get ready for bed? I'll finish up."

*　　　　　*　　　　　*

"I am so sore. I never want to move again," Micah groaned, lying on the smooth planked bedroom floor.

Wren and Stu sat nearby, sorting over their belongings. Each boy had a trunk full of their things. Wren opened his black trunk, and Micah sat up. Wren had a wide selection of combs and a mirror attached to the lid.

"Jeez, did you bring enough combs?" Micah said, opening his own trunk.

Stu reached over to take one of the combs, to which Wren playfully slapped his hand away. "Don't touch. These are my babies. My hair's my life."

Counselor Grace and Pearl appeared in the hallway and entered the girls' bedroom. Micah leaned over to catch a glimpse of Pearl but instead got a good look at Counselor Grace's ample backside.

Quinn appeared at the door, startling Micah. He was carrying several odd bits of clothing. "These are what I found lying around on the deck. I expect you boys to take better care of your things.

I'm not your mother, and if I find them lying around again, I'll have you do push-ups to get 'em back."

He stood over the boys, frowning at the strewn shoes, socks, and shirts. He was about to say more when Penelope and Twitch flew in through the portal.

Penelope was in her usual orange hornbill form. Twitch was now a green bird with a long slender beak and a long curving tail. The two transformed into their tiny human form with perfect timing, landing on Quinn's head.

There was a loud thump at the window, and for a brief moment, Bosco's head and toothy beak frantically poked in. Wings and claws wildly flapped and scraped against the hull of the ship. With a loud, "Caaahh!" Bosco's head suddenly whipped back out of the window, and there was a muffled splash outside.

"I told you, no matter what I turn into, he *always knows it's me!*" Twitch said angrily.

"He's just trying to tell you he loves you," Penelope giggled. She bent over and smiled down at Quinn. "Hi, handsome," she said, fluttering her eyes.

Quinn pursed his lips and exhaled without taking his eyes off the boys. His breath blew upward, making Penelope's pink lock of hair flutter. He spun around and marched out of the bedroom.

Stu looked over his blistered hands. "Quinn tried to kill us today. I don't know what his problem is. No matter what we did, we were doing it wrong. He even made Sariah cry."

"Really? She seems too stubborn to cry," Micah said.

"Well, she did."

"At least you two don't have to work with Gertie," Wren said. "She hit me with a spatula. Jeez. All I said was she was burning a pot of water. She didn't have to attack me."

The boys compared their bumps and scratches of the day when

Stu suddenly let out a loud sneeze, which drew the attention of Counselor Grace. "Sounds like you need another dose of allergy medicine, young man. Oh, look at your hands. Let's put some ointment on those and we'll get you back in good shape. It can be a little rough the first while."

"I haven't sneezed or coughed all day," Stu said happily. "That pill you gave me really worked."

"That's good, dear. How 'bout you two?"

Micah and Wren said they were fine. Counselor Grace puttered around the room, showing the boys removable panels that hid shelves for their clothing and other belongings. She told them she was especially proud of the work they had done for the day because there were fewer kids this year to help with chores.

"Why are there so few of us?" Stu asked.

Counselor Grace gave Micah a sharp look. "There were some unexpected setbacks this year. So some of the parents held their kids back until next year. It's happened before."

"Is it because of what happened with that meteor shower the night we registered?" Stu pressed.

"You were there too?" Micah asked. "I didn't see—"

"This is nothing you three need to worry about. It's time for you boys to get ready for bed. The morning comes soon. Oh, and if you get sick, do yourselves a favor and aim out the port window. Good night." Grace left and closed the door.

Stu looked concerned. "I don't know what to expect on this trip," he said finally. "I think some of the leaders are worried."

"Why do you say that?" asked Micah.

"When we were working on the dock, Melbourne was pestering Chief Hawkins on how they expected us to do all of the duties on board the ship with so few numbers. I asked him how many they usually had, and he told me the fewest he ever remembered were twelve kids."

Wren thought for a moment, adding on his fingers. "Between us and the officers, there are only thirteen for the whole crew. Alfred said we were his thirteenth class. Isn't that unlucky?"

Micah and Stu scoffed.

"Are you superstitious?" Stu said.

"I don't know," Wren said.

The three turned their attention back to their things.

Micah's mother had neatly packed his trunk. There were towels, socks, underwear, shirts, and other items. The neatness of the packing disintegrated as he rummaged through the trunk. He finally found what he was looking for: his pajamas. Putting them on, he threw his clothing in a heap and dragged the trunk to the corner under his hammock.

Micah noticed a pouch in the lid of the trunk. It contained several items, including a fresh pad of paper and pencils. On the pad, Micah's mother had written:

Micah,
Be sure to write once a week. We miss you.
Love,
Mom and Dad
PS Please give the letters and the photo back to Alfred.

There were several family photos tucked in the pouch. Micah suddenly felt the urge to cry. Embarrassed, he stuffed them away. In a sleeve, he discovered the bundle of letters he'd found in Alfred's mansion. He had forgotten about those. They had been tossed, like everything else he ever found, under his mattress back home. How had his mother found them?

Micah opened the bundle and out fell the black-and-white

photo. "Who's this?" Wren asked, picking it up.

"I found that in Alfred's mansion on the first day of school. That day I kicked Jack's football over the fence, remember?"

"Like I could forget," Wren said. He related to Stu the story of the football incident and Jack Farnsworth. Stu laughed at the part where Micah shredded Jack's football in half.

"That's Alfred in the picture," Wren said.

"Yeah, and look at the man with the ball cap. That's Bassam, the janitor at the school."

Stu took the photo and studied it closely. "This was taken aboard this ship," he said. "You can see the door to Alfred's cabin on the deck, and that man is Melbourne."

"Hey, you're right," said Micah.

"There's something familiar about the lady," Stu said.

There was a knock at the door, and the door creaked open. "Evenin', boys." Alfred and Chief Hawkins beamed down at them.

Micah gathered up the letters and snatched the photo away from Stu. His face turned red with embarrassment as he handed the bundle to Alfred. "I found these a while ago. I'm supposed to give them back to you."

Alfred took the bundle. "Well, I'll be—I lost track of these," he said, grinning at the photo. He passed the picture to Hawkins, who gave it an amused acknowledgment.

"I never read your letters," Micah said. "Besides, I can't read cursive."

"Well, at least you're honest, Mr. Fennly," Hawkins said.

Twitching his eyebrows, Wren asked, "So, who's the *lady*?"

"That would be Miss Darby Clemens," Alfred said. "She was my girl at the time."

"Miss Darby?" Wren asked. "Hey, that's like your ship."

"That's right, Mr. Kinglsey. The ship was named after my lady-friend here."

"So what happened to her?"

"Let's just say she wasn't thrilled when I intended to take up residence here in Astoria. I kept tabs on her for a while. She ended up marrying a fella named Harold Moon and had a small family. She passed away just a few years ago."

"Moon? I know someone named Cornelia Moon," Micah said.

"That's Darby's oldest daughter. I met her a couple of times. She'll leave a sour taste in your mouth if you get on her bad side," Alfred said, nodding.

"Sour? She's more like tangling with a rakish," Hawkins said.

"So who are the others?" Micah asked.

"The one with the cap, you recognize. That's Bassam. This fellow right here you should recognize by now. That's Melbourne back in the early days. Here's a little history lesson for you boys. Do you know what his real name was back then?"

The boys shrugged.

"Astoria. Believe it or not, his bunch decided to name this whole world after him. It's funny how things work out like that."

"Really?" Micah mused.

"Yessir. Melbourne is a piece of walking, talking history. Oh, and this gentleman here with his hand on my shoulder—this might interest you Fennlys. He's your great-grandfather, Ernest."

Micah and Stu jumped up and looked again at the photo with renewed enthusiasm.

"May he rest in peace," Hawkins said reverently.

"Yes," Alfred said. "It was Bassam, Melbourne, your great-grandfather, and Ramalah that all took me in until we got things settled."

"Ramalah? Grace's father?" Hawkins asked. "He had more hair back then. I didn't know you two were close friends."

"In the beginning, we were. We're still on speaking terms these days, but it's not like it once was."

From the girls' room came shouting. "No, I'm sleeping by the window!" yelled Lilly.

"No, I am! And who said you could use my hair clips? Don't touch my things!" Tiyana shouted.

"Girls, girls. Is this fighting I'm hearing in here?" Alfred said.

"Of course not," Hawkins laughed. "It's just a little steam-blowing. It's been a hard day, and they're all just a little tired. That's all."

Alfred and Hawkins visited with the girls, leaving the boys to climb into their hammocks. Micah closed his eyes and listened to the muffled chatter of the girls next door. Hawkins lectured the girls about how much luggage they'd brought.

"*Miss Darby* doesn't pull a trailer, ya know," Hawkins said.

The boys snickered.

Suddenly, Wren sat up, nearly flipping out of his hammock. "Oh, my gosh. I only went to the bathroom once today in that outhouse by the dock. What if we have to go while on the ship?"

Micah and Stu both shrugged.

"Captain?" Wren called out.

Alfred stepped back in. "What can I do for you, Mr. Kingsley?"

"What do we do when we have to…you know, go?"

"I knew there was something I was forgetting! Listen up, class. Let's talk about the bathroom situation aboard the ship. *Miss Darby* doesn't have indoor plumbing like you're accustomed to. So when you need to go, you go upstairs to the sick bay—that's directly above us. There are two small areas off to the side called the head. It's where you can do your business."

"So where does the stuff go?" Stu asked.

"Well, it's direct plumbing. Goes right into the water."

A frenzy of panic came from the girls' room.

"Are you telling us that we have to stick our keisters out the side of the ship?" Wren said.

Hawkins' laughter exploded from the girls' room.

"It's not quite that primitive," Alfred said. "There's a board with a hole in it."

Soon, the laughter and chatter died down. Alfred and Hawkins dismissed themselves with a cheerful, "Good night."

As the night settled, the lights dimmed. Within minutes, Wren was snoring loudly.

Chapter 30
Melbourne

Micah and Richard sat on their bikes with only one newspaper left in their bags. Grabbing the paper, Micah aimed to throw it onto Cornelia Moon's front porch. Just then, he noticed a hundred lazy cats sleeping on the porch. It would require a delicate throw.

He let the paper fly and hit the screen door. The porch exploded with frightened cats leaping in every direction. Cornelia Moon burst out the door and charged at Micah, waving her broom until she towered over him.

"You'll never see home again! Never!" she screeched.

Micah shot up in his hammock, searching frantically around the dark sleeping quarters. Waves crashed outside the port window with an occasional bell clanging up on deck. The ship creaked on the unsettled waters of the lagoon.

The sleeping quarters weren't completely dark. Set at regular intervals of the baseboards, luminescent crystals cast a dim blue light. There was little comfort in the light, however. Ominous shadows were cast on the walls from swaying fixtures and the hammocks.

Micah had no sense of what time it was. He laid back, closing his eyes. He blanked his mind, hoping for sleep to return.

It was then he first noticed the swirling feeling welling up in his chest. The burning sensation provided neither worry nor comfort. It was just a feeling—a lingering weight that he could almost touch when he put his hand to his chest. He tried to dismiss the sensation as heat trapped under the covers. But when he pushed the blanket to his waist, the warmth remained.

A quiet scratching stole Micah's pondering.

In the dark, it was difficult to pinpoint the location of the sound, but it was coming from somewhere below. It stopped briefly then came again. It sounded like tiny claws on wood with an almost hissing quality. After his experiences with the gompums, Micah's imagination wandered dangerously close to panic.

There were no rats in Astoria, he thought.

The scratching stopped, and there came the ding of a tiny bell. The sound came from his trunk resting below him. He leaned over. In the pale-blue light, he saw Mariam's open diary on top. Her number 2 pencil was resting on the first page, where there was new writing.

Micah climbed out of his hammock, making quite a commotion

in the process. Wren snorted, swaying back and forth on his hammock, his leg dangling over the edge. Stu churned in his hammock, looking back at Micah. Stu's cheeks glistened with tears. He wiped his face with a big, slurpy sniff and rolled back over.

Micah removed the diary, squinting at the writing in the dark. The words were written in his spidery penmanship and read:

September 20, 2019. Monday. Promontory Point, aboard Miss Darby with Wren and Stu sleeping nearby.

I'm worried.

I dreamed I was standing in front of Cornelia Moon's house with Richard. There were many cats. When I threw the paper, the cats ran off, and Cornelia Moon screamed at me that I'd never see home again.

The cats represent the many concerns I have and the despair over leaving home. I deeply fear I may never see home aga—"

The writing ended where the blunted tip of the number 2 pencil had broken.

Micah buried the diary and pencil in his trunk. While digging, a faint glow caught his eye. At the bottom was the key he'd found that day in Alfred's mansion. Picking it up, it felt warm to the touch. He tossed it back in with his things.

He wondered if it was worth struggling back into his hammock. With the ship's swaying, Gertie and Wren's dinner of charred biscuits and bland stew was threatening to come back up. He decided not to risk it.

Tiptoeing out of the bedroom, he paused at the door when he heard sobbing from the girls' sleeping quarters. He continued down the narrow hall, trying to be quiet. It would be difficult to sneak around *Miss Darby*, as each footstep was announced with a creak. The mess hall had the same blue crystal light. Cookware swayed on their hooks, gently tapping each other.

From nowhere in particular, Micah heard the voice of *Miss Darby*.

"*Miss Darby?*" Micah whispered.

"If you eat rocks, you deserve to get a bellyache. Try the red ones. They're delicious," she babbled.

"*Miss Darby*, I need to go to the bathroom."

"…remember not to put my sails on backward. It tickles," *Miss Darby* tittered.

Was *Miss Darby dreaming?* He passed through the mess hall and climbed the steep stairway up. He surveyed the deck. High above on the main mast, the blazing sun flag lit the cavern around the ship. Giant insects fluttered around the light, creating enormous zipping shadows on the cragged walls. Many indistinguishable shadows flitted around in the air currents above.

At first, Micah thought they were birds or bats. Until one of the things landed before him. It was a branch of leaves.

He navigated around the debris scattered on the deck. The ship rolled, and he nearly lost his balance. A renewed sense of urgency hit. Rushing to the fore of the ship, he climbed to the sick bay and discovered the bay was little more than an enclosed area up against the bowsprit. Hammock netting and several boxes were secured to the wall. Four small doors flanked the two sides of the bowsprit. He yanked one of the doors open, revealing a nook just large enough to seat one person. Indeed, there was a board with a hole in it. He stuffed his head in and wretched.

For a long while, he knelt over the hole, staring into the inky black. He missed the conveniences of light and running water in his bathroom at home. Relieving his stomach of Gertie and Wren's dismal dinner did make him feel better, however.

Heading back, Micah reached the stairway leading back down

to the mess hall. A very Oregonian smell wafted around him—the smell of tobacco smoke.

He looked for the source. Above, he saw the silhouette of a man rocking on a chair on the poop deck. The fat end of a cigar flared briefly bright orange. The man leaned forward, catching the light. It was Melbourne.

"Ya be feelin' better now?"

Micah nodded.

"There be some fresh water and a ladle in that barrel over there. Just secure the lid unless'n you like bugs in your liquid refreshment."

Micah took Melbourne's advice. The water was cool and refreshing. He drank two big ladles and swished his mouth out, spitting the water onto the deck of the ship.

"Don't n'you go spitting on Alfred's ship, mind ya. That'n could bring down the wrath of Master Higgins."

"Oh, sorry. I'm new to this whole ship life."

Melbourne chuckled. "It be alright. Ya young ones always be a bit awkward. It won't be noticed anyway. Look at the mess that's comin' down. You'll be picking leaves off the *Miss* 'til ya be coming back."

"Is it always like this?"

Melbourne flicked the ashes off the cigar. He motioned over his shoulder to the open sea. "Haven't seen one like this in these parts for years. I'll see my entire summer spent cleaning up topside."

"You're not coming with us?"

"No, young one. Melbourne and the sea be no longer mates." Taking another long puff on the cigar, he sat back and rocked on his chair.

Melbourne wore a ragged shirt that revealed his sinewy arms

and shoulders. A glow briefly appeared on his chest just above his heart. It was a tattoo that Micah swore glowed. Just as he started to get a good look, it faded away.

"Me not supposed to be smoking these around ya little ones," Melbourne apologized.

"My mom told me if she caught me smoking, she would ground me for a month."

Melbourne laughed with a wet coughing fit. "Ya be the other of the two Fennly boys, are ya?"

Micah nodded.

"It's an honor to meet the offspring of me long-departed friend Onitah. Ya be Kimble's boy?"

"I'm Micah."

"Ya have the eyes of your grandfather."

"Alfred told us you knew Grandpa."

"I did more than know 'im. I owe my life to him. Onitah was my closest friend. A man of courage he was—fear was a stranger to him, it was."

Micah smiled. He'd heard stories about Grandpa Fennly around the dinner table. One, in particular, was a story his dad related about a hike the two went on in the mountains when he was a little boy. They got caught in a thunderstorm. Kimble told how his grandpa could outrun lightning, which Micah always thought was a joke.

Melbourne peered down hawkishly and studied Micah. His ancient eyes glittered in the pale light of the blazing sun. "There be something curious about you, grandson of Onitah."

Micah felt self-conscious under Melbourne's scrutinizing gaze.

"I see it—ya have the Radiance, you have," Melbourne said, patting his chest.

The warmth in Micah's chest throbbed steadily. *Can Melbourne see it?* he wondered. He didn't know where to put his hands and finally just folded his arms.

"Ah, don't be shy about it, me young friend. 'Tis a gift from the God of our fathers. Your ol' Grandpa Onitah had it."

"What does it mean?"

Melbourne's expression darkened. "It brings the omens."

Micah met Melbourne's tired eyes. White light streamed from Melbourne's face. Ever since Micah had got the Macabre Ring, he had experienced heightened sensitivity to feelings. But now, feeling this warm feeling—the Radiance, as Melbourne called it—something stronger was happening. Like a vision, he saw into Melbourne's heart. The old man was a pure soul trapped in an ancient body. He felt Melbourne's love and respect for his grandpa, and his sorrow for his loss.

Memories came. There were laughter and tears. Mingled in these memories, Micah saw war, suffering, and fear. A memory flashed by—the moment his grandpa had sacrificed himself so others could live. Like searching through a maze, Micah sifted through other memories of his grandpa. Most were vague and ordinary. But one memory was strong and caught Micah's attention.

Melbourne stood on a ridge by the sea. Except he wasn't known by that name then. He was Astoria. The sky was dark, and Micah tasted blood. Fires were raging, and the air was thick with smoke. Micah saw his grandpa wearing strange wooden armor and holding a sword.

"Astoria, stay down," his grandpa whispered. Grandpa wasn't Ernest Fennly. He was Onitah.

Onitah waved his sword downward. Astoria and five other companions, all holding weapons, crouched down. Names and faces passed through Micah's mind—these men Astoria knew well. One was meaningful to Micah: Bassam Amun, whom Astoria only knew as Amun.

If Astoria had been looking a few degrees more to his left, he would have missed it—a brief flash of light in the sky. He glanced over, expecting to see the enemy advancing, but saw something else. A man fell from the sky. He landed just out of sight from Astoria's view.

"Onitah," Astoria whispered.

Onitah was focused on the battle over the ridge. Astoria looked to the other soldiers; none of them had seen the light.

Astoria crept down the ridge. He paused, hearing a mighty roar nearby—a rakish. There were screams and an eruption of lightning and fire.

In the brilliance of the lighting, Astoria saw a body floating face down just out where the ocean waves began to break. The beach was dangerous and exposed. Astoria waited for the light to die down. He approached the body cautiously. Was it an enemy?

Wading into the waist-high water, Astoria caught the arm of the man. He was lying face down and unconscious. Astoria paused, judging if the man might be dangerous. He slapped the man's head. It bobbed lifelessly in the water.

Exposed on the beach, Astoria had little time to think. He grabbed the man's arms and slung him over his shoulder. Charging back out of the water, another bolt of lightning lit up, and the creature's roars came again. Astoria dove into the bushes. The stranger tumbled to the ground, landing on his back.

Astoria looked over the man. His clothing was strange, like none he had ever seen among his people or his enemies. Around his neck, he wore a gold chain with a jagged tooth-shaped nugget of gold. At the tip, the gold changed into the familiar amber crystal of Deity Stone.

Dangerous, Astoria thought. He yanked the chain off the man and stuffed it into his pouch. When Astoria looked into the man's face, Micah instantly recognized Alfred.

Leaning closer, Astoria checked the man's breathing. He wasn't. Placing his hand on Alfred's chest, he uttered the word, "Utcha."

Alfred's eyes snapped open, and with a mighty cough, he expelled seawater.

Melbourne looked away, and the vision vanished.

"You saved Alfred?" Micah said softly.

Melbourne leaned back on his chair, grinning, and took a long, satisfied puff on his cigar.

The tattoo on Melbourne's chest caught Micah's eye again. It glowed brighter this time as the tobacco coursed through Melbourne's veins. It was the Rashaar eye with the pupil gouged out—just like the one Micah had seen on Morty Crowther.

Micah was about to ask about the tattoo when there came a commotion from below deck.

"Come here, little fella. You need to go back downstairs." It was *Miss Darby*. She began to whistle softly. A jingling came up the stairs. Seeing Micah, Grubb charged and leaped up into his arms.

Miss Darby's face appeared on a nearby water barrel. "Micah, what are you doing up at this late hour?" She looked up and frowned at Melbourne. "Is that a cigar you're smoking? You know the rules. If my timbers reek of that—"

"Don'tcha be lecturing me, ya old Betty. I was up here minding my own business."

Miss Darby looked around the deck, and her face went stormy. "Look at this mess! Micah, be off to bed, sweetie. It's a big day tomorrow, and you need your sleep."

"Can Grubb sleep with me tonight?"

Micah waited for *Miss Darby* to answer. He looked about and saw she had wandered off to another part of the ship.

"How did this get here?" she grumbled.

Micah looked up at Melbourne. The old man winked, motioning him away.

Micah climbed into his hammock with Grubb in his arms. Grubb nestled under the covers as Micah squared his blanket over them. For the first time since arriving in Astoria, something felt like home.

Chapter 31
The Radiance

The morning began promptly at 5:00 a.m.

Quinn burst into the boys' bedroom with a bugle pressed to his lips. He blasted out a rise-and-shine that spun Micah and Stu out of their hammocks. Grubb flew out of the bedroom. Wren didn't move.

Annoyed, Quinn stomped over, taking a deep breath. He blew

a long, forceful note into Wren's ear. "Get up! The Shiner's spoken!" Quinn shouted.

"What the heck was that?" Wren exclaimed, hands to his ears. Losing his balance, he violently crashed out of his hammock, much to Quinn's delight.

"There's work to do. Wren. You're on cooking detail with Gertie."

The boys got dressed and went to the mess hall. The brightlings plopped down to the empty table one by one without saying a word. Yellow light filtered through the portal windows, illuminating the dense, swirling fog that enveloped the *Darby*.

"Look how foggy it is," Tiyana finally said, breaking the silence.

"Can we sail in this?" Stu asked, sticking his head out the port window.

Quinn came down the deck ladder and found the children gathered at the windows. "What are you all waiting for? Wren and Gertie, you two get with Pearl in the galley to start breakfast. Micah and Lilly, go downstairs to feed those animals. The rest are up top. We've got a mess to clean up."

The children groaned, to which Quinn cast a threatening scowl. Micah and Lilly went down to the hold. Grubb rooted around in the straw near his cage, where a large hole had been chewed out of the chicken wire.

"Grubb, you've got to stop ruining stuff," Micah said and began bending the wire back into place.

Lilly hummed to herself.

"Did you sleep last night?" Micah asked.

"Not very good. Sariah slept next to Gertie to get her to stop crying. She misses her mom. We all miss home. But Gertie was hysterical."

"Wren snored all night," Micah said.

"Yeah, we know."

Lilly took a bucket of grain over to feed the animals and stopped in front of the radmal cage. Four extra-large eggs were lying in the hay. She reached in to take one. A radmal charged and nipped her hand.

"Ouch!" she yelped.

The other radmals took defensive postures, their tiny heads lowered while emitting soft, throaty growls.

Lilly rubbed her hand. "I was told to collect the eggs. How do I do that when they attack like that? That's way worse than chickens!" She looked over the radmals and counted. "Hey, weren't there ten in here last night? What does Grubb eat?" Lilly asked, eyeing Grubb suspiciously.

Grubb playfully sniffed at a small beetle scuttling in the hay. He leaped and dove on it, wagging his tail. When he noticed Lilly looking at him, he raced over to her, nuzzling her foot affectionately.

"We just fed him dog food. Do you think he might've eaten them?" Micah asked.

"Well, three are missing. And he was pretty vicious with that gompum yesterday," Lilly said, scratching Grubb's head.

A thump came from a nearby crate. Grubb perked up, sniffing. Tiny eyes poked out behind the crate, and Grubb charged.

Screeching came as one of the escaped radmals suddenly leaped up on the crate, its sparse tufted wings flapping frantically as it scolded Grubb. Meanwhile, down farther in the hold, Micah and Lilly noticed two more radmals fleeing into the shadows.

Capturing the wily creatures proved to be difficult and demanded stealthy coordination. Grubb was little help. He would charge in when the two had one cornered. Radmals, with their powerful legs, could jump, sometimes conking themselves on the low ceiling.

After finishing their chores in the hold, Micah and Lilly went up on deck. Quinn was barking out orders with his hands on his hips. Penelope was on his shoulder with her hands on her hips, mimicking every move Quinn made.

"Took ya two long enough," Quinn said, his temper flaring. "Get up in the ropes and untangle those branches."

"Yeah, you two," Penelope said, winking at Micah.

Micah and Lilly looked at each other like they were being mugged.

"You heard me. You two are on line duty today. Where are your grippers? You *always* bring your gloves when on deck. Get down and give me ten push-ups, both of you."

"Yeah, ten push-ups!" Penelope demanded, though she was doing jumping jacks on Quinn's shoulder.

Micah looked around the deck and saw Alfred and Counselor Grace at the ship's wheel, ignoring the confrontation. On the dock, Chief Hawkins was shouting directions to Armin and Melbourne, who were somewhere off in the fog.

"Don't look at them. Look at me. I'm in charge of cleanup, and I said ten push-ups!"

"Yeah, ten!" Penelope shouted. Now, she was doing sit-ups.

"Are you serious?" Micah said.

"Make that twenty," Quinn snapped.

"Twenty?" Penelope frowned. "That's a lot of push-ups, and they're hard."

Quinn's shoulders slumped. "Fine, fifteen push-ups."

Penelope leaped up, hugging Quinn's neck. "Oh, you're such a softy."

Reluctantly, Lilly and Micah went down and started doing push-ups.

"I want real push-ups, though. None of those sissy kind."

"Yea, no sissy push-ups!"

Micah glanced over to Stu, who was pushing a wheelbarrow of tree limbs. Stu gave Micah a rude gesture meant for Quinn.

"And that'll be ten more from you, Stu!"

Stu's shoulders sank.

*   *   *

It took an hour to clear the deck of the debris. Just as chores were wrapping up, Wren and Gertie came up on deck clanging a dinner bell.

"Breakfast!"

The brightlings sat around the table looking glum. The tablecloth was askew. Cups stuffed with cloth napkins and spoons were placed on the table in a disorderly fashion. At the end of the table was a stack of seven bowls. Without any prompting, Sariah straightened the tablecloth and arranged each place setting neatly.

Brightlings gathered around Tiyana as she sketched. She was drawing pictures of Grubb—and doing a good job of it. Everyone was amazed at how quickly she captured Grubb in different poses.

The aroma of bacon, cinnamon, and bread made their mouths water. The galley door swung open with Pearl and Armin carrying large plates of bacon, eggs, pancakes, and a pitcher of juice.

"Mornin'," the two greeted cheerfully.

Faces brightened as they passed by to an adjoining smaller nook with a neatly set table for seven. They arranged the food to picturesque perfection and went off in different directions.

Tiyana stopped sketching. "Were we supposed to sit over there? There are seven of us and seven places over there."

"I don't think so. Pearl said we sat here," Sariah said.

"So what do we eat?"

Yelling came from the galley.

"I don't care if it's heavy! I told you, you made too much. Carry it to the table," Gertie demanded.

"We should just make 'em come in here and serve themselves. This thing weighs a ton."

"No, we're not!" shouted Gertie.

The galley door burst open and out came Gertie wearing a white apron, carrying a plate full of burned toast and a bowl of fruit. Behind her came Wren, grunting, carrying an enormous pot of oatmeal.

"Hot! Hot! Hot!" Wren cried, racing to the table. In his haste, he shoved Gertie. Fruit and toast went everywhere. He barely made it. The pot crashed down, sending a thick splat of porridge across the table.

"Wren, you did that on purpose!" Gertie spat.

"I did not. I told you it was too big and hot to carry." The two began arguing fiercely over their cooking adventure that morning.

Sariah and Lilly collected the scattered fruit and toast and sat it in the middle of the table.

"There. Breakfast," Gertie said with a forceful nod.

They all looked at the giant pot.

"Jeez. How much of that stuff did you make?" Micah said.

Gertie and Wren glared back.

"I followed a *recipe*," Wren said, whipping his fingers through his hair. It said to use one pound of oats per person."

"It didn't say a *pound*, you idiot! I told you to use a *cup*!" Gertie said.

"A pound, a cup. What's the difference? I just boiled water and threw in handfuls until it thickened up." Wren took a spoon from a nearby hook and began slopping portions into the bowls as they were passed to him one by one.

Gertie retreated to the galley, returning with a pitcher of milk and shakers of cinnamon and sugar. Micah and Stu took their bowls and sipped at the hot porridge.

"Wow! That's really salty," Micah said with a scowl.

Gertie went around the table, pouring milk into the porridge. "Maybe you'd like to explain why, *Wren*," she said, annoyed.

"So I dropped the salt shaker into the water. Big deal. A little salt won't kill you."

There was clinking on crystal nearby. The bickering ended as the children realized the staff had taken their places at their table. Everyone was there, including Melbourne. "Look at that fresh lot. Barely stepped 'way from their mother's knee, they did."

"Did we look that young back then?" Pearl asked.

"Ya still do, young miss."

Chief Hawkins and Grace both nodded with a grin.

Alfred stood. "It's good to see everyone so chipper this morning. It was a stormy night. Looks like it's mostly passed now. But, like we told you yesterday, don't overeat. The sea will be rough today. Your meal might not be very impressive this morning, but you'll thank us if it comes back up. Now, before every meal, it's customary to take a moment and give thanks. Sometimes you don't know where your next meal will come from."

The staff and brightlings bowed their heads. After a short pause, everyone began to eat. Gertie sat next to Sariah, who gave her a big hug and thanked her for making breakfast.

"Hey, what about me?" Wren said, sitting next to Micah. "I made the main meal here. She helped Pearl make their stuff."

"And we thank you, too, Wren," Micah said, pouring a giant scoop of sugar and cinnamon on his porridge.

"So does anyone know how long it will take us to get to Boshii Campus?" Tiyana asked.

"I asked Quinn," Stu said quietly. He glanced over to the staff table, where they were consumed in talk of the day's duties. He was glad to see Quinn was sitting farthest away. "He told me it was none of my business until we got done with chores."

The others nodded.

"Armin told me," Lilly said shyly. "He said it can take up to a week. It's on an island called Neitah Island."

"Neitah Island? What kind of name is that?" Wren asked.

"I don't think you're going to like what it means," Lilly said.

"It sounds like neat-o. That can't be too bad."

Lilly smiled widely. "Armin said the English translation was Spider Island."

"Spider Island!" Wren and Gertie said in unison.

"I wonder why they don't just fly us there?" Micah said, stirring his porridge.

"I asked Armin that. He said with the number of kids that needed to travel, it used too much Deity Stone to fly. He said the second-year students left three days ago by boat. Access to the island is restricted."

"Restricted? Why?" Gertie asked.

"It's the spiders, isn't it?" Wren said with a shiver.

Lilly shrugged.

"Everything will be fine," Sariah said, hugging Gertie.

Talk turned to the previous night's rest. They discussed the hammocks and how small the sleeping quarters were. They joked about Wren's snoring and shared experiences about adapting to the absence of showers and other bathroom amenities.

"I miss home," Gertie finally declared, tears welling up in her eyes. The girls all scooted around her.

"Home. That's all she talked about. I finally told her to get over it," Wren said privately to Micah and Stu.

"What did she say?" Micah asked, pulling several hairs out of his porridge.

"Oh, I don't know. She cried—*a lot*. That's why she got to help Pearl."

"We all miss home, Wren," Stu said.

"Yeah. But this is only the second day. What's she going to be like in a week?"

The boys ate in silence.

"Where does the staff sleep, anyway?" Wren finally asked.

"Their quarters are at the back of the ship below Alfred's cabin. Pearl and Counselor Grace share one cabin, and Chief Hawkins shares the other with Quinn and Armin. Quinn took me down there earlier to look over the ship's computer," Stu said.

"The ship has a computer?" Micah asked.

"Yea. It's in a waterproof closet—a bunch of electronics are wired to Deity Stone. *Miss Darby* was down there talking to it like it was a person. When she saw me and Quinn, she got all embarrassed and left."

"What was she saying?"

"Not sure. She was talking to someone named Beatrice, but she left before I heard much. I did see the screen, though. It was compiling something. I've written code before and used the same software. Looked like C code to me. I asked Quinn about it, and he got mad and shut the screen off."

Micah and Wren were impressed.

"So, is *Miss Darby* just a computer program?" Micah asked.

"I don't think so. Quinn told me they installed the computer just a few years ago. *Miss Darby*'s been around a lot longer than that. He said the computer serves as some kind of relay. They don't have satellites here."

"You're just a big nerd like Micah," Wren said, taking a comb from his back pocket and running it through his hair.

"About your hair," Micah said, showing Wren the hair he'd pulled out of his porridge.

Wren was indifferent. "It's clean."

*   *   *

After breakfast, Alfred had the mess hall cleared of tables and benches. He went over the duty roster, reminding the crew to be prepared for departure and to stow their things properly.

Pearl and Armin left briefly and returned carrying a wooden chest.

"Ah, thank you, you two," Alfred said, motioning for the box to be placed before him. "Let's talk about our journey. To what lurks in that ocean outside, we're a floating buffet. You've all heard stories about old Oregonian sailors and sea monsters. Here, those stories are true. The sea is the most dangerous place we'll be taking you...this time. And just like the land maws, those under the sea are larger than any you've ever imagined. To fall into the sea in some regions is almost certain death, and we'll be going through those regions on our journey."

Everyone was solemn. Gertie looked pale.

"To protect you, we have these." Alfred removed the blue jeweled necklace from his neck. The blue crystal suddenly glowed brilliantly. The other staff showed that they, too, were wearing the same jewel.

Armin and Pearl presented each of the children with their own necklaces.

"This is the seafarer's jewel," Alfred said. "Think of it as a life preserver. It will protect you from drowning if you happen to fall overboard. But more importantly, it will repel creatures in the water. *You'll wear the jewel at all times* while on the seas—no exceptions. If you're found without it, Quinn here has some chores waiting to help you remember."

"Push-ups!" Quinn said enthusiastically.

Micah slipped the necklace on. Once the necklace was around his neck, the crystal stopped glowing.

"Why does it glow?" Tiyana asked. Finding something new and exciting, she pulled out her sketchbook and started sketching.

"So you can find it if it comes off," Counselor Grace said, inspecting the brightlings.

"Very good. Now, ol' *Miss Darby* has some new tricks this year that Chief Hawkins will introduce," Alfred said.

Hawkins stood up with his typical wide grin. "As you know, Quinn, Melbourne, and I are in charge of maintenance and equipment. Over the summer, we installed new communication hardware aboard *Miss Darby*. We're going to be testing it during the trip. Depending on what job you're assigned, you'll be granted access to one or more of the systems. Being docked here, we have access to the island's main system. Let me demonstrate how it works. I want each of you to repeat after me. 'Abracadabra.'"

"Abracadabra," the kids said together.

"Wow!" the others brightlings exclaimed. Everyone looked around the room with wonder.

Micah didn't see anything.

"Abracabra… Abracaba…" Micah tried to say the word but couldn't quite pronounce it right.

Armin stepped over to Micah. "Saying the word is not required. It just usually helps you focus. You can also think of the password. The system reads your mind."

Abracadabra, Micah thought. Suddenly, he was standing in the middle of a perfect three-dimensional model of the island. He stepped to the edge of the mess hall where the others were gathered and surveyed the miniature model before them.

They stood in the ocean like giants, peering down on the shark-tooth-shaped island. The details were exquisite. They could make out small features like swaying trees, paths, and birds. At the tip of the tooth was the time gate and Alfred's mansion.

Micah and Stu got their bearings and followed the trail they'd taken to get to the cavern. They walked around the room and peered into Belmont Cavern. There, they could see *Miss Darby* bobbing in the glistening water. Micah got on his hands and knees and looked closely at the boat. He could even see the crew looking at the map on the ship. He waved, and the tiny version of himself waved.

"This is augmented reality," Stu said. "I've never seen it this good before. What kind of video card are you using?"

"Video card? There's no video card involved here," Hawkins scoffed. He tapped his temple. "It's all happening in your mind. Take your ring off and see."

Micah took his ring off, and the map vanished. Putting it back on, it instantly reappeared.

"This is the Antilles map. It shows the status of the island. You can manipulate your bearings on the map by willing yourself around. It takes a bit of practice, but to you kids, it should come naturally."

Micah wished he could see the details of the *Darby* closer. It suddenly enlarged to the size of the room. He quickly adapted to the map's controls, whisking around the island and finally stopping at Alfred's home. He followed the walkway that led to the time gate, wondering if there was a way to get more information about what he saw. Suddenly, brilliant labels appeared. The largest appeared over the school building and read *Time Gate 20% Capacity*.

The island model captured the brightlings' attention for several minutes. They each studied the map from their unique perspective.

"Unify," Hawkins commanded, taking back control of what the crew could see. Now they all saw the island from Hawkins' perspective. "Weather," Hawkins added.

The island shrank as the view pulled away. Clouds appeared layered on the map. Statistics like wind current and direction appeared. Most of the water immediately around the island was colored red, indicating hazard—except for a narrow way that led out of Belmont Cavern.

"Here we are at Promontory Point. You can see the storm's heading northwest. We prefer to sail along the coast when we can—the waters are calmer. The storm has altered our original plans. We will begin our journey heading east, but our destination is to the southeast."

The map pulled back, revealing the coastline of the continent.

"Oregon," Hawkins commanded.

A ghostly outline of the western coast of North America appeared over the Astorian coast. Where Promontory Point was now would eventually be part of the land mass in the future. Oregon—the actual state of Oregon—was mostly buried under the sea.

Three red lines snaked their way from Promontory Point. They went out taking different courses in the watery expanse, but all ended on a heart-shaped island down the coast. A label appeared reading *Neitah Island*. Time estimates and distance appeared above each of the three routes.

"You can see our journey would take two days if we could travel directly to the island with a good wind at our backs," Hawkins said. "Factoring in the weather, we need to choose an alternate route. These are the routes recommended by the computer. The fastest would take three days, but it also would be the choppiest. I suggest a more leisurely route that will take us down the coast. It could be up to a five-day journey, but it will go the easiest on you young ones. If all goes according to plan, we should meet up with the *Majesty* and the rest of the convoy around here." Hawkins touched the map and a three-dimensional model of the *Majesty* appeared fifty miles north of Neitah island.

He released control of the map, and Micah regained his position on the map where he had been earlier.

"Isn't this incredible?" Stu whispered to Micah.

"Yeah, imagine the video game this could make," Micah said.

Armin lit up. "Funny you say that. Most of this tech was provided courtesy of some of our people who work on games in Oregon. Don't expect it to always be this good, though. It gets pretty primitive once we get out to open sea."

A tiny flicker at the edge of the island caught Micah's eye. He leaned over for a closer look. It was at the opposite end of the island behind the time gate. He zoomed in, and the image behind the time gate glitched with static.

This wasn't particularly noteworthy, and he almost skipped past it without further thought—that was until the Radiance in his chest suddenly lurched. It almost took his breath away.

"What's wrong with this spot?" Micah said, unable to ignore the Radiance that now burned hot.

Hawkins and Quinn moved the map to Micah's vantage. They both looked at each other, puzzled. "Maybe the sensors are damaged? It's the side of the island that took the brunt of the storm last night," Quinn said.

"Possible," Hawkins agreed. "But they've never given us trouble before. I did a full diagnostics check this morning. Everything was in the green. Melbourne, come look at this."

Melbourne hobbled over and studied the glitch for a moment.

"Lamptor's almighty! Give me a guard maw any day over this new-fangled security system. When I'm topside, I'll give it a kick. I can hear the home office now wond'ren where we've been off to."

"Home office?" Micah asked.

Alfred stepped into the conversation. "The island is monitored on both sides of the gate. The Oregonian side is home office—it's quite an operation these days. We hear from your mother some-times, Micah. She's one of the controllers. Nothing happens on this island without someone noticing. But this will have to keep for now. We need to be heading out while the tide is low. If we don't get on our way, we won't clear the cavern. Everyone. It's time to depart."

*   *   *

Ten minutes later, the crew were at their posts, readying to leave the cavern. Micah had been directed back up into the crow's nest with Armin at his side.

From the fog below, Alfred shouted, "*Miss Darby*! Pull up an-chor. All eyes look sharp now!"

A strong gust of wind came howling down the cavern, broad-siding the starboard side of the ship. Micah and Armin held tight to the crow's nest as the *Darby* heaved away from the dock.

Below, Melbourne threw lines to Tiyana and Stu, who were pulling them aboard with the help of Hawkins and Quinn.

Melbourne stepped back on the dock and waved. "Be off with ya! Ol' Melbourne will be here when you get back!"

Alfred stood at the wheel with Sariah and Pearl.

"What is Counselor Grace doing?" Micah asked, poking Armin.

The two looked down to the poop deck where Counselor Grace

stood alone with her arms raised high.

"She's an elemental. It's one of the ancient arts—runs in her family. That downdraft we just felt is her handiwork."

"She can control the weather?"

"In limited ways by herself. But you bring three or four of them together, you'll see something..."

"Micah, Armin, pay attention up there! We're coming about. Watch that mast," Alfred shouted from below.

Armin reached down and pulled up two long poles that were fastened nearby. He handed one to Micah.

Miss Darby appeared on the mast, looking nervous. "Oh, it worries me so when we leave the lagoon. That's when all the accidents happen," she said, shaking.

The ship came about with her bowsprit, heading toward the great crack in the cavern. Micah could see by the waterlines that the tide had lowered in the lagoon by about eight feet. But even being lower, they needed to maneuver carefully. The crack narrowed at the top to a gap about ten feet wide.

Micah felt the *Darby* lean forward. Getting close to the cavern exit, a grip of panic hit as it appeared they were going to collide.

"It's going to be tight!" Armin shouted down.

Following Armin's lead, Micah used his pole and pushed away from the cave ceiling.

"Oh, dear!" *Miss Darby* cried, closing her eyes.

The tip of the mast scraped rock, and then...they were clear.

The ship pitched down as the wave sank. The fog was thick again. The channel leading from the cavern was full of colossal rocks and was very treacherous. Voices below were lost in the roar of the wind and surf. A loud bell clanged from a passing buoy.

"That's how it's done!" Armin shouted, slapping Micah on the back.

"Oh, thank heavens," cried *Miss Darby*.

"*Darby*, drop sails!" Alfred shouted below.

The sails unfurled and stiffened from the wind coming off the cliff. The ship pitched and rolled mightily into the frothy channel.

They were now traveling at the mercy of the wind, heading out to sea.

Chapter 32
Out of Time

"*Miss Darby*, we need you," Alfred called from the deck.

"I'm so relieved that's over," *Miss Darby* said, breathing out a sigh of relief. She smiled at Micah and Armin, dismissing herself.

The two looked forward into the orange, soupy fog. The air was wet and salty. Occasionally, a buoy would ding somewhere below.

"That's the fifth buoy. We've cleared the channel," Armin declared.

"Isn't it dangerous to sail in fog?" Micah asked.

"It would be in unfamiliar water. But *Miss Darby*'s been this way a thousand times. The fog shouldn't go out more than a few miles from the island."

The Radiance raged in Micah's chest. The feeling burned deep in his heart, whispering and demanding.

Melbourne's words echoed in Micah's mind. *I see it—ya have the Radiance, you have. Your ol' Grandpa Onitah had it.*

Micah tapped his ring on the railing of the crow's nest nervously. He wondered what value such a gift was if it only filled him with anxiety. Shouldn't it come with an interpreter, even just a hint? Should he hide or prepare to defend himself? He checked his pockets for the Urmin Stone and remembered he left it in the sleeping quarters.

It brings the omens.

Micah searched the fog with unease, feeling exposed and vulnerable. A certainty came that, at any moment, something was going to be there. He tapped his ring hard on the wood.

The fog suddenly brightened. He nearly leaped from the crow's nest.

"Take it easy, Micah!" Armin Cried, grabbing a fistful of Micah's shirt. "It's just the light from the lighthouse, see?"

The fog dimmed and then re-brightened rhythmically.

"Why are you so jumpy this morning?"

Death-gripping the railing, Micah looked Armin in the eyes. Armin's expression was hard with concern. Even his odd eye, which normally looked in a different direction, was looking straight at him.

Micah saw into Armin's mind. He saw memories—kids pointing fingers and laughing. Armin had been teased ruthlessly about his eye, the one that didn't quite look straight. Cross-eyed Alby was the cruel nickname he'd been branded with.

But kinder memories came. Armin had spent countless hours with animals and insects. He understood creatures far better than people. He loved learning and discovery. Among these memories, Micah saw a man Armin looked up to like a father who shared Armin's passion.

"Micah, snap out of it," Armin said.

"Fexly," Micah said involuntarily when the name drifted to the forefront of his mind.

Armin stepped back. "You know my uncle?"

"What?"

"You just said my uncle's name. Uncle Fexly."

"I did?"

Armin nodded, eyeing Micah curiously. "Funny, I was just thinking about him. Have you run across his work before? He's published several books about animals in Astoria—that's his true love in life. When I was little, he took me places around Oregon. One of my favorite memories was when he took me to Africa. He's great, you'd like him," Armin went on about his uncle. Micah didn't mind. Armin's stories brought relief from the Radiance.

Sailing due east, the rising sun appeared as a bright disc in the fog. It hung for a long while, comfortably viewed by the naked eye. Its brilliance intensified until the *Darby* emerged out of the mist. The ship was a mere speck fleeing into the crystal-blue sea. Behind them, the cloud bank rose a thousand feet. The cloud looked like a fortress wall that went for miles at the *Darby*'s flanks.

A bell rang six times at the front of the ship.

"What does that mean?" Micah asked.

"It's seven o'clock. *Miss Darby* rings the bell in a rolling pattern. See this chart…"

Armin scooted around the crow's nest, directing Micah to a brass chart mounted on the mast. Micah had seen it before, but he didn't understand it. It was just a bunch of numbers, times, and bell counts.

"On even bell counts, you know you're at the top of the hour. Odd counts mean every half hour. Have you ever heard the saying 'eight bells, and all's well'?"

Micah shook his head.

"It's an old sailor term usually said at the end of a shift. Everyone will get a turn up here. We take four-hour shifts. Well, my friend, the time has finally come to pass the mantle to my successor," Armin said, rummaging in his pouch. He drew out a pair of brass binoculars.

"Successor?" Micah asked.

"When I was a brightling, I became the ship's lookout captain. I inherited the job from Jake Tompkins, one of the junior officers over me. Now, I'm passing this responsibility on to you. I guess it's a tradition. As lookout captain, it will be your duty to schedule the lookout. I'll take care of today, but from here on out, the duty's yours."

He ceremoniously put the binoculars around Micah's neck and bowed. Micah tittered at Armin's pomp but graciously accepted the gift.

"These aren't just ordinary binoculars. Her name is Peep," Armin said.

"Her?" Micah looked over the brass binoculars. They were heavy and durable, etched with fancy scrollwork around the cylinders. Micah's eyes narrowed as he inspected them. *Is it crying?* he wondered, putting it up to his ear.

"She's just a little upset. We've been partners for a long time. Peep, don't be shy. Say hello."

A tinkly tiny voice sniffed, "Hello, Micah."

Micah's eyes widened.

"Peep, what did I tell you about this? I told you all about Micah. He's going to take care of you now. And besides, I'll still be here. We'll always be friends," Armin said, petting the binoculars.

"I know. But you've been the best friend I've ever had."

"Well, Micah is going to even be better, right, Micah?" Armin said, giving Micah a pat on the shoulder.

"Peep, I'm your friend," Micah said, feeling silly talking to binoculars.

"You are? Promise?" she said timidly.

Micah put Peep to his eyes and scanned the horizon.

"Oh, your eyes are so blue," Peep said.

Micah glanced at Armin, and Armin grinned back.

Peep made everything remarkably clear. Micah looked down to the deck, and it focused perfectly.

"You've got good vision, Micah. I can tell. Would it be helpful if I displayed the distance? I just learned how to do that."

"Sure," Micah said.

"I added this over the summer," Armin said, showing Micah a tiny lens mounted at the front of the hinge of Peep's brass cylinders. "It's amazing how a little technology enhances the natural power of the Deity Stone."

Micah focused on Pearl below. She was showing Tiyana and Gertie how to tie knots. The display read *42 feet*. Pearl's hair blew in the wind as she delicately handled the rope. She tied it around a wooden dowel, threading the rope skillfully. She had a tender expression on her face as she was explaining the knot.

"Pearl's sure pretty, isn't she?" Peep said.

"No. Um...er. I didn't notice. I was testing to see how good your lenses were."

"Were you, now?" Peep said curiously.

"Yes, well, besides looking at Pearl, Peep has other things she can do," Armin said sarcastically. Micah's face reddened. "Look over there." Armin pointed to a disturbance in the water off the port side of the ship.

Micah focused Peep on the disturbance. Though the water wasn't entirely gone, Peep penetrated several meters below the water's surface. Micah could make out a school of large yellow fish with broad, blunt faces thrashing about.

"Those are trondle mee feeding on a school of krill," Peep said.

"Now, look back there," Armin said, pointing back at the fog.

Peep penetrated the fog, and Micah saw the island looming over them. He focused on the flashing lighthouse. They were one mile from Promontory Point.

Appearing at the cragged edge of the island, the first of the great towers could be seen coming into view with its tip aflame.

"When were those tall towers built?" Micah asked.

"We're not sure. My uncle calls them the Four Sentinels. Similar towers appear all up and down the coastline. Many of them are damaged. They were here long before we arrived," Armin said. "No one knows who built them. We think they may have been markers to tell sea travelers they were entering the Endless Sea."

"Endless Sea?"

"We're sitting at the edge of the continental shelf here, and it's shallow—only fifty feet or so. But beyond those towers, its deep water, and where there's deep water, there are some truly immense sea creatures. Even Alfred won't go out there without good reason."

Micah followed the horizon and saw Nikola Island eight miles away. "I see Nikola. Looks pretty quiet. Has everyone left?"

"They left yesterday. I contacted one of my classmates this morning, who's a junior officer aboard the *Ark Royal.* He said the fleet got an early start and is about a hundred miles out. The *Majesty* was escorting them. He said the seas are pretty choppy and to expect delays."

Micah retraced the shoreline of Promontory Point. The island had scores of birds nesting in its craggy rocks. They were on the broad side of the island on the opposite side of the time gate and Alfred's home.

"Armin, we need you to help us with these ropes," Hawkins shouted.

"Aye, aye, sir!" Armin shouted back, putting his hand on Micah's shoulder. "Are you going to be alright if I leave you here alone?"

Micah nodded. Armin climbed over the edge of the crow nest, leaving Micah alone.

The Radiance once again demanded Micah's attention. He scanned the horizon several times but soon got bored.

"So, Peep, what else can you do besides show how far things are?"

"Hmm. I record what I see. I can zoom in and out and even see in the dark."

"Like night vision?"

"Yup."

Micah looked down to where Armin went. Lilly had created quite a mess from the foremast's ropes when she got them tangled up. *Miss Darby* retracted the fore sail onto its boom so Armin, Quinn, and Hawkins could examine the bundle of ropes jammed in the winches. Lilly was distraught, with her hands over her face, bawling.

With the foresail no longer employed, Micah could feel the loss of speed. "Peep, how fast are we going?"

"Let me check… *Miss Darby* says we're doing two knots. We have a contrary wind at the moment."

"You talk to *Miss Darby*?"

"Yes. She's one of my friends."

"You have other friends?"

"Sure I do."

"Really? Like who?"

"Let me think…" Peep's tinkly voice said thoughtfully. "There's Goldie, Honey, and Nani. They're all other lookers like me that belong to Alfred, Chief Hawkins, and Counselor Grace. There's Oggy, he's a book that belongs to Penelope and Twitch, but he's grumpy."

"Wait. You're telling me there are a bunch of other things aboard this ship that can talk like you?"

"Uh-huh. Is that strange to you?"

"Well, it used to be." Micah thought for a moment. "How fast is two knots?"

"It's about two miles per hour."

"We're only going two miles per hour? I can walk faster than that."

"Really? Can you walk on water?"

"Of course not."

"Then you can't complain about *Miss Darby*," Peep said defensively.

"I'm not complaining. I just didn't—" Micah began, but Peep cut him off.

"After all, it's not her fault. She depends on wind and currents. Do you see that ribbon above you? It shows the direction the wind's coming from. There's not much she can do when the wind stops."

Micah looked up. He saw a couple of things he hadn't noticed before. A bell with a rope was attached to the clapper just within reach. Above the flag was a long red ribbon at the top of the mast. It was twelve inches wide and six feet long. The ribbon lazily fluttered off the port side of the ship.

"*Darby* says the wind is light, blowing from the south, and we're traveling east. She says sorry."

"Sorry? For what?"

"For being so slow. I told her what you said."

"Peep. You shouldn't... Oh, never mind," Micah said, resting his chin on the railing.

The sun warmed his back as he admired the wall of fog. The sea was calm, and he wondered if his previous anxiety was unfounded. With little else to do, he lazily kept an eye on what the others were doing.

Alfred was at the helm with Stu and Sariah, explaining ship navigation. It was apparent by the way the three were acting that they were looking at the Antilles map. They gestured and walked around, scanning the horizon.

Pearl sat with Tiyana's head on her lap. Tiyana held her sketchbook to her chest as Pearl dabbed her head with a damp cloth.

Micah found himself most entertained watching Wren and Gertie. The two were mopping the deck where Tiyana had thrown up. Grubb was there too. He was trying to lap up the water they were cleaning with. They took turns guarding the bucket with their mops to keep Grubb away.

"Missed a spot!" Micah shouted.

Wren and Gertie both threw Micah an annoyed look. "Yeah? Why don't you come down here and teach Grubb not to drink throw-up water!" Wren yelled back.

"Bah!" Micah said, waving dismissively. Next, he searched for Counselor Grace. From his vantage point, he had a good sense of where everyone was on the ship, but she was notably missing.

Maybe she's below deck, he thought.

"Peep, do you know where Counselor Grace is?"

"Hmm. Let me ask… Nani says they're on the poop deck."

Micah looked back. The rear mizzen sail blocked his view. The wind changed slightly, causing the sails to turn a few degrees. He saw Counselor Grace behind the sail. Micah was puzzled over what she was doing. He climbed onto the railing and straddled it between his legs to get a better look.

Counselor Grace stood with her arms behind her back, staring into the fog. Something was unsettling about how detached she was from the others.

"Micah."

"Yes, Peep?"

"Something's coming down from the sky."

Micah looked up. A black dot appeared in the sky. Through Peep, he saw Bosco coming down, eventually leveling out and circling the ship. He landed on the tip of the main mast.

Bosco peered down at Micah. "Micah, Micah," he cawed.

"Stupid bird," Micah said.

"Stupid bird," Bosco mimicked, making Micah laugh.

Bosco leaped off the mast and threaded through the ropes. He banked and then crashed into netting near Counselor Grace. Micah expected she would throw a fit. But instead, she remained stoic, gazing back at the fog.

Bosco pecked at the netting until a green bird suddenly darted out. Seeing Micah, the bird flew straight up, landing on his shoulder. Breathing frantically, Twitch changed into his tiny human form. "Save me! It's Bosco!"

Bosco flapped wildly, untangling himself from the netting. He finally jumped onto the railing and leaped over the ship's edge. With the light breeze, he flapped his wings hard to gain altitude.

Twitch dove down Micah's shirt, peeking through the flap of his shirt. "Don't tell."

With a clumsy thud, Bosco landed on the crow's nest railing. His egg-sized yellow eyes blinked, regarding Micah curiously. Bosco was a lot larger up close than Micah realized before.

Micah began to giggle as Twitch burrowed down by his armpit. Bosco growled, spreading his wings defensively.

Penelope fluttered up to the crow's nest. She landed on the railing and turned into her curvaceous female self. "Go home, Bosco. Go home!" she shouted, stamping her tiny foot.

Bosco blinked at Penelope. With an amusing waddle, he paced on the railing and then sat. Penelope hugged him around his thick neck. The giant creature set his head down next to her and cooed.

"I'll miss you too," Penelope said soothingly, rubbing Bosco's head.

"I won't!" Twitch's muffled voice shouted.

With a dramatic burst, Bosco leaped up and dove off the crow's nest. He stayed with the ship briefly, then banked back toward the island.

"He's gone. You can come out now," Micah said, undoing his shirt to let Twitch out.

Twitch used the shirt buttons to climb onto Micah's shoulder.

"Why does he chase you?"

Twitch was silent.

Thinking Twitch hadn't heard him, Micah repeated, "Twitch, why does Bosco chase you?"

Twitch leaped off Micah's shoulder next to Penelope. Mumbling, he kicked his tiny toe into a crack in the wood.

"Louder, Twitch, use your words," Penelope said.

"Because I teased him when he was little," Twitch spat, glaring at Penelope. "When we found him, he was a baby. Alfred said we could keep him because his mama abandoned him. He was even smaller than us back then."

Penelope put her hand to her waist, showing how small Bosco had once been.

"We fed him real good, too—worms, eggs, rocks, fish. You know, all the stuff his kind eat. He grew fast. Soon, he was bigger than P'nel and me, but he couldn't fly for a long time. That's when I learned he was *terrifi*ed of gompums. So sometimes—*sometimes*—I would turn into a gompum and chase him around. He would squeal and run around flapping his silly little wings. It was so funny. I couldn't help myself."

Penelope nodded, confirming Twitch's story. "And what did I tell you was going to happen?" she said in a motherly tone.

Twitch's expression sank as he looked down at his tiny feet. "One day, I'd be sorry for teasing him."

Penelope smiled widely at Micah. Micah laughed.

"It's not funny, you two!" Twitch said.

"I never fed him rocks," Penelope laughed.

"Well, I did…"

The two started arguing. Twitch jumped off the crow's nest, with Penelope about to follow.

"Penelope, wait," Micah said, hastily retrieving the locket from around his neck and removing the coin.

Penelope's smile disappeared. "That dreadful thing," she spat. "It nearly got us killed getting it back home. But we owed Mariam. You were the one who gave her hope, Micah. She talked about you all the time. She worried about her little brother who was too afraid to climb trees. We couldn't let her down." Penelope looked over the edge of the crow's nest. "She'd be proud of you if she could see you now."

"Do you think she's still alive?"

"Yes."

"How can you be sure?"

"Because the angel that helped us get home told us you'd see her again."

Penelope dove off the edge and disappeared.

Micah tucked the coin away, taking in a deep breath of sea air. The simple life he once cherished was gone and would never return. Hermit Cove felt like a lifetime ago. Looking out over the water, he thought of everything that had led him here. His troubles with Jack, Ben, and Kamran were nothing more than blunted thorns. He had wiped away so many tears. He vowed going forward that he would rather fight than live in fear again.

An hour passed.

The excitement from the departure and visits in the crow's nest had worn off. Boredom set in as the *Darby* cut through the seemingly endless glistening sea. When they were seven miles from Promontory Point, the main sail turned.

Miss Darby appeared briefly. "That should make you happy," she said, motioning to her sail. "The winds picked up and have changed in our favor. We're doing seven knots now. I bet even you can't walk seven knots."

Micah tried to apologize, but *Miss Darby* vanished before he could say a word. He looked up at the red flag. It fluttered tightly from the steady wind at their backs.

Eight miles from Promontory Point, Hawkins announced they had reached the outer edge of the time gate. They passed a chain of rock formations teaming with life, and Peep identified the different animals. She told Micah that many of the birds in the region were carnivorous. She explained there were two categories of birds—aped and kosh. Apeds were harmless and considered safe to be around. Kosh were the carnivorous kind—one was usually not a worry. But a flock of kosh was dangerous if he were alone. The birds they encountered thus far had been the kosh kind. They came in all different sizes, colors, and shapes, but they usually had one common feature—snouts full of sharp teeth.

The rope situation had worsened. Hawkins and Quinn dismantled several pulleys frozen up from months of idleness. New ropes were brought up from the hold and laid out the length of the deck. Hawkins and Quinn had become more agitated as the morning wore on. Micah overheard them secretly complaining to Alfred that the shortage of crew had made for a hasty departure. They were still only utilizing the main sail and the smaller mizzen sail.

The crisis required the attention of everyone. Alfred went to the aft of the ship to talk to Counselor Grace. She hadn't moved the entire time.

Miss Darby rang five bells. It was ten thirty. Micah had another half hour before the end of his shift.

Looking back at the distant fog bank over Promontory Point, his eyes drooped. He kept nodding off as the ship rhythmically rocked like a cradle.

It was then that Micah noticed something peculiar. A black-haired boy wearing a familiar yellow fleece jacket climbed the rear mast. When the boy reached the top, he secured his footing, and while holding the mast with one hand, he leaned out to survey the ominous cloud that cloaked Promontory Point.

"Richard?" Micah called. He rubbed his eyes, and the vision disappeared.

Moments later, Micah felt someone standing next to him. Richard leaned on the crow's nest railing next to him with a fresh haircut from his mother—nicks and all.

"Hey, buddy," Richard greeted, nodding at the distant cloud bank. "Remember I told you to be careful? You can't sleep now."

Micah jerked awake and found he was alone. The burning in his chest was now all-consuming, and he struggled to catch his breath. When he thought he couldn't take anymore, the Radiance suddenly released him and drifted away. The feeling had been with him since he awoke that morning, and its sudden absence created a terrible sense of worry.

Below, everyone was preoccupied with the sails. They were cleaning up and even Counselor Grace was helping direct the girls to pick up the bits and pieces from the overhaul of the ropes and winches.

Micah scanned the horizon with Peep. They were ten miles out from Promontory Point.

The first sign of trouble came when a swarm of kosh erupted from the islands they'd passed earlier. Hundreds of the squawking sea birds flocked over the ship.

Silently, the distant cloud blanketing Promontory Point blackened and churned as though it were shaking off its cloak. Bursts of lightning flared, revealing the island's shadow.

The water became turbulent. Fish broke the surface and dove frantically past the ship. Micah scanned the water with Peep. Below the surface, sea life swam erratically in great confusion.

"Does that seem strange to you?" Micah asked Peep.

"I've never seen this before."

Surveying the horizon again, glints of white caught Micah's eye.

"Peep, can you zoom in?"

The image in the binoculars zoomed, enlarging the white glints. Hundreds of ships bearing the Rashaar's blood-red ankh rose and fell in the choppy water, with blustery plumes of billowing mist rising from their sails. Water crashed over their bows as they pursued the *Darby*. In the lead ships, men stood with drawn swords.

"Captain, Captain!" Micah shouted, but his voice was tight and dry from the salty sea air, and no one could hear his cry. He had wondered why there was a bell on the mast. He now understood. He rang it loudly and desperately.

Everyone looked up.

Armin shot up the ratlines. "What is it?" he asked.

"Look, ships are coming!"

Armin removed his monocle from his pouch and scanned the horizon. "Holy…"

A deep groan, like a creaking door, came from the sea. Suddenly, a straining, muffled crack rolled across the water. The *Darby* pitched violently as the sea floor thrust upward. Caught in a great tidal wave, the galleon rolled as it was swept back.

The crow's nest erratically swayed as the ship tossed back and forth. Micah and Armin desperately clung to the mast, with every moment a certainty they would be flung into the sea. Screams were heard below from the rest of the crew.

As the *Darby* crested the tidal wave, it began to settle. Armin clambered to his feet, looking back at the colossal wave speeding toward Alfred's home. His eyes widened as his expression turned to horror.

Micah regained his footing just in time to see a great fireball erupt on the horizon.

Promontory Point exploded.

About the Author

Karl Loveridge grew up in Utah until the age of fifteen when, on a whim, his dad decided to change careers to become a gold miner. On July 4, 1983, his dad drove his family in an old Datsun truck to Winnemucca, Nevada. The adventure was supposed to last only a week. Instead, Winnemucca became their new home. Though the gold industry wasn't as kind to them as it was to Alfred Quentin, it played a contributing role to the plot of *House of Massan: The Edge of Time*.

The central plot of this book, the bullying, was inspired from experiences Karl had as a sixth grader. While he didn't have the benefit of a Deity Stone, sixth grade gave him insight into human nature and how life has nothing to do with being fair. He hopes anyone who reads the *House of Massan* series might find inspiration to rise above the injustices of life.

Karl survived his childhood and went on to marry the love of his life, Janna. They had three kids, Megan, Bailey, and Jace, who have since grown up and have lives of their own now. Karl made a career making video games that has spanned nearly three decades. Writing is his escape from the exhausting world of technology.